Scandal in Sydney

MARION LENNOX
ALISON ROBERTS
AMY ANDREWS

MILLS &
BOON

Published in Great Britain 2015
by Mills & Boon, an imprint of Harlequin (UK) Limited,
Eton House, 18-24 Paradise Road, Richmond, Surrey, TW9 1SR

SCANDAL IN SYDNEY © 2015 Harlequin Books S. A.

Sydney Harbour Hospital: Lily's Scandal, *Sydney Harbour Hospital: Zoe's Baby* and *Sydney Harbour Hospital: Luca's Bad Girl* were first published in Great Britain by Harlequin (UK) Limited.

Sydney Harbour Hospital: Lily's Scandal © 2012 Harlequin Books S. A.
Sydney Harbour Hospital: Zoe's Baby © 2012 Harlequin Books S. A.
Sydney Harbour Hospital: Luca's Bad Girl © 2012 Harlequin Books S. A.

Special thanks and acknowledgement are given to Marion Lennox, Alison Roberts and Alison Ahearn for their contributions to the *Sydney Harbour Hospital* series

ISBN: 978-0-263-25234-7

05-1015

Harlequin (UK) Limited's policy is to use papers that are natural, renewable and recyclable products and made from wood grown in sustainable forests. The logging and manufacturing processes conform to the legal environmental regulations of the country of origin.

Printed and bound in Spain
by CPI, Barcelona

SYDNEY HARBOUR HOSPITAL: LILY'S SCANDAL

BY
MARION LENNOX

With thanks to the fabulous Alison Roberts—a gorgeous friend who wears truly awesome boots! And to the rest of the authors in this series—you're brilliant to work with and I love you all.
Aussie and New Zealand authors rock!

CHAPTER ONE

LUKE WILLIAMS had been operating since dawn. All he wanted was bed. Instead he was coping with stinking tallow, teenage hysteria and the director of surgery and the representative of the founders of this hospital thinking pistols at dawn.

'You said multiple burns. Four children. I've spent most of the night with a kid with a collapsed lung, and you wake me for this...'

Luke's boss, Finn Kennedy, the taciturn head of surgery at Sydney Harbour Hospital, was practically rigid with fury, but Dr Evie Lockheart, emergency physician, was giving it right back.

'I was told four children fell into a vat of boiling tallow from the meatworks. You think that's not worth getting you and Luke down here? I wanted the best.'

'Luke has other things to do as well. Like sleeping. And boiling? It must have been barely warm. You should have checked.'

'And waste precious time? Pull your head in, Kennedy.'

Luke sucked his breath in at that. These guys were powerhouses in this hospital. Evie Lockheart, of Endowing-the-Hospital-with-Serious-Money Lockheart fame, and Finn Kennedy, the Do-Not-Cross Director of Surgery, had personalities to match their egos. Powerful intellects, serious commitment, serious…conflict. Conflict getting worse.

Could he back away?

No.

School holidays. A meat-processing operation out in the suburbs, with inadequate security. Four teenaged boys, fifteen or sixteen, egging each other to walk the plank—on rollerblades!—over a two-thousand-gallon vat of tallow being rendered down.

They were lucky the heat had only just been turned on. They'd fallen into the equivalent of a bath that was a bit too hot.

Through the office window, the kids and their frightened parents looked a pool of misery. The stench was unbelievable, but it could have been much worse. A pert little blonde nurse was swabbing tallow from one kid's legs, exposing only minor scalding.

He couldn't leave, he decided, not until things had calmed down. Meanwhile he had a choice. Join in the fight. Look at the kids. Look at the nurse.

This was a no-brainer.

The woman was cute, he thought, even in her ER scrubs. Her blonde curls were wisping from under her cap. As he watched, she tucked them back in, and then glanced through the window.

He caught her gaze and saw laughter, quickly suppressed.

She'd be seeing the conflict, he thought, even if she couldn't hear it. Was she laughing at these two? Not a good idea, he told her silently. Laughter would be really unwise right now, even for him, and he'd been working here for nearly ten years. He fought—quite hard—the urge to smile back.

He also fought the urge to hold his nose. This stink was permeating the whole floor.

'The gastro outbreak has given us nursing shortages through the whole hospital,' Evie was snapping. 'I didn't have the nursing staff to clean and check each of these boys before calling you. Possible burns, possible major trauma, it's my job to call for back-up.'

'They're not traumatised,' Finn snapped back.

But they were, Luke conceded, looking through at the very-sorry-for-themselves kids. It looked to him like their parents had initially been terrified and then expressed shock in the form of anger. He'd seen it time and time again in this job, fright finding vent in fury.

A couple of the kids had been crying. Tough teenage boys, scalded and scared… They should do a bit of reassuring.

But first he needed to defuse the battle of the Titans. How to stop World War III without accidentally escalating it?

'You think your power gives you the right…' Finn Williams was growling to the Lockheart heiress.

Luke gave an inward groan and thought, Here we go.

The little blonde nurse had disappeared into the storeroom. Good idea, he thought. Could he follow?

Not so much. Finn was his direct boss. Evie was the granddaughter of the founder of this place.

If he valued his job he needed to stick around while these power-mongers tore each other's throats out.

In truth he wasn't so worried about his job. As head of the plastic surgery team at the Harbour his credentials made him pretty much unsackable. But as well as being his boss, Finn was also his friend, or as much of a friend as either of them wanted. The last few weeks, he'd watched Finn's perennially short fuse grow even shorter.

Finn and Evie had sparked off each other from the moment they'd met. As a junior doctor, Evie had dared query one of Finn's decisions. She'd been wrong, she'd apologised, but Finn had mocked her family's right to power, and their relationship had been...*interesting* ever since. But now, even for Finn, his anger was over the top.

It was messing with staff morale. It was also worrying, and Luke didn't like being worried. Luke Williams was a man who held himself apart. He didn't get close to people.

He was worrying now about his friend.

And through the window...

He hadn't seen this nurse before.

Pretty. Great eyes. They were a blue that made you feel like diving into clear, sunlit water on a hot day. It must be her first night on the job, he decided. He would have noticed those eyes.

Where was she?

Maybe she'd gone to get a hose.

'There may well be second- or third-degree burns under that mess,' Evie was saying, almost hissing her anger.

'There's no sign of shock. All they need is a good wash.'

'And then assessment,' Evie snapped. 'So then I'll call you back?'

'You won't need to call us back. I'm guessing first-degree burns at worst.'

'Could we find out?'

It was Blue Eyes, out of the storeroom, popping into their private war with her arms full of plastic. 'Sorry,' she said, blithely, as if she hadn't noticed any anger. 'I know it's not my place but I've spent the last couple of years working in a country hospital where all staff step in at need. I'm thinking we have four kids here, and four medics if you count me. How about we all put on protective gear, get each of these guys in a shower cubicle and do an individual check for any burn that needs attention? Split up the work from there.'

Whoa. Luke's jaw practically hit his ankles. Did she know who she had here? Only three of Sydney Harbour Hospital's most influential doctors. Head of Surgery. Head of Plastics. Member of the Lockheart family.

She wasn't wearing the Harbour uniform. *She was an agency nurse?*

She was holding out the protective gear as if she was expecting them to take it.

But… What choice did they have? There were no nurses spare. The gastro outbreak had badly affected the hospital, plus there'd been a brawl early in the night; he'd seen it on his way off duty. Drunk casualties. That meant intensive nursing, guys who'd been stitched up but who were still affected by alcohol.

So Evie had been left with one lone nurse and four filthy kids with possible burns. An emergency department full of hysterical patients, parents and stink. No wonder she'd called for help, even if she'd called for help a bit high up the food chain.

Maybe the nurse was right, this was the fastest solution. And, besides, those eyes…

'I'll take the beefy one with the scowl,' he said, taking a set of waterproof gear.

Evie gazed at him, speechless. 'You…'

'You called me,' he said mildly. 'I assume you need me.' He grabbed another waterproof set and tossed it to Finn. 'It'll do us good,' he said. 'Bit of stress release. You want to take the little guy with freckles?'

Finn caught the waterproofs. Looked flabbergasted.

'I'll do the skinny one,' Blue Eyes said, and handed the last set of overalls to Evie.

There was a moment's pregnant pause. Very pregnant.

Blue Eyes calmly hauled on her waterproofs, then bent and started putting on boots.

She had wispy blonde curls on the back of her neck, Luke thought. Cute. Really cute.

Was that the reason he hauled on boots as well?

No. This was sensible. He didn't succumb to testosterone when it came to cute, not any more, but this place was clogged with stinking kids. They all needed checking, there were no nurses free and this way... Blue Eyes had it right, in the time they spent arguing they could get them checked and out of here.

'I'll ring the cleaning staff and tell them we need this place cleared while we're showering,' Blue Eyes said, now clad all in waterproofs. She tugged open the door, allowing contact between doctors and patients. *Before she even had Finn's okay.*

'Ross, you go with Dr Williams, Robbie, you're with Dr Lockheart, Craig, you're with Mr Kennedy and, Jason, you're with me,' she said. She turned to the parents. 'Could you leave the kids with us? They're in the best of hands; we have the most senior doctors in the hospital working with them. We'll clean them, check there are no problem burns and then get them back to you. Maybe you could find an all-night supermarket and pick up some loose clothes. Is that okay with everyone?'

But before they could answer they were interrupted. 'Excuse me...' The night receptionist edged into the emergency area like a scared rabbit. Of course she was nervous, Luke thought. Everyone in this hospital was nervous around Finn Kennedy, and for good reason. 'The police are here,' she ventured, and before she could say more two cops pushed past her.

Uh-oh. They hadn't realised, Luke thought with grim humour, that they'd just entered Finn Kennedy territory. Facing gun-toting drug dealers might be safer.

'These youths are facing charges of breaking and entering,' the older policeman said, looking at the boys as if they were truly bad smells. 'The orderly outside said they don't seem badly injured. Can we get the paperwork out of the way so we can get on with our night's work?'

Uh-oh, indeed. Luke held his breath. Finn's fuse, already short, was suddenly down to the core explosive, and he had a target.

'Breaking and entering?' His voice was icy.

'That's right, sir.' The cop still didn't see the danger— but here it came.

'These kids have fallen into exposed hot fat,' Finn snarled. 'A life-threatening hazard to anyone who comes near it. An unsecured environment. Unlocked windows. You know as well as I do that a simple padlock on a closed door doesn't begin to cover such a risk. Breaking and entering... You can tell whoever's thinking of pressing charges that he can go back to whatever stinking wormhole he crawled from and expect a visit from Occupational Health and Safety, with lawyers following. These children are traumatised enough, and you're adding more. Now get out of this hospital before I phone someone with enough clout to have you thrown out.'

Then, as the cops backed out with astonishing speed, he turned to Luke. 'What are you waiting for? Get those waterproofs on and get these kids clean. Do what the nurse says. Now.'

* * *

The really good thing about being a nobody was that it didn't matter whose toes you stood on. You were still just a nobody.

These guys were all big-wigs. Lily knew it, but she'd watched the outburst of sound and fury with dispassion, not really fussed if the anger turned on her. What was the worst that could happen? She'd move on.

There were other hospitals. Her credentials were good. She could go somewhere else and be anonymous all over again.

The feeling was extraordinary. She felt like she was floating, light and free. She'd escaped.

She'd return eventually to Lighthouse Cove, the tiny community that judged her mother and who judged her. She knew deep down that this was a momentary escape. A promise was a promise. But right now her mother was in the middle of a dizzying affair with the local parish vicar, the whole town was on fire with gossip and Lily was staying right here, in nice, anonymous Sydney.

She was a bank nurse, employed by an agency. She was sent where she was needed, so if she stood on toes, if she wasn't needed, if these Very Important Doctors decided they wished to dispense with her services, then so be it.

She practically chuckled as she led Jason into a shower cubicle and along the line of cubicles three Very Important Doctors followed her lead.

Two of them looked grim. The other…not so much. He was the head of plastic surgery, she gathered. Luke Williams looked lean and ripped, hovering above six feet, with sun-bleached brown hair and deep green eyes that glinted with repressed laughter. Very repressed, though. She caught his gaze and she could have sworn he was laughing, but he averted his eyes fast. It wouldn't do to laugh out loud.

There wasn't enough laughter in her life, she thought, and she needed it. But she'd taken the first step, and it had felt good to exchange her first attempt at laughter in her new job with a doctor as hunky as Luke Williams.

There's an inappropriate thought, she chided herself, but she was still smiling inwardly.

'Will this hurt?' Jason quavered, and she gave him a reassuring smile.

'I suspect mostly just your pride. We need to get those clothes off. Are you hurting?'

'Stinging,' he admitted. 'A bit.'

The meatworks proprietor should have washed them straight away, Lily thought, growing serious. If the tallow had been really hot, they'd have been facing a nightmare. The owner of the meatworks hadn't checked. He'd simply threatened them with police and they'd fled. Their parents had brought them straight here, with hot tallow still intact. If it had been boiling it would have kept right on burning.

They'd been so lucky. Apparently the vat had only just started warming. The boys had climbed in through a high window, seen huge planks laid across to skim off impurities and dared each other to rollerblade across. The stupidity left Lily breathless. She'd heard the outline. One kid falling, clutching his mate as he fell, both grabbing the planking, which had come loose, tumbling their mates in after them.

Lily turned the shower to soft pressure, skin temperature. She put Jason's hands on the rails and produced scissors.

'Just to my knickers,' Jason whimpered.

'There's nothing I haven't seen,' Lily told him. 'If you've burned anything personal, you'll need it fixed.'

Another whimper.

'There's nothing to this,' she told him cheerfully. 'These jeans are going to stink for ever so we might as well cut 'em off. So…rollerblading over steaming tallow. Quite a trick. How long have you been blading?'

'A…a year.' The water was streaming over the kid; his clothes were falling away and so was the muck that was covering him.

'You any good?'

'Y-yeah.'

'So of the four of you, who does the neatest tricks?'

Luke was in the next cubicle. He was scissoring clothes from his own kid. Ross had been blustering when Luke had first seen him, whinging to his parents that it wasn't his fault, that his 'expletive' mates had pressured him to do it, Craig had pushed him, his dad should sue.

Under the water, with Luke scissoring off his clothes, he calmed down. His legs were scalded. They were only first-degree burns, though, Luke thought, little worse than sunburn. He'd sting for a week but there'd be little long-term damage.

He'd been swearing as Luke had propelled him under the shower, but when Luke had attacked with scissors… the boy had shut up. 'We need to check down south,' Luke had told him. 'Check everything's still in working order. Steamed balls aren't exactly healthy…' Luke wasn't reassuring him just yet. He liked him quiet, and, besides, with him quiet he could hear the conversation in the next cubicle.

'I've been blading since I was twelve,' Blue Eyes was saying.

'Girls can't blade.' That was her kid—Jason.

'You're kidding me, right? I suspect you'll need to come back in a week or so to make sure these scalds have healed. You bring your blades; I'll organise time off and I'll meet you in the hospital car park. Then we'll see who can't blade.'

Luke blinked. An assignation…

'What, you can blade fast?' Jason had been shakily terrified but Blue Eyes had him distracted. He sounded scornful.

'Fast?' Blue Eyes chuckled, and it was a gorgeous chuckle. 'I do more than fast. I do barrel rolls, grapevines, heel toes, flips, you name it. I'm no gumbie, kiddo.'

'You're kidding.'

'Would I kid about something like blading? My skates were the most important thing in my life for a long, long time.' Blue Eyes suddenly sounded serious. 'It took my mind off other things and I loved it. I can't say I ever bladed over tallow, though.'

'I bet you could.' There was suddenly belief—and admiration—in the kid's voice and Luke found himself agreeing. If this slip of a girl could get Evie and Finn to don waterproofs and wash off tallow, she might be capable of a whole lot more.

He wanted, quite badly, to explore the idea.

Bad idea.

She was an agency nurse. Her uniform told him that. She was one of the casual nurses employed to fill gaps at need in any hospital in the city.

After tonight he might never see her again.

But…she'd made an assignation with Jason in a week.

That might mean the agency had positioned her here for more than a night.

She had a great chuckle.

No. Beware of chuckles. And blue eyes. And twinkles. He thought of Hannah.

He always thought of Hannah. Of course he did. Her memory no longer evoked the searing pain it once had, but instead was a basic part of him, a knowledge that he'd messed with the most precious thing a man could be given. The emotions that went with the sort of involvement he was briefly considering with Blue Eyes were gone. They were left behind in a bleak cemetery with what was left of his wife and his little son.

'Me balls…' Ross whimpered. 'They gunna be okay?'

'They're gunna be fine,' he told the kid he was treating. 'They're a bit pink but they'll live to father sons.'

'I don't want to father kids!' The thought was obviously worse than hot tallow.

'No,' Luke said soothingly. 'I guess you don't, but one day you might. Meanwhile everything's in working order for when you want them to do what they're meant to do. For when your chance in life happens.'

Ross and Jason were sent home. Robbie and Craig were admitted. They'd been in the centre of the vat. It had taken them longer to get out, which meant they had patches of second-degree burning. No full-thickness burns, though. Evie took them in charge, patching them up before admitting them. Luke somehow found himself doing the paperwork while Lily gave Ross and Jason's parents instructions on how to deal with minor scalds.

She then headed off to fill in a police report. Finn might have moved on, but Luke heard Blue Eyes asking questions, getting the boys to sign statements, and he knew because of her the open vats would be covered and there'd be no prosecutions of kids who were just being…kids.

Lily was some nurse.

She wasn't your normal agency nurse. Most agency nurses were looking for a quiet life. They were mums with small kids who worked when they could find someone to care for their children. They were overseas nurses, funding the next adventure. They were older women who worked when grandkids and aching legs permitted, or they wanted funds for a few retirement treats.

Lily, though, didn't seem to fit any of these categories. She was in her late twenties, he decided, nicely mature. Competent. She had the air of a nurse who'd run her own ward, and who didn't suffer fools gladly. And the way she'd talked to Jason… She didn't sound like a young mum, wearily getting the job done.

He badly needed to get to bed. He had a full list in the morning. He shouldn't be awake now, but first… First he finished the paperwork and casually dropped by Admin. And while he did he just happened to retrieve the fact sheet that had been faxed through with the notification that Blue Eyes had been allocated to work at the Harbour.

Blue Eyes.

Lily Maureen Ellis. Twenty-six years old. Trained at Adelaide. Well trained. He flicked through her list of credentials and blinked—hey, she had plastics experience. She was trained to assist in plastic surgery.

Plus the rest. Intensive care. Paediatrics. Midwifery. He knew the hospital she'd trained in. This woman must be good.

According to the sheet, she'd left Adelaide two years back to run the bush nursing hospital at Lighthouse Cove.

He knew Lighthouse Cove. It was a tiny, picturesque town less than an hour's drive from Adelaide.

Fishing, tourists, pubs and not a lot else.

So what had driven Lily Maureen Ellis to pack up and leave Lighthouse Cove and put her name down as an agency nurse in Sydney?

Maybe she was following a man.

Maybe he needed to get some sleep.

'Why the hell aren't you in bed?' It was Finn, scaring the daylights out of him—as normal. The Harbour's Director of Surgery had the tread of a panther—and night sight. Word in the hospital was that there was nothing Finn didn't know. He knew it before it happened.

'Why aren't *you* in bed?' Luke managed back, mildly. 'Have you been giving Evie more grief?'

'I haven't…'

'Yeah, you have,' he said evenly. 'You're tetchy, and you're especially tetchy round Evie. What's eating you?'

'Nothing.'

'Headaches? Sore arm?'

'Why would I have headaches?'

'Beats me,' Luke said mildly. 'But you keep rubbing your head and shoulder, and if anyone puts a foot wrong…'

'Dr Lockheart had no business waking us up,' Finn growled.

'She had four potentially serious burns and one agency nurse. Cut her some slack.'

'She drives me nuts,' Finn said, taking the fact sheet. 'So this is the girl handing out waterproofs.'

'She's got guts.'

'I'm sick of guts,' Finn said. 'Give me a good pliable woman any day. So why are we reading her CV?' He raised an eyebrow in sudden interest. 'Well, well. It's about time…'

'No.'

'No?'

'No.'

'Hannah's been gone for four years now,' Finn said, gentling. 'A man can't mourn for ever.'

'Says the whole hospital,' Luke said grimly. 'It's driving me nuts.'

'So have an affair.' He motioned to the CV. 'Excellent idea. Get them off your back. Get a life.'

'Hannah didn't get a life.'

'It wasn't your fault.'

'So whose fault was it?' he demanded, explosively. 'Fourteen weeks and I didn't even know she was pregnant.'

'You were working seventy hours a week and fronting for exams. Hannah knew the pressures. She was also a nurse and she knew her way around her body. To lock herself in her bedroom and suffer in silence at fourteen weeks pregnant… She was fed up that you were caught up in Theatre. It still smacks of playing the martyr.'

'Don't.'

'Speak ill of the dead? I say it like it is. If one stupid act of martyrdom stops you from getting on with your life…'

'I don't see you getting on with your life.'

Finn stiffened. Finn was his boss, Luke conceded, but their relationship went deeper. He knew as much of Finn's background as anyone did. Finn had a brother who'd been killed in combat. He'd been wounded himself. There'd been a messy relationship with his brother's wife, then a series of forget-the-moment flings.

Was he about to throw those in his boss's face? Maybe not. Not at two in the morning, when they were both sleep deprived—and when a cute little blonde nurse had suddenly appeared in the background behind Finn. Waiting for an opportunity to break in.

'Don't make this about me,' Finn snapped. 'Meanwhile, you…' Finn waved the folder. 'An agency nurse, ripe for the picking. That's what you need. A casual affair and then move on.'

The blue eyes widened.

Luke stifled a groan.

'Excuse me, doctors,' the Agency-Ripe-For-The-Picking nurse said, in a carefully neutral voice. 'The paging system doesn't appear to be working down here. Dr Lockheart has asked me to find you, Dr Williams. Not you, Mr Kennedy. Dr Lockheart's words were, *"Keep that man out of my department at all costs"*. But a child's been admitted with facial injuries from dog bites. Dr Lockheart says to tell you, Dr Williams, that this is serious and could you please come now.'

CHAPTER TWO

JESSIE BLANDON was headed for Theatre—if he made it that far.

He was four years old. He'd woken in the middle of the night, needing his mother, the bathroom, something. He'd stumbled through the living room. His mother's boyfriend's Rottweiler had been on the couch.

As far as Lily could see, he'd lost half his face. Or not completely lost; it was hanging by a flap. How he'd not bled to death, she didn't know.

Lily didn't have time to think about what she'd just overheard. She flew back to Emergency with Luke.

'Tell me,' he snapped as they strode down the corridor at a pace practised by most emergency medics. Never run in a hospital. Walk—exceedingly fast.

She outlined what she'd seen and Luke's face grew grim.

'Dogs and kids,' he muttered. 'No matter how trustworthy... Hell.'

It was hell. Lily had seen the mother and her boyfriend as the ambulance had wheeled the little boy in. They looked shattered. This would be a great goofy dog, she guessed, normally quiet, startled from sleep into doing what dogs were bred to do. Attack and defend.

How good was this man beside her?

She was about to find out.

She'd not dealt with a case like this at Lighthouse Cove. For the last two years, in her tiny hospital, any serious case had been transferred to Adelaide. Still, she had the training to back her up. Those long years, travelling back and forth from Lighthouse Cove to Adelaide Central, struggling to do her training yet still support her mother, they'd been hard but they'd provided her with skills, so that when Luke Williams said, 'You've done plastics, you trained with Professor Blythe? You'll work with us on this?' she could nod.

But she wasn't nodding with confidence that they'd save the little boy. He was desperately injured. She was only confident that she could back up this man's skills.

If he had the skills.

He did.

To say she was impressed with Luke William's professionalism was an understatement. This was a life-and-death emergency. Every minute they wasted meant this little boy had a smaller chance at life, yet Luke exuded calm from the moment he saw him.

First and foremost he made sure Jessie was feeling no pain. He had an anesthetist there in moments and Jessie was placed swiftly into an induced coma. He assessed what needed to be done. He gave curt, incisive directions with not a word wasted. He even found a moment to talk to the couple outside.

'Things are grim,' he told them. 'There's no way I can assure you your little boy will be okay. I don't know. No one knows. But he's in the best of hands, and we'll do everything we humanly can to save him. Meanwhile, I want you to ring a reliable friend and ask them to bring in Jessie's favourite things, a bear maybe, his blanket from his bed? Reassuring stuff. The paramedics will have informed the police. Tell your friend not to go near the house until he's sure the police have the dog under control.'

'The dog's a pussy cat,' the man said, brokenly.

'No,' Luke said grimly. 'He's a dog. And your son...' He closed his eyes for a fraction of a moment and when he opened them Lily saw something behind his eyes that looked like pain. 'Jessie,' he said. 'It's up to us now to see if we can save your Jessie.'

She'd come on duty tonight as an unknown nurse, expecting to be treated as very junior. In fact, she'd kind of wanted to be junior. Anonymous. Working steadily in the background, a tiny cog in a big wheel, disappearing as soon as she was off duty, coming on duty tomorrow on another ward, knowing no one, no one knowing her. Bliss.

What she hadn't expected was to be part of a close-knit, highly skilled team, working desperately to save one little life.

That weird conversation she'd overheard in Admin was put aside. For some reason Luke had been checking her credentials. Whether the conversation between Finn and Luke should have the pair of them up before the medical board for sexual discrimination was immaterial right now. What was important was that Luke knew she was up to the job in hand and he let the rest of the team know it. The hospital was desperately short-staffed, so she was no doormat, standing in the background. She was scrub nurse, working with every ounce of her knowledge and skill.

They all were.

The child's face had been torn from chin to forehead. A vast flap of skin and flesh was hanging from his cheek. Among the blood and mess, they could see bone.

His eye socket, his nose, the side of his mouth… Unspeakable damage…

But the flesh hadn't been ripped away entirely. If Luke had the skills he might…he must…

The alternative was unthinkable. If the flap couldn't be replaced, this little boy would be facing years of grafts, even a face transplant. A life of immuno-suppressant drugs. If he lived.

The alternative was that Luke sorted this mangled mess and teased it all back into place. That he keep the flap alive, re-establish blood supply, leave nerves undamaged…

A miracle?

No. Pure skill.

Her initial impressions of the man were that he was… okay, a womaniser. He'd been laughing with her. Eyeing her appreciatively. Talking with the director of surgery about her in *that* way…

Now every speck of concentration was on what he was doing. Jessie's face was an intricate jigsaw puzzle that had to be fitted together before the blood supply was compromised. Every tiny torn piece had to be sorted, cleaned, put into careful, cautious position.

The nursing team of the hospital might have been hit by gastro but there was no hint of understaffing now. This was priority one, a child's life. Luke was assisted by a surgical registrar, a paediatric anaesthetist, two scrub nurses and two junior nurses. All were totally focused.

And in their hands was a little boy called Jessie. Redheaded. Freckled on the tiny part of his face that wasn't damaged. He was intubated, heavily anaesthetised. He'd been lucky he hadn't drowned in his own blood.

Every person in the room was totally tuned to what they

were doing. This was the most important job in the world, saving a child's life…piece by piece…

Lily thought briefly of a case she'd worked on three years back. A professor in Adelaide, trying to save a man's lips. Problems with drainage afterwards. Like Luke, the professor's total attention had been caught in what he was doing, but afterwards he'd talked through what might have helped.

She turned to the closest junior nurse.

'Slip out and find Dr Lockheart,' she said. 'Tell her we may need medical leeches. Tell her priority one.'

'I don't have authority…' the girl said, casting a worried glance at Luke, but Luke's attention was all on what he was doing. He might not have the head space to think beyond his current actions, Lily thought.

The anaesthetist, the registrar, the senior scrub nurse were totally focused as well.

'Just say leeches are needed urgently,' she told the nurse. There was no need to say the agency temp had ordered them. 'Be it on my head if they're not.'

And it would be her head, too, she thought. Leeches were kept in only a few medical facilities around the country. Her order might well involve helicopter, urgency, cost.

So sack me, she thought grimly, and went back to what she was doing. Elaine, the senior scrub nurse, needed to back off a little; there was only so long that she could hold the suction tube steady, that her fingers would do as she bid.

Luke's fingers didn't have a choice, they had to keep going.

'Lily, move in,' Luke growled, and he'd sensed it too, that the older nurse was faltering.

She moved in and kept on going.

* * *

Two hours later her decision was vindicated. The flap of skin was finally closed around the nostril and left lip. Luke was working under the little boy's eyelid but he rechecked the lip and swore.

'The blood's coagulating,' he said. 'I need drainage. Hell, I didn't think we'd get this far.'

'We have leeches on hand if you can use them,' she said diffidently, and the nurse in the background was already unfastening the canister.

'How the…?' Luke was momentarily distracted. 'Did Dr Lockheart order these?'

'Lily did,' the junior said, and grinned, the atmosphere in the theatre lightening as the outlook improved. 'She's not bad for an agency temp, is she?'

'Not bad at all,' Luke said, and caught Lily's gaze and held, just for a moment, a fleeting second, before he went back to work.

Lily went back to work, too, but she was flushing under her mask.

Not bad at all.

His glance had unnerved her.

Luke Williams was a womanising surgeon, she told herself. She was here as a temporary nurse, knowing no one, wanting to know no one.

But his gaze…

It did something to her insides. Twisted…

She didn't have time for anything to twist.

Work. Anonymity. Just do what comes next.

At five in the morning she was totally drained.

'Go home,' Dr Lockheart told her. 'We've thrown you in at the deep end tonight. I know you're not off duty until six but no one's expecting anything more of you now.

'And if you'd like to change agency nursing for permanent nursing at the Harbour, you'd be very, very welcome,' Elaine said warmly. 'Dr Williams is already asking that you be made a permanent member of the plastics team.'

'I don't want to be a permanent member of anything,' she said wearily, and went to change and fetch her gear from her locker.

Home.

Problem. She didn't actually have a home. Not until ten o'clock.

She'd arrived in Sydney yesterday, fresh from her mother's dramas, wanting only to escape.

Her mother was, even by Lily's dutiful daughter standards, an impossible woman. She drifted from drama to drama, and the small town they lived in had labelled her as trash, for good reason. She wasn't trash, Lily thought. She was…needy. She needed men. And in between needing men, she needed Lily.

This last fling, though, had pushed the townspeople to the limit. It had pushed Lily to the limit. Two days ago—had it really been only two days ago?—the wife of the local vicar, a woman who was also the head of the hospital board, had stormed into Lighthouse Cove hospital and slapped her. As if her mother's actions were Lily's fault.

'Get your mother away from my husband. You and your mother… She's a slut and you're no better. She needs a leash! You think you can be a respectable nurse in this town while your mother acts as the town's whore?' She'd slapped Lily again. A couple of patients' relatives had had to pull her away and she'd collapsed in shock and in fury. Lily had caught her as she'd fallen, stopped her from hurting herself, but there had been no gratitude. No softening of the vitriol.

Why would there be?

'Get out of my sight,' the woman had hissed as she'd recovered. 'Get out of our hospital. Get out of our town.'

She'd had no right to sack her. It was her mother who'd played the scarlet woman, not her.

But in a tiny town distinctions blurred.

She'd sat in the nurses' station with her stomach cramping, feeling sick, knowing she couldn't live with this stress a moment longer. She was being unfairly tarred with the same brush as her mother, and she knew she didn't deserve it. But it was a small town and so far she'd always stuck up for her mother…that couldn't go on.

On the way home she'd stopped to buy groceries. Walking into the general store had been a nightmare. Shocked, judgmental faces had been everywhere.

The Ellis women.

Then she'd tried to use her card to pay for groceries. 'Declined: Limit exceeded.'

Her mother had been using her credit card?

Speechless, she'd gone home and there was the vicar, pudgy, weak and shamefaced, but totally besotted with her mother.

'Make yourself scarce for a while, there's a good girl,' her mother had said. 'We need time to ourselves. It'll be okay, dear,' she'd cooed as Lily had tried to figure what to do, what to say. 'We were going to go to Paris but we've run out of money. It doesn't matter. If Harold can just borrow a little bit more from his relatives we'll leave. We're in love and everyone just needs time to accept it.'

Enough. What had followed had been the world's fastest pack. She'd driven eight hundred and fifty miles from Adelaide to Sydney. A seventeen-hour drive, her stomach cramping all the way. She'd had cat naps at the side of the road, or she'd tried to, but sleep had refused to come. She'd arrived in Sydney late in the afternoon, trying to figure how she could survive on what little money she had.

She'd walked into the nursing agency before it had closed and they'd fallen on her neck.

'All your documents and references are in order. There's a job tonight, if you're available. Sydney Harbour Hospital is desperate.'

She'd found a cheap boarding house, dumped her luggage and booked accommodation for the next night. That was tonight, she thought, glancing at her watch. She could have the room from ten.

But it was five hours until ten o'clock, and she was so tired she was asleep on her feet.

Her stomach hurt.

She stared at her locker, trying to make her mind think. The thought of finding an all-hours café until then made her feel ill. There'd be an on-call room somewhere for medical staff, she thought. Probably there'd be a few. There'd be rooms for obstetricians waiting for babies. Rooms for surgeons waiting for their turn in complex multi-specialist procedures.

Rooms to sleep?

Just for a couple of hours, she thought. Just until it was a reasonable time to find breakfast and book into her boarding house.

Just for now.

He had a whole hour of thinking he'd done it right. One lousy hour and then the phone went off beside his bed.

'Problem.' It was Finn. Of course it was Finn—when did the man ever sleep?

When did Finn ever wake him when it wasn't a full-blown emergency? Luke was hauling his pants on before Finn's next words.

'It's Jessie,' Finn snapped. 'It seems he has a congenital heart problem. No one thought to tell us, not that it would have made a difference to what you did anyway. His heart's failing. You want to come in or you want me to deal?'

'I'm on my way.'

She woke and he was right beside her. Luke Williams, plastic surgeon. He looked like he'd just seen death.

The on-call room was tiny, one big squishy settee, a television, a coffee table with ancient magazines and nothing else. She'd curled into a corner of the couch and fallen asleep. Until now.

The man beside her wasn't seeing her. He was staring at the blank television screen, gaze unfocused.

She'd never seen a man look so bleak.

'What's wrong?' she breathed, and touched his arm.

He flinched.

'What are you doing here?' His voice was harsh. Breaking. It was emotion that had woken her, she thought. Raw grief, filling the room like a tangible thing.

'I don't get into my boarding house until ten,' she told him. 'So I'm camped out, waiting. But what is it? Jessie?'

'He died,' he said, and all the bleakness in the world was in those two words. 'Cardiac arrest. He had a congenital heart problem and no one thought to tell us. As if we had time to look for records. The admission officer didn't even read the form, she was too upset. We patched him up, we made him look like he might even be okay, and all the time his heart was like a time bomb.'

'There was no choice,' she managed, appalled.

'There was a choice. If I'd known...I could have taken

the flap off, thought about grafts later, concentrated on getting his heart stable first.'

She took a deep breath. What to say?

This man's anguish was raw and real.

A congenital heart problem...

If Luke had known he might well have decided not to try and save his face, but without that immediate operation Jess would have been left with a lifetime of skin grafts. With a face that wasn't his.

'What sort of life would he have led?' she whispered.

'A life,' he said flatly. 'Any life. I can't bear...'

And she couldn't bear it either. She took his hands and tugged him around to face her.

There was more to this than a child dying, she thought. This man must have lost patients before. He couldn't react like this to all of them. There was some past tragedy here that was being tapped into, she guessed. She had no idea what it was; but she sensed his pain was well nigh unbearable.

'I killed him,' he said, and for some reason she wasn't sure he was talking about Jessie.

'The dog killed him,' she said, trying to sound prosaic. 'You tried to save him.'

'I should have—'

'No. Don't do this.'

He shuddered, and it was a raw and dreadful grief that took over his whole body.

Enough. She pulled him into her arms and held him. And held and held. She simply held him while the shudders racked his body, over and over.

This couldn't just be about this child, she thought.

Something had broken him.

He was holding her as well now. Simply holding. Taking strength from her. Taking comfort, and giving it back.

A man and a woman, both in limbo.

The events of the past two days had left Lily gutted. Her mother… The vicar.… Losing her job. The judgement of the town.

The Ellis women.

She held to comfort, but he was holding her as well and she needed it.

Jessie's death. The trauma of finding what her mother had done, planned to do. Forty-eight hours with little sleep.

If she could give comfort…

If this was what they both needed…

He shouldn't be here. He shouldn't be holding this woman.

But he wasn't thinking of now. He was thinking of Jessie, four years old and red-headed.

The past was back with him. Four years ago, walking into their apartment after surgery that had lasted for fourteen hours. Exhausted but jubilant. Calling out to Hannah. 'I'm home. It's over and she'll live. Hannah…'

Walking into the bedroom

Ectopic pregnancy, the autopsy said. Fourteen weeks pregnant.

By her side, a letter to her mother in Canada.

'Tonight I'm finally telling Luke I'm pregnant. I've been waiting and waiting—I thought a lovely roman-tic dinner, but there's no chance. He's been so busy it's driving me crazy but now he'll have to make time for us. I want a son. I'm hoping he'll be red-headed like me. I want to call him Jessie.'

Tonight, four years later, he hadn't been able to save a red-headed boy called Jessie.

The woman in his arms was holding him. She smelled clean, washed, anonymous, clinical.

But more. The scent of faded roses was drifting through, like some afterthought of a lovely perfume. The silken threads of her fair hair were brushing his face.

She was an agency nurse. She didn't know him.

She was warm and real and alive.

He'd come in here to sit, to try and come to terms with what had happened. He had two hours before his morning list started. He needed to get himself under control

Jessie.

Hannah.

They were nothing to do with the woman who was holding him.

She shuddered and he thought, She's as shocked as I am. He tugged away a little and searched her face.

Her sky-blue eyes were rimmed with shadows. Her shock mirrored his. She looked like she, too, was in the midst of a nightmare.

'Lily...' It was the first time he'd used her name and it felt like...a question?

'Don't,' she said. 'Just hold me. Please.' And she tugged him back to her.

He should back away.

He didn't. He couldn't. He simply held. And held and held.

A man and a woman—with a need surfacing between them as primeval as time itself.

Stupid. Crazy. Wanton?

It didn't matter. It couldn't matter.

His hands were slipping under her blouse, feeling the warmth of her, the heat. He needed her heat.

Her breasts were moulding to his chest. Skin was meeting skin, and conscious will was slipping. Their bodies were meeting, in a desperate, primitive search for…

What?

For life?

That was a crazy idea. He was crazy.

It didn't matter.

For now, for this moment, he was kissing her, holding her, wanting her, with a desperation that was so deep, so real that nothing could interfere.

They were only kissing. They were only holding. They were only touching.

No. This was much, much more. This was a man and a woman come together in mutual need, giving, taking…

Holding desperately to life.

'Luke…'

'Just hold me,' he ordered, and she did, she did. She held.

Fire to fire. Need to need.

They held—and two minutes later a junior nurse looking for something to read in her coffee break slipped into the room and saw two entwined bodies.

One passionate embrace.

The girl stared, dumbfounded, as she realised who it was. The solitary Luke Williams. Head of Plastic Surgery. A man who walked alone.

Kissing an agency nurse. Slipping his hands under her blouse.

And, oh, that kiss…

She gasped in disbelief and backed out, her magazine forgotten.

Who needed magazines when there was much better fodder right through the door? Boy, was this juicy titbit about to fly around the hospital.

CHAPTER THREE

LILY had signed up for four weeks at Sydney Harbour. That was approximately three weeks and six days too long. She knew it the moment she turned up for duty that night. Gossip reached her the moment she crossed the threshold.

From the lady in the florist shop on the ground floor, to the orderlies, to the nurses and interns working in Emergency where she'd been rostered, it seemed they all knew what had happened that morning.

They didn't know her—many of them hadn't even been working last night—but they knew Luke Williams and it seemed the gossip machine was in overdrive.

A mutual offering of comfort had turned to something stronger, and the hospital gossip machine had flamed the story to the next level. Even before she'd walked out this morning she'd realised the news was flying all over the hospital—that she and Luke Williams had indulged in wild sex in the on-call room.

It had taken sheer willpower to walk back into the Harbour tonight—plus the fact that, thanks to her mother, she was broke. She'd agreed to four weeks and if she didn't fulfil her contract she'd have to find another agency. This was the only agency that dealt with acute-care hospitals and she didn't have the money to leave Sydney.

The alternative was to go back home to her mother. And the vicar.

No way.

So get over it, she told herself. She'd been caught in a clinch with the head of plastic surgery. So what? Who cared what these people talked about? In four weeks she could pick up her pay and move on.

How far did she have to run to escape gossip?

For ever if she brought it with her, she told herself, keeping her chin deliberately high. What had she been thinking, letting Luke hold her as he had? She was just like her mother.

Um…no. Her mother would never do what she'd done. Her mother would now be declaring to the world that she was in love, and she'd be destroying anything and anyone she needed in order to get what she wanted. Her mother would get her heart broken and launch herself into suicidal depression when it was over.

Lily had simply made one mistake. She'd been emotionally shattered and she'd fallen into the arms of someone who was equally shattered.

There was no need for everyone to look at her sideways.

They did anyway.

'Wow.' Elaine, a woman who'd looked intimidating and severe last night, relaxed enough to greet her with laughter as she appeared at the nurses' station. 'Who's on your list tonight?' Then at Lily's expression her smile softened; becoming friendly. 'Don't look like that. Lots of women in this place would offer to comfort Luke Williams any way they know how. That man is a walking suit of armour. I don't know how you managed it but his armour was well and truly pierced last night, and thank heaven for it. Maybe now he can move on.'

'Move on?'

'You didn't know?' Obviously things were quiet right now, because the senior nurse was ready to talk. 'Luke's wife died four years ago. She was gorgeous, a redhead with a temper to match. She had an ectopic pregnancy, went into septic shock and died, and Luke didn't even know she was pregnant. Since then it's been like he's built the Great Wall of China around himself. No one gets near. And then you did.'

'I don't usually…' she managed.

'Nobody gives a toss what you usually do,' Elaine said. 'The fact is that our mighty Dr Williams has been shagged by an agency nurse.'

'I did not…'

'It doesn't matter whether you did or didn't,' Elaine said bluntly. 'Gossip is truth as far as this hospital is concerned, and we're delighted. Let him try and keep his armour after this. A girl with accommodating morals was just what he needed. Now…we've just got word there's been a boat crash on the harbour, two guys with suspected spinal injuries and a girl with deep facial lacerations expected any minute. I suspect we'll want you in Theatre again. Scrub?'

'I… Yes.' At least this was a vote of confidence. She'd expected to be treated like a pariah. Here she was being handed a position of responsibility.

'You did great last night,' Elaine said. 'In more ways than one. But hands off the rest of our male staff, at least until you're off duty. You've done us a favour with our Luke, but let's not push things too far.'

And that was that.

A girl with accommodating morals… Everyone was looking at her.

Aaagh.

* * *

He'd come close to having sex with an unknown nurse in the on-call room. It was like being a member of the mile-high club, he thought. Sordid and stupid.

Only it hadn't felt like that at the time.

But that's how his colleagues were treating it, as a huge joke. Medics had black humour at the best of times. Jessie's death last night had upset them all and Luke's out-of-character behaviour was a welcome diversion.

Even Finn commented. 'About time,' he growled. 'Now take her out properly and do it again.'

Huh? He didn't date. Ever.

He wasn't starting now.

What had happened? He'd been gutted by the events of the night; he'd found himself in the on-call room simply because he hadn't had the strength to get back to his apartment without getting some sort of grip on himself, and she'd been there.

He'd lost himself in holding her. She'd felt...

Amazing. Just amazing. From a night where all he could see was black, he'd been lifted into a world of warmth, and strength and laughter. Yes, even laughter. She'd made a gentle joke as the world intruded, she hadn't let him apologise, she'd slipped away and he'd thought he might not even see her again.

What would have happened if they hadn't been interrupted? He should feel grateful that they had been—they'd both been well out of control. Instead, strangely, he felt an empty regret. And worry for her. The gossip machine in this hospital was ruthless.

When he'd finished his day's list he'd gone back to the agency sheet, checked for her address and found a simple 'To be advised'. So he couldn't find her even if he wanted to. She was an agency nurse. She might not even turn up tonight.

She did.

Evie called him at dusk.

'Your lady's back. She's contracted to us for four weeks. Are you popping into Emergency tonight by any chance?'

Evie was laughing.

'I might,' he conceded.

'To introduce yourself?' Evie was definitely laughing.

'What makes you think I don't know her?' he growled before he could stop himself.

'You know her? I thought this was lust at first sight.'

'Leave it alone,' he told her. 'I'm coming in.'

'The lady's busy,' Evie said. 'We're run off our feet. She goes off duty at six; you can come and take her home.'

They met before that. The woman with lacerations needed someone with real skill if she wasn't to be scarred for life. Once again he found himself in Theatre, with Lily as second scrub.

This wasn't a life-and-death situation. Becky Martin would survive with barely a scar from her drunken joy ride in a powerboat, and the mood in the theatre was a far cry from last night's trauma.

But it was also a far cry from the usual relaxed theatre. Everyone was watching Luke—and Lily. One glance between them and it'd start again.

No. They didn't even have to glance for the gossip to keep going, Luke thought. This hospital used gossip as a means to dispel tension, and what they'd done last night had started a wildfire that only time would extinguish.

Or Lily leaving.

She might. She looked strained and flushed.

She was working with professional competence, anticipating well, displaying skills he valued. Even so, he wasn't sure he wanted her here. He didn't like his staff distracted and they were distracted by her.

That wasn't fair, he thought grimly. She was being judged because she'd tried to comfort him.

His colleagues thought his actions were amusing. They saw her as…easy.

That was a harsh judgement by any standards.

He put in the last suture, stood back from the table and sighed.

'Well done, Luke,' his anaesthetist said. 'Great job. You deserve a wee rest. I hear the on-call room's free. Nurse Ellis, maybe you're free, too?'

'Leave it,' he growled, and watched in concern as Lily started to clear.

The junior nurse was sniggering.

He needed to talk to her, he thought. He needed to apologise.

Not in the on-call room.

He was due to sleep. Lily was on duty all night. He'd come in at change-over, he decided. He'd see her then.

Not in the on-call room.

Luke disappeared and she could get on with her night's work. Which was just as well. The guy was distracting, to say the least, and the staff reaction was well nigh unbearable. With him gone she could lose herself in what needed to be done.

She felt mortified. She was also feeling…ill? Her stomach cramps were getting worse, and now there was nausea on top of them.

She'd left Lighthouse Cove to get rid of the tension that

was making her sick. In two days here, she'd only created more tension.

'You're looking pale,' Elaine said in passing. 'You'd better not be coming down with gastro. Half this hospital's had it, but I thought we were past the worst. Are you feeling okay?'

'I'm just tired,' Lily said. 'I've had a hard…' She caught Elaine's gaze and stopped. 'I mean…'

'No, no, I understand,' Elaine said, grinning. 'You and Luke… I'd imagine he can be very tiring. But according to Dr Blain, who heard it from Dr Lockheart, word is you already know him. Is that right? Why did you make me tell you about him if you're old friends?'

'I—'

'I know he keeps to himself, but if he pairs up with someone who does the same thing we're in real trouble,' Elaine said. 'Apparently he's coming to take you home at six. If you make it that long.' Her eyes narrowed. 'You're looking sick as a dog. Tell you what, you stick round the nurses' station until handover and finish the paperwork there. If you're coming down with gastro, we don't want you near patients.'

'I'm just tired—and I don't need anyone to take me home.'

'It's not anyone, it's Luke Williams. Paperwork for you, my girl, and then let your lover take you home to bed.'

Lily had felt bad before. She tackled her paperwork feeling infinitely worse.

Luke found her in the locker room, preparing to leave.

He could have gone the whole four weeks of her contract without seeing her again, he thought. With the gastro outbreak almost over, staff levels were nearly back to normal. He could easily arrange for her not to be rostered to Theatre with him.

He could pretend the encounter had never happened.

Finn used women to forget, Luke thought. Maybe he could, too.

Only…there was something about Lily that made him think it hadn't been a casual embrace. That her need had been almost as great as his.

A lesser man wouldn't need to ask why, but for some reason this didn't feel like a simple matter of honour. It was how she'd made him feel. It had been the generosity of her body, the smile behind her eyes, the touch of her…

He'd remember it, he thought, and he honoured her for it.

And she was being labelled because of it. The least he could do was thank her and apologise.

He opened the locker-room door and she turned to face him. She looked white faced. A bit unsteady on her feet. Wobbling?

He crossed the room in four long strides to reach her. Gripped her shoulders. Steadied her.

'Hey…'

'It's…it's okay,' she said, and hauled away to plonk herself down on the wooden bench. 'I'm just having a queasy moment.'

'You're not pregnant, are you?'

She gave him a look that would have withered lesser men. It was the look he deserved.

What had made him say that? Of all the ridiculous…

'We didn't make it that far, Superman,' she retorted. 'You don't get pregnant by kissing, no matter how hot you think you are.'

'I'm sorry,' he said, with feeling. 'That was dumb. Plus offensive. But you're ill.'

'I suspect,' she said with as much dignity as she could muster, 'that I'm coming down with this blasted gastroenteritis that half this hospital seems to have suffered. You should have a huge skull and crossbones on the entrance with a sign saying "Abandon hope all ye who enter here".'

'Or abandon the contents of your stomach.'

'Don't,' she begged. 'Go away.'

'Let me take you home.'

She glared. 'Tell me you don't have a car with leather upholstery and I might be interested.'

'I do,' he admitted. 'But we can go via Emergency and get a supply of sick bags. I had it last week so I won't get infected.'

'You might have infected me.'

'Then that'd be yet another thing I need to apologise for,' he said grimly, and took her elbows, propelling her up. 'We'll organise you a shot of metoclopramide for the nausea. Then we'll take some paper bags and take you home and to bed.'

'No.'

'No?'

'I mean, yes, please,' she said with as much dignity as she could muster. 'Only I need to spend ten minutes in the bathroom first.'

They didn't speak on the way to the address she'd given him. She didn't lose her dignity, but he could see she was holding onto it with every shred of effort she could muster. One shot of metoclopramide was barely holding it.

She wasn't what she'd seemed. Questions were crowding in, but his medical training told him that breaking her concentration would be unwise. So he focused on driving, found the address, pulled up in front of a boarding house that looked as if it had seen better days and watched in astonishment as she struggled out of the car.

'You don't live here?'

'No,' she said, closing the car door with care, as if it was a really tricky task. 'I'm staying here. Thank you for bringing me home.' And she headed for the gate.

He was out of the car, through the gate, stopping her.

'Don't stop me,' she pleaded. 'I need…'

'I know this place,' he said. 'When I was an intern we averaged one drug overdose a week from this dump.'

She was trying to shove past him, looking increasingly desperate. 'It's only until payday. It has a bathroom. Please…'

She was nothing to do with him, he told himself. This was none of his business. He'd brought her home. He'd done what he had to do.

But…she'd held him. She'd stopped his grief from stripping him raw.

She'd lightened his life.

That had to be an overstatement, he told himself. One crazy impulse did not mean emotional change. She'd simply been there when he'd needed her, had responded to his need, had maybe used him to assuage her own needs.

Her own needs were pretty apparent now. She'd broken from him and was doubled over behind a scrubby hedge. The garden was filthy.

Questions.

She was a skilled theatre nurse from a town he remembered as being quiet and beautiful.

His colleagues had her labelled as wanton.

She'd held him.

Whatever she was, he couldn't leave her here.

She was crouched, trembling, in the filthy garden, sweaty and sick, and he knew he had no choice.

He waited for the spasms to cease. Then, giving her no chance to argue, he stooped and lifted her into his arms and carried her back to his car. He deposited her back into the passenger seat before she knew what he was doing.

'What's your room number?' he demanded.

'T-twelve.' She could barely speak. 'But—'

'Give me your key.'

'I don't…'

He took her purse from her limp grasp and retrieved the key.

'Don't argue and don't move,' he said, and headed for the house.

She didn't go anywhere. How could she? That last episode had left her wanting to do nothing so much as to lie down and die. Her bed in the boarding house was lumpy and none too clean, but it was a bed and right now she wanted it more than anything else in the world. Only her legs didn't feel like they'd take her anywhere.

After the week she'd had, it needed only this. Of all the stupid hospitals she had to temp in, it had to be Sydney Harbour Hospital during a gastro epidemic.

She wanted to die.

Why was she sitting in Luke's car?

It was too hard to do anything else.

She closed her eyes and he was back again, carrying her suitcase. That got through…sort of. 'What…?' She was trying to get her thoughts in order. She wasn't succeeding.

'You're not staying here,' Luke said grimly. 'This place is drug bust central.' Then his face sort of…changed.

He slid into the driver's seat and pushed up her uniform sleeves.

She got that. No matter that she was dying...*he thought she was a crackhead*?

Enough. There were some things up with which a girl did not put. Or something. She wasn't making sense even to herself, but as he tried to check her pupils she found the strength to haul back her hand and slap him. Straight across his cheek with all the strength she could muster. Which wasn't actually very much. He recoiled but not far, then caught her hands in his before she could do it again.

'Just checking,' he said, mildly.

'I drink champagne every time I get a pay rise,' she managed through gritted teeth. 'I'm addicted to romance novels and chocolate. I once got a speeding ticket and a parking fine all in the one month. Evil doesn't begin to describe me—*but I don't do drugs*.' She tried, very badly, not to sob, as she hauled her hands away from his and fumbled for the door catch.

'No.' He leaned over and tugged the door closed, took her shoulders and twisted her to face him. 'I'm sorry.'

'Me, too. Let me out.'

'I'm taking you home.'

'I am home.'

'My home.'

'You don't want a junkie at home.'

'You're not a junkie,' he said wearily. 'I've seen enough to know I've mortally offended you. Can I start making amends?'

'There's no need...' But her stomach wasn't up to arguing. Another cramp hit and she doubled over.

He handed her a paper bag but she didn't need it. There was nothing left.

He waited for the spasms to cease, then magically produced moist wipes. 'Paper bags and wipes from Emergency,' he said softly as he cupped her chin in one hand and washed her face. She was so limp she couldn't argue. 'You get parking tickets. I steal wipes. Criminals both. You want to do a Thelma and Louise and run for the border?'

'I… No.'

'Thought not,' he said, and fastened her seat belt for her. 'Let's find you an alternative.'

His surgical list started at eight and he made it only fifteen minutes late. This morning was his private list, cosmetic surgery. The woman he was treating had travelled overseas to get cheek implants, a reshaped nose and liposuction for her thighs. She'd got what she'd paid for and she hadn't paid much. She'd ended up with a perforation of the nasal septum, a nasal obstruction and nasal deformity. One of her cheek implants had slipped, which meant her face was weirdly lopsided and her thighs were…undulating. She had lumps and bumps all over the place.

He wasn't working on her legs this morning. He'd remove the cheek implants first—he wasn't the least sure of their quality and the last thing she needed was one to burst. Then he needed to focus on revision rhinoplasty and repair of the septal perforation.

She'd need further procedures and he couldn't be sure she'd look as good as she had when she'd started.

Cosmetic surgery could sometimes be brilliant, restoring self-image, but this time it had been a disaster.

The surgery he'd had as a child had been brilliant.

Luke's childhood had been made miserable by a massive port wine birthmark almost covering one side of his face. His parents, cold and emotionally detached, had decreed it was simply 'character building', but when he'd been fourteen his uncle had stepped in.

'I've arranged the best plastic surgeon I can afford,' he'd told his father. 'The kid's getting that off his face whether you like it or not.'

His uncle was a bachelor, taciturn, unsentimental, refusing thanks. He and the plastic surgeon he'd found had changed Luke's life and had set him on the path he was on now.

His uncle's farm had been lifesaving as well. It still was. Even though his uncle was as emotionally distant as the rest of his family, his farm had been a retreat from the world.

He hadn't been to the farm for two weeks now and he was missing it. Maybe he could take off for a few days. Leave his apartment to Lily. Whoever Lily was.

Not a junkie. An unanswered question.

Don't get close.

'So tell me about your lady of the night.' Finn's voice from the doorway to his office made him start. Dammit, he should be used to it. He wasn't. 'My what?'

'Your one-night stand. Or your one-morning stand. You planning to make it two mornings?'

'Leave it,' he growled. He thought of Lily as he'd left her, huddled in his bed, so sick she could hardly acknowledge he was leaving. He'd stayed with her for an hour and made sure the retching had stopped. He'd left her with fluids, and he knew all she needed was sleep, but still he'd hated leaving her.

And somehow…for some reason he hated this hospital thinking she was…his one-night stand.

Sydney Harbour Hospital. It should read Sydney Scandal

Central, he thought. Any hint of gossip was through the place in minutes. A team of skilled medics working long hours under intense pressure, in teams where they were thrown together in emotionally charged scenarios over and over, made for a hotbed of scandal. Up until now he hadn't added to it.

It drove him crazy, though, the fact that he was being watched all the time. 'When's our aloof Dr Williams going to crack and prove he's human?'

He was aware he was a target; he was aware there were bets—first woman to break his icy barricade. Even a couple of the gay guys had tried.

The gossips would be relentless now, he thought. A one-night stand… They wouldn't stop.

And Lily? She'd signed up for four weeks' work and she was labelled from this moment forth.

She was in his bed. They'd find that out in about two seconds flat. Other medics lived in his apartment block, Kirribilli Views. Hell, his cleaning lady was due in there this afternoon. By the time she'd finished dusting, the news would be all over Sydney.

'She's not a one-night stand,' he found himself saying, before he even knew he intended saying it. 'I already told Dr Lockheart that. I've known Lily for years.'

'Years?' Finn raised his brows in disbelief. Finn Kennedy made stronger doctors than Luke nervous, Luke thought. The man just had to raise one of those supercilious eyebrows and minions were supposed to quake.

But Luke was still thinking of Lily retching. This was no time for quaking. Or for disbelief.

'Why do you think she's here?' he demanded. 'We wanted to see if we could make a go of it.'

'You were checking her records.'

'I was making sure they'd got her address right. We used a boarding-house address as cover, intending to keep our relationship private a bit longer.'

'By snogging on the on-call couch?'

'Yeah, that wasn't exactly wise,' he admitted. 'She was waiting for me after finishing work. I found her and...' He closed his eyes. 'The kid had just died. Sure, what happened was inappropriate, but Lily's a big-hearted woman. She held me first, asked questions later.'

'You're in a relationship. What the—?'

'This hospital thinks it knows everything about me,' Luke said wearily. 'It doesn't.'

The door to his office was open. Their voices were carrying, which was just what Luke intended.

Everyone knew what had happened in the on-call room. They were labelling Lily because of it, but if they thought Lily and Luke were in an established relationship she'd be treated with respect. He'd already hinted at it to Evie. Why not take it further?

Maybe this was the least he could do. Where women were concerned he always did the least he could do, he thought grimly, but this time...

'You bring your woman to work here without telling us about the relationship?' For some reason Finn's disbelief was giving way to anger.

'What of it?' It was Evie, just passing. Like half the hospital. How many medics used this corridor, and how carrying was Finn's voice?

Answer—very carrying.

'It's deception,' Finn growled.

'What, not telling us who he's sleeping with?' Evie demanded. 'What gives us the right to know?'

'We're a team.'

'If we are you have an odd way of treating team members,' Evie snapped. 'Leave Luke alone. It's his business.'

'If he wants to bring his—'

'Luke's your friend,' Evie said, closing the door. 'You want to make this worse?'

'I have a patient being sedated,' Luke said warily. Sparks flew whenever these two got close and he didn't want to be in the middle. He needed to leave. Now.

'I'm so pleased,' Evie was saying warmly, and she hugged him. 'She's a very competent nurse. I agree you should have told us, but…' she cast a disparaging glance at Finn '…I can see why you wouldn't. She looked bad though when she left this morning. Is she okay?'

'She has gastro,' Luke said. 'Remind me to speak to Admin. She'll have got it here; she'll get paid for time off or I'll take it further.'

'She needs time off?'

'Yes.'

'Where is she now?' Finn growled, and Luke fixed his friend with a challenging stare.

'At home,' he said. 'In my bed.'

'How wonderful,' Evie said happily. 'Lily and Luke… Ooh, I love it.' She cast a cheeky look at Finn. 'Maybe it's time you tried a solid relationship, Mr Kennedy.'

'In your dreams,' Finn snapped.

'Aren't you having one?' Luke asked.

'He's been seen with Mariette from Accounts,' Evie said, disparagingly. 'Not exactly a long-term proposition, that one.'

'Will you butt out?' Finn was almost explosive.

'Like you butted out of Luke's love life?' Evie retorted. 'Certainly, Mr Kennedy. Can I walk you to Theatre, Dr Williams?'

'Yes,' Luke said with relief.

'And tell me about Lily on the way. Leave nothing out. First sight, first touch, first kiss. The whole romantic fantasy.'

Fantasy, Luke thought. She had it right there.

Lily woke as someone was vacuuming right through the door.

There were sunbeams on her counterpane. *Her counterpane?*

She was lying in the middle of a king-sized bed, on down-filled pillows, ensconced in crisp, white sheets and fleecy blankets.

The room was spacious, painted in cool soft greys, with white drapes—masculine but not too harsh.

The focus of the room was the floor-length picture windows, and through the windows Sydney Harbour.

She could see the Manly ferry chugging across the harbour. She could see the opera house.

A sunbeam was on her nose.

The cramps had stopped. She wriggled, very carefully. The nausea had gone as well.

She'd died and gone to heaven.

She was in Luke Williams's bed.

It didn't matter whose bed she was in, she decided. Anyone with a bed like this was a friend for life.

Was she more like her mother than she'd thought?

Even that concept wasn't enough to spoil what she was feeling right now. Like life might be possible again.

A tap on the door. 'Come in.' She hauled her sheets to her chin, expecting...Luke? Instead a chubby little lady in a floral pinafore peered round the door, looking anxious.

'Are you awake, dear? I didn't want to disturb you, only

I popped my nose round the door an hour ago and saw you hadn't drunk anything. I think Dr Williams would like you to drink. Would you like a cup of tea?'

Lily thought about it. She had many things to think about, but right now tea was pretty much the limit of her brain power.

'I'd love one.'

'With lots of sugar.' The lady beamed. 'I'm Gladys Henderson and I do for Dr Williams. I do for other doctors in this apartment block as well but he's my favourite. But he's in my bad books for not telling me you were coming. They tell me you've had quite the romance and then you just start doing night duty and no one knew. And now to get this nasty bug… But we're all so pleased for Dr Williams. He's ever so nice and we've been thinking he goes up to that farm of his all the time with only his old uncle, and he stares at nothing and just thinks and thinks about that poor young wife of his. But she's four years dead, and we're so pleased…well, not pleased she's dead, of course, but pleased as Punch that he's got a young lady. And that's enough from me; you don't want me standing here gabbling for ever. I'll make you a nice cup of tea and plump your pillows and then you settle down and sleep until the doctor comes home. Ooh, I do love a good romance.'

CHAPTER FOUR

LUKE'S list went overtime. There were always complications, he thought. The problem with being a plastic surgeon with a decent reputation was that he was sent other people's mistakes. Repairs of repairs... He hated it.

His real work, his passion, was repairs that made a huge difference to people's lives. Birth defects, accidents, improving the aesthetic results after disfiguring cancer surgery.

He'd refused at first to do cosmetic surgery but there was a need. The lines blurred between vanity and distress and he couldn't say no.

Regardless, he left the hospital as he always did on a Wednesdays, feeling that his time could be better utilised. Feeling that there should be something more.

Like going home to Hannah and their little boy?

No. Time had left him ceasing to miss Hannah. In truth, their marriage had been...problematic. He didn't miss her as if he was missing part of himself. He missed what could have been without even knowing what that was.

He was going home now to another woman.

She might not still be there. She might have had her sleep and gone back to that appalling boarding house.

He'd fetch her back.

Um…no. It was none of his business where she was living.

But now half the hospital believed she was his long-term lover. And it was his business. He'd compromised her reputation. Maybe some kind of primitive instinct was kicking in, making him feel…

Dumb? Too chivalrous for words? He hadn't even had sex with her.

But the whole hospital thought he had, and he wasn't doing logic right now. He swung into the underground car park as Mrs Henderson was loading her buckets into the back of her cleaning van.

'Oh, Dr Williams, I'm so pleased you're home,' she said. 'I've been popping in to check on your young lady all afternoon and I didn't like to leave until you got home so I thought I'd do Dr Teo's spring cleaning. His place has been wanting a good going over for ever. But she's looking a little better. I gave her a nice boiled egg and she managed to eat most of it. She wanted to get dressed an hour ago but I said you wouldn't hear of it and if she tried I'd ring you. So she's gone back to sleep like a good girl. And she's lovely.' She beamed. 'Just lovely. I knew you'd find someone someday but I had no idea that you'd already found her… Lovely, lovely, lovely.'

He opened the door looking like a little boy expecting a bogeyman. If she wasn't so discombobulated, she would have laughed.

The last time she'd seen this man he'd been totally in control and she very much hadn't been. She still wasn't, but he looked like a man thrown overboard without a lifeline.

She shoved herself up on her pillows…on *his* pillows, she reminded herself…and tried to look dignified.

Gladys had helped her shower and change into her nightgown. It was quite a respectable nightgown. It wasn't respectable enough for greeting the man the whole hospital thought she'd slept with. Who'd held her paper bag.

'Thank you for the bed,' she said with as much dignity as she could muster. 'I'll get up now. I would have left sooner but Gladys was threatening strait-jackets.'

'And you didn't feel well enough?'

'There was that. It's a powerful little bug.'

'It hit most people harder than you.'

'Gee, that makes me feel better.'

'Sorry.' He wasn't sure where to take it from here, she thought. Neither was she.

'I will get up now,' she said.

'There's no need.'

Really? The thought of wriggling further down on these gorgeous pillows was almost irresistible—but this wasn't her bed. It was Luke Williams's bed.

'Gladys seems to think I'm your long-lost lover,' she managed. 'The sooner I'm out of here the better.'

'The whole hospital thinks you're my long-lost lover. It's not such a bad idea.'

She thought about that. Or she tried to think about it. Her brain was ever so fuzzily…well, fuzzy.

What he'd said was a very fuzzy statement.

'From whose point of view?' she said at last.

He ventured further into the room, looking suddenly businesslike. Professional. Doctor approaching patient with an action plan. 'From both of our points of view if you intend fulfilling your contract,' he said briskly. 'We were caught in a position that was less than dignified. If we were long-term lovers, the hospital grapevine would think it was funny and get over it. For a man and woman who met each other only hours before, it's like a great big neon light's appeared over your head saying "Condemn".'

There was much in that to think about. Condemn. It was a heavy word. Condemnation was how she was thinking of herself, in the fragments of time the gastro had given her to contemplate the matter.

But her self-image wasn't this man's problem. She'd held him. She'd wanted him as much as he'd wanted her. It was up to her to handle the consequences. 'I can handle a bit of condemnation,' she said, wondering if she could.

She thought of all the insults thrown in her direction since her father had died. She was her mother's daughter, therefore she was a Scarlet Woman by default. It had even ended her relationship with Charlie the Accountant, the man she'd dated for three years but who'd jibbed when expectations had turned to marriage.

'*Sorry, Lily, but I can't handle your reputation.*'

'*You mean my mother's reputation? My mother's behaviour makes me a whore, too?*' Her voice had risen... maybe more than she'd intended.

'*No but people look at you. I'm not sure I can handle that for the rest of our lives; people expecting you to turn out like your mother.*'

She'd thrown something at him. Something large and unwieldy that had just happened to be full of water and half-dead Christmas lilies. It had been a satisfactory moment in a very unsatisfactory interview, one that had left her feeling sullied. Mostly because she'd thought she'd loved Charlie and he'd loved her, and how could she have loved someone who thought her mother's reputation was more important than their relationship?

But her mother's reputation was important. It made a difference. Like her reputation was important now, if she was to continue working at the Harbour.

She was only at the Harbour for four weeks. She *could* handle this.

'I need a favour,' Luke said and sat on her bed.

His bed. She inched back on the pillows.

She'd held this man, why?

She knew why she'd held him. It had been the culmination of an appalling time, an appalling emotion. She'd felt a matching need in him and their mutual need had exploded.

There was no longer mutual need. They were strangers. There wasn't even attraction.

Um…yes, there was. He was rumpled after a long day at work. He'd hauled off his tie and his top shirt button was undone, revealing a hint of lean muscle underneath. His dark eyes were shadowed with weariness, and his five o'clock shadow was toe-curlingly sexy.

If he leaned forward and touched her…

She'd be out of here so fast he wouldn't see her go. What she was feeling scared her witless.

She was not going to become her mother.

What had he said? *I need a favour.*

'I don't owe you,' she said, cautiously. 'Or not very much. I mean…it was lovely that you helped me this morning, and you gave me a gorgeous bed to sleep in for the day, but—'

'I'd like you to sleep in it for a month.'

That was enough to take her breath away. A girl could be properly flummoxed with a statement like that.

'No,' she said.

'No?'

'It's a very nice bed,' she managed. 'But despite all evidence to the contrary, I keep myself nice.'

'I'm not propositioning you. I have a sofa bed in the living room. This apartment has two bathrooms. This bed can be yours for a month.'

'I have a bed of my own.'

'You're not going back to that doss house.'

'It might be a doss house,' she said with as much dignity as she could muster, 'but it's a prepaid doss house. It's okay. My bedroom's almost clean.'

'There are bedbugs.'

'Nonsense. I would have been bitten by now.'

For answer he tugged her arm forward, slid her sleeve to her elbow and exposed a cluster of red welts. They both looked down at them. Irrefutable evidence. 'I saw these this morning,' he said. 'I rest my case.'

She stared down at the welts, perplexed. Bedbugs. She *had* been itchy, she thought. She'd just been too preoccupied to notice.

'Yikes,' she muttered. 'And double yikes. I'll buy insect spray.'

'You don't get rid of bedbugs with inspect spray. You get rid of them by moving out.'

'Not an option.'

'You have an option. Here.'

'I'm not in the market for a relationship,' she snapped.

'I told you, I have a very comfortable sofa bed. I'm not in the market for a relationship either.'

'I didn't even mean to kiss you.'

'Neither did I.'

They were glaring at each other. He was still holding her arm. A frisson of something…electricity?…was passing between.

She couldn't figure it out.

Why had she kissed him?

She wanted, quite fiercely, totally inexplicably, to do it again.

Get a grip, she told herself frantically. Even if her body was operating at ten per cent capacity, she had to think.

She was so tired. She wanted to go back to sleep.

But a woman with no money, a woman who was dependent on her next pay cheque, *a woman like her*, couldn't sleep.

She glanced at the bedside clock. Seven-thirty. She was due back at the hospital at eight. She went to toss back the covers and then thought better of it. Her nightgown wasn't all that long. She didn't intend to make this situation more personal than it already was.

'I need to get to work,' she said, with as much dignity as she could muster. She glanced at her suitcase in the corner. 'Thank you for bringing my stuff. Would you mind giving me some privacy while I get dressed?'

'You're not getting dressed.'

'Says who?'

'Me. And there's no need. You're not required at work again until Monday.'

'Monday!' She gasped. 'Are you out of your mind? I've signed on for four weeks. If I don't go to work tonight, I've broken my contract. No pay. Do you know what that means?'

'The hospital's paying,' he said. 'Their barrier nursing clearly isn't working; they took out the controls too soon. The least they can do is pay you while you're sick. I've already organised it. Standard leave for this bug is four days—barrier nursing requires it. They don't want you back there before Monday but you'll be paid regardless.'

Whoa.

No work until Monday.

Four days with pay.

She could sink…

She couldn't sink. *She was in this man's bed.*

'You're looking paler every minute,' he said conversationally. 'You don't want to be sick again. Put your head down and sleep.'

'No!' It was practically a wail.

Why did he want her here? She was starting to feel like a white slave trader was standing at the end of her bed. *His bed.*

'I'm not holding you here against your will,' he said.

'Yes, you are.' She was having trouble making herself speak. 'If you won't let me get dressed…'

'Your baggage has been cavorting with bedbugs,' he said, prosaically. 'I'll take it down to the basement and fumigate it while you sleep.'

'But why?' It *was* a wail this time—she was reaching the point where the world was starting to blur.

He knew it. He took her hands in his before she could resist, his strong fingers holding hers. The strength of him was infinitely…masculine. Infinitely seductive and infinitely comforting.

How long since someone had held her to comfort her?

He wasn't holding her to comfort her, she reminded herself, trying frantically to defuzz her thoughts. He was holding her to have his wicked way…although how he could want to have any sort of way with a woman who'd just stopped throwing up…

'We can help each other,' he said, quite gently, and she blinked and tried to think of something other than the feel of his hands holding hers. His gorgeous eyes; his gaze meeting hers, pure and strong. The strength of his jaw, the strong bone structure of his face, the shadow of a smile that was gentleness itself.

He'd make a gorgeous doctor, she thought. He *was* a gorgeous doctor.

'You're already helping me,' she muttered. 'Your housekeeper gave me an egg and toast soldiers.'

'Good for Gladys. I hope they helped.'

'I kept 'em down.'

'All the more reason why you should help me back. Stay here for a month.'

Her eyes weren't working properly. They kept blinking.

She was seeing him in soft focus. He was a beautiful man, she thought, and he was proposing that she stay with him for a month. Like a sheik and a desert princess.

Princesses didn't wear shabby nightgowns and smell of... She didn't want to think of what she smelled of, despite her shower. A night on duty, followed by gastro...

'I think you're weird,' she said. 'Go find a princess, instead of—'

'I'm not in the market for a princess,' he said, the gentleness fading a little. 'That's why I want you.'

'Pardon?'

He sighed, looked down at their linked hands and carefully disengaged. The gentle look became grim.

'I don't do relationships,' he said.

'I see that,' she said cautiously, casting a quick look round the sparse bedroom. This was such a male domain.

'But everyone in the hospital wants me to.'

This was important, she decided. She had to get to the other side of the fuzz. Figure out where reality and nonsense merged. 'You don't think that's just a wee bit egotistical?' she demanded, and his smile returned. It was a truly gorgeous smile.

His smile could make a girl's knees turn to putty—if a girl's knees weren't already putty.

'Sydney Harbour Hospital is gossip central,' he said. 'Too much intense emotion, too many people working long hours, thrown together over and over... Everyone at the Harbour knows everyone else's business.'

'You're kidding,' she said faintly. 'I'd thought it'd be a huge, anonymous hospital.'

'The Harbour?' He gave a hollow laugh. 'Anonymous is not us. Big or not, we're made up of individual teams. Everyone knows everyone else's business, sometimes I think right down to the jocks we wear. Actually, that may well be the literal truth; Mrs Henderson does my washing. This apartment block is home to at least half a dozen Harbour medics who also use Mrs Henderson, so I guess that's public knowledge as well. But since my wife died four years ago...'

'I'm sorry.'

'It's history,' he said harshly. 'But that's the problem. The hospital, the grapevine, the whole gossip network has decided it's time for me to move on. Even my boss keeps pushing women at me.'

'Gee,' she said cautiously, her interest caught through the fuzz. 'So you're being besieged with women. That must be tough.'

'I've been married,' he said, maybe more harshly than he intended because he paused and softened his tone. 'What I mean is that I have no intention of going there again. I'd like everybody to lay off. You're in Sydney for a month?'

'Yes.'

'Then where are you going?'

'Brisbane?' It was the first place that came into her mind. It sounded a lot more fun than Lighthouse Cove.

'A month would give me head space,' he said. 'I've told them we've been in a relationship for a while.'

'You did that?' The fuzz was thickening.

'It protects your reputation.'

'Thank you.' She didn't feel like saying thank you. She felt…like she didn't know what to say.

He was being businesslike, a surgeon outlining an action plan. 'Apart from protecting your reputation, if we let everyone know what happened yesterday was the result of a long-term relationship, it helps me. I'm having four weeks with you and then you can go to Brisbane, you can do anything you like, but from my point of view you can be my absentee girlfriend for as long as I can carry it off. I'll tell them you need to care for an ailing mother or something similar. I can tell them we met on holiday a couple of years ago. That you come to the farm whenever you can. That I'm a very loyal lover. I'm thinking I might get two years out of this.'

'Two years…'

'Two years without matchmaking. Two years where I'm left alone.' He ran his fingers through his already rumpled hair and sighed. 'Believe me, in this hothouse, that's worth diamonds. And in return you get board for a month. You have to admit anything's better than that dump you were staying in. So…deal?'

The fuzz was everywhere, but his gaze was on her. Firm. Businesslike. Like what he was suggesting was reason itself. 'Platonic,' he said. 'No sex. Promise.'

'Of course there'd be no sex, but…' But her head was spinning. This was crazy. She'd be a pretend lover?

He was proposing an affair of convenience. No sex.

He really did have the most beautiful...pillows.

Oh, she was tired.

'You,' Luke said, with a certain amount of contrition, 'are wrecked. You need to sleep. I have another bathroom off the living room. We're independent. You sleep your bug away and then settle in for a month of businesslike contact. Would you like anything before you go to sleep?'

What was happening?

Sense was telling her to get out of this man's bed now; get out of his life.

If she did, she'd have to leave the pillows.

And... He'd just asked her if she'd like anything. What she wanted more than anything else in the world...

'Another cup of tea?' she murmured, figuring it couldn't hurt to ask.

He grinned. 'Your wish is my command.'

And five minutes later she was tucked up in his bed with a fresh cup of tea, plumped pillows, a spare blanket, the night settling in over the apartment. Five minutes later she was Luke Williams's Lover of Convenience.

CHAPTER FIVE

SHE slept for almost twenty-four hours. Mrs Henderson popped in during the day with sympathy, tea, more eggs and toast soldiers, and some gentle probing.

Where had she come from? How long had she known 'our lovely Dr Williams'? Were they engaged?

She acted shy. She acted sleepy, which wasn't all that hard.

She slept.

The events of the last week had left her exhausted. In truth, the events of the last few years had left her exhausted.

She'd been her mother's keeper. It had been a full-time job.

Right now, her mother didn't know where she was and she couldn't contact her. When Lily left town she'd stopped at the headland overlooking the bay and tossed her cellphone as far as she could throw it.

If her mother had a drama—and she would certainly have a drama—Lily wouldn't even know about it.

She could guess.

Would the vicar stay with her? Would her mother be able to ride out the town's condemnation? Would her mother be able to operate the microwave?

Her father had treated her mother like a Dresden

doll. He'd died when Lily had been twelve, and Lily had promised...

Enough.

She lay in Luke's bed with no cellphone, no way her mother could know where she was, and she felt...weightless.

She could even manage pretending to be Luke's lover for this luxury, she told herself. And Luke was serious about what he wanted. He'd slept in the living room, then carefully packed everything up before he'd left for work, checking and rechecking so Mrs Henderson would have no hint they'd slept apart.

Mrs Henderson supported her into the shower, clucked over her and helped her into a clean nightgown. Apparently Luke had gone through her baggage and given instructions that everything should be cleaned. She should be offended but she didn't have the energy. She lay in the vast bed on the crisp linen Mrs Henderson had insisted on changing. She gazed out of the windows at the glorious vista of Sydney Harbour.

Four days of nothing, nothing and nothing.

Apart from being Luke Williams's pretend lover.

'Wouldn't your mother want to know that you've been ill?' Mrs Henderson asked as she bustled back in to say goodbye for the night.

'No,' she said sleepily. 'I don't want to worry her.'

And her mother wasn't worrying *her*. Luke Williams's lover wouldn't have mother worries.

Luke William's lover didn't.

'So how long has this been going on? Why haven't we heard about her before this? Where have you been keeping her? And where is she now?'

To say he was besieged was an understatement.

Luke's Thursdays were always frantic—it was the day he did his kids' list, birth defects, procedures that took all his skill and emotion. Today he was doing graft work on Ruby May Ellington's left thigh. Ruby May was four years old. Born as a conjoined twin, her sister had died at birth. Her sister's death had meant there had been no hard ethical decisions to be made, but the surgery to separate them had been performed urgently. There'd been no time for preparation of excess skin flaps, and the grafting still was ongoing.

Luke had been working on this case when Hannah had died. The day she'd died, his team had saved Ruby's life.

The medical imperative tore a person in two. Like now, when he was concerned about the woman he'd left in his apartment. She was suffering from gastro but instinct told him it was more. She was too thin. Too tired. Too…shadowed.

She was running from something, he thought, but what?

He worked on, but the questions kept coming.

And they kept coming from the people around him.

Who was this Lily he'd kept so dark?

'Why didn't you tell us?' The head of paediatrics, Teo, a Samoan with a heart almost as big as his body, had been involved in Ruby's care from the beginning and, like Luke, he was willing the little girl a good outcome. It wasn't, however, deflecting him from hospital gossip. 'You've had this woman for how long?'

'That's none of your business.'

'Hey, this is the Harbour,' Teo said mildly. 'Everything's everyone's business. And now you've installed her in Kirribilli Views… You expect to keep her to yourself?'

'Until she's better, yes.'

'You have the next three days off, right?' With the procedure over, Luke was stripping off his theatre garb. Teo had hitched himself up onto the sinks and was regarding him thoughtfully.

'Yes.' What was coming?

He knew what was coming. Teo had a huge extended family and he treated the hospital as part of it. He shouldn't be a paediatrician, he should be a party organiser.

'I'm having a party on the beach on Saturday night,' Teo told him. 'My aunties are bringing food. You've knocked me back now one hundred and seventeen times…'

'A hundred and seventeen?'

'I've been counting,' Teo said. 'You disappear every time you have time off, and now we know why. But since you've introduced your Lily into the medical team, the least you can do is bring her along.'

His Lily? 'No.'

'No?'

Finn walked in and Teo turned to him. 'He's not co-operating,' he complained. 'Tell him letting us in on this lady is in his contract.'

'It's not,' Finn said shortly, and Luke glanced sharply at his boss. Was he in pain? His voice was tight, tense. Luke had seen a lot of pain in his professional life. There was something wrong.

'Leave him alone,' Finn snapped before Luke could get any further. 'He chose to flaunt his woman once, it doesn't mean he has to do it again.'

'I didn't…flaunt,' Luke said, and Teo grinned.

'Having it off in the on-call room? I'd call it flaunting. Bring her on Saturday. You're going to spend the whole weekend fending off visitors anyway. Word is Ginnie Allen's already figured out she's Lily's new best friend.

She'll be knocking on the door asking for a cup of sugar right now. So…party it is.'

'Party it isn't,' Luke growled.

'Are you taking Mariette to Teo's party on Saturday?'

Finn Kennedy groaned. Surely as Surgical Director he should have privacy. He'd been back in his office for a whole two minutes and now Evie Lockheart was leaning on the doorjamb, surveying him with sardonic amusement.

'No.'

'No?' She raised her brows. 'Just as well. Everyone's tiptoeing around you but maybe someone ought to let you know David Blackmore, the new paediatric intern, is breaking his heart over Mariette.'

'What does that have to do with me?' The pain in Finn's shoulder was driving him nuts and this woman was driving him nuts. She had no power in this hospital. She was one cog in a very big machine.

Her family money meant she could lean on the doorjamb and look…sardonic.

She also looked concerned. 'Is there something wrong with your arm?'

'No. Butt out.'

She butted, but only so far. 'Mariette's afraid to break things off with you because she's scared you'll sack David.'

'I won't sack David. And Mariette…'

'Has a reputation,' Evie said evenly. 'Which is why you're using her. You don't use women you can hurt. All I'm saying is that David's smitten and Mariette's worried enough to be not backing off from you for his sake. David might be the making of her. They say love cures all…'

'You're telling me this why?'

'Just so you know,' Evie said blithely. 'You're the ogre around this place. No one stands up to you.'

'Except you.'

'And Luke,' she said thoughtfully. 'There's another case in point. Love conquers all. He has a lady and he's taking her to the farm this weekend. I'm thinking we should change the quarantine rules so neither can come back to the hospital for a week. It wouldn't hurt to give them a push.'

'If you think I have time to waste…'

'On romance? I know you don't,' she said, and straightened. 'Just saying. Just going. Think about Mariette, though. She's a good kid at heart. And as for interfering with Luke's hot weekend—'

'I have no intention—'

'Excellent,' Evie said. 'I do like a man with no intentions.'

Every second Friday Luke had off. Every second Friday was tomorrow.

Luke's normal routine was to work for eleven days straight. He was happy to be rostered on public holidays, Christmas and Easter; in fact, he preferred it. But at the end of every two weeks he had three days off for the farm. For his sanity.

His farm was his place, his sanctuary, his solitude.

Solitude? Lily?

The entire hospital now believed he was taking Lily there.

In the brief moments he'd had to himself since settling Lily into his apartment, he'd decided that he'd go to the farm as usual this weekend and that she'd stay where she was. Only now he'd started a lie.

Lily was deemed his long-term lover. He'd hardly go away to the farm the moment she arrived.

If he did, everyone at Kirribilli Views would know she was 'home alone', and what's worse, he wouldn't put it past them to drop in on Lily. To sympathise? To check on her for him?

He could see Teo dragging her to his party whether she willed it or not. The man's charm was legendary.

He didn't mind if Teo's charm was second to none, he told himself, but…

But his thoughts wouldn't go further than that one word.

One lie and a whole skein of deception had appeared.

Should they both stay here?

If he stayed here he'd be either pacing the hospital with nothing to do or he'd be pacing the apartment. With Lily.

So… Farm?

Would she come?

How did you persuade a stranger?

But she wasn't a stranger, he told himself grimly. She was his lover for a month.

Including farm time.

'John says you're going to the farm for the weekend. Oh, that's lovely. What's it like? He never tells us anything about it. He keeps everything so quiet. He's kept you so quiet.'

To say Lily was bewildered was putting it mildly. She'd opened the door, hoping the doorbell signalled a delivery or something equally innocuous, and an immaculately groomed woman with eyes darting everywhere swept right in.

'I'm Ginnie Allen. My husband's a clinical psychologist at the Harbour. We live in the apartment on the next floor up. I'm so happy to meet you. Oh, he's wicked, your Luke, fancy keeping you to himself. Has he told you Teo's having a party this weekend? Everyone's aching to meet you but he says you're going to the farm. He always goes to the farm. Surely you'd prefer the party?'

Lily clutched her bathrobe round her. Actually, it was Luke's bathrobe. Big and black and masculine, it fell to the floor and made an ungainly train.

She'd just woken. Her hair was ghastly. She was wearing no make-up. The woman before her looked like she'd just stepped out of *Sporting Vogue*.

To say she felt at a disadvantage was an understatement.

'And you're Lily…?' Ginnie waited for her to complete the name.

'Yes,' Lily said discouragingly, backing away slightly. 'And I'm sorry, but I've been ill. If you could excuse me…'

'Oh, of course, you tuck yourself straight back into bed and we'll talk there. Would you like me to make us both a nice cup of tea?'

Tea had suddenly lost its appeal. 'I'd rather—'

'Coffee? No, dear, tea's much better. And toast? You need to keep your strength up if you're going to spend the whole weekend with Luke.'

'Hi, Ginnie.'

Luke. He stepped out of the apartment elevator in his suit and tie, with his briefcase in hand. Doctor coming home from work—to be greeted by the little woman in his bathrobe, and her new best friend, Ginnie.

'Luke!' Ginnie gave a crow of delight and hugged him before he had a chance to defend himself. 'Oh, wow, congratulations. You and Lily… I had no idea.'

'We're hardly announcing diamonds,' Lily said dryly,

thinking she'd better nip this in the bud. 'Are you congratulating Luke on sharing his bathrobe?'

'I've no intention of sharing,' Luke said, and looked across Ginnie's head to smile at Lily.

And that smile...

Oh, that smile. She really was her mother's daughter, she thought, suddenly feeling frantic. If Luke had been the vicar...

She thought suddenly of the vicar, and for some stupid reason the thought made her want to chuckle. And wince. How could her mother fall for someone like the vicar when there were men like Luke in the world? Men who owned bathrobes like this. It must be cashmere, she thought. It was a caress all on its own.

His smile was a caress all on its own.

'I can't believe you're not coming to Teo's party,' Ginnie said reproachfully, letting Luke go and regarding him with huge disappointed eyes—and Luke's expression became a bit hunted.

He always goes to the farm... Lily wasn't sure what was happening here, but he didn't look the least bit like he wanted to go to any party. Well, neither did she. She didn't know what was going on but he'd lent her his bathrobe. He'd lent her his bed. Maybe she could afford to be generous.

He always goes to the farm...

'I'm not a city girl,' she told Ginnie. 'That's why I've only agreed to come and stay here for a month. That's why Luke and I can't be...as together as we'd like. But now I've been ill I'm—'

'Pining,' Luke finished for her, his smile still lurking. 'For the fjords.'

She cast him a look that was meant to put him in his

place. 'For fresh air,' she told him. 'For the smell of… sheep.'

'Horses,' Luke said.

It was becoming more difficult to be generous. Especially when he was still smiling.

'Especially for the smell of horses,' she amended. 'Eau de horse will cure me faster than anything.'

'You like farms?' Ginnie sounded incredulous.

'What's not to love?'

'Well, horses for a start,' Ginnie said, and shuddered. 'They bite.'

'Not my horses,' Luke said.

'Well, we wouldn't know,' Ginnie said, suddenly wasp-ish. 'We've been practically next-door neighbours for four years and not one invite. You know we'd all love to see your farm. It's like you're keeping it a secret. It's like you've been keeping Lily secret.'

'It's because I know you hate horses,' Luke said blandly. 'Lily loves horses. She rides 'em to the manor born.'

Lily blinked. She loved horses?

Actually…she did.

A farm with horses. She thought suddenly…what was being proposed here? A couple of days on a farm with horses.

She might even put up with Luke Williams for that.

'Well, I think you should stay here,' Ginnie said crossly. 'Look at her.' She motioned to Lily-In-The-Bathrobe. 'She looks sick.'

'Gee, thanks.' But she *was* wobbly.

'My car's lovely,' Luke said reassuringly. 'Aston Martin, deep leather seats, pure luxury. And Lily even managed to protect them with her paper bag,' he told Ginnie. 'She's a heroine, my Lily. I'm thinking she can sleep all the way there.'

My Lily. The words hung.

This was getting out of hand, Lily thought, starting to feel hysterical. She'd agreed to this, why?

'How long have you guys been an item?' Ginnie demanded of Lily. '*Have* you been to his farm?'

Was now the time to back away? Lily wondered, hysteria growing. Pack and leave for Brisbane?

It'd have to be Brisbane. She couldn't go back to the Harbour after confessing this lie.

Luke had started the lie. Not her. She glanced at Luke, who glanced right back. Their eyes locked. His gaze was... almost a challenge?

Are you about to tell the truth?

Oh, for heaven's sake, why should she? she thought. What right did this nosey woman have to the truth?

Whatever, she decided. Go with the flow.

But maybe...not lie unless she had to?

'Merrylegs is my very favourite horse,' she said, tangentially.

'Merrylegs?' Ginnie blinked.

'She's given me years of joy,' she said and somehow, between Ginnie's prurient interest and Luke's bland withdrawal, she found herself remembering her first and one true love. 'She's beautiful. I know her so well she's almost part of me, and I wish I could be riding her now.'

'She's on Luke's farm?'

'All my horses are on my farm,' Luke said, sounding suddenly...wicked. 'Even though Merrylegs is Lily's favourite, all my horses are her horses.'

'How long have you two been an item?' Ginnie demanded.

'Years,' Luke said. 'Like Lily said.'

'How many years.'

'Three?' Luke said. 'I think. Isn't that right, dear?'

'Have you been staying on Luke's farm for three years?' Ginnie was almost speechless. 'That's not even a year after Hannah died.'

'I never met Hannah.' Lily faced Luke's wickedness head on. What had he called her? *Dear*. She lowered her voice, talking respectfully about her lover's deceased wife. 'Would Hannah have loved Merrylegs?' she asked Luke. 'Dear?'

'Hannah was more a cat person,' Luke said. The smile behind his eyes was challenging. Dangerous.

She rose to meet it. Challenging right back.

'You never talk to me about Hannah. I think you should.' She turned back to Ginnie. 'He never talks to me about Hannah,' she said, sounding aggrieved. 'I think our relationship would be better if he let it all out.'

'That's what John says,' Ginnie managed. 'So…'

'So, farm,' Lily said, trying hard to sound brisk when, in fact, all she wanted to do was retreat to Luke's bed and pull pillows over her head. 'We can pack pillows,' she told Luke. 'Your beautiful car might even be comfortable enough to sleep in. Mind, I'm more accustomed to the farm truck,' she confessed to Ginnie. 'But when in the city, act like a city girl, that's what I say. You might like to pack some more paper bags…*sweetheart*.'

'I guess we'd better start packing,' Luke said faintly. *'Darling.'*

'You start packing,' Lily said tartly, long-term-lover-like. 'I'm poorly. Ginnie, would you like to help? Maybe you could make me that toast you were offering?'

'Are you offering to make us dinner?' Luke asked, full of hope, and Ginnie backed out as if burned.

'I'll leave you to it. We'll miss you tomorrow night. Come back better, Lily. We'll have a lovely long chat on Monday.'

'I can't wait,' Lily muttered as Luke closed the door behind her. 'I just can't wait.'

To say the silence was loaded was an understatement. Luke closed the door carefully and then snibbed it, as if even now Ginnie might return.

Lily backed to the closest dining room chair and sat. Whatever energy she'd had had been spent.

'I'm thinking,' she said at last, trying hard to breathe so she didn't gasp, 'that communication seems to be lacking. So we're a couple. Congratulations are in order. We've been dating for years. We're about to leave on a romantic weekend to some farm I've never heard of.'

'Where you ride a horse called Merrylegs.' He seemed just as winded as she was. 'I believe two of us are playing this game.'

'It's not a game,' she snapped.

'I'm not laughing,' he said, and suddenly he wasn't. All this time he'd been holding his briefcase. Now he set it down, carefully, like it might explode.

That's what the atmosphere felt like, Lily thought. Loaded.

'I'm feeling a wee bit trapped,' she said, and hauled his bathrobe tighter round her.

'That's the part I don't understand.'

'What?'

'The trapped bit. You're an agency nurse. You could pack up and leave.'

'If I break my four-week contract.'

'I understand it'd make it hard to find another agency to take you. But there are other cities.'

'I don't have enough money to move to another city.'

'Would you like to tell me why you're in trouble?'

'No,' she said. She thought about it, thought about all the conclusions he might be jumping to, thought that maybe hiding any more conclusions wasn't a good idea. 'My mother's maxed out my credit card,' she said. 'She's done…well, let's just say savings I thought were in my account no longer are. She's taken a lover. We live in my tiny two-bedroom apartment and the walls are thin.'

'Ouch.'

'Her lover's the local vicar, husband of a prominent citizen, I'm a scarlet woman by association.'

'Double ouch.'

'Lighthouse Cove is too small.'

'I can see it might be.' He looked at her, not so much sympathetic as interested. Doctor inspecting patient. Looking at strange symptoms. 'So why not Adelaide? You trained there. You could get a job there.'

'And my mother would be on my doorstep within days, weeping, asking for money, needing support. Or worse, walking into the ward where I'm working, weeping, asking for money, needing support. She's done it before and she'll do it again.'

'So Sydney.'

'For as long as I can manage,' she said wearily. 'For as long as I can get by until I need to go home and face the mess. I hadn't counted on running into a mess myself.' She sighed, and looked longingly at the bed. 'I'm really very tired.'

'You are,' he said, gently this time, as if the physician

had made his diagnosis and was moving to treatment phase. 'But this apartment block is almost an extension of the hospital. We'll be watched all weekend. The farm is best.'

'I don't want to move,' she admitted.

'It'd be better if I went to the farm and you stayed here,' he conceded. 'Only you'd get visitors and questions. At the farm you can sleep for three days straight. So what I suggest is that you sleep now for a couple of hours while I finish some patient notes, then I'll tuck you into my car and you can sleep all the way to Tarrawalla.'

'Tarrawalla?'

'It's where my elderly uncle lives,' he said. 'And the phantom Merrylegs.' He smiled. 'And the rest of my horses, all of which you ride like the wind.'

That smile…

She shouldn't.

Shouldn't what? Go to his farm? Sink into that smile? No, she thought wearily, but her body was caving in.

'You're beat,' he said softly, and before she could guess his intention he lifted her and carried her to the bedroom.

'Put me…put me down…'

'Of course I will,' he said softly. 'I won't do anything you don't like, Lily Ellis. We've been unwise enough. Now's the time to be sensible.'

She didn't feel sensible. She felt…she felt…

Like Luke Williams was carrying her to his bed and there wasn't a thing she could do about it.

Travelling in Luke's car was almost like travelling in his arms. She lay back in her glorious leather seat, padded with pillows, ensconced in a soft cashmere blanket and felt…cherished.

'I feel like your ancient grandmother, being taken on a nicely padded outing,' she told him as he negotiated his way up into the hills north-west of Sydney. It was well past dusk. They were driving into the night and the passenger compartment was a pool of luxurious intimacy.

Luke's face was a focused profile against the moonlight shining through the driver's window. His face had such strength… He'd been hurt, Lily had decided after a few covert glances at him. Even if she hadn't known his wife had died, his face told her that. It looked…forbidding.

She was fighting an overwhelming urge to reach out and touch his hand on the steering-wheel, as a lover might, as a wife might.

Or an ancient grandmother ensconced in woolly cashmere.

'My grandmother wouldn't have been seen dead under a cashmere blanket,' he said, and she blinked.

'Past tense?' she said cautiously. 'Your grandma?'

'She died young; cirrhosis of the liver. Too much champagne.'

'I'm sorry.'

'There're worse ways to go. She was the society matriarch of Singapore.'

'Is that where your family live?'

'Yes.' Blunt and hard. The meaning was clear. Don't go there.

She wouldn't. But he had family. The thought jolted her. He'd seemed isolated.

He still seemed isolated.

And…he'd mentioned an uncle at the farm. Maybe it was time she learned more, even if she couldn't ask directly about his parents.

'So why aren't you in Singapore?' she ventured.

'I was sent to Sydney to boarding school when I was ten and I've stayed. A couple of visits home were enough for me, to be honest. My uncle did all the caring needed. He left Singapore when he was twenty as well, pleased to be shot of them.'

'So the Harbour is your de facto family,' she said thoughtfully. 'No wonder they matchmake.'

'They won't any more.'

'Because I'm the match.' She retreated under her cashmere and watched the car eat white lines. 'So after I leave…will you go back to being heartbroken?'

'I haven't decided.' He sounded amused. 'But I'm thinking I won't give up on you. You'll be heading into the sunset to find yourself and I'll be faithful for years, waiting hopelessly for you to return.'

'Wow,' she said. 'Like Miss Havisham, sitting in a pool of mouldy wedding dress.'

'That'll be me,' he said, sounding cheerful. 'So your family. One nutty mother. Who else?'

'Not a sausage.'

He shook his head. 'Everyone has a sausage.'

'Nope. My parents were both only children of elderly parents. My dad died when I was twelve. There's just been me and Mum ever since.'

'Cheap on birthday gifts,' he said, cautiously.

'Not so much. This year Mum's self-administered birthday gift was a trip to Paris for her and her vicar. She's disgusted because apparently I didn't have as much in my bank account as she thought. That's why she's still stuck in Lighthouse Cove, until her vicar finds the extra money— or her vicar gets tired of her.' She grimaced. 'It's a merry-go-round. I'll put more safeguards in place next time.'

'Next time… You'll go back?'

'I promised my dad I'd look after her and I will, but I need a break for a bit.'

'Of course,' Luke said, cheering up. 'For now you're my lover, or my ancient grandmother. But it doesn't matter. My farm's a haven Tom and I have created, a place with no obligations at all. My farm's for being whoever you like.'

Whoever she liked.

His lover or his grandmother?

Hmm.

She snuggled under the cashmere and thought, This could be a very long weekend.

CHAPTER SIX

THE farmhouse was tiny, remote, perfect.

Lily gazed in awe at the moonlit valley; at the tiny house set high above a creek meandering through bushland. Mountains loomed in the background, blue-black in the moonlight.

A trail of smoke wisped from the chimney and a warm glow of light spread from the veranda.

'Who lives here?'

'I do.'

'But…the fire…the light…'

'My uncle lives in the big house. He likes his privacy. I bought the adjoining land so this is mine. Tom knows when I'm coming. He'll have brought in supplies, lit the fire, got the place warm.'

The night was warm and still. A mopoke was calling from the gums around the house. She could hear water rippling over stones, and frogs.

She climbed out of the car and the beauty of the place felt breathtaking. To have had the week she'd had, and then to find herself in a place like this…

Her eyes were suddenly filling with tears and she swiped them away with desperation. Luke was carting her suitcase up the steps. He stopped and looked back. 'What's wrong?'

'I… Nothing.'

'There are no padlocks here,' he said, mistaking her hesitation. 'I promise.'

I wouldn't mind if there were, if I got to stay here, she thought, filling her lungs with the gorgeous night air.

She could smell horses!

A million memories were crowding in. Her father, their farm, the horses she'd grown up with.

'When can I meet Merrylegs?' she managed, and made her feet head for the steps. All she wanted to do was stand and sniff the air.

'Merrylegs might be a bit hard to arrange,' he told her. He grinned. 'Though come to think of it, Tom told me we have a new colt since last time I was down. Merrylegs… Shall we take a look tomorrow and see if the name suits?'

'You'd name a colt for me?' She practically gasped.

'Think about it in the morning,' he said gently. 'You're shaking.'

How had he known? But she was. This stupid bug had left her so weak she was struggling not to cry.

She was out of control. But no. It was simply that she wasn't under her own control. Luke was calling the shots and for the first time since her father had died someone had lifted responsibility from her shoulders.

She was back on a farm, without the burden of care.

She thought suddenly of the day of her father's death. Of him sitting at the kitchen table, a mass of bills around him, his face as bleak as death. 'Lily, if anything ever happens to me, you'll take care of your mother? Promise!'

She'd promised.

'Coming?' Luke said, and she looked up at this big, stern stranger, whose eyes were gentle but whose voice was inexorable. If she didn't move he was quite capable of striding down the steps, lifting her up and carrying her to bed.

The thought was…

Unwise. She made herself walk up the steps, into the beautiful little house, then up the stairs, into the made-up spare room and into bed.

She was asleep in an instant.

How could he sleep?

He didn't sleep much anyway. He lay staring into the night. So what was new?

Lily sleeping in his spare room was new.

He didn't invite people to this house. Hannah had made it beautiful, but he only used his bedroom and kitchen. He'd made the bed up because last year when the local stock and station agent's car had broken down a few miles from the house, he'd decided having the spare bed ready was sensible—but there was no question that this was his place.

To have Lily here was even more disconcerting than having her back at his apartment.

Why should it be disconcerting? She was a guest, a stranger in the next bedroom. A colleague. She was no different from the stock and station agent.

Or not.

Lily of the gaunt face. Lily who had been too thin even before the gastro. She seemed shadowed.

She needed this weekend. What harm was there in giving it to her? So what reason was there, then, to stay awake and be aware that she was just through the wall?

The whole hospital thought they were an item.

It'd been a spur of the moment deception but now…the thought seemed to be closing in on him. Deception or not, he didn't connect with people. Especially with complicated women.

Lily.

Hannah.

'Stand on your own two feet.' His father's voice seemed to boom from the darkness.

Luke's father and also his paternal grandfather were wealthy, foul-mouthed bullies. Luke's mother and grandmother were society gadflies, only interested in social standing. It was amazing they'd come together for long enough to produce children. Luke's father certainly hadn't wanted him. A son with a disfiguring birthmark had meant contempt from the day he was born.

What a family! His Uncle Tom had escaped Singapore as soon as he'd been old enough to emigrate, and Luke had been sent away at ten. Even though Tom had taken rough care of him since he'd arrived in Australia, Tom didn't seem like family. Neither uncle nor nephew knew what that was about.

Stupidly, Luke had tried family with Hannah. He'd spent four years thinking it might work; knowing it wouldn't. Then disaster.

Family was disaster. Emotional attachment was disaster.

'I have my farm and my medicine,' he told the darkness. 'That's enough.'

Whether Lily Ellis was his make-believe lover or not.

She woke and had to pinch herself to think she wasn't dreaming.

The bed was high, cast iron, the kind you'd expect in your grandmother's attic with a chamberpot underneath.

There was no chamberpot. There was a tiny bathroom

right through the door. Lush towels hung from antique towel rails. Her patchwork quilt was gorgeous. The thick lemon carpet meshed beautifully with the soft blue walls.

This was no garret. This whole wee house was beautiful.

Had it been furnished by Hannah? Certainly there was a woman's touch—this was a far cry from the cool greys of Luke's city apartment.

She'd gone to sleep listening to mopokes and night owls.

Now there were kookaburras right by her window, their raucous laughter making her smile. How come they hadn't woken her until now?

She rolled over and reached for her watch. And practically yelped.

Ten o'clock in the morning? What the…?

Where was Luke?

She glared at her watch like it had betrayed her. What sort of guest was she? He'd think…he'd think…

Why worry? He already thought she was loose and fast; why not let him think she was a total slob? The damage had been done. She could sleep until midday.

Or not. Kookaburras. Sunlight on her coverlet. Smells, pure country.

It was Friday. She was here until Sunday; three whole days of farm.

She was out of bed, heading for the shower before she finished the thought.

They needed to be independent. Luke decided this at dawn, when he woke, headed to the kitchen for his standard eggs and bacon, and then hesitated and thought he should wait for Lily to wake.

No. She needed to sleep. Independence was the go. He

needed to ride the boundaries, head over to the big house, spend a bit of time with Tom, do what he normally did on his first day here.

Lily needed to sleep for as long as her body required.

So he headed for Tom's but he made a phone call first. There was enough in what Lily had told him to think maybe some intervention might be needed. Without pushing the thought further, he called a lawyer mate in Adelaide. Then he left a note directing Lily to breakfast and headed out.

He found Tom, out with his dogs, eager to be doing things. Even though Tom was fiercely independent, he usually greeted Luke with a list of jobs the length of his arm. Today was fencing.

Excellent, Luke thought. Building fences, a man could get his thoughts together. Building fences, a man could forget about a woman with shadows, who'd melted into his arms and who'd…

No. Concentrate on fencing. He'd made the call to the lawyer. His conscience didn't require he worry any further.

Funny things, consciences. They had a will of their own.

The horse was young, Lily thought, watching him skittering toward her. Full grown. A gelding—he wasn't big enough, tough enough to be a stallion. He didn't look tough but he looked…bad? He pranced toward her and she could almost see challenge.

'Oh, you're beautiful,' she breathed as he came closer. She stood motionless against the fence, letting him assess her.

He was wearing a halter of tooled leather with a metal name-plate attached.

Glenfiddich.

He'd have been called Glenfiddich because he was pure spirit, she thought, and couldn't resist reaching to touch.

Or not. The contact had him skittering back, rearing, then tearing round the paddock at full gallop. His coat gleamed in the morning sun, every muscle clearly delineated. He was glorying in his strength, in the morning, in the sheer joy of being alive.

Which was exactly how Lily was feeling. The sun was on her face. She was out of the city. For now her mother was the vicar's responsibility. She felt like she'd shed a too-tight skin.

'Did he rescue you as well?' she whispered, and the big horse dashed past her once, twice, and then paused. Slowed.

Decided to investigate.

She stayed absolutely still. He reached her and touched her cheek with his nose. He blew against her hair.

She swung onto the fence-rail, slowly, but he didn't shy away. He nuzzled her again, pushing his nose into her armpit.

She scratched him behind his ears and he threw back his head, backed away again, then tossed his head and came back for more.

He was a wild, beautiful thing.

She looked at the halter. Maybe not so wild.

Wildish.

He looked at the gate. So did she.

Dared she?

This was Luke's horse.

What had he said to Ginnie? *All my horses are her horses.*

There was soft rope by the gate; rope that could be looped as makeshift reins.

At twelve there wasn't a horse she couldn't ride. She'd helped her father break them. He'd taught her well.

She hadn't been on a horse since.

Oh, he was beautiful.

She slipped down from the rail and he started nudging her toward the gate.

She giggled and he shoved her in the chest. Hard. Like, hurry up, there's a world out there. Let's go.

Let's go…

They might find Luke. He had to be somewhere. On this horse she could go anywhere.

Not since she was twelve…

'Don't you dare throw me,' she told the nose shoving her toward the gate. 'My pride's at stake.'

Luke spent four hours with Tom. Thirty satisfactory fence posts later he decided he needed to check on his guest.

He swung himself up back onto Checkers, his favourite horse, elderly, big, black and docile, with the gorgeous white blaze that had given him his name. He needed to head back to the house and make some lunch. He'd take Lily for a gentle stroll over the more accessible places on the farm.

Or not. For suddenly he saw her, over the ridge, cantering down along the track toward them. And she was riding…Glenfiddich.

His breath caught in his throat. Glenfiddich was a half-broken yearling, as spirited as his namesake. Lily was riding him without a saddle, with the halter he always wore but no bridle or reins. She was using rope as reins.

The last time Luke had ridden Glenfiddich it had taken

him an hour to settle him; to make him trustworthy. But here was Lily, her canter turning to gallop.

Was she crazy?

Even as the question hit, he was flying. Checkers was almost an extension of himself. He touched his flanks and his big horse flew toward Glenfiddich, veering at the last moment so Luke could grasp his halter. Glenfiddich tried to rear—of course he did—but Luke had him in a grip of iron. He swung off Checkers so he could take full control.

Glenfiddich objected—and so did Lily. 'What are you doing with my horse?' Even though Glenfiddich had reared back she hadn't shifted on his back.

'He's not your horse,' he said through gritted teeth. He was fighting Lily for the rope-cum-reins. 'Give me the reins and get off. Tom,' he yelled to his uncle. 'Come and lift Lily off.'

'Does Lily want to be lifted off?' Tom asked mildly, strolling up to meet them and raising his battered hat to Lily. 'Seems to me she's got a pretty good seat. Pleased to meet you.'

'Get off the horse,' Luke snapped.

'So…you didn't mean what you said about me being free to ride whatever horse I liked?'

'He's not trained.' When he thought of what could have happened…a slip of a girl on a half-trained gelding…he felt sick.

'And I've forgotten my training as well,' Lily said happily. 'So we suit.'

'Get down!' His anger reverberated through the bush.

Lily stared at him in dismay and then slid expertly from Glenfiddich's back.

'I haven't hurt him.'

'You're lucky he didn't kill you.'

'I know horses.'

'Not this one. Of all the stupid, risk-taking behaviour… You're just like those kids, rollerblading over tallow.'

'You don't think you might just be overreacting?' she ventured.

'I didn't give you permission.' He had both horses in hand now, keeping them well clear of Lily. Glenfiddich was objecting but Luke was in no mood to let him show it.

'I believe you told Ginnie I rode every horse here,' Lily said, sounding angry herself now. 'I ate breakfast as your note said, but there were no instructions after breakfast. I inspected the creek, the home paddock, the horses close by, and then I thought I'd like to go further. Glendiddich asked me to ride him, so we've been exploring and here we are.' She smiled at Tom and carefully ignored Luke's fury. 'You must be Luke's Uncle Tom. I've very happy to meet you.'

Glenfiddich asked me to ride him…

He tried to take it in. This morning Glenfiddich had seemed to take his decision to ride Checkers as a personal insult. He'd kicked out as they'd left the paddock, and it was only because Checkers was an old and wise horse that there had been no damage.

To see Lily flying along the track toward him, bareback…

Gorgeous didn't begin to describe her, and fear didn't begin to describe how he'd felt.

'You're out of your mind, riding a strange horse,' he snapped.

'He's not a strange horse. We introduced ourselves before we got familiar.' She tilted her chin defiantly. 'Not like you and me.'

It almost defused his anger. A lesser man would have blushed. He almost did.

'Let the girl back up,' Tom said from behind them. 'She looks a picture on horseback.'

'I'll find you a quiet mare,' Luke snapped.

'Or a tractor?' Lily said, suddenly teasing. 'Tractors are safe but they're not nearly as much fun.'

'You're not here to have fun.'

Her smile died. 'Of course I'm not. I'd forgotten. Sorry.'

'Lunch,' he said, tugging the horses round to face the house.

'I guess we're not riding, then.'

'No. I'll find you a safe horse after lunch.'

Her smile died completely. 'It's okay. I guess I don't need to ride. I should have learned that a long time ago. Tom, are you joining us for lunch?'

Tom shook his head, but amazingly he looked almost tempted. 'No, but let the girl back on,' he told Luke.

'And have her break her neck? In your dreams. I've had one woman die on me; there'll not be another.'

'Hey,' Lily said, startled. 'I'm not your woman.'

'Of course you're not,' he said shortly, and he led two horses along the track to the house without saying another word.

Luke worked with Tom again in the afternoon and Lily wandered the farm alone. She dropped by to chat—to Tom. She offered to help and when Luke said she should be resting she seemed rebuffed.

'She's a decent woman,' Tom said, eyeing Luke sideways. 'Good seat on her, too. Find her a horse.'

Luke had quiet horses but Lily's reaction had been blunt. 'I don't ride,' she'd said flatly. 'Forget it.'

He'd hurt her but he couldn't help it. He wasn't about to let her risk her neck.

But he did feel bad—and he had a foal she needed to see. Toward sunset, as Tom headed off to feed his cattle, Luke joined Lily on his veranda.

'I'm sorry I snapped,' he told her. 'I don't like people taking risks.'

'I wasn't taking risks,' she said mildly. 'But apology accepted.'

'I have something I need to show you.'

She looked at him, considering whether to take the conflict further. She shrugged, moving on, and he was relieved.

What he had to show her should lighten the atmosphere, he decided, and led her over to Tom's home paddock to visit Zelda.

Zelda was a roan with soft white markings, a lovely gentle mare. The foal by her side was a tangle of spindly legs with his father's markings. Checkers's markings.

'Meet Zelda,' he told Lily, and Lily gazed at the foal in delight. 'And Merrylegs. Just named this morning.'

Tension was forgotten. 'He's beautiful,' she breathed. 'Is Checkers his dad?'

He nodded.

'A family,' she breathed. 'Mother, father, son. How lucky are you!'

'It's all the family I ever want.'

'Really?' she said, sounding startled. 'Why?'

Why?

He hadn't intended to say it. It had been a dumb thing to say.

So why had he said it?

Because she was too close.

Because she was too beautiful?

He'd hurt her today. He didn't intend to hurt her again. He didn't intend to be hurt himself.

He forced himself to recall the day Hannah had died. She'd been unwell at breakfast but she'd thought it was the take-away meal she'd eaten the night before. She'd eaten too much of it, she'd snapped, because he hadn't arrived home in time to share.

'Ring me if you need me,' he'd said, knowing she was angry but not knowing what to do about it. He'd kissed her goodbye, intending to come home at lunchtime and check.

And then there'd been cojoined twins, one dead, one close to death, surgery impossible to delay. Fourteen hours in Theatre. At some stage he'd asked a nurse to ring and let Hannah know what was happening.

'The call went to your answering-machine,' the nurse had told him. 'I left a message.'

She must have gone out, he'd thought, relieved, and then all his thoughts had gone back to saving one little life.

While his wife and son had died.

So why had he said it? *It's all the family I ever want.* He watched Lily stroke Merrylegs's soft nose, he watched Lily fall under the spell of the tiny colt and he knew that he'd been warning himself.

'I don't do relationships,' he growled, and Lily cast him a look that held amusement.

'Good, then. Except pretend relationships. They're my favourite. So what will happen to Merrylegs? Will he be sold?'

'No.'

'So this farm…' she said cautiously. 'It makes a lot of money?'

He smiled at that, tension defusing. 'Not so much as you'd notice. We make a bit on the beef cattle.'

'I've seen your beef cattle,' she said. 'World's fattest beasts. I'm betting when they droop with age you move them into cattle nursing homes where they're pushed round in bath chairs until they die. And I've counted six horses I reckon are twenty years old or more. Plus you've bred Zelda with Checkers when anyone can see…'

'That's practical,' he told her. 'Checkers is getting too old to carry me and I'm used to a checkered blaze. It's like a flag on the antenna of your car how I pick my horse out in a crowd.'

She chuckled. The little colt nudged her chest and she hugged him. Zelda nudged her so she gave Zelda a hug for good measure.

'What a softie,' she murmured. 'You know your reputation around the hospital is cool and grumpy. And solitary.'

'That's the way I like it.'

'You could never be solitary with these guys.'

The sun was setting low in the west. Lily was stroking Zelda while the colt shoved her for his share of attention. The last rays of the sun were glinting on Lily's hair the soft evening breeze was making it ripple like silken waves.

Zelda was usually wary of strangers. She wasn't wary of Lily. She wanted to get closer. Touch.

Same with Luke. Maybe he could…

He raised a hand…and let it fall. No.

Talk about something else. Something to break the moment.

He had it. A reality check.

'I made some phone calls for you this morning,' he said. 'I went through university with a solicitor from Adelaide. He's made enquiries on your behalf.'

She straightened and stared. 'You…what?'

'Firstly the money. What your mother did was illegal. The bank wasn't authorised to transfer your money.'

'I didn't ask you—'

'I know,' he said. 'But it seemed…you're in such trouble.'

'That's my business.'

'But you can reclaim your money.'

'No,' she said, suddenly angry. 'I can't. Of course I know Mum's action was illegal but the bank won't refund money without wanting it back from somewhere. They'll have Mum arrested for fraud. Do you think I want that?'

'If she's stolen—'

'She's my mum!'

'She's an adult. She's stolen—'

'Luke, my mum can't help herself,' she said, anger giving way to weariness. 'She was indulged by doting parents and then by my dad. He adored her. All men adore my mother,' she conceded. 'But apart from my father, she never sticks to them. Dad committed suicide when I was twelve, lumbered with a mountain of her debt. He made me promise to look after her and I will. I know she can't help it. It's just the way she is.' She took a deep breath. 'So, no, I won't claim, and I won't have her arrested. I'll be more careful in future. In a while I'll go home and sort out the damage. But not…not yet.'

'You could go home now,' he said gently.

'I don't want to go home.' She said it with a vehemence that was startling. 'Mum's vicar will leave,' she said, weary again. 'But not until my mother gets tired of him, which won't be long. Meanwhile I'm staying as far away as possible.'

'I'm sorry.'

'Yeah.' She gave him a shame-faced smile. 'I'm sorry, too. You were trying to do good.'

'Gerald says he can get you damages.'

'Damages?'

'That's the second thing,' he said. 'According to Gerald, you were publicly slapped and dismissed without cause. Assault and public humiliation, with witnesses. The hospital board should pay damages.'

She thought about that. Her weariness and anger seemed to fade.

'The hospital board,' she said slowly, 'consists of five judgmental toads. I'm judged a bad lot by association. They only gave me the job because my qualifications beat every other applicant fourfold.' She considered a bit longer. 'Damages, eh?'

'It'd be a statement,' he said. 'A line in the sand.'

She considered a bit more. 'She did have cause,' she said. 'Vicar's wife discovering vicar with Mum.'

'Was that cause to hit you?'

'No.' She grinned, bouncing back. 'Does it cost to sue?'

'With the evidence as clear as it is, Gerald said one letter should do it, sent to the board with a promise to copy it to the press if damages aren't forthcoming. He reckons they'll be falling over themselves to limit fallout.'

'Ooh…'

'Do I have your permission to go ahead?'

She beamed and it was as if the sun had come out. 'Yes.'

'And the bank…'

'No.' Her humour faded. 'Mum's not going to jail on my account.'

'How long do promises last?' he said softly. 'A promise made by a twelve-year-old…'

'I know,' she said. 'It's ridiculous, but I loved my dad.

I do this for him. Thank you for what you've done already but I won't take it further. My mum, my problem.'

He glanced at Zelda and at Merrylegs. Then he looked at Lily, at her expression of acceptance of a load that seemed almost too much to bear. He'd yelled at her, he thought, and he was sorry. 'Are you sure I can't organise you a quiet horse tomorrow?' he asked.

'Not Glenfiddich?'

'No.'

'Because?'

'I will not watch you take risks.'

'So don't watch.'

'Lily…'

'Okay, sorry,' she said, and held up her hands. 'You're trying to protect me. Thank you very much, but I don't need it.'

'You could enjoy a quieter ride.'

'I guess I could,' she said, but then managed a rueful smile. 'I know, it doesn't make sense, even to me, but I'd rather not. Not having been on Glenfiddich.' She took a deep breath. 'It's just… Luke, I don't want to be protected. For now I just want to be me.'

She seemed to wilt a bit after that. The gastro had knocked her, he thought, or maybe it was simply life that had knocked her. A crazy mother and a promise to the father she'd adored… She'd faced it alone since she was twelve.

He bullied her into toast and soup. She sat by the fire and gazed into the flames and he thought he shouldn't have let her out today. She should have stayed home by the fire. He should have stayed home with her.

I don't want to be protected…

What else was a man to do?

'Go to bed,' he said gently, and she cast him a look he couldn't understand.

'I like it by the fire.'

'You're exhausted.'

'Yes, but—'

'But you don't sleep?'

'I slept last night.'

'Gastro would make anyone sleep. Is that why you signed up for night duty?' he asked. 'To keep the demons at bay?'

'I don't have demons.'

'I think…living with your mother must be nigh on impossible.'

'Like having your wife die? And the fear of facing that sort of tragedy again?'

'I'm not afraid.'

'I think you are. Wasn't that what today was all about?' She rose, a little unsteady on her feet, and he jumped up fast to steady her. He took her shoulders and held on.

He could draw her closer.

He didn't. He simply held.

A common bond—two nightmares?

It was enough to forge a friendship. This could be touching from mutual sympathy—but it felt much more than that.

The fire crackled in the grate, a sort of warning. That was a dumb thought, but right now anything was acting as a warning.

He should let her go.

He couldn't.

'Maybe you could curl up here and watch the flames while you go to sleep,' he suggested, and the tension around them escalated. Maybe he could stay here, too. The flames…the warmth…this woman.

He knew how this woman could make him feel. She could drive out his demons.

He couldn't make her safe. He knew she wouldn't let him.

'I will go to bed,' she said, and somehow she managed to step back from him.

'Count mopokes to go to sleep?' he suggested, and she smiled.

'Or frogs?'

'You don't have enough fingers and toes to count frogs.'

She chuckled and the desire to draw her close again was almost irresistible.

She stepped back fast, as if she felt it too.

'Goodnight,' she said.

He couldn't help it. He touched her hand, a feather-like touch, nothing more, but in that touch fire flared. It was contact that burned.

She tucked her hand behind her back. 'Luke…no.'

'No,' he said, and let his own hand fall.

They were pretend lovers. Nothing more.

'Goodnight,' she said again, gently, and she walked out of the door, closing it after her.

He stood staring at the closed door. Thinking, How much courage would it take?

Too much.

He wasn't tired. He headed out again, around the paddocks, following the line of the creek. How many times had he followed this route since Hannah had died?

It was different tonight. He was here because of Lily. She touched such a chord… A woman keeping a promise at all costs. A woman of honour and intelligence and skill and laughter.

But...

The moment he'd seen her on Glenfiddich's back, he'd been hit with the knowledge that there was nothing he could do to protect her...

She'd guessed right. She'd known that his fear had been all about Hannah.

He looked over toward his uncle's house, where a solitary light burned on the veranda.

His uncle had learned the same hard lessons. He was like Luke.

They didn't do relationships. Not now. Not ever.

CHAPTER SEVEN

LILY woke without the joy of the day before.

She could hear Luke moving downstairs. She heard Tom calling, dogs barking in the distance, and those dratted kookaburras.

Her stomach was cramping again. She'd talked to the doctor at home about the cramps. Tension, he'd said. Avoid stress.

Stress was sharing a house with a guy who was drop-dead gorgeous. Stress was playing pretend lovers with Luke.

She shouldn't have come. This was a stupid deception, designed to protect a reputation she didn't have and to add another level to Luke's armour, but by coming here a layer of her own armour had peeled away.

This farm…these horses…

Luke.

Okay, there was the problem. She was feeling what she had no right to be feeling.

He was feeling it too, she thought, but…

But she'd seen his panic when she'd been on Glenfiddich, and his reaction had scared her. He'd yelled at her through fear. Shadows of a dead wife.

She was being dumb, she thought. This was an over-reaction.

It was an overreaction because she was scared.

Because she was falling for Luke?

Maybe falling for anyone would be scary.

Growing up in her mother's dramatic shadow, she'd never thought of romance. Of falling in love. Drama, emotion were to be avoided at all costs. She knew the devastation they caused and it wasn't something she wanted.

Her relationship with Charlie had been like a comfortable pair of old socks. They'd been friends at school, they'd fallen into dating and they'd kept dating until suddenly Charlie had woken up one morning and realised he was heading for marriage with the daughter of the town tramp. When he'd cut her adrift she'd been hurt and angry, but she hadn't been heartbroken. Sometimes when she looked at romantic movies, seen friends marry, she'd felt like that part of her had simply not been formed. She'd been born without it.

Now… What she felt for Luke…

It was as if she knew him at some level she couldn't possibly understand.

She knew Luke's story—between Gladys and the Harbour night shift she knew more than she'd ever need to know—but this went deeper than that. She'd instinctively joined the dots. Last night she'd said his fear for her was all about his dead wife and she knew it was. A lonely child, a tragic marriage… A man who walked alone.

He made her feel…

She didn't know how he made her feel. She felt… She felt…

She felt like she had cramps in her stomach, she decided. She felt like she needed to roll over in bed and put her pillows over her head, which was exactly what she did.

Avoid stress? Ha!

* * *

Luke worked with Tom, stringing wires between the fencing posts they'd put in the day before, then going on to re-wire fences further along the creek.

All the time he worked he expected her to come.

She didn't.

'You two still fighting?' Tom said at last.

'We're not fighting. She's had gastro. She overdid it yesterday. She should spend the day in bed.'

'Then why are you wiring fences?' Tom asked bluntly. 'With a woman like that in your bed.'

'She's in the guest bed.'

'More fool you. She's a good 'un.'

'There speaks an authority on all women,' Luke said. 'Curmudgeonly old bachelor that you are.'

'Had a woman once,' Tom said reflectively, astonishingly. 'Liseth.' He sighed. 'I thought maybe I had a chance, that our family hadn't stuffed me completely. But with parents like ours you don't rush into relationships. Anyway, I got drafted; Vietnam War. I was stupid enough to tell her to go out with other guys while I was away. I met her twenty years later, married to a car salesman. I walked into the office and she was there. She told me about her husband and her kids. All very polite. Then at the end when her husband was shifting the car she turned to me and exploded.

'I would have married you,' she said. 'In a heartbeat. Even if we'd only had those two months before you went overseas, it would have been enough.'

'Tom...' The vehemence of his uncle's voice shocked him.

'Yeah,' Tom said. 'I was a fool, like you were a fool with Hannah; but in your case the fool part wasn't one-sided. So we've made mistakes, do we have to keep making them? Enough. All I'm saying, boy, is life's short and she's a good 'un. Now let's get this wire done. And I want to talk to you about my arm. I damn near dropped the chainsaw on Friday. I reckon I might have tennis elbow.'

'Chainsaw elbow,' Luke said, and the old man grinned.

'You doctors have fancy names for everything.'

'Hi.'

The men turned and saw Lily at the edge of the clearing.

Uh-oh. How much of the conversation had she heard? Just the end, Luke hoped, though the silence in the bush meant sound travelled.

'I'm feeling better,' she said. 'I wanted to stretch my legs. And, no, Luke, I'm not about to ride another of your horses, even though I had to duck round Glenfiddich's paddock so he wouldn't see me. And I'm not here to interfere. I'll keep on walking.'

'Keep walking with Luke,' Tom growled. 'He's done enough for one day.'

'So must you if you have chainsaw elbow,' Lily said, teasing a smile from the old man.

'Nah, I'm fitter than the pair of you,' he retorted. 'You head off and do what a young feller and his lady ought to do.'

Luke looked at Lily and Lily looked at Luke, and Luke put down his tools.

What was it that a young feller and his lady ought to do?

They walked slowly back to the house. She was walking a bit gingerly.

'Your tummy's okay?' he asked.

'Recovering nicely.' Her tone said not to go there.

'Rest this afternoon.'

'You should tell Tom to rest,' she said. 'Not that he will when you're around. He's lonely.'

'Tom—lonely!'

'He's like you,' she said softly. 'He drives people away. I met Patty Haigh up on your north boundary fence when I was walking…'

'Patty!' Patty was the cheerful next-door neighbour who cooked and cleaned for Tom. She was the mother of seven sons. She was always ready for a gossip—not that he and Tom gossiped.

'She worries about Tom,' Lily said.

'Tom's okay.'

'She doesn't like him being on his own.'

'Neither do I,' he said. 'That's why I bought adjoining land.'

'Why don't you commute?' she asked curiously. 'Patty says you can get to the Harbour in forty minutes from here.'

'An hour and a half at peak hour.'

'Since when do doctors travel at peak hour? You can fit your hours around traffic.'

'Tom doesn't want me here.'

'That's not what Patty says. He needs family.'

'He doesn't want family. Neither of us do.'

What did Lily know about Tom? he thought. Lonely? Tom was as fiercely independent as he was. But… Tom's revelation of moments ago had shaken him.

Regardless, it was nothing to do with Lily.

The chainsaw revved up behind them. He winced. He hated Tom using power tools when he wasn't here; it was a risk, the price they both paid for independence.

He blocked it out. Or tried to. He tried not to care.

'You want to go back and help?' Lily asked, looking concerned.

'He wouldn't thank me.'

'Like my mum doesn't thank me for caring,' she whispered. 'Sometimes you have to do what you have to do.'

'And sometimes you need to back off.'

'Like you have from everyone?'

'Butt out,' he said, trying to sound good humoured. If she was to pry into his personal life, the next four weeks would be endless.

'You made phone calls on my behalf,' she said mildly. 'Do you call that butting out?'

'That's…'

'Different,' she said cordially. 'You can butt into my life, but I can't do the same in yours.' She glanced back along the track. 'That chainsaw…'

'He doesn't want us! He's vowed not to want anyone.'

'Like you?'

'I wouldn't know. Tom and I don't talk of it. What business is it of mine?'

'All your business if you love him.'

'Then you end up where you are with your mother.'

'Are you saying your uncle Tom is like my mother?'

'No, but…' He raked his hair. 'You can care too much. It leaves you open for hurt, like you've been hurt. It sounds to me like you should have backed off years ago.'

'Like you,' she said cordially. 'And Tom. Living in your emotion-free bubbles.'

'I like emotion-free bubbles.'

'Good for you,' she said, and smiled, and it was an entrancing smile. Enchanting. Beguiling. It made him want to…

Step right out of his emotion-free bubble.

It wasn't going to happen. *It was not.*

The chainsaw was roaring in the background. They walked on in silence, using the noise as a silent excuse not to talk.

He was so aware of her, a slip of a girl with an enchanting smile, with judgment written all over her. And challenge.

He thought of Tom. Was she right? Was the old man finally admitting he needed people?

The chainsaw was biting through wood. It really wasn't safe, he conceded.

He had talked to Tom about it. Tom had told him where he could put his worries.

Suddenly the chainsaw's motor whined sharply, differently, rising in pitch as if it had been jerked free of wood. The wood was rotten. If Tom was pressing against solid wood and met rot…

Even as Luke thought it, the chainsaw motor cut out as it was meant to do the moment pressure was released from the hand hold.

And as the motor died…a scream.

Luke was running almost before his brain had processed the sounds.

They'd been replacing fence posts. The old ones had been hauled out and stacked.

Tom had balanced the first post against the pile, then started slicing it for firewood. Now he was sprawled on the damp grass, the chainsaw tossed beside him. The dogs were whimpering in fear.

A pool of bright scarlet was blooming out from Tom's leg.

Lily wasn't as fast as Luke. By the time she reached the clearing Luke had rolled Tom from curled and clutching his leg onto his back so he could see the damage.

In that one instant, she knew what had happened. He'd swiped the chainsaw downward. Maybe the wood was more rotten than he'd expected—maybe he hadn't needed as much pressure as he had exerted. For whatever reason the saw had sliced far further than he'd intended, smashing into his upper thigh.

He must have hit the femoral artery. It had to be cut, she thought with horror. There was no other explanation for this amount of blood.

Luke was searching for pressure points, one hand pressing, the other ripping at his shirt to try and get a wad, a tie, anything.

Her shirt was off in an instant, folded, handed to him. Then she grabbed Luke's sleeve and ripped with a strength she hadn't known she had. She ripped the sleeve right off, then ripped again from shoulder to cuff.

It gave them padding and a tie.

'Let me…let me…' Tom was gasping, trying to see.

'Lie still,' Luke snapped. There was no time for reassurance, not while the blood was pumping as it was. 'Tom, lie still. You've cut an artery and we have to stop it.'

'Bloody fool,' Tom muttered, and subsided.

His face was ashen.

So much blood.

The pad was doing nothing, no matter how hard Luke pressed. Lily was twisting the tie above the wound but making no difference at all to the blood flow. Already Tom was looking clammy, a sheen of cold sweat on his face.

He'd bleed out in minutes.

If they were back at the hospital they'd have tools to cut down, to find the artery and clamp it off. Here they had nothing.

'I can't locate it,' Luke snapped, and the agony in those words was desperate. 'Your hand's smaller. You try.'

It was a desperate request. He had nothing else to try.

He took the tie, while she shoved her fist into the wound, hard, as tight as it'd go. Was her hand small enough? She was searching for the source of the blood, pushing with a desperation born of terror.

Harder…

The blood welled around her fingers…and slowed.

Slowed more.

But in time?

She had to be in time.

'Hey, she's stopped the bleeding,' Luke told his uncle. Until now it had been impossible to disguise the panic. 'Lily's hit the spot. Don't you move, not a whisker.'

'I wouldn't dream of it,' Tom whispered. 'Oh, girl, I'm making you all mucky.'

'I love horses and I love nursing,' Lily told him, trying to match Luke's reassurance, trying to keep the strain from her voice, as if holding back blood like this was routine. Knowing how close to disaster they still were. 'I like a bit of muck.'

Tom tried to laugh but it didn't come off. He looked…

Like he could go into shock at any minute.

It was a real possibility.

Lily couldn't move. Her fist was a ball curled tight against damaged tissue, pressed hard against the pulsing artery. Somehow she'd hit the spot, somehow she'd blocked the blood supply. If she moved a fraction…

Luke was tightening the tourniquet with one hand, holding his phone in the other. Snapping details to an emergency service.

'Air ambulance, helicopter, code blue. GPS co-ordinates…' He lifted his uncle's phone from his pocket—a new model, Lily saw, and read the positional co-ordinates off. Thank goodness for technology. 'There's a clearing a hundred yards to the north. I'll secure it before you get here. If you can break the sound barrier I'd appreciate it. Move.'

He flicked the phone off.

There were sheets of paper-bark hanging from the massive gums along the river. While Tom—and Lily—stayed motionless Luke hauled a dozen of the soft bark sheets, folded them into a wedge and manoeuvered them with extraordinary care underneath Tom's hips and legs. He had to be careful; there was no way he was interfering with Lily's position. But it had to be done. Any available blood needed to flow to Tom's head and not to his lower limbs. His hips had to be higher than his heart.

Done. He twisted the shirt tighter around Tom's thigh and Tom grunted in pain.

'I have emergency gear in the car,' he told Lily. 'Catheters. Saline. Morphine.'

'Then why are you here?' She was impressed by how calm she sounded. Luke needed to get an IV catheter in now, if not sooner. If Tom's veins collapsed, resuscitation would no longer be possible.

They both knew that point was close.

'I'm going.' Luke sounded agonised. He'd hate to leave but he couldn't stay. He touched his uncle's face, then he touched Lily on the shoulder—a feather-light brush.

Then he was gone.

They were the longest minutes of Lily's life, keeping pressure on the wound, praying Tom's condition wouldn't worsen. Trying not to let Tom see she was terrified.

The dogs, Border collies, lay and watched and she sensed their fear as well.

'I hope Luke can run,' she ventured, and Tom tried a smile.

'Like the wind,' he whispered. 'He spent half his childhood running on this farm. Most weekends. All his school holidays. Ran all over this farm.'

'Did he never go back to Singapore?'

'Parents sent him to boarding school to get rid of him,' Tom muttered. 'He had a ruddy big birthmark on his face. His parents hated looking at it. My brother was too mean to get it fixed, though. Told the kid it was character building but in truth he was fixated on money. Like that bloody wife of his...'

He broke off and gasped and Lily wished she could hug him, wished she could move. Selfishly she also wished she could alleviate the pins and needles in her hips.

She could do nothing.

They were totally dependent on Luke. He needed to fetch equipment. He needed to check for a safe place for the helicopter to land. It was maybe a ten-minute run back to the house. Ten minutes there, ten minutes back, time to get land cleared...

All she could do was sit.

It was killing her. It *was* killing Tom. With every moment his chances grew slimmer.

Then, before she imagined it was possible, she heard the roar of a motor revving through the trees, crashing... and Luke's Aston Martin broke into the clearing, bushbashing like he was driving an ancient SUV rather than a sports car. No matter, he was here. He was out of the car almost before it stopped, hauling his bag with him.

'Tom…' She heard the catch in his breath, knew how terrified he'd been of what he'd find.

'We're fine,' Lily said quickly. 'And we always knew Aston Martins were offroaders.'

He managed a fleeting grin as he hauled a catheter from his bag.

'You drove that thing through the bush?' Tom gasped, and Luke's smile became genuine. Luke would have run thinking the worst, Lily thought. He'd have known that if Tom had gone into cardiac arrest while he was gone there'd have been nothing she could do—not when taking her hands from the pressure point meant blood loss would resume.

But now…

Luke was inserting a catheter. He had IV fluids! Not blood product, she thought, that'd be too much to hope from most emergency kits, but he had saline, and any fluid was a lifesaver.

Could be a lifesaver.

Please.

The catheter was inserted in seconds. An IV line was set up.

'There's morphine going in, Tom,' Luke said. 'Any minute now you can stop gritting your teeth.'

'I'm not gritting my teeth,' Tom said, indignant. 'Or not very much.'

Lily let out her breath, not knowing until then that she'd been holding it. There was a chance…

'I'm releasing the tourniquet for a moment,' Luke said. 'I'm not saving you only to lose that leg. You might want to grit those teeth.'

'Pansies grit teeth,' Tom said, though the expression on his face said the pain was bad. 'Me and Lily aren't pansies.'

'You and Lily can face the world with your heads held high,' Luke said. 'Pansies? I don't think so. Heroes, both of you.'

'It's our Lily. I'm just lying here thinking of England.'

'Well, think of England a while longer,' Tom said. 'I need to get the paddock cleared for the chopper. Harbour Hospital, here we come.'

'Hey, we might even be in time for Teo's party,' Lily managed, desperately striving for lightness. 'Tom, there's a party on the beach tonight. You want to get stitched up and come?' They all knew how impossible it was, but the thought was a good one.

Tom groaned. 'Parties,' he whispered, trying to sound withering. 'Mind, if alcohol's involved, I wouldn't mind a wee drop.'

'Neither would I,' Lily said, with meaning. 'And not so wee at that.'

The helicopter arrived soon after with a team of paramedics from the Harbour who knew Luke by name.

Jack Stephens, trauma specialist, was in charge. The team must have understood the call was deadly serious to have sent a physician of Jack's standing. In her two nights in the Harbour Lily already knew this guy's reputation and he was with a team who were just as awesome. They worked with competence and speed, and a light-hearted banter that made Tom relax as nothing else could.

'For years we've been trying to wangle an invitation to see the place where Luke hides out,' Jack told Tom as he replaced IV saline with blood product and set up another line in case of need, then checked Lily's position and placed a hand on her shoulder—a silent message not to move. 'Thanks for organising it. I guess you're not quite up to guided tours.'

'Maybe another time?' Tom said weakly, and Luke gripped his hand and held.

'Don't agree to anything,' he urged. 'This guy's a free-loader from way back. He'll have conned you into bed and breakfast in no time.'

'I'm guessing it's you who needs the bed and break-fast,' Jack told Tom. 'Let's get you back to the Harbour.' He cast an uncertain look at Lily, looking closer at where her hand lay. 'And I'm thinking we're taking Lily as well. You've got a pulsing artery there, Tom. Lily has her hand on exactly the right spot and it's hard to reach. If we try to clamp it here we risk more blood being spilled and you've made enough of a mess already. Lily, can you stay where you are while we work around you?'

Luke made an involuntary protest. To have Lily hold that position during transfer…

But it was the only way. Where she was now, not only was she holding the blood flow back but somehow she'd lucked onto a position where a tiny amount of blood was seeping through to Tom's foot. To take Lily away, to slice down, to tie off the artery, keeping the blood supply to the foot uncompromised…

It had to be done in a well-equipped theatre to give Tom any chance of keeping his leg, as well as his life.

'I've never ridden in a helicopter,' Lily said. 'Cool.'

She was amazing, he thought. She was as pale as a ghost, still shaken by gastro. Her jeans were blood-soaked and she was only wearing a bra on top. She wasn't moving. She knew what needed to be done and she was doing it.

'We can't fit you in as well,' Jack told him, and grinned at the look on Luke's face. 'This is cool indeed. Our team has the whole ride back to grill Lily and Tom about our Dr Williams's secret love life and secret farm life. The hospital's been bursting with questions since Wednesday. Now, you, Luke Williams, can butt out and calmly drive your poncy little car back to the Harbour while we do our interrogation as we ride in real transport. We'll do our best to save your uncle's leg while we're at it. By the way, you might want to stop and collect pyjamas for your uncle on your way. That'll give us more time to interrogate. Okay, guys, let's move.'

The Aston Martin, loaded now with two subdued dogs, took a lot more time getting back to the road than it had taken getting to his uncle.

He'd hit a couple of small trees, bush-bashing in his desperation to get back to Tom and Lily. His front fender was bent. He stopped at Tom's house and had to do a bit of rebending in order to protect the wheel. He didn't want any hold-ups on the way back to hospital.

He was thumping the fender one last time when his neighbour Patty arrived, looking scared.

'I saw the chopper,' she said. 'From the Harbour. What's happened?'

He told her, and she offered to pack Tom's bag while he got the car sorted.

'I'll take care of the dogs and the rest of the place as well,' she said. 'Tell him Bill and I will drop in and see him as soon as he's well enough for visitors.'

'He won't want—'

'He always says he doesn't want,' she said. 'But what men say and what men mean are different things. Like telling me he doesn't need me bringing him casseroles and pies. Like telling me he doesn't want you living here. He's a lying hound but he's *our* lying hound so we'd be grateful to have him home safe and sound.'

He left her, but her words stayed with him.

What men say and what men mean are different things...

If he and Lily hadn't been there today...

Tom couldn't stay on the farm any more. Not alone. They'd have to find him a live-in housekeeper.

He'd hate it.

Could *he* finally decide to commute?

Tom would hate that, too. He'd put up with him as a kid, because he'd felt sorry for him. He tolerated Luke owning the place next door and he appreciated his help, but essentially he was a loner.

Tom didn't want Luke close, like Luke didn't want anyone close.

Anyone like Lily.

His thoughts should have only been on Tom. Instead they kept drifting to a shadowed girl with bloodstained clothing and a courage that defied belief.

Riding Glenfiddich yesterday.

Holding Tom today.

Facing down the gossip of the Harbour.

Coping with a mother who sounded like a nightmare.

Wasn't he supposed to be worrying about Tom?

He was feeling sick about Tom. No matter that he was in good hands, there was still a chance...

Don't go there.

He was going as fast as the speed limit and a slightly buckled Aston Martin allowed. The chopper would be back at the Harbour by now. Jack and his team would be doing their utmost to save Tom.

Would they have released Lily?

She'd go into Theatre with them, he thought. They'd leave her hand in position while Tom was anaesthetised, while they put every tool in place so they could work with speed to cut down, clamp, tie off, without compromising what little was left of the leg's blood supply.

Then Lily could step away.

He needed to be there when she stepped away.

How fast could he make this car go? Not fast enough.

He hit the phone. Evie.

'He's here and he's still with us,' Evie said before he could say a word. 'Jack's taken him straight through into Theatre. He had everyone lined up before he got here. Finn's supervising. Judy's on her way. You have the best surgical team the Harbour can provide.'

'Lily…'

'Lily still has her hand in place. We're not shifting her until we're sure we can get in fast enough.'

'Can you be there when she's no longer needed?'

'I'll have one of the nurses—'

'I want you, Evie,' he snapped. 'I don't ask favours, but I'm asking for one now. She's had gastro. I'm worried about her as well. It'll be twenty minutes before I get there. Be there for Lily for me.'

'If it means that much…'

'It means that much,'

'Well, well,' Evie said gently. 'And I thought it was mostly gossip. You really do care. Don't worry, Luke, of course I'll be there.'

CHAPTER EIGHT

LILY woke and someone was holding her hand.

That someone was Luke.

She blinked but she wasn't dreaming. Luke Williams was leaning over, smiling, and he was definitely holding her hand. Her fingers were on the coverlet. His were entwined with hers.

Sunlight was streaming in the window, or rather the rays of a tangerine sunset. She was warm and cosseted and...

Luke Williams was holding her hand.

'Hey, sleepyhead,' he said softly, and his hold on her hand tightened. 'I thought you might be intending to sleep until morning. Mind, you have the right.'

His voice was low and husky, tense with emotion. His face was drawn.

It definitely wasn't a dream. The day's events flooded back and with it, dread.

'Tom...'

'Tom's fine,' he said, and he didn't release her hand by a fraction. 'Judy Nerolin, our senior vascular surgeon, has decreed his leg will be okay and no one argues with Judy. He's out of Theatre. He's still in Intensive Care but all the signs are that he'll make it and even make it with his leg intact. Thanks to the team from the Harbour—and one amazing nurse. One nurse called Lily.'

'Hey, I didn't do anything,' she said sleepily. 'Except put my fist in a hole. Like the boy with his thumb in the dyke in Holland. Highly skilled stuff.'

'You fainted,' he said ruefully.

'But not until Judy took over,' she said with pride. 'I told myself I couldn't and I didn't.'

'You mean you knew you were going to faint.'

'By the time they rolled us into Theatre I was feeling a bit light-headed,' she admitted. 'But then Dr Lockheart brought me up to this cool bedroom.'

It was indeed a cool bedroom. This suite was for the Harbour's wealthiest, most influential patients. It was more a suite of rooms than a bedroom.

Dr Evie Lockheart's family were principal benefactors of this hospital. They were Sydney's answer to royalty and what royalty decreed, royalty received.

Royalty had obviously decreed Lily deserved this bedroom and Luke wasn't arguing.

He should pull his hand away. He didn't.

He'd been sitting here for the last ten minutes, watching her sleep. Her curls were sprawled over the pillows. She was stained and battered.

She'd fought and she'd won. For Tom.

He wasn't supposed to feel like this. Had Tom taught him nothing?

He remembered the first time Tom had come to collect him from boarding school. It had been his first week there, aged all of ten, and to say it had been ghastly was an understatement.

'You teach yourself you don't need anyone,' Tom had growled. 'You grow up tough and you stay tough.'

That's what his father had said when he refused to pay for the removal of the birthmark. 'It'll make you tough.'

He'd sent him away, though. Tom had been raised with the same philosophy, had learned the hard way how it worked, but he'd bent the rules.

He'd cared for Luke.

Luke now cared for Tom in a way he hadn't realised. He'd thought the only person he'd ever fallen in love with was Hannah. It wasn't true, though. Seeing Tom's life hang so precariously, he knew he was exposed to pain all over again. And now this slip of a girl, who'd hung on for over an hour, knowing if she moved a sliver of an inch they'd lose…

It was her bravery that moved him, he told himself, not the woman herself, but he knew it was much more.

He thought of her suddenly on Glenfiddich, and the dread surfaced. He thought of Tom and the chainsaw.

When Luke had been fifteen Tom had been bitten by a snake. He'd recovered but Luke remembered thinking, If he dies I have no one.

'Don't watch me if you're worried,' Tom had snapped, and Luke had been trying not to watch ever since.

It wasn't working.

'I'm sorry I overreacted about Glenfiddich,' he said. 'Give me another six months to train him and you can ride him all you like.'

'All by myself?' she demanded, mock-awed. 'Will you buy me a stepladder to climb up with?'

'Lily…'

'No, it's a very generous offer,' she whispered. 'Sorry. I should have asked before I rode him.'

'And I should have stayed home with you.'

'Watching me in case I did anything dangerous?' she asked, her eyes clouding. 'Is that the problem? Is that why you can't stay with Tom—because you can't bear that he does dangerous things whether you're watching or not?'

'That's deep,' he said, and tried a smile. 'Have you been talking to John Allen?'

'I don't need a psychologist to figure out something's wrong. Luke, go away.'

But her hand didn't disengage from his.

'You want me to leave?'

'I need to take a shower. I'm fine. Fainting was just a reaction. Even the strongest woman might have been tempted to faint, so a wuss like me...'

She was laughing again! After all she'd been through...

She was enchanting.

Love...

Whoa. Step away now, he told himself.

Don't watch.

He could no sooner not watch than fly.

'I could help you shower.'

'In your dreams, Dr Williams.' She grinned. 'Since when do plastic surgeons shower patients?'

'Three nights ago a very bossy nurse said I should do just that.'

Her lips twitched. 'That was some cheek.'

'I think you're wonderful.'

The laughter in her eyes faded. She met his look square on. 'Luke, don't.'

'Don't?'

'You want me to share your apartment for a month. That's not going to work if you make me feel...'

She didn't finish but he knew what the words were.

Their eyes locked, and something was happening. A link, a connection, growing stronger every second.

He wanted to lean forward. He wanted to take her in his arms and...

The door opened and Lily flinched. He pulled back, not sure whether to be glad or sorry.

No. He was definitely sorry.

Evie Lockheart opened the door with caution. She smiled as she saw him, and she smiled even wider when she saw Lily was awake.

'Hey,' she said. 'We were worried about you. Nurses collapsing in Theatre does our safety record no good at all.'

Lily smiled back, looking embarrassed. 'I'm sorry.'

'No need to be sorry. The whole hospital's in awe of what you did. Saving Luke's uncle...' She glanced at Luke and grinned. 'And the hosital's on fire with the story. In one fell swoop we've met your lady, your uncle and your farm. Where's your precious privacy now?'

'Shot to pieces,' Luke admitted.

But Evie was focusing on Lily. 'How are you feeling?'

'Fine.'

'You don't look fine.'

'Because I'm covered in blood,' Lily said with dignity. 'If I could have a shower...'

'I'll send a nurse to help you.'

'I don't need—'

'Tell me what you need when I'm interested,' Evie retorted. She elbowed Luke out of the way and felt Lily's pulse.

'She's had gastro,' Luke reminded her. 'The plan was for her to rest this weekend.'

'Yeah, like that worked,' Evie said dryly, assessing Lily with professional concern. 'You're too thin.'

'I'm always thin.'

'No other symptoms?'

Lily hauled her hand away and tucked it under the covers. 'I'm okay. Honestly, gastro and this afternoon would make anyone faint.'

'I guess.' Evie turned to Luke. 'Look after her.'

'I will.' And he surprised himself by how much he meant it. 'She won't let me help her shower, though,' he complained, and Evie grinned.

'Good. She needs to rest.'

'I wouldn't…' He practically blushed.

'You're male,' she said darkly. 'Of course you would. I'm with Lily. I'll send in a nurse.'

'I don't need help,' Lily said.

'You'll take it. Shower and back to bed for the night.'

'I'm going home,' Lily said, and then hesitated. *Home.* The word had connotations for them both.

But Evie was being efficient. It was up to him to be the same. 'I'll collect you as soon as you're clean,' he said. 'I'm going to check on Tom but I'll be back in half an hour, Lily. I'll bring the car to the discharge area.'

'I'm not a patient.'

'No,' Evie said. 'You're a heroine. The Harbour takes a while to accept people as its own, but what you've done this afternoon…you're now one of us, like it or not. We might gossip, we might be in your face, but we do look after our own. Luke takes you home or you stay here, like it or not.'

'Fine,' she said helplessly. 'I mean, thank you.'

'You're welcome,' Evie said, and grabbed Luke's arm and steered him out of the room. 'Expect a nurse. Luke, let's leave the lady to get on with what she needs to do.'

The nurse took a while to come. That was fine by Lily. She watched the sun set over the distant harbour and she felt as if she was floating.

Luke was taking her home.

She could still feel the pressure of his fingers on hers. He didn't know his own strength, she thought.

He'd almost kissed her.

She'd wanted him to.

Which was really dumb. It must be because she was still tired and overwrought. Today—or, to be honest, the last few days—had taken it out of her.

Her stomach still hurt. Stress?

Maybe she should have said something to Evie.

No. She simply needed to give herself time to get over the gastro. To get over today. And more, she needed to *stop stressing*.

How could a girl do that when she was heading to Luke's apartment? What had she got herself into?

She sighed and closed her eyes. At least her mother wasn't here, and with that thought came more. How was her mother coping?

Her father's voice… 'You will look after her?'

She was so tired.

A young nurse peeped round the door. 'Dr Lockheart said you'd like help to shower. Dr Williams has given me a bag with some clothes. Are you up to showering now? Dr Lockheart says if you'd like to have another sleep first then Dr Williams will wait.'

'No,' she said, pushing herself upright. Reluctantly. 'No, it's okay. I need to go home.'

Wherever home was.

Home with Luke?

'So why's she looking like she's been hit by a train?'

To say Evie was blunt was an understatement. She said things as she saw them.

'She had gastro.'

'You and I both know gastro doesn't make you look like that. There's no underlying medical problem? She went out like a light in Theatre. She scared the hell out of Judy.'

'She's been under strain.'

'Because of your relationship?'

'Will you butt out?' He turned to face her head on. Finn had labelled her Princess Evie. The staff still called her that, not to her face but as a gentle reminder to themselves of the power she wielded. Evie was one doctor among many, but her family money meant she was unsackable. Her grandfather had brought her in here when she was tiny, she'd practically lived in his office and she thought of the place as home.

So this hospital was her home and she didn't like mess. She was trying to tidy Lily up, he thought. Pigeonhole her. Figure exactly where she fitted.

'She almost looks abused,' Evie said conversationally, and he practically spluttered.

'You're accusing me of abusing...*my girlfriend*?' It took him a while to find the last two words but he managed it.

'I'm not saying anything of the kind,' Evie said. 'That's why I'm asking. I said almost. What other explanation is there?'

He groaned inwardly. There was no way she'd leave this now; no way she'd stop pestering him. If he didn't give her what she wanted then he had no doubt she'd march right back and ask Lily. If she thought a woman was in trouble...

She might be Princess Evie, but she had courage and honour.

Almost as much as Lily?

He had to give her the truth, he thought, or as much as he needed to divulge to get her off both their backs.

'Lily's having trouble with her mother,' he said. 'Major trouble.'

'Illness?'

'Her mother's stolen her savings and has taken up with the local vicar. And if you repeat that to a soul I don't care who your family is, I'll hang you out to dry. I imagine Lily would kill me if I told anyone.'

Evie stared at him, stunned. 'All her savings…'

'Yep.'

'So that's why she's finally staying with you. Oh, the poor girl.'

'I'm fixing it,' he said heavily.

'You're fixing it?'

'As much as she'll let me.'

'You?' she said, and he wondered what exactly the staff did think of him.

'Leave it,' he said, and her face creased into a smile.

'Our Luke, fixing it,' she said happily. 'How about that? Falling for a woman with problems.'

He wasn't.

Or wait…maybe he was.

He needed to get things in perspective.

He wasn't sure what perspective was.

'Luke, while you're in fixing mode…' Evie said

And he thought, Uh-oh, here we go. He did not have this kind of conversation with Evie. He didn't have this kind of conversation with anyone.

Did Evie suddenly think he'd changed?

'It's Finn,' she said. 'I'm worried.'

Here was another jolt. Evie wasn't a worrier; she was a brisk, efficient doctor with the weight of the Lockheart fortune behind her.

Finn.

The niggle of worry he'd been feeling about his friend surfaced again, and turned into something more substantial.

But this was Finn Kennedy they were talking about, and no matter how much money Evie's family had, he wouldn't thank Luke for crossing boundaries. A junior doctor was talking to him about his boss. 'I don't think he'd thank you for worrying about him,' he said dryly.

'You're his friend,' Evie snapped.

Was he? Finn didn't do friends. Still… He'd been there when Finn had been released from the army. He'd spent time with him whether Finn wanted him or not. The number of bottles of single malt they'd consumed…

There was a good reason why Finn had hit the bottle, Luke conceded. His brother had died in front of him. He'd been wounded himself. There was trauma, deep and never spoken of.

He didn't want to get involved.

Too late. He already was.

'So why are you worried?' he growled, and started walking again, but Evie took his arm and made him stop. Here in the carpeted corridor of the private suites they could have some privacy.

'He dropped his clipboard.'

He dropped his clipboard. He let her words sink in. There wasn't a lot of basis there for worry.

But this was Evie, talking about Finn. Evie didn't do worry lightly.

Evie and Finn sparked off each other. Evie gave as good as she got. They'd make a good pair, Luke thought, but, wow, there'd be some fights.

Maybe that's what Finn needed. Fights. Someone to stand up to him.

His thoughts were flying tangentially. He was thinking about Finn. He was thinking about Tom.

He was thinking about Lily.

He didn't do personal concern. Or he hadn't. Suddenly he was surrounded on all sides.

In half an hour he had to take Lily home. Put her back into his bed. Make her something to eat…

Keep her safe.

No. Focus on Finn. Of the three worries, this was the easiest.

'Tell me what you're worried about.'

Evie exhaled and he thought this seemed liked a major decision, to talk to him about it.

'Wednesday night…he was walking down the corridor in front of me, carrying patient notes in one hand and a clipboard in the other. Heavy pile in the left. Clipboard in the right. He dropped the clipboard. I… We've been a bit tense with each other so I stood back; hoping he wouldn't turn around and see me. He stared down at the clipboard and then he stared at his hand. Swore. He set the notes down, put the clipboard on top of the notes and lifted them all in his left arm. Then he kept going, everything in his left arm, his right arm sort of tucked against him. And, Luke…yesterday in Emergency we had a guy who needed urgent stitching and I was flat out. Finn was passing. You know how he's always passing. I called for help and he stitched for me. It was tricky. This was a guy's face but Finn's good. Anyway, fifteen minutes later I finished what I was doing, went to the cubicle where Finn was working and he handed back over to me. "This is your job," he snapped. Okay, that's his usual style. But, Luke, I'd swear his right hand was trembling.'

Silence.

Luke stared out of the window and watched the Manly ferry chug slowly across the harbour.

His boss. A shaking hand.

It was probably nothing—only Evie didn't worry for nothing.

No matter how convoluted the gossip network of the Harbour became, Luke stayed detached. He liked to think he'd taught himself not to care, only of course he did care. From a distance.

Finn was a bad-tempered, surly, uncommunicative surgeon. He was one of the best surgeons Luke had ever worked with.

He was, like it or not, his friend.

How much of the single malt was he putting away?

So what to do? Head to Finn's office and say, 'I hear your hand's shaking?'

There was not one snowball's chance in a bushfire of that happening, and of getting back out of the door if he did.

Besides, he needed to check on Tom. And then take Lily home.

Lily, of the gaunt face. Lily, who was too thin even before the gastro.

She'd needed this weekend to recover and it had ended like this.

'That's all I wanted to say,' Evie said, brisk again. 'I just thought...someone else should know.'

Gee, thanks, Luke thought morosely. Hand over your worries to me, why don't you?

But that wasn't fair, and he stopped himself from saying it. Evie could have taken her concerns straight to the medical director. Eric would then be bound to take them further. The legal implications of an impaired director of surgery would make Eric act whether he wished to or not.

Evie had chosen the kinder path.

'Thank you,' he said heavily.

'I'm sure you mean that,' she said dryly. 'Sorry, but I had to tell someone. Short of counting the whisky bottles in his garbage and confronting him with it, I didn't know what else to do. So can you fix Finn as well as Lily and her mother? I'll see to Uncle Tom.'

'That's hardly a fair division of labour.'

'No, but otherwise you're landed with everyone,' she said softly, and then she smiled. 'Because you care. I thought you'd escaped it but it seems even the great Luke Williams has to succumb to caring eventually.'

Lily wouldn't leave the hospital without seeing Tom. Luke had just come from Intensive Care but he detoured back again with her, carrying Lily's overnight bag, feeling strange. Feeling like a relative rather than a doctor.

As they walked through the corridors staff were watching, and as they neared ICU Lily took his hand.

The sensation was unnerving to say the least.

Once upon a time he and Hannah had had a relationship within this hospital. She'd held his hand whenever she could. Or rather her action had been...proprietary. From the time they'd started dating she'd announced their relationship in no uncertain terms.

Like Lily was doing now. Not like Hannah, who'd deliberately kissed him where colleagues would see, touched him whenever she could, called him sweetheart in the wards, but, still, she was holding his hand and that was possessive enough.

Maybe she needed it for support. He glanced down at their linked fingers and her hold tightened.

'Don't,' she said.

'Don't what?'

'Look at our hands. Act as if it's normal. Isn't this what you want? For the staff to think we're a long-term couple? If we are, then holding hands is something we'd do all the time.'

It was.

It was also hard to get his head back to where it had been two days ago, to the idea that this was a pretend relationship so he could go on as he wanted to: independently.

'You think we should kiss, to make a bigger impression?' he said, thinking of Hannah.

'Long-term couples wouldn't,' she said. 'Kissing in corridors is tacky. Being caught in the on-call room was bad enough. Holding hands will do nicely, thank you.'

'We wouldn't want to seem tacky.'

'No, we wouldn't,' she said serenely. 'This couple has class.'

And then they were in ICU, and their hands could separate because all focus was on Tom. He still looked ashen, hooked up to every conceivable piece of technology the Harbour could throw at him, but amazingly he was smiling to see them.

'Here's trouble,' he whispered. 'I s'pose you're here to give me a lecture.'

'Not me,' Lily said roundly, and kissed him. 'I have more respect. Though I suspect Luke might be a bit angsty about his car.'

'His car?'

'He used it as a farm bike,' she said. 'I like it better now. It looks pre-loved.'

'That's me,' Tom whispered. 'If pre-loved looked battered.' He hesitated. 'Doc says I'll keep the leg, thanks to you guys.'

'I know you have two,' Lily said, still smiling. 'Trying to cut one off might seem a saving on socks, but think of all those left-foot shoes you'd have had to ditch.'

And Tom actually managed a grin. He was enchanted, Luke thought.

He wasn't the only one.

'I'm taking Lily home now,' he said, maybe more roughly than he intended. 'She's had a bit of a shock, too. She needs to rest.'

'Back to the farm?' Tom demanded.

'To my apartment.'

'Who's going to look after the farm?' No matter how battered he was, Tom's focus would be on his horses.

'I'll drive up tomorrow,' Luke said. 'I'll sort something with the neighbours.'

'I'll come with you,' Tom said, and grimaced.

'No,' Luke said gently. 'Sorry, Tom, but with the damage you've done to your leg you'll need a while to get over it. You'll need a few days' physiotherapy.'

At least. Maybe a few weeks. It'd take time to get full function back.

'A few days…' Tom sounded appalled. He tried to sit up but Lily pressed him back on his pillows.

'Don't think about worst-case scenarios,' she said. 'For now you need to sleep. When the anaesthetic wears off properly, you'll be able to assess the damage for yourself.'

So stop worrying now, was her silent message, and she sent a warning glance to Luke.

She was right. What was he doing, talking long term

when Tom was still in a post-operative haze? When things could still go wrong.

'But the farm…' Tom whispered.

'I'll go up every day,' Lily said, and Luke blinked. What?

'One of the mares is about to foal,' Tom whispered. 'Larkspur. And your little'un's too young to be left.'

'Merrylegs,' Lily said, smiling again. 'You reckon I'd let him fend for himself?'

'I know you wouldn't,' Tom said, and reached out and gripped her hand. 'You're a good kid. I dunno where Luke found you but I'm glad he did.'

'Me, too,' Lily said in a voice that was suddenly unsteady. 'And I bet he is, too, so that's three out of three. Aren't we all lucky?'

They didn't speak then until they were home. Home at Kirribilli Views, a two-minute drive from the hospital; home that wasn't a farm forty minutes' drive away.

There didn't seem much to say—or rather there was a lot to say and neither felt sure where to begin. Lily certainly didn't. She stood by Luke's side in the elevator. Luke was still carrying her bag and she thought, I've just taken over his life.

He rescued me from bedbugs and here I am, his live-in lover. About to lecture him about the care of his uncle.

It shouldn't be her business, whether he cared for his uncle or not, but it was. She'd lain still for an hour saving Tom's life and she was darned if she'd let him risk it again. She'd say something.

Soon.

The silence was getting oppressive.

And then the elevator door opened and Ginnie was in front of them and there was no such thing as silence.

'There you are!' It was a cry of triumph. 'I've been down and knocked three times already. I told John to let me know the minute you were discharged, Lily, because I wanted to catch you before Luke put you to bed.' She peeped a smile at them, and Lily groaned inside. 'As soon as I heard about the accident I dashed down to Pete's. His chef does the best beef and Burgundy pie. I've bought one for you because I expect you still won't want to come to Teo's party tonight. John tells me you were awesome,' she told Lily. 'You saved Luke's uncle. And he says the chopper guys say your farm's awesome as well,' she told Luke. 'I was thinking… I mean…not yet, obviously, while your uncle's unwell, but as soon as he's back on his feet John and I could drive up there. We could bring our own Sunday lunch. Do say yes. Now I'll just dash up and get the pie.'

'We don't need—' Luke started.

'Of course you do,' Ginnie retorted. 'Lily needs to try it. She needs to try everything. We can't believe you've hidden her for so long. Pete's Bar is right over the road from the hospital,' she explained to Lily. 'It's home away from home for half of the staff. Pete has half-price drinks on Wednesday, not that that's important. What is important is that John and I thought tomorrow night we'd take you both there for dinner. It's time you got to know us.'

That was said with a glare at Luke, like he'd somehow conspired to keep her hidden. Which, come to think of it, was just the impression he'd been after.

'Lily's still recovering from gastro,' Luke said, brusquely.

Lily thought, He hates this. Involvement.

Gossip?

Luke and Lily both.

'And as soon as I'm over it I'll be staying back at the farm,' Lily added. 'While Tom's recovering someone has to care for the horses.'

'What, alone?' Ginnie demanded. 'By yourself?'

'I'm an independent woman.'

'But John says it's only forty minutes from the hospital.' Ginnie was clearly struggling with information overload. 'The way Luke explained it, we thought it was hours away.'

'It's longer in peak traffic,' Luke said, but Ginnie wasn't listening.

'You could have come back for parties from there. I can't believe you'd live so close and not want to be part of the hospital scene. It has to stop. Lily, you don't like being isolated, surely?'

'It has advantages,' Lily told her.

'Like being allowed to go to bed when she needs to,' Luke said, and put his arm around her waist in a gesture that was almost rough. 'The pie's great, thank you, Ginnie, but I'll come up and collect it later, after Lily's settled.'

'You make me sound like a baby.' Lily tried to tug away but failed. 'We can both pop up and get the pie now.'

'No, we can't,' Luke said, sounding goaded. 'Bed.'

'Ooh,' said Ginnie.

'Ginnie…'

But Ginnie was grinning. 'I'm just going,' she said airily. 'I know when I'm not wanted. Tell you what, I'll pop the pie into the parcel box in the lobby. That way you can fetch it when you're fin…when you're ready.'

'Thank you,' Luke muttered, and turned Lily toward the door.

'Think nothing of it,' Ginnie said as Lily choked on sudden laughter. Ginnie backed into the elevator, Luke managed to get his key in the front door and propel her inside, he slammed the door behind them…

Lily couldn't help herself. The bubble of laughter wouldn't stay down one second longer.

Luke leaned on the door and glared at her, but it was so…it was so…

'It's not funny,' Luke growled.

'It's just what you want,' she managed. 'It couldn't be more perfect.' She smiled and smiled. 'Now that Tom's going to be okay.'

'There is that,' he said, and the trace of a smile appeared behind his glower.

'And you well and truly have a lover.'

'I do, don't I?' he said.

Her laughter caught. She met his gaze. Something locked. Held.

Laughter died.

'Lily…'

'They know about your farm,' she said, suddenly uncertain. The way he was looking at her…

'They do.'

'And your Uncle Tom.'

'Yes.'

'Can you bear it?'

'If I must,' he said softly, and instead of leaning against the door he was suddenly holding her by her shoulders. His gaze hadn't wavered.

'It's a hard call,' she whispered.

'It is,' he said. 'A package deal. The farm, Uncle Tom, and you.'

'Luke…'

'Enough,' he said. 'Enough, my beautiful Lily. Even though no one's watching, even though this doesn't corroborate our story one iota, even though it doesn't matter at all…I believe I need to kiss you.'

'Really?' She sounded hopeful, she thought. She sounded like a silly teenager.

But this was Luke.

'Really,' he said and proceeded to do just that.

CHAPTER NINE

His kiss was strong and sweet and wonderful.

It was just like that first morning. Just like…

No. It was just like nothing.

It was just like now.

To say she was blown away was an understatement. The day's events had left her disoriented, wobbly, like her legs didn't belong to her. Now it seemed her body didn't belong to her. She was dissolving into a haze of heat and aching desire.

What was it with this man?

Charlie hadn't made her feel like this. Not even close.

Luke.

His hands were holding her close, and she felt like she was melting into him. Her breasts were crushed against his chest, and he felt like iron. Strength mixed with tenderness, she thought, dazed. It was the sexiest of combinations.

Restraint and desire.

For he was simply kissing. His mouth was exploring hers, nothing more. He held her close, and he kissed as if he wanted nothing more than simply to have this connection—and she felt fire.

For fire it was. The heat between their lips was indescribable. She was fusing to him, melting into him, wanting him with every shred of her being.

She was on tiptoe, wanting to be closer, closer…

Her hands were holding his face, feeling the roughness of his five o'clock shadow, loving the strength of his bone structure, quite simply…

Loving Luke.

As plain and as simple as that.

This man was like no one she'd met before but he wasn't a stranger. Something in him resonated as nothing had ever done before. The other half of her whole?

As simple and as complicated as that.

She was falling in love.

It was crazy, crazy, crazy, but it was there. She was falling in love with this man.

Or she would if he kept kissing her and no way did she want him to stop. She didn't care if this kiss broke records. She was holding him as hard as he was holding her. What was the record? Two days? Three? She was willing to give it a shot.

But he wasn't. Of course he wasn't.

She wasn't sure how long it lasted but it was Luke who finally broke the contact. He tugged back and she almost glared. Only she couldn't quite glare. Not at Luke. Not at this man who'd just kissed her.

He was looking kind of fuzzy.

Her whole world was looking kind of fuzzy, she conceded. She'd just been kissed by Luke Williams. This man was seriously…

Hers.

She'd been thinking sexy. She'd been thinking hot. But when the word framed in her head it didn't come out like that.

Definitely the word was *hers*. Her man. She met his gaze and her heart twisted and she felt like she knew him better than she'd known any other living person. She felt like she was looking deep inside him.

And she saw shock. Dismay?

'Hey, it was you who kissed me,' she managed, but there was no way she could stop a tremor in her voice wobbling through. 'There's no reason to look like that. I'm not about to eat you.'

'Look like what? I wasn't thinking—'

'Yes, you are. Like I'm about to jump you. I'm not. Though it was a very nice kiss.' The tremor was getting better. She was getting better. More in control.

Liar. She was so out of control she wasn't sure what week it was.

'It was a very nice kiss,' he said, and his smile returned. Keep it light. That's what his smile said. Fine by her.

It had to be fine by her.

'But maybe not all that wise,' she said.

'No.'

'Not if we're living together. Mind, no one outside these walls would know.'

'Everyone outside these walls already knows,' he said, and the wariness was still there. 'They think we've been an item for years.'

'Well, then,' she said.

Where to take this from here?

What to do in a one-bedroom apartment on a Saturday night when you were pretending to be lovers?

When your body said you weren't pretending?

'I might head back to the hospital and do a ward round,' Luke said.

'A ward round on a Saturday night.'

'My current registrar's a bit unsure.'

So am I, she thought, but she didn't say so.

'Fine,' she managed. 'And you'll go back and see Tom?'

'Of course.' Things were formal. Absurdly formal.

'Remember to pick up our pie for dinner on the way back. It's in the parcel post in the foyer.'

'Yes, dear,' he said, and his smile was definitely back.

'That's good, then,' she said. 'I'll just watch the telly. I might do a bit of knitting on the side. Then…I don't know…dust the mahogany?'

'We don't have any mahogany.'

'That's a shame. It's my splinter skill.'

'Like rollerblading and horse riding.'

'That's right.' She hesitated. 'But far less dangerous. No one's ever yanked me off mahogany dusting, so you needn't worry at all. Luke, do tell Tom I'll go out to the farm tomorrow. I can't bear to think he'll worry about the dogs and horses. I can easily commute.' You could, too, she thought, but she didn't say it.

'You're not going to the farm. I'll drive up tomorrow and and organise things with Patty. She has a couple of sons who'll feed the animals.'

'You think Tom will be content with a neighbour's sons feeding his horses?'

'He doesn't want us up there.'

'Of course he does.'

'He likes his independence,' Luke snapped.

And Lily thought, Whoa.

'So…he's like you,' she said.

'He learned his lessons the way I learned mine. We don't depend on people.'

'No,' she said softly. 'You don't. But you do care for people.'

'Of course I care.'

'So kissing me now…'

'Wasn't such a good idea. Call it the culmination of one heck of a day.'

'I'd call it a lot more,' she said frankly. 'I've never felt like you made me feel just then. All wobbly at the knees.'

'You were wobbly at the knees before.'

'I was,' she admitted. 'But, then, I met you four days ago. My knees have been wobbly ever since.'

'Not because of me.'

'No.'

'Lily…'

'I know—it was an aberration.' She sighed. 'You're right, we're grown-up people and you have your independence and I have my mother. So the intersection of two worlds is impossible—except that we're still pretending it's possible.' She cocked her head to one side and considered. 'Luke, the way I'm feeling…'

'Wobbly kneed?'

'Yes,' she admitted. 'And it's not just gastro and Tom that's made them wobble. There's something about the way you make me feel… I know it's dumb but I can't help it and four weeks staying here… I think the sensible thing is for me to stay at the farm. Tom may well need four weeks of rehabilitation. I'm used to commuting a lot further than Tarrawalla. I can stay there happily until it's time to go back to Lighhouse Cove.'

'You can't go back to Lighhouse Cove.'

'I don't have a choice.' Her flash of being in control faded and she backed until she was leaning on the settee. She really was feeling wobbly.

'It's time you walked away from your mother.'

'And here's me thinking it's time you walked towards your Uncle Tom.'

'He doesn't need me.'

'He does. He just doesn't admit it.'

'And your mother admits it all the time.'

'At least I know where I stand.'

'Tied by the apron strings.'

'Don't,' she said wearily. 'I know she's difficult, but I've tried walking away in the past and I feel worse than if I stay. I loved my dad…'

'This is not your dad.'

'No, but—'

'It's past history. A promise made when you were twelve.'

'As your wife's death is past history,' she said softly. 'And the panic about losing people. It's not as easy as it sounds; ignoring history.'

'No.'

'So I can go to the farm.'

'You can go to bed.'

'Luke—'

'Enough,' he said roughly. 'Rest and then pie and leave any other decisions until morning. I'll fetch the pie on the way back. And no opening the door to visitors. I've had enough nosy-parkers in my life this weekend.'

'Am I included in that?'

'No,' he said roughly. 'Or at least…I'm not sure where you're included and I'm not sure I want to find out.'

He went back to the wards. Contrary to what he'd told Lily, his registrar was excellent. Evening visiting hours were in full swing. No patients wanted or needed to see him.

He ended up in Intensive Care. Tom was looking more

stable by the moment but was fast asleep. Judy popped in; they discussed muscle and nerve damage, the need for rehab, and Judy's pride at how little residual damage she expected.

It was such a far call from where they'd been at midday, Luke felt dizzy.

'With the drugs I've given him, I doubt he'll surface until tomorrow,' Judy said. 'You needn't stand by his bed worrying he'll wake in pain. I promise it won't happen. You need to get back to Lily.'

'I…'

'She's a great girl,' Judy said softly. 'The whole hospital's happy for you.'

'Thank you.' He couldn't think what else to say.

'Will you stay at the farm and commute while Tom's in here? I gather that's where Lily's been hiding. Is her mother such a horror?'

Whoa… Evie. Surely she hadn't…

'This hospital has ears,' she said, grinning at the expression on his face. 'I was up seeing Hank Oliver in Six South, just about to walk out of his door, when I heard you and Evie talking.' She hesitated. 'What you said about Finn, too. It's not only Evie who's worried.'

'Nerve damage through drinking?'

'Unlikely,' she said. 'But possible. He'd never let me near to check.'

'Me neither.'

'Yeah, well, good luck with that one,' she said. 'Do your best. He might be an ill-tempered grouch but he's our ill-tempered grouch, and he's a fine surgeon. So…off to pack for the farm?'

'No.'

'Because of Lily's mother?'

'No!'

'Okay, none of my business,' Judy said, raising her hands in surrender. 'It doesn't help, though. You know as well as I do that keeping things to yourself in this hospital is impossible. Seemingly you've kept Lily to yourself for years but now you have every nose in this hospital twitching and they won't stop twitching until All Is Revealed.' She grinned and picked up her notes. 'Good luck and goodnight and welcome to the world of exposure. You know, it doesn't actually hurt. Sometimes it's even a power for good.'

He went back to the apartment. To Lily. They ate pie. They watched the grand finale of *Eurovision* on TV, one amazing, Lycra-clad act after another. Lily giggled.

He listened to Lily giggle and felt…like he needed not to feel.

Lily went to bed and closed the door behind her. He slept—badly—on the settee.

In the morning he woke at dawn, wrote Lily a note and left for the farm. He'd do what needed to be done and be back by lunchtime. Then he'd check on Tom, and spend the afternoon in his office catching up on medico-legal work. His day was thus mapped out, without Lily.

He reached the farm as the early morning sun was still glistening through the trees. The leaves were wet with dew. The mountains were majestic in the background, the creek was rippling across the stones, the kookaburras were greeting the day and he felt the familiar tug of love he always had whenever he reached this place.

So why didn't he commute?

His uncle didn't want him to.

Or he didn't want to?

He thought back to the first lot of school holidays he'd spent at the farm, ten years old, and desperately lonely. It had been his first term break.

'It's too short a time to come home,' his mother had told him. 'Maybe you can come back here in summer.'

Maybe. The word had left him feeling sick.

He'd been the only kid left in the boarding house. The boarding master had been kind, but even Luke had been able to see he hadn't wanted him there. Finally, with a bravery that he still didn't believe he'd possessed, he'd rung an uncle he'd only heard of in conversation. 'I don't want to stay here…' He'd struggled not to cry but he hadn't succeeded.

'Your father doesn't want me messing in what's not my business,' his uncle had snapped, and hung up, but the next day his battered truck had pulled up outside the boarding house.

'The kid'll be better at my place,' he'd told the boarding master, and had broken every rule in the book by simply loading Luke into the cab of the truck and leaving without parental permission.

Back at the farm Tom had barely spoken. He'd shown Luke a bedroom and told him he was expected to look after himself.

The next day he'd given him a colt and shown him how to train him. Checkers. Luke's life had looked up from that moment.

But rough kindness apart, they'd lived separate lives. Tom had barely spoken to him, but at the end of each term—and finally most weekends—the truck would turn up at school and Luke would find himself back at the farm. The deal was Luke didn't get in Tom's way and Tom didn't get in his. When Luke had been able to afford it he'd bought the place next door, which Tom seemed to approve of, even if he only signified it by a grunt.

Today's outburst by Tom, his approval of Lily, his story of an old love affair…that had been the most he'd heard from Tom, ever.

He'd held Tom up as an example. How to live without needing people.

Maybe it was an illusion.

Was it okay to admit to needing people? Needing Lily?

No. He didn't need Lily, he knew that.

But maybe Lily needed him.

He could keep her safe.

Right. Like he'd kept Hannah safe.

Lily on Glenfiddich… The fear…

He wasn't making sense, even to himself. He raked his hair and wondered what he was doing staring at mountains when there was work to be done. He needed to head over to Tom's and feed the dogs. He need to check the cattle, put out the hay, check the horses.

And tomorrow?

Lily had offered to come up here. She was working nights. She could be here in the daytime, he could be here at night. Every night.

But…it seemed dangerous, just as it had when he'd first bought this place and wondered whether he could commute.

'Every night,' Tom had said, startled. 'What would you want to do that for? Your work's your life, boy. Don't you forget it.'

He'd forgotten it for a bit, and his work had killed Hannah.

His head felt like it was going round in circles. To let Lily come up here, day after day, to be here by herself…

It wasn't going to happen. He'd speak to Patty, employ one of her sons, get on with his life.

He headed off to feed the cattle, knowing he had a fight on his hands. He'd known Lily for, what, four days, and already he knew she wouldn't take this lying down.

She had to accept it. This was none of her business. The plan was she was to stay in his apartment for four weeks. Period.

He needed to stay in control. He needed to keep Tom's wishes in mind. He needed to maintain independence for both of them.

Despite Lily.

Plans didn't always come off, especially when three people were making them and Luke was only one of three. On Tuesday morning Lily finished work, took her suitcase from Luke's apartment and headed for the farm. Luke had no say. She'd organised it directly with Tom.

'I know you don't want me on your place,' she told Luke. 'So I won't be on your place. You've organised Patty's son to feed the animals. He can keep on looking after your place but Tom's asked me to look after his. I'm sleeping at his house. This is an arrangement between me and Tom so, as you're very keen on saying, butt out, it's none of your business.'

'You can't commute.' She was looking better but she was still pale. Still too thin. A weekend of bullying her to eat could only achieve so much.

'Yes, I can,' she said. 'You could too if you wanted, but you needn't worry. All the hospital knows why I'm doing what I'm doing, and they all think our love affair's still going strong. Knowing I'm helping Tom just adds to their belief that ours is a truly authentic love affair. With you working days and me working nights, and me living at the farm and you here, we can have a love affair without ever seeing each other. That's just the way you like it.'

Just the way he liked it. It wasn't. Neither did he like it that he saw Lily only in passing, as she arrived or left for work, or when he chanced on her in Tom's ward. It wasn't enough.

Tom was recovering well, accepting the need for rehabilitation, knowing he wouldn't be back at the farm for weeks. He was tickled pink that Lily was staying in his house.

Lily was making him talk. A week after the accident Luke walked in on Tom in the rehabilitation ward and Tom was chuckling.

Tom didn't chuckle. He was a recluse. A loner. But there was something about Lily…

'You didn't go up to the farm for the weekend,' Tom said accusingly.

'I was on call.'

It was Monday morning. Lily must be about to go off duty. She was wearing her agency uniform. She looked neat and prim and cute.

The farm must be doing her good, he thought. She looked much more relaxed than she had last week. She'd gained a bit of colour. Maybe she'd been riding one of Tom's horses.

Not Glenfiddich. The thought of her on his half-wild colt when she was on her own on the farm was unthinkable. He'd made her promise not to go near.

'You needn't worry,' she'd said. 'I get the boundary thing. Over your boundary I will not step.'

But Tom had horses, too. Was she riding them with no one around?

He wanted to ask.

He knew she'd react with anger.

He stood in the doorway and thought about retreating.

'Hey,' Tom said. 'Luke. You want to see me walk?'

There was no retreating from a statement like that. He watched as his uncle proudly manoeuvred the walking frame to the door, then let it go, held the rail along the corridor and made it all the way along to the nurses' station.

He and Lily stood side by side, like two proud parents. Lily clapped him on.

As Tom reached the end, he glanced down and Lily was smiling and sniffing back tears.

She'd only known Tom for a week. She was that involved?

'Isn't it wonderful?' she whispered.

And he thought, Yes, it is. And, yes, she was. But to wear her heart on her sleeve...didn't she understand about being hurt?

Didn't she understand how much love hurt?

'Tom's enjoying this,' she said softly, as Tom inched his way back to them. 'Despite his leg. He's making friends. Are you sure he really wants to be a loner?'

'He's made a good fist of it if he doesn't.'

'Maybe he's just good at disguising need,' she told him, and went back to encouraging Tom.

Tom was trying so hard, Luke thought, and then he thought I'd try hard, too, if Lily was expecting it of me.

'I have tomorrow off,' Lily was telling Tom. 'If the physio okays it, would you like me to take you to Coogee? Do you know it? I've only just discovered it; it's the most gorgeous little beach only twenty minutes from here. We could do your exercises in the ocean baths. Fun!'

Fun? This was Tom she was talking to, Luke thought. Tom didn't do fun.

But Tom was looking at Lily with delight. 'Ocean baths?'

'Rock pools,' she said. 'They're fabulous. What if I pick you up at ten?'

'You'll need help getting into the water,' Luke said, and then, before he knew it, he found himself offering. 'I'll come with you.'

'I don't want you bothering with me,' Tom growled—but he hadn't said that to Lily.

'It's okay. I can arrange time off.'

'There's no need,' Lily told him. 'Tom and I will manage. Meanwhile, I'm off to the farm to sleep.' She kissed Tom, an extraordinary gesture to Tom, who treated invasion of privacy with horror. 'I haven't slept so well in years as on your farm. It'll be hard when I have to leave.'

'Maybe you could stay,' Tom said, to Luke's further shock. 'I mean…you need somewhere to board, right?'

'I'll be returning to Lighthouse Cove,' Lily said, sounding regretful. 'But it's a lovely offer. Thank you.'

She left—and Tom watched her go with regret.

'Do something,' he snapped. 'She's gold. You'd seriously let her go back to this Lighthouse Cove she talks about?'

'I don't have a choice,' Luke said. 'It's her business.'

'Bunkum. It's our business. I made a fool of myself once, and you messed around with that selfish woman you married. But this time… If I was forty years younger…' He shoved himself from the corridor railing and lurched toward his walking frame, only just managing to grab it.

'Leave me be,' he growled as Luke moved to help. 'Go after your woman if you want something to do. Her business? A man'd be mad to think that.'

CHAPTER TEN

AT TEN on Tuesday Lily arrived at the Harbour to take Tom to the beach.

She was growing really fond of Tom.

So much for anonymity, she thought ruefully as she passed through the hospital on the way to Tom's ward. She'd come to Sydney aching to be a nobody and here she was, involved up to her neck. She was part of the Harbour team. She was Tom's friend. She was Luke's pretend lover.

But her involvement was an illusion, she thought as she was greeted by staff members all through the hospital. It was a part of the deception that was her relationship with Luke, but at the same time it was a taste of something she'd never known.

Until now, gossip had seemed vicious and hurtful. Here it was a way of life. A part of belonging. The Harbour was closing round her, enfolding her as one of its own, and the sensation was extraordinary.

At Lighthouse Cove she'd been the daughter of a man who'd died owing money to half the town and of a woman whose morals were questionable. She'd been shunned as a 'bad lot' all through her teen years. During her training in Adelaide, at the end of every shift she'd faced the long drive back to Lighthouse Cove. She hadn't had time to join in social fun. She was considered an outsider. She was used to being an outsider. When she'd come here what she'd wanted was to be anonymous, but now…

She was a member of the Harbour team.

Tom's friend.

Luke's lover.

The concept of belonging was an illusion, she told herself savagely. It had to end but it was messing with her head. It was like a siren song, dragging her in.

Luke had it for real, she thought, but he didn't want it. He didn't know how lucky he was. She had to go back to Lighthouse Cove. She had to leave Luke and everyone around him.

She walked into Tom's ward—and Luke was there.

Both men were casually dressed. Tom was already settled into a wheelchair. Luke had a bag full of beach-towels slung over his shoulder. They looked relaxed and happy and ready to go.

They took her breath away.

Luke took her breath away.

'You're two minutes late, Nurse,' Luke said, mockingly severe. 'Tom and I have been waiting and waiting.'

He was wearing jeans. His short-sleeved, open-necked shirt displayed a hint of the muscles of his chest. His hair looked ruffled.

His hair always looked ruffled, Lily thought. He had the most gorgeous hair. He had the most gorgeous smile…

'I've borrowed John's SUV,' he said, while her thoughts flew everywhere. 'I figured it'd be easier to get the wheelchair in and out.'

'You're coming with us?'

'I said I would.'

'But I didn't think…' She drew in breath. 'I mean… don't you have surgery?'

'I have an excellent registrar and an easy list,' he said. 'I need to be back by three for a cleft lip and palate but Tom will be ready for a sleep by then.'

'I won't,' Tom said indignantly. 'But if you need to be back by three, why are we hanging round here? Push.'

Luke chuckled and pushed.

Lily followed, feeling flummoxed.

She hadn't intended this. She thought, It's dangerous. But then Luke was the one who worried about dangerous.

They passed Reception on the way out and Evie was there.

'It's the Williams family.' Evie smiled. 'Have a lovely day.'

'Thank you,' Lily said, and glanced at Tom and then at Luke and saw similar expressions on both their faces.

The Williams family...

It didn't exist. Another illusion.

Dangerous.

The beach was gorgeous. The day was gorgeous.

They wheeled Tom down the ramp, helped him into the water. Tom's legs were white from years on the farm where long protective pants were the norm. The scar on his thigh stood out stark and dreadful. Luke expected him to sit in the shallows and do his exercises.

Instead he swam. Luke hadn't even known he could swim. Lily swam too, and he watched.

He watched as they swam, then he watched as Lily helped his uncle go through his exercises, then he watched as they duck-dived for stones.

'I'm playing lifesaver,' he told them when Tom accused him of laziness, but he wasn't.

He was watching Tom come out of his shell. And he

was watching Lily. In her simple, green, one-piece bathing suit, with her wet curls spiralling down her back, with her eyes sparkling...

She was entrancing.

He was watching his uncle fall under her spell.

He was falling under her spell himself.

He should join in, but if he duck-dived he'd brush against her body. He wanted it—but he wasn't going there.

Need. Desire. Things he'd put away for a lifetime were suddenly front and foremost.

'What is it?' she demanded as she surfaced and saw him watching. 'You're watching me as if I have two heads.'

'One head's enough.'

'So's one and a half legs,' she retorted, after a thoughtful stare back at him. 'That's all Tom has and he's beating me at duck-diving every time. You don't want to compete?'

'No.'

'More fool you,' Tom said, and chuckled, tossed the next stone and dived.

He abandoned lifesaving. He went and swam in the bay, hard and fast and long.

Alone.

They swam until they were exhausted. They ate fish and chips on the foreshore and Tom started drooping. Lily brushed the sand from her toes and slipped on her flip-flops, decreeing time out was over.

'Back to the Harbour,' she said. 'Tom, you need a sleep, and you, Dr Williams, have surgery scheduled.'

'Luke!'

'Luke,' she said, and smiled.

Oh, that smile...

'Are you going back to the farm tonight?' he managed.

'Of course.'

'Let me take you to dinner here instead.' Where had that come from?

He knew where it had come from. From need, pure and simple.

'She has to feed the horses,' Tom said.

'Okay, then,' Luke said, driven against the ropes. 'We'll have dinner at the farm. I'll stay the night and come back early tomorrow.'

She surveyed him with caution, as if he'd just proffered a peace offering and it might just explode. 'But you don't like commuting,' she said at last.

'I'll make an exception.'

'That's big of you.'

He ignored the sarcasm. 'I'll bring up a couple of Pete's pies.'

'They are good,' she said, weakening. 'Okay.'

She'd accepted.

Dinner. On the farm. With Lily.

He thought of the restaurant meals Hannah used to love. Dinner in any restaurant within a mile of this hospital meant every mouthful, every nuance was reported back to the gossip machine. Hannah had thrived on gossip.

Lily was different. He could see dinner on the farm with Pete's pies was a temptation where dinner anywhere else wasn't.

'We'll stay in separate houses,' Lily said, cautiously.

'A man'd be a fool…' Tom retorted, and Lily grinned.

'You stay out of this. Isn't the older generation supposed to keep up moral standards?'

'What fun is there in moral standards?' Tom demanded. 'And the whole hospital thinks you're sleeping together anyway.'

So even the patients thought it. Luke rolled his eyes—and caught Lily doing exactly the same.

He laughed and Lily laughed and things suddenly lightened.

Filled with hope?

'Okay,' Lily said. 'If you bring pies, I'll supply wine. Tom's veranda at eight?'

'We have a date,' he said gravely.

'Excellent,' she said. 'Pete's pies are awesome.'

And that was that.

He watched Lily feed the last of the chips to flying seagulls, going to enormous effort to make sure a one-legged bird was well fed.

That was Lily, he thought.

Hope?

Suddenly he had it in spades.

'Exactly how long have you known this woman?'

It was Finn—of course. The man was always where he was least expected to be.

Luke had less than an hour to get to the farm. He'd just repaired a cleft lip and palate, the procedure had taken longer than expected and even for his boss, he wasn't interested in stopping.

'I can't remember,' he lied. 'I need to get on.'

'The way you look at her…you're thinking of making it legal?'

'What, marriage?' That was enough to make him pause.

'That's what the grapevine's saying. The girls in Accounts are taking bets on you having another society bash. Will your parents come over again?'

In your dreams, he thought. A wedding like the last one…

Hannah's parents had serious money. His parents had come from Singapore. He still woke in a cold sweat thinking of that wedding.

'If anyone's to be married it should be you,' he told Finn. 'I've done my time. You haven't even stuck your toe in the water.'

'You can have a lot more fun without marriage.'

'I don't see you having fun.' He surveyed his friend with concern and decided to be blunt. 'It seems to me you're using women to distract yourself from something else. Pain?'

'Leave it.'

'So…you can talk to me about Lily and marriage and I can't talk to you about the pain in your right arm?'

'Who said anything about pain?'

He wasn't landing Evie in it. 'This is the Harbour,' he said mildly. 'Knowledge permeates its walls and then oozes out again.'

'The walls have it wrong.'

'The walls don't think so. What exactly hurts?'

'I've strained a muscle,' Finn snapped. 'It's getting better.'

'So who's seen it?'

'No one needs to see it. It's healing.'

'Can I take a look?'

'No.'

'Finn…'

'Get out of here. Go find your woman,' Finn snapped. 'They help.'

Luke hesitated. *They help.* The statement hung. That's what he'd thought, that Finn was using women to blot something out.

Physical pain or mental?

'Maybe you need to talk to a shrink,' he said softly. 'Hell, Finn, what you've been through... Let me make you an appointment.'

Uh-oh. He'd got that wrong. Finn's face tightened with anger. If looks could kill, Luke would be dead right now.

But Finn was his friend and he wasn't backing down. 'You know you need help,' Luke said. 'Why can't you admit it?'

'You know where you can put your help.' Finn stalked to the door, lifted his right arm—which didn't shake—and swept it hard across the bench.

Patient notes went flying, and Finn was gone. The door slammed so hard behind him it almost came off its hinges.

That went well, Luke thought. *Or not.*

He stared at the closed door. He thought about going after him. Thought it'd be useless.

Besides, he was having dinner with Lily.

He collected the pies—beef and burgundy, and chicken and leek. They smelled fantastic. Pete wrapped them in cloth with directions about reheating. 'Put 'em in a microwave and I'll come after you with a cleaver. Treat 'em right. You'll never win a lady with a soggy pie.'

'Who said anything about winning a lady?' he demanded. But Pete had already moved on to his next Harbour client, his next piece of gossip.

About twenty pairs of eyes followed him out the door of the pub. Counting pies.

Tomorrow they'd know he hadn't come back to Kirribilli tonight, he thought, and then he thought, So what?

One way to stop gossip—pretend to be in love.

A better way to stop gossip... Acknowledge you were.

He stopped short, feeling...discombobulated.

In love.

He drove all the way to Tarrawalla and the two words stayed with him all the way.

Lily was waiting. She had the table set on Pete's veranda.

He wasn't to be invited inside?

She took the pies and sniffed her appreciation. 'I'll put them in the Aga to reheat,' she said and he blinked.

'You're using the Aga?' As far as he knew, the slow combustion fire stove hadn't been used in his lifetime.

'Why wouldn't I? It's fabulous.' She slipped inside and returned with wine.

She was wearing jeans and an oversized windcheater. She had mosquito coils burning by the table.

Romantic dinner by candlelight?

Dinner by mosquito coils.

'How did the cleft palate repair go?' she asked, and that took him back all over again. He hadn't told her what he'd been doing.

But, then, those Harbour walls…

'He'll be okay. We'd been hoping to wait until he was a little older but his local hospital rang this morning. He was starting to suffer respiratory distress so we had to bring it forward. His mum's been beside herself but it's gone well; she can sleep easy tonight.'

'That's great,' she said simply. 'Those pies will take fifteen minutes to reheat. You want to take a walk, or just sit and listen to the frogs?'

'Frogs are great.'

'Aren't they?' she said, and shut up and listened.

She wasn't expecting him to talk, he thought. She wasn't expecting him to do anything.

Nothing.

He'd spent four hours this afternoon in nerve-racking surgery. He'd made the best possible job he could of tiny Joshua McFaddon's disfigured mouth. He was delighted with the result, but it had taken it out of him. He'd been up since five.

He was physically exhausted and Lily was simply saying listen to frogs.

The silence deepened, and the thought that had been playing in his head all the way up here grew louder. And louder.

'I believe I'd like to try living with you,' he said, before he even knew what he intended to say.

The words hung.

I believe I'd like to try living with you.

Where had that come from? The desire.

It had just happened. He wanted to live with Lily. Simple as that.

He didn't want the huge emotional roller-coaster of courtship, engagement, wedding. Not the romantic fantasy. But this need was growing more powerful by the moment. To have this restful woman beside him.

But she was looking…flabbergasted.

'Live,' she said, floundering. 'You mean…like housemates? Your bedroom at one end of the house, mine at the other?'

'No,' he said. For she might be restful but she was also beautiful. And sexy. And so desirable she made a man burn. 'I believe I mean live together as in what the Harbour believes we're doing right now.'

'For three weeks?'

'I suspect I'd like to make it permanent. It feels like it would be great—being permanent.'

She was looking at him like he was nuts. Maybe he was.

He shouldn't decide he wanted a permanent relationship when he'd known her for less than a week, he thought, but it felt like he'd known her for much longer. She seemed... the part of him that was missing.

If she was, she wasn't about to join up again. 'You've lost your mind,' she said.

'I'm just saying what I'm feeling,' he told her, trying to figure it out as he went. 'I've never met anyone like you. When I'm with you I feel like I've come home.'

She tried to smile. 'That's because I smell of the hay I've been hauling.'

'There is that,' he conceded.

'So you agree it's nonsense.'

And suddenly he thought, I've scared her.

'Lily, I'm not pushing for anything you don't want,' he said hastily. 'I'm simply saying what I feel. With Hannah... we were an item for two years before I proposed. We were engaged for another year while she organised the wedding of the millennium. For all that time I didn't feel like I'm feeling now. Like this is where I should be.'

'On the veranda of your uncle's farm?'

'With you,' he said softly. 'If you'll agree, I'd love you to come back to my apartment,' he said, urgently now. 'Lily, we decided to be pretend lovers. Let's see if we can be real ones.'

'Lovers.' She still thought he had a kangaroo loose in the top paddock, he thought. This woman was a highly trained medic. Any minute now she'd produce a strait-jacket to stop him hurting himself.

'I know it's fast...'

'Yeah, I feel like I've missed something,' she said warily. 'The process that goes before. Like dates and stuff.

We haven't actually slept together yet, have we? I mean, I haven't forgotten anything important?'

'I… No.'

'There you go.' She sounded like she'd decided to humour him. 'No matter what the Harbour thinks, one kiss does not a relationship make.' She took a deep breath, moving on. 'Luke, I'm hungry. Maybe that's your problem. Hunger makes people do weird things. Stay where you are. Don't move. I'll see if the Aga's done its magic.'

The Aga had. So had Pete. The pies were wonderful.

Lily ate hers with one eye on the pie and one eye on him. That was in case he suddenly developed strange twitches, he thought, or saw dancing elephants.

He found himself smiling as he ate. This really was ridiculous. He was out of his mind.

But he still felt exactly the same, like the woman across the table was part of him.

She wasn't eating enough. He wanted to bully her to eat more but he thought he had more important things he wanted her to agree to tonight.

'Walk?' he said when they'd eaten, and she was still watching him. He rose and held out his hand. 'Please.'

'I need to do the dishes.'

'Blighty,' he called. 'Patch.' As the dogs hared up the veranda steps he put dirty plates down and the washing up was done. Sort of.

'Sorted,' he said, and she choked.

'Of all the… Typical surgeon!'

'What?'

'No finesse. You were supposed to offer to wash, thus earning brownie points.'

'Would you consider living with me if I washed them?'

'You're ridiculous.'

For an answer he held out his hand again. 'Walk. Please.'

She hesitated, and then cautiously took a step forward.

Excellent. He took her hand and he led her down the veranda steps, down to the creek and into the night.

They walked silently, the dogs following at their heels. Silence was almost their usual state, he thought. That was fine by him; he'd been raised in silence and it was a friend.

His fingers were linked with Lily's. In a moment the silence would end, her fingers would withdraw and the moment would be gone, but in the silence was a promise of a future.

Hope.

They followed the creek along the bank, skirting trees, boulders, fallen timber. At one point they had to cross the creek to get further, stepping over widely spaced rocks. He wanted to help her but she was intent on coping herself.

She reached the other side and he took her hand again.

She didn't resist.

'I've fallen in love,' he said gently, at last, and the words hung in the night sky.

'That sounds…easy to do,' she said cautiously. 'People do it all the time. Only not with me.'

'A man'd be mad not to.'

'Because I helped your uncle?'

'Because you're wonderful.'

'Okay, I helped your uncle and I'm wonderful,' she said, and he could tell she was struggling to sound placid. 'Two compliments do not lovers make.'

'I know,' he said ruefully. 'It's too soon. But I'd love you to come back to my apartment, to see if we can make it work.'

She stopped then, turning in the moonlight so she could see his face. She looked troubled.

'That's another thing I don't understand. Why would you want to go back to your apartment when you could stay here?'

'Maybe we *could* stay here,' he said, thinking that with this woman anything was possible. Even a home was possible. 'But not while you're working nights. I don't like this. I'm away during the day. Tom's not here. What if something happens?'

'I'm not Hannah,' she said, and he flinched.

'I know that.' He raked his hair, knowing he needed to get a handle on what he was feeling. Knowing it was too huge for any handle. 'But I'd never want a marriage where I couldn't reach you.'

'Who's talking marriage?' she demanded, astounded.

'Okay, I'm not,' he said hastily. 'Not yet. But even now, when we're little more than friends, I hate you being here by yourself.'

'We're *nothing* more than friends,' she said, calm and sure. 'And I love being here. I don't need you to know that I'm safe. I'm a big girl. I'm responsible for my own safety. I don't take risks—or not many. You know I won't ride Glenfiddich, even though I'd love to, but even if I did, I don't want anyone wrapping me in cotton wool. If that's the kind of relationship you want, then thank you very much but no.'

'I think,' he said carefully, 'that right now I'd be content with any relationship you'd be prepared to give.' He took her hand back in his and looked down at their linked fingers in the moonlight. She looked up at him, and he knew her answer was no.

'I have my mother,' she said, and it was like saying, 'Step away.'

He didn't. He held her more strongly still. 'I won't let your mother hurt you.'

'You'll protect me from my mother as well?'

'From anything that threatens you. The way I'm feeling...'

'Well, you can stop feeling,' she said, suddenly angry. She tugged back as if he'd suddenly shown signs of the plague.

'Lily...'

'I'm my own person,' she said. 'Or I'm trying to be. I'm struggling really hard to have a life. With Mum like she is, I only manage it in snatches, but in those snatches I'm not about to be cocooned.'

'I wouldn't—'

'Of course you would,' she said. 'That's why you don't commute from here, isn't it—because you think that if you live here then you and your Uncle Tom might learn to depend on each other. You both hold onto your precious independence because anything else is too scary. And me? You'd take me back to the Harbour, back to the Sydney Scandal Central, you'd ensconce me in your sterile apartment and you'd keep me safe. You'd bring me up here when you're free to watch me. I bet you'd even offer to buy me a nice quiet mare.'

That idea had crossed his mind. She met his gaze and saw.

'Ha!' She tried to smile but it didn't come off.

'Do you think,' he said cautiously, moving sideways, 'that apart from the safety thing, a relationship might be possible?'

'Do you mean do I find you sexy? Of course I do.'

He reached for her hand again but she stepped away fast.

'Of course you're sexy,' she said. 'You're so sexy you make my toes curl. And you're kind and clever and a brilliant doctor, and I love the way your hair does that really cute kick at the sides. And you have the best horses. But you won't let me ride them. You come with a past, and that past is problematic. And I come with a mother and she's more so.'

'I can fix—'

'Your past? I don't think so. How do you walk from the shades of a dead wife and child? Hannah will always be with you. I suspect you'll always want her to be.'

He thought about that, trying to be fair. In some ways, she was right.

Hannah had been a gorgeous, vibrant girl who'd pulled him from his studious, solitary life and introduced him to fun. It hadn't worked—he'd been too infatuated to see past her glossy exterior until it was too late—but he was grateful for what she'd given him. She'd died carrying his child.

She would always be a part of him.

'And I'll always be with my mother,' she said, softly, watching his face. 'Of the two, I'd choose Hannah. At least you can keep the parts of her you loved and let the rest go.'

'You can't do that with your mother?'

'No,' she said, and sighed. 'Enough. This was a lovely walk. It was a huge compliment, saying you'd like what's between us to go further, but I'm old and wise enough now to know what's possible and what's not.'

She took his hands back in hers and looked down at

them, steadily, surely. She was bracing herself, he thought, and here it came.

'Luke, let's be honest,' she said. 'You wouldn't want to be tied in a relationship with me. You'd want to cocoon me and I'd kick against the traces and you'd hate it. My mother would be included and you'd hate it. The threat of what happened to Hannah would always hang over us and our lives would be impossible. Tonight we had great pie, some lovely wine, a gorgeous walk, but now it's over.'

And before he knew what she intended, she stood on tiptoe and kissed him, lightly, a feather touch, her lips brushing his so fleetingly it was as if he was imagining it. And when he went to hold her close she backed away.

'Your house is thataway,' she said, pointing through the trees where he could just see his veranda light. He'd left the car and walked to Tom's. 'Mine's in the opposite direction. The dogs will take me home. You need to go home by yourself. You and Tom have lives apart. You only know two extremes—apart or so close you'd cage me. But with my mother I'm already caged, and that cage is a long way from your side.'

She didn't sleep. Of course she didn't. How could a girl sleep after such a night?

She lay in the dark and thought about living with Luke Williams. Sharing his bed. Sharing his life.

Impossible, impossible, impossible—but, oh, to be asked…

For him to feel as she was feeling seemed a miracle. A miracle that couldn't be taken further.

Maybe she should try it, she thought in the small hours. She could return to his apartment and see if she could make it work.

But if she put one toe in the water her whole body would follow. If she slept with him…

She knew she'd melt.

'I'm weak,' she whispered, and she knew she was.

'And I can't be,' she said. 'I'd break my heart. To let myself love him and then have to walk away…'

Oh, but to let him walk away now…

She rolled over in bed and stared across the valley. She could still see his veranda light in the distance.

Was he lying in bed thinking the same?

Thinking about sharing his life?

He wasn't talking about sharing. He was talking about tugging her into his life and holding her close. They were two different things and she was wise enough to see it.

Sleep wouldn't come. Her stomach was hurting. Avoid stress? Ha. She gave up, warmed a hot-water bottle to alleviate the cramps and headed out onto the veranda, where the dogs lay on an ancient couch. They roused and wagged their tails and shifted along, as if this was her place as well.

She lay, and the dogs sprawled on top.

'See, I'm hopeless at being alone,' she told them. 'Is it time I went home to my mother?'

He dropped by the next morning, just at dawn. She woke to find him staring down at her, woman under dogs.

To say she felt at a disadvantage was an understatement.

'Do you mind?' she managed. 'This is my bedroom.'

'So I see.' He sounded stunned.

He was looking gorgeous, she thought, in tailored pants and his crisp, white shirt. He wasn't wearing a tie but it'd be in his car, she decided, ready to be popped on at need.

She was in her ancient nightgown. She'd be smelling

of mosquito repellent. The only thing she could put on at need was dog hair.

She wanted, quite desperately, to be in her nice, anonymous, nursing uniform. On level pegging. Right now she felt like a charity case. Someone to be looked after. That was how he thought of her, wasn't it?

'You've slept with the dogs,' he said.

'Mmm.' She tried to act casual. She yawned and stretched and the dogs yawned and stretched with her. 'We like it out here.'

'You sleep outside when you're here by yourself?' He sounded appalled.

'I have the dogs.'

'I'm commuting,' he said grimly. 'I'll stay at my farm until Tom comes home.'

'Until…'

'Okay, maybe I'll commute after he comes home as well,' he snapped. 'Maybe I need to. He's even more pig-headed than you.'

'That'd be hard.'

'I'll see you tonight,' he said, brusque again.

'I'll be going to bed early tonight. I'll thank you not to check on me.'

'Lily—'

'Independence,' she said.

'It's your mantra. You want it for yourself, so give it to me. Say byebye to Daddy, guys.'

She lifted two dog paws and waved them at Luke. Luke spun on his heel and left.

Discombobulated didn't begin to describe how she felt as he walked away.

CHAPTER ELEVEN

THE next night Lily went back to the night shift. She put her head down and worked. She tried to put Luke out of her mind.

That was pretty hard when the entire hospital was treating them as a couple. 'Would you and Luke like to come out with us? What are you and Luke doing at the weekend? Can we come up and visit?'

She got pretty good at avoiding invitations, and she assumed Luke was doing the same. 'Sorry, we're a bit overwhelmed with work now that Tom's in hospital. Maybe when he's better…'

When Tom was better, she'd be gone.

But still there was this insidious sweetness. Belonging. She'd never felt it before and it was almost overwhelming her. If she really did belong here… If she really was in love with Luke…

No. Reality was very different. She'd aimed for anonymous; she had to keep reminding herself that anonymous was what she wanted.

Luke was doing the same, knocking back invitations and trying to avoid being with Lily in a work capacity.

Professionally they hardly saw each other. Lily worked the night shift, Luke worked days. He made sure she wasn't rostered to Theatre— 'Personal relationships distract me when I'm working,' he told Elaine, and Elaine raised her brows but made sure his theatre roster didn't include Lily—and he didn't need to see her at all.

But he did need to check she was still okay. He dropped by Tom's farm every morning, making sure she was safe home before he left for work. She didn't seem to appreciate it but he did it all the same.

Twice there were late-night lacerations where he was called in and Lily needed to assist. She was kindness itself to the patients but she was businesslike in her dealings with him.

'I can see why you can't have her in Theatre,' Elaine told him, thoughtful. 'When you see each other it's like you both put on masks. Mr and Mrs Rigid. I don't understand. The whole hospital knows you're an item—why not relax and enjoy it?'

And then, toward the end of the second week, she probed deeper. 'You two haven't had a fight, have you? It'd be such a shame if we finally found out about your love life only to have it end. Your Lily makes every patient feel like the sun's come out, but when you come into the room it's like a cloud descends. I'm sensing domestic disharmony.'

Everyone was probing. Nurses, Luke thought dourly. Once upon a time they'd known their place, but Elaine was ten years older than he was, she'd been at the Harbour for ever and the only doctor she treated with deference was Finn.

There was another problem. Finn.

He couldn't do anything about Finn, as he couldn't do anything about Lily. Nothing but worry.

And, of course, this was the Harbour. He wasn't the only one worrying.

'Is Lily eating okay?' Evie was probing, as seemingly the whole hospital was probing about Lily. 'She's still looking pale. She shrugged it off when I asked but, if I were you, I'd push for blood tests. We should have had them done when she fainted.'

'She's under stress,' he said shortly, knowing what Lily's reaction would be if he pushed any such thing.

'Because of her mother?'

'Yes. And she shouldn't be driving back and forth to the farm.' He raked his hair. 'But I can't stop her.'

'Why doesn't she shift from agency to permanent?' Evie suggested. 'The hospital would employ her in a minute. We could organise her onto the day shift and you could travel back and forth together.'

'She doesn't want permanent work.'

'Because?'

'Evie…'

'Okay.' She held up her hands in surrender. 'I know. Relationships are out of bounds. I should know that—I'm hopeless at them. I'll butt out. But she's pale, Luke. Fix it.'

She *was* pale, Luke thought.

She didn't want him interfering.

When Tom had been in hospital for two weeks—another week and he'd be ready for home—Luke dropped into his ward and found Lily perched on his bed. They were intent on Tom's exercises, and for a moment he could watch them both, unnoticed.

Tom was looking great.

He tried to see Lily as the rest of the staff were seeing

her—and Evie was right. She looked…strained. Just how much was her mother's behaviour weighing on her?

He wanted to pick her up and take her home—only it was seven at night and she was about to start the night shift and he was about to go off duty. She was Lily the Independent, as was her right.

'How's it going?' he asked from the doorway, and Tom saw him and beamed, and Lily turned and smiled but her smile was much more contained.

'Brilliant,' Tom said. 'I can bend every single thing that needs bending. I'm fully weight bearing. I don't know why they won't let me home.'

'They won't let you home until they're sure you're strong enough not to fall,' Lily said severely. 'You go home early, you risk coming back in with a broken hip. Is that what you want?'

'No, but—'

'And Luke and I are caring for both farms like champions.'

'Have you cut down the dividing fence yet?' Tom demanded.

Lily smiled but her smile was forced. 'You guys haven't cut down the dividing fence in the whole time Luke's owned his farm,' she said. 'I don't see why I should make a difference. Luke, is it okay if we have a birthday party for Tom in your apartment next Saturday?'

'A birthday party…'

She fixed him with a look that would have withered stronger men. 'Tom turns seventy-five on Saturday, and he's due to go home on Sunday. He's made so many friends here we need to do something to celebrate. We can't do it in the ward so I thought we could have a bash at your place. We could invite anyone from here who's grown fond of him. Maybe we could invite Patty and the boys from the farm.'

'They won't want to come,' Tom said, startled.

'We'll never know until we ask,' she said serenely. 'Pete's Bar does catering. I checked and he said no problems—and Ginnie says they do awesome cakes. I'll get balloons and—'

'Hey,' Tom said, starting to sound uneasy. 'How many people?'

'I don't think,' Luke said carefully, 'that Tom's ever celebrated a birthday in his life.'

'Why not?' She looked astounded. 'Why ever not?'

Because they'd never thought about it, Luke thought. Tom had grown up in the same sterile environment he had. His parents and grandparents didn't notice birthdays. After Luke had come to Australia, Tom had occasionally given him gifts, things he'd noticed he might like. They'd been awesome gifts; Checkers to start with, a trail-bike, an amazing sound system, furniture for his student digs at university. None of those gifts had been for his birthday.

He'd known when Tom's was, though. Once, when he was in his early twenties, he'd made an effort, brought a card and a cake and a bottle of whisky and gone back to the farm for it.

'Should'a rung before you come,' Tom had said. 'I'm clearing blackberries from the back paddock today. Could use a hand, though.'

He'd ignored the birthday card. They'd eaten the cake without lighting the candle, and he'd put the whisky away for later.

'Birthdays are fool nonsense,' Tom said now, and Lily glared.

'I like fool nonsense. I can't believe you've passed seventy-five birthdays without being forced to blow candles out. Right, you have a week's notice to develop some lung power. Seventy-five candles is huge.'

'Just you and Luke,' Tom said, belligerent.

'*And* your friends.'

'I don't have friends.'

'If you don't have friends I'll eat my hat,' she declared. 'Let's see what happens.'

'Are you out of your mind?' Outside in the corridor Luke let fly. 'Of all the stupid... Tom's been a loner all his life. What sort of a statement is that—*If you don't have any friends I'll eat my hat.*'

'The statement of someone who knows he has friends,' she said evenly. 'And the statement of someone who knows he needs them. If you're going to stay aloof for the rest of his life, the more people he has around him the better.'

'He wants me to stay aloof. He trained me in the art.'

'No,' she said flatly. 'His parents trained him and your parents trained you. I'm seeing two guys who haven't got the courage to decide what they want for themselves.'

'At least we've figured where we stand. Not like you, letting your mother get away with making outrageous demands.'

'As your parents' training makes outrageous demands on you,' she snapped.

'Then you crack first,' he said. 'Call the bank and re-claim your money.'

'Go in and hug your uncle,' she said. 'No? I rest my case.'

'He doesn't want—'

'Doesn't he?'

'A birthday party...' He raked his hair. 'Honestly, Lily, no one will come.'

'Patty's coming.'

'You've already asked her?'

'She's bringing lamingtons. I know I should have asked first, but it'll be fun. How are you at blowing up balloons?'

'I wouldn't know.'

'You're about to find out. Now I need to find Elaine. She says her Graham makes fantastic piñatas. You think Tom would like one in the shape of a horse?'

'This is not a kid's party,' he snapped.

'No,' she said, thoughtfully. 'But if it's the first birthday party Tom's ever had it needs to be a good one. I think it'd be best if we both stay here on Friday and Saturday night—or at least I'll need to stay. There'll be stuff to organise. Patty will take care of the animals for us, then we can both take him home on Sunday. He'd like that.'

'This is all about what Tom wants.'

'Of course,' she said, meeting his gaze head on. 'What else would it be about?'

'Lily...'

'Dr Williams!' Cathy, the lady who delivered ward meals, was heading toward them with her trolley. 'This party on Saturday...'

'You didn't,' Luke said, and Lily shrugged.

'This is the Harbour. I hardly needed to spread the word myself.'

'I'm so happy it's happening.' Cathy was beaming. 'Your Uncle Tom's lovely—and when he's out of hospital he says I can take my little boy up to see his horses.'

'He said that?' Luke felt winded.

'So of course we'll come,' Cathy told him. 'I make great

fairy cakes, with red jelly and cream. Would you like me to bring some?'

'Yes, please.' Lily said, beaming back at her. 'Can you make lots? I have a feeling we're going to need them.'

'A birthday party. In your apartment.' To say Finn was hornswoggled was an understatement. 'I assume you're not expecting me to come.'

'Not if you don't like piñatas, lamingtons and fairy cakes,' Luke said.

'I don't.' Finn surveyed his friend with care. 'You're letting them get to you.'

'Them?'

'Women.'

'No,' he said but he was. One woman.

'You're not sleeping with her,' Finn said, and it wasn't a question.

He sighed. Finn the omnipotent. 'Enough with the commentary.'

'But you're nuts about her.'

He thought of Lily as he'd just seen her, beaming, excited, happily making Tom happy. There was only one way to answer Finn's question. 'Yes.'

'You going to tell Papa what's wrong?'

'I suspect Papa wouldn't be interested. Besides, you won't tell me about your arm.'

'It's getting better, whereas you and Lily… You're playing some game.'

'We're not.'

'She's only contracted here until the end of the week. Then she leaves?'

That brought him up with a jolt. After the party she'd be gone?

That's the plan, he thought, and said so.

'I see,' Finn said and Luke thought he did see. Far more than he wanted. 'Then it's back to normal?'

'I hope so,' he said, thinking he wasn't hoping anything of the sort. He should be—but he wasn't.

'Whisky's a cold bedmate.'

'Yeah,' Luke said, and suddenly he'd had enough of this conversation. 'You'd know,' he said savagely and walked away.

'I love a party!' Ginnie was practically squeaking with excitement. To give her her due, Ginnie had taken it upon herself to visit Tom every afternoon while he was in hospital. Lily wasn't sure how much Tom appreciated her visits, but Ginnie chatted and Tom let her, and they seemed to have formed a sort-of bond. So of course she needed to be invited. She was delighted, but she had reservations. 'But your apartment's so dreary. Can I decorate?'

'Of course,' Lily said, thinking, Hmm… Luke seemed to like grey.

'Jungle theme,' Ginnie said decisively. 'What sort of cake are you getting? No, don't worry about it, you have enough to sort. I'll talk to Pete. And I'll tell the guys to sort the drinks.'

'The guys?'

'The boys from the chopper rescue will be coming,' Ginnie said, as if it was a given. 'And the physios, and the nurses from Tom's ward. Ooh, it's just as well you have a big balcony. How many are coming from the farm?'

'I'm not sure.'

'Don't worry, we can cope, no matter how many.' Ginnie waved an airy hand. 'I'll haul Teo in. He's head of paediatrics, you must have met him. He's only met Tom once—I dragged him in to visit last week—but if there's a party there's Teo. I bet he can persuade his aunts to do some cooking. Do you think Tom would like his aunts?'

'I have no idea,' Lily said faintly.

'This hospital is so good at parties,' Ginnie declared. 'Saving lives and giving parties.' She giggled. 'It's a great mix. I couldn't bear to live anywhere else. I've never really thought that Luke liked being part of it, though. Isn't it lucky he finally has you to drag him into it?'

Friday was huge. Luke's operating list was long already and two emergency cases stretched him to the limit. It was nine before he had finished.

He wasn't going back to the farm. Lily would be in his apartment. Despite his fatigue it felt okay. More, it felt good.He headed back to Kirribilli, opened the apartment door—and was met by a jungle. Ferns, foliage and jungle growth was everywhere. Green netting, pith helmets, spears were hanging from the ceiling. A hulking plaster tiger was about to pounce from behind the settee.

He stood, stunned.

'It's from Kipling,' Lily said happily from under a mountain of green balloons on the floor. 'Do you like it?'

'Kipling?' he managed.

'*Jungle Book* was Tom's very favourite childhood book,' she said. 'I asked him when I was looking for a theme. Ginnie's been helping. Do you think we've succeeded?'

'Yes,' he said, trying to get his breath back. His lovely cool apartment. A jungle.

'You want to blow up balloons? Ginnie says we need to hang them in the foyer and on the letterboxes downstairs. Elaine was helping but Graham rang to say he knows where he can get a gorilla suit. They've gone to find it.'

'Great,' he said, and sat on the floor and started blowing up balloons. He couldn't think what else to do.

'You needn't look like that,' she said.

'Like what?'

'Like your life's been taken over. It's one party. Tom will be back at his farm next week, I'll be gone and you can get right back to your nice solitary self.'

'I've given up on my nice solitary self,' he said. He blew up two balloons while he watched her blow up four. He thought about what he needed to say. What he should say. What he had to say. 'Did you know you're beautiful?'

'So are you,' she said, and she put down the balloon she was blowing and met his gaze, direct and true. She smiled. 'Luke, I'll sleep with you tonight if you want.'

If he wanted…

There was a statement to take a man's breath away.

'My mother rang,' she said, dropping her gaze, tying string to her balloon. 'She found me. She must have rung every hospital in the country. Admin has this apartment as my address so she rang here. She was almost hysterical. I've told her I'll be home on Monday.'

'No,' he said, and it was a gut reaction.

'I don't have a choice,' she said, only a faint tremor in her voice betraying emotion. 'But I've been thinking. I'd really like to sleep with you before I go. It just seems… wrong not to. In so many ways we seem so…perfect.'

'We are right.' It was practically an explosion.

'No,' she said, and sighed. 'Sadly we're not. We have two insurmountable obstacles, my mother and your crazy idea that I need protection. But if they didn't exist… I'd really, really like to sleep with you. That is, if you'd like to sleep with me. Would you?'

And how was a man to answer that? He looked across

at her, in her faded jeans and sweatshirt, her tumbled hair, her mountains of balloons.

She looked back at him, calm and sure, and there was no need for an answer.

Balloons were forgotten. Party organisation was forgotten.

Everything was forgotten but this woman. He kissed her and then he rose and tugged her up with him. He kissed her again, long and deeply—and then he lifted her and carried her to his bed.

She woke and sunbeams were drifting over her nose. She was spooned into the curve of Luke's body. He was holding her as if she was the most precious thing in the world.

She'd never felt so alive, so wonderful, so loved, in her entire life.

The cramps had subsided. Where was stress now? She felt amazing.

She didn't want to move.

Any minute now she must. She had a party to organise. Guests were arriving at midday. Balloons still needed blowing up.

She wasn't stirring for balloons. She wasn't stirring for anything.

This was an illusion, she thought, and then she thought this whole month had been an illusion. Pretending they were a couple.

The night hadn't been an illusion. The night had been mind-blowingly, wondrously perfect.

The alarm went beside the bed. She'd set it last night when she was moving her gear into the bedroom.

Before Luke had come home.

Home. It was where she felt right now. Her perfect place.

'You're not a dream.' He was awake, his hold on her tightening. 'Whose idea was it to set the alarm?'

'It'll stop ringing in a minute,' she whispered. 'If we ignore it.'

Like the world might not intrude. If they ignored it.

'What has to be done?' he asked, and she outlined her list, her body not losing contact with his for a moment. Skin against skin, spooned against the man she loved.

She'd asked him to take her to his bed and she didn't regret it for a moment. Yes, she had to leave, but for this last weekend…not to make love with him…she would have regretted it for the rest of her life.

Now she was only sorry she hadn't relented three weeks ago.

Tomorrow she'd told Tom she'd go with him back to the farm. Then she'd return to Lighthouse Cove. But for now…

For now Luke was going through her items, one by one.

'Balloons?' he said, kissing the back of her neck. 'First guests here get to blow up ten apiece. There's nothing worse than standing around as an early guest with nothing to do. Sausage rolls? I'll get Teo to come early; we'll tackle them as a team. Hoovering? Why on earth would we hoover when the place will be covered with people?' He reached over and the alarm was firmly turned off and then she was even more firmly taken back into his arms.

'So what shall we do with all our spare time?' he asked, and he kissed her nose, her hair, her mouth. 'Oh, wait, I can think of something. It's a big job, it'll take two of us to complete, but it's totally essential. It involves me telling you how much I love you and you listening. And then there's a demonstration. So do I have your permission to swap your list for mine?'

She smiled. She held him close, she felt him kiss her, hold her, take her.

This had no future, she thought. There was only now.

For now, though, who could think of a future?

There was only Luke, and there was only now.

They showered and dressed—very hurriedly—just in time to let Teo in for sausage-roll making. Luke was heading over to the hospital to do a fast ward round and collect Tom. Lily was trying to remember a mental list that seemed to have vaporised.

Luke kissed her goodbye, which didn't help at all.

'You're not leaving,' he growled into her ear. 'You're my woman.'

My woman. The words hung.

'I think I'm a feminist,' she said cautiously, as Teo whistled loudly in the kitchen and pounded out pastry.

'It works both ways,' he said. 'I'm your man. We'll work it out,' he said, and kissed her again, and then he really had to go.

She set out glasses and plates and tied balloons into bunches. She moved onto the sausage-roll assembly line. Teo joked and chatted and she joined in, but her thoughts weren't on the party.

You're my woman. Possession. Worry.

We'll work it out.

How?

It wasn't possible. Last night had been a farewell gesture, she thought, pure indulgence.

There might be one more night, but then it was over.

* * *

From the moment Luke escorted Tom into the apartment and assorted guests shouted, 'Happy Birthday,' the party was a success. Tom's face said it all.

The first to greet him were his dogs. Patty had brought them from the farm, cleaned, brushed and wearing ribbons with balloons attached. They'd been subdued when Patty had brought them into this strange environment but one sniff of Tom, who they hadn't seen for weeks, had them unsubdued. Luke had had to hang onto Tom or he'd have ended on his back under their weight.

Luke steered him to a chair and when Tom stopped laughing and emerged from under the dogs he could see who was there.

The place was packed. There were hospital people, the people he'd got to know in the last few weeks, Luke's friends.

There was Patty, who he'd expected.

There were more.

Almost every farmer within a 'cooee' of Tarrawalla was here. People he waved to over the fence, kids he saw getting on and off school buses, the local stock and station agent, the guy who sold him hay…

Patty had done the rounds, letting people know, and almost always the response had been the same.

'Tom Williams… Why didn't you let us know he was in hospital? Of course we'll come; what can we bring?'

In his own quiet way, Tom was beloved, Lily thought, watching people crowd round him, watching his eyes fill with tears. His neighbours had simply been waiting for permission to show it.

They were showing it now.

Luke put his arm around her waist and held her close.

'This is some gift,' he murmured. 'I would never have

thought of it, but it's a miracle. How did you know he'd like it?'

'How many people really choose loneliness?' she asked softly. 'You and Tom had loneliness thrust upon you.' She smiled across at Tom, loving his reaction, loving the feel of Luke holding her even more. Even if it was transient, she was loving it. 'Tom told me about your childhood,' she said. 'It sucks. I thought mine was bad, but your loneliness must have been so much worse.'

'Yeah, but it's long past.'

'It's not past. It's holding you still,' she said. 'And it will until you get perspective. There's loneliness, there's crowding and there's friendship. The third doesn't necessarily mean the second.' She took a deep breath, deliberately lightening. 'Enough introspection. There's work to be done. I need to take more sausage rolls from the oven and you need to make a speech.'

'A speech.'

'Absolutely,' she said. 'Teo says you're good.'

'I would have liked some warning.'

'I'm giving you warning,' she said. 'Right after the smashing of the piñata, ready or not.'

He tried to figure out a speech. He moved among the crowd in his apartment, enjoying the buzz. He marvelled at Tom's happiness.

He watched Lily.

She was wearing a simple crimson dress and crimson sandals. Her curls were brushed and shining. She smiled and smiled.

He'd asked her to move in with him. She'd refused even that, but now he wanted more.

Somehow he had to persuade this woman to marry him.

For that to happen…

First, there was the obstacle of her mother. Second, he had to figure how to relax. How to let her be her own woman. How not to watch her every moment.

He knew why she'd refused when he'd asked her to live with him. He could see it; the anxiety he'd learned from Hannah would stifle her. But how to get past it? She was seeing that he couldn't—that there was no use pretending.

He would learn, he told himself. He must.

But first…her mother.

He'd never met her but he'd imagined her.

He didn't have to imagine her much longer.

They'd just finished smashing the piñata on the balcony. Sweets were scattering over the rail and down to the street below and kids were wondering whether they could reach street level in time to retrieve them when the doorbell went.

Luke was closest. He opened the door—and there was a woman. And a vicar.

He didn't need to ask who they were. Some things spoke for themselves. The man was in his fifties, flaccid, weak faced, wearing a religious collar. The woman was a diminutive version of Lily.

She was tiny, with shiny, jet-black curls, exquisite make-up—and not very exquisite clothes. Clothes that said *Look at me* in the worst possible way.

The plastic surgeon in him noted the lines around her neck, the skin on the back of her hands, age signals impossible to hide. He also noted the flawless complexion, nary a wrinkle, and he looked for—and found—the tiny scars under her ears.

She was sixtyish, he thought, but she was aiming for thirty. Good cosmetic surgery.

I bet Lily paid for it, he guessed grimly as the woman walked in, towing her vicar behind her.

'I'm Gloria Ellis,' the woman said brusquely to the room at large, her gaze darting everywhere. 'They said at the hospital that my daughter's here.' Luke turned to Lily, and Lily's face had blanched white.

'Mum.'

'Lily.' Gloria dropped the vicar's hand and headed for her daughter. 'Of all the selfish…! Do you know how long it's taken me to find you?'

'You rang yesterday,' Lily said dully. The sounds of the party were fading around them as everyone realised who this was. Rumours of this woman had swept the hospital and probably beyond. Everyone knew Lily's mother was trouble. The whole room was listening. 'I said I'd come home on Monday.'

'Yes, but the thing is that Lighthouse Cove is ghastly,' Gloria told her, ignoring the people around them, focused only on her own need. 'The things people are saying… Harold and I decided it's impossible to stay there a minute longer, and we can't get to Paris as we planned. So we need a nice place to stay. The girl on the switchboard at the hospital said this is a nice place.'

She took time then to gaze approvingly out of the windows to the harbour beyond, and she gave a decisive nod as if the thing was decided. She took Harold's hand again and faced Lily. 'It was wrong of you to run away,' she said severely. 'You knew I'd be worried. However, I've decided to forgive you and rather than you coming back to Lighthouse Cove we'll stay here with you. This looks much more fun.'

She smiled then, a cat-got-the-cream smile that turned Luke's stomach. 'So you're having a party.' Her smile encompassed the whole room. 'Are you all Lily's friends? I look like her sister, but I'm really her mother. I know, it's unbelievable but I was a child bride.'

She giggled.

No one giggled back.

The Harbour might be Sydney Scandal Central, Luke thought, but the team was a close-knit community. It protected its own.

As did Tarrawalla. Lily had been living in Tom's house for only a few weeks, but she'd been seen as Tom's family and therefore she belonged.

Consequently she had two communities who were looking at Gloria with outright mistrust. They were moving imperceptibly toward Lily. Their body language spoke of protection.

Gloria was beaming at Teo now, a full-on beam which made Luke see exactly what Lily contended with. Gloria thought she was a sex goddess, as simple as that. She was wearing a tight-fitting, leather dress, which pushed her cleavage to impossible limits, stiletto heels and fishnet stockings. She beamed and pouted all at once, and even though she stood beside the vicar, her eyes were darting from male to male, and her invitation was obvious.

This was the woman Lily had promised to protect, Luke thought, feeling ill. He thought of Lily as a child, a twelve-year-old, being asked to commit her life to the impossible.

He thought of all the things he wanted to say to Lily's mother. He glanced at Lily and he thought, Not here. Not now.

Lily had wanted to be anonymous, he thought, and now he knew why. That's why she'd come here. She'd embraced—and been embraced by—the Harbour community, she'd abandoned her anonymity, but things needed to be said now without an audience.

'Let's take this to the foyer,' he said in a voice that brooked no argument. 'Now. Ginnie, make sure the door's shut behind us.'

'Sure,' Ginnie said, and suddenly Gloria and her vicar found themselves propelled outside. Luke towed Lily out after them, and Ginnie closed the door behind them.

Lily was so white. He put his arm around her waist but she was rigid in his hold. She was helpless against a promise made when she'd been twelve.

Enough. If Lily couldn't say it, he'd say it for her.

'Gloria, Lily's promised to care for you,' he said into the deepening silence, and Gloria's seductive smile turned onto him straight away. She'd seemed stunned when he'd ushered her outside but she was making a good recovery.

'Yes, she did,' she agreed. 'She's a good girl, my Lily.'

'But did you know,' he said, and his voice took on a ruthless edge because ruthless was how he was feeling, 'that a promise made under duress is not legally binding? Neither is a promise made by a minor. A minor, Gloria. That would be someone under the age of eighteen. Lily made her promise when she was twelve. The way I see it, Lily's promise to care for you was made to reassure her father, who was under such pressure that he killed himself. If that's not duress, I don't know what is. And she was twelve. She was six years under the age when a promise is valid.'

'Luke, don't,' Lily said, distressed. 'Go back to the party. This is my business.'

'No,' Luke said. 'It might not be my business but I care, and because I care I need to speak the truth. Lily, this is line-in-the-sand time. You should have this out with your mother, right here, right now. You're sixty years old,' Luke said to Gloria. 'How can you still live your life dependent on the promise of a child?'

'I am not sixty years old,' Gloria snapped, aghast. 'How can you…?'

For answer Luke flicked her dyed black curls from her face, exposing the scars of myriad past cosmetic surgeries. He wasn't in the mood for games.

'I'm a plastic surgeon,' he said. 'Sixty? I was being generous. I'm thinking older.'

'How dare you?' It was a scream of outrage. 'What gives you the right?'

'I have the right because I love your daughter,' he said, 'and Lily needs to see you as you really are. Lily also needs to see her promise for what it really is. It's unjust and unreasonable and she shouldn't be bound by it for a moment longer. She's cared for you almost all her life but it's time it stopped.' He turned to the vicar. 'You love this woman?'

'Y-yes,' Harold said, but he sounded doubtful. 'But Gloria needs her daughter.'

'Nonsense,' Luke said bracingly. 'How can one grown woman need more than you? And, Lily…are you saying that your father would have seen your mother settled with a man of the church, and not said you've done your duty and more? That you've fulfilled his promise over and over, and now it's time you stopped? It is time you stopped, love. Right now.'

'What are you suggesting?' Lily looked aghast.

'That you let your mother go,' he said, his voice softening. 'Not completely. I know you won't do that. But I also know you own the apartment in Lighthouse Cove—that somehow against the odds you've bought it and managed to pay for it. But it's in your name and your name only.

So what I suggest is that your mother takes Harold back there, that you give her permission to live in your house, that you're happy to chat to her once a week or so on the phone but that's it. That's your twelve-year-old's promise fulfilled with honour, and with a lot more courage than your father ever could have expected of you.'

And then, as Gloria stared at him, speechless, as Lily stared back, white-faced, he took her hand.

'Tell her, Lily,' he said. 'Your dad did his best for your mother but he reached his limit and he couldn't take any more. Think about your dad right now. You loved him and he loved you. If he's looking down now he's seeing his ex-wife with another man. He's seeing his daughter who's been robbed blind. He'll be thinking…what will he be thinking, Lily? What would he be asking that you say right now? And more. What do you want to say?'

She looked at him and he met her gaze, pure and strong. You can do this, his gaze said.

She must.

And finally, finally, she did.

'Luke's right,' she whispered, and then her voice firmed. 'No. I should say that louder. Enough, Mum. I've done enough for you and more. Yes, you're my mother, but we're both grown women with independent lives. Go home to Lighthouse Cove with your vicar.'

'You have to come home.' Gloria was suddenly as ashen as her daughter. 'You can't leave me.'

'You have Harold,' Lily said, her voice growing more sure by the moment. Luke linked his hand with hers and she held on, but she didn't need it. He knew she didn't need it. The strength was there.

'You have Harold and whoever else replaces him,' she said. 'But I'm not there as a stopgap any more.' She glanced at the unfortunate Harold. 'Harold seems nice. Solid. What about holding onto him?'

'You're expecting us to go home?' Gloria's voice was a screech of outrage. 'We can't. How can you expect us to? Besides,' she added and there was triumph in the outrage, 'we flew here on one-way tickets. And we don't have enough money to get home.'

'*What have you done with my money?*' Lily closed her eyes, but then opened them and shook her head, as if shaking off a nightmare. 'No. It doesn't matter. It's past. Mum, when I was twelve I promised Dad I'd look after you. Dad was so distressed… All I wanted was to fix it and I would have promised him anything. But I can't fix it. He couldn't and neither can I. But that's it. I don't know how you're getting back to Lighthouse Cove but it's not my problem.'

Luke tugged her tight against him and she let herself be tugged.

'There's no need for you to feel bad,' he said, holding her close. 'Your mum's not on her own. She has her vicar.'

'And help from me.' It was Finn—of course it was Finn—appearing without notice from the elevator. 'My secretary's buying one-way tickets back to Adelaide as we speak,' he said jovially. 'Don't thank me, Luke,' he said, expansively. 'This is a birthday party, isn't it? Don't all guests bring presents? If not, we'll call it an early wedding gift.'

He turned to Gloria and the full force of Finn Kennedy power focused on her and her alone. 'Mrs Ellis, I have a hospital car waiting outside to take you to the airport. Lily, give your mother birthday cake to go, and two balloons— it'd be sad if the Harbour was seen as less than generous. Luke, escort your future mother-in-law to the car to make sure she's properly gone. Right, I need a whisky. Enough. Are you intending to let me into this party or not?'

Finn escorted her back into the party while Luke took her mother to the car. To her amazement there was no buzz of gossip; no one talking behind her back. The room sort of closed in around her. She had approval and warmth and support. She was hugged by people she hardly knew.

So much for being anonymous. Why had she ever wished for it?

'Good girl,' Finn said, gripping her hand. 'One problem fixed. Now fix Luke.'

'So what about you, sir?' she asked, wondering at her temerity. She'd seen him wince as she'd taken his hand, and she'd heard the talk. 'Rumour is you have a problem you won't do anything about.'

'Nothing that this won't cure,' he snapped, motioning to his whisky, but then he shrugged and smiled. 'And we can't fix everything in one day.'

Luke returned. 'She's gone,' he said.

Lily felt... Actually she didn't know how she felt. Weightless? Happy?

Free.

Luke hugged her and she hugged him back and she thought...she thought...

That he needed to make a speech. And that this was only part one of a two-part problem.

But as Finn had said, '*We can't fix everything in one day.*'

Tom returned to his ward, exhausted but happy, looking forward to a long sleep to celebrate his last night at the Harbour. The birthday party went on without him.

Luke's colleagues weren't abandoning this excuse to celebrate Luke's long-awaited inclusion into their social network. Hints failed. Threats failed. It was two a.m. before the last giggling partygoer staggered towards the elevators.

'That was some party.' Lily turned and looked at the carnage of the living room. 'This is some mess.'

'You want to clean up now or go to bed?' Luke said into her hair, and she thought about it. For about a nanosecond.

'Bed. But, Luke…'

'Mmm?'

'Thank you,' she said softly. 'I should have done that so many years ago. It seemed impossible. For you to make me see…'

'Think nothing of it, my lady,' he said, sweeping her into his arms. 'Have I asked you to marry me lately?'

'No,' she said, her heart seeming to skip a beat. 'I don't believe you have.'

'I don't have a ring,' he said, settling her on his bed with care. 'But hypothetically…' He kissed her long and deeply, and lowered himself onto the bed beside her. 'If I was to go down on bended knee with a crimson box…'

'I'd probably giggle.'

'And then say yes?'

'I'd say I'd think about it,' she said, trying to make herself think when he was doing truly delicious things with his tongue; with his fingers. 'And I can't think about it at two in the morning surrounded by chaos.'

'I can't see any chaos,' he said, searching for the zip to her dress. 'I can only see you.'

'That's a problem as well,' she said, and she tugged him close and held him tight. 'How can I think about anything when all I see is you?'

CHAPTER TWELVE

SUNDAY they were due to take Tom back to his farm. Home.

They planned to collect Tom at ten and take him in Luke's car, with Lily following behind.

'We need a bigger car,' Luke said as they woke, and Lily stirred in his arms and thought she didn't need anything at all.

But… A bigger car?

'A family car?' she ventured, feeling like she was on the edge of a precipice. A warm and delicious precipice.

But… 'No,' Luke said, revolted. 'But something like John's SUV. If I'm to cart uncles and women around the countryside…'

Keep it light… 'Buy a roof rack, then,' she suggested. 'It's cheaper. And one of those luggage pack things. Tom and I can pack down small.'

'Ridiculous,' he said, kissing her nose. 'Lily, will you stay at the Harbour? You have a permanent job here any time you want. We could try living together.'

'You mean before you think of giving me that little crimson box?'

'I mean before you accept it,' he said. 'The crimson box is metaphorically on the table already.'

'That's a very big word for the day after the night before.' She snuggled into his arms and felt delicious. 'I guess...' She thought about it. 'Tom has an attic room with a huge cast-iron bed. Maybe we could set up there,' she suggested.

He frowned. 'Live with Tom, you mean?'

'He'll need us.'

'I guess...for a week or so.'

'A week or so.' She stilled. 'Luke, he needs you.'

'Not permanently. We'd drive him nuts if we shared a house.'

'You're very sure.'

'I'm like him.'

She stilled. 'Would I drive you nuts if I shared a house?'

'No!'

'I might,' she said. 'I hog the bathroom. My mother calls me a selfish cow.'

'Your mother's gone,' he said, kissing her. 'We have each other. We'll do what we need to do for Tom, and then we can come back here.'

'And leave Tom?'

'Not while he's unsafe, but after that... We'll install a housekeeper. Someone. We're loners, Tom and I. This is huge for me, loving you.'

'I should be grateful?'

'No, but—'

'Luke, Tom isn't like my mother,' she whispered. 'We love Tom because he's special, like I love you because you're special. You shouldn't love me because you think I can fit into a niche in your life, leaving the rest undisturbed.'

'Lily—'

'No,' she said, closing her eyes for a second, coming to a decision. 'You've made me see the problems in my life but I don't know how to do the same for you. But until you do… All I know is that you need to leave that crimson box in the undecided basket.' She took a deep breath. Regrouped. 'Right. Let's get Tom home and settled. I'll take on another month at the Harbour…'

'Not night duty.'

'Okay, not night duty.' She glowered at him. 'Is that because you want to be with me or you'll worry about me when you're not with me?'

'Both,' he admitted.

'We do need time,' she said softly, and she tugged him back her arms. 'I shouldn't stay. I know I shouldn't. I see this whole black chasm where hope should be. Oh, but, Luke…'

'I do love you,' he said, strong and sure, and she kissed him and held him tight.

'I'm figuring that out,' she said. 'I just need to know what it means to be loved that much.'

They made love. They dressed and headed to Tom's ward with Lily feeling more confused than she'd ever been in her life.

Things felt so right, yet there was a niggle of doubt that wouldn't disappear.

Love without conditions… That was the dream, she thought, but Luke's love seemed to be conditional. On her being safe. On him keeping her safe. On him keeping his boundaries with Tom. On him keeping his own boundaries.

Maybe I need to change, she thought. He won't.

Still…she thought back to where she'd been four weeks ago and she wondered why on earth she was worrying. She'd met Luke and she'd fallen in love. Luke had rescued her in true heroic style. He was, quite simply, the most gorgeous guy she'd ever met. He wanted to marry her.

She should be over the moon.

A niggle…

The cramps were back again. That was another niggle.

Tom. She put niggles aside and greeted Tom with smiles. They gathered his belongings. With Luke on one side and Lily on the other Tom walked slowly out to the doctors' car park and almost half the Harbour's staff wished him well on the way.

But they weren't leaving yet. They'd just reached Luke's car when Evie came flying out the emergency entrance.

Walk, don't run. It was a medical mantra.

Evie was running.

'Sit in the car,' Lily told Tom, and Tom sank gratefully into the passenger seat, unaware of impending problems.

'Luke…' Evie called. She looked…scared. 'Thank God I caught you. Can you come?'

'What's happening?' Luke was already striding to meet her.

'Road trauma,' she said. 'Four guys, all needing Theatre. I had to call Finn in as back-up. He was to cope with a ruptured spleen. He started—but he's just downed tools.'

'Downed tools…'

'His hand's shaking, Luke. Carl's doing the anaesthetic—he's got the guy under but Finn's backed from the table. Carl said he tried to pick up forceps but his hand shook and he put them down again. Luke, it's Sunday morning and there's no other surgeon who can step in. If you come now we can keep this under wraps, we can get a good result, but if you can't, we need to transfer him now.'

Lily saw Luke's shock.

A ruptured spleen…a patient already anaesthetised…

And it was road trauma. There'd be other injuries as well, she thought. Even though Luke was trained in plastics, he'd have been thoroughly trained in general surgery. He could deal with whatever had to be dealt with.

'It's okay,' she told him. She fished in her pocket and handed him her car keys. 'Tom's in your car now and it's much more comfortable than mine. I'll take him out to the farm. You bring my car later. Just get on and do what you need to do.'

Luke turned and faced her, looking torn. 'If anything happens…'

'What will happen?' she demanded. 'Don't you trust me with Tom?'

'Yes, but—'

'Then stop with the hang-ups and go fix a spleen,' she snapped, and held her hand out for his car keys. 'Go.'

'Yay,' she said as she turned Luke's little car out of the car park. 'Hooray for us. We have a sports car and the open road. Do you want to put the hood down?'

'We might get dust in our eyes,' Tom said dryly. 'Luke'd have our guts for garters.'

'He is a worry wart,' she said cautiously.

'He is,' Tom agreed. 'He drove me nuts when he first came to the farm. Used to watch me all the time. I know it was because he didn't have anyone else, but it drove me crazy. I kept telling him to clear off.'

Which wouldn't have helped at all, Lily thought. What ten-year-old Luke had needed had been a hug, but Tom had never learned hugs either.

'And then that wife of his died,' Tom said. 'It was like

his worst fears were realised. I tried…you know…to get close a bit, but he wasn't having any of it. But you, lass… he's letting you near.'

'Maybe too near,' she said. 'I kind of like the freedom to get dust in my eyes when I feel like it.'

'Then we put the hood down,' he said.

'Let's live dangerously,' she said, and they did.

She wasn't enjoying it much, though. Her stomach hurt.

By the time he finished surgery it was almost dusk. One ruptured spleen plus the rest, he thought wearily. He'd finished with his guy, then assisted Brian with another.

He was exhausted.

Evie turned up as he dumped his gear and turned to leave.

'Sorry,' she said. 'I had no choice but to call on you.'

'I know. How's Finn?'

'Angry. He says he thinks he's torn a ligament and he's taking time off. He's not talking about it.'

'I'll talk to him.'

'You won't get any further than I did.'

Torn ligament? He didn't believe it for a moment. What to do about his friend?

He looked at Evie and she looked steadily back and he thought, She cares as much as I do.

The Harbour. A whole network of carers.

It was a shock, he thought, and what came next was more of one.

'And what's wrong with Lily?' Evie asked. 'Luke, is she pregnant?'

Pregnant. The word hit him like a slap.

'No,' he said, and then, more cautiously as he thought of the night before, 'I don't think so.'

'Why is she losing weight? That dress she was wearing last night was a size too big.'

Was it? He'd thought she looked gorgeous. But if Evie said so…

'Blood test,' she said. 'Insisting with Finn's impossible. With Lily at least you have some control.'

'Do I?'

'I imagine you do,' she said. 'I'd imagine Lily would have the sense to know her health's important. Are you going up there now?'

'To the farm? Yes.' And then he paused. His phone was ringing. He flipped it open.

The call was from Lily.

'I thought you should know before the Harbour grapevine tells you,' she said, and he could tell she was speaking through gritted teeth. 'I've just rung the chopper for an airlift. I know it's dramatic but I'm not facing those winding roads again in an ambulance. Luke, I've got rebound. I'm thinking my appendix has burst. I'm on my way in.'

'Lily—'

'Don't you dare panic,' she told him. 'I'm in control, we're managing nicely and if you panic I'll panic. I'm safe and I'm in control. Deal with it. And, Luke…'

'Love…' It was a hoarse whisper.

'Tell me you love me.'

'I love you,' he said, with all his heart.

She woke and the pain had stopped and Luke was holding her hand.

She felt peaceful and warm and safe.

Luke was holding her hand.

'Did I die?' she asked cautiously.

'No.' The growl made her smile. Luke's voice was so-o-o sexy.

'Someone took my appendix out?'

'Brian Lassiter. Evie assisted.'

'I thought you might,' she whispered. 'But I'm glad you didn't.'

'So how long,' he said through gritted teeth, 'have you been harbouring a grumbling appendix?'

'I suspect months,' she said, and he almost groaned.

'Of all the stupid—'

'Hey,' she said. 'Don't call me stupid. How was I to know? I've been having rumbling tummy cramps, nothing major. My doctor back at Lighthouse Cove thought they were caused by stress, and how could I argue with that? Then I had what we all thought was gastro. I saw Marnie Chrysler and she thought I might have picked up a bowel infection. She gave me anti—'

'You saw Marnie?' Marnie did the family medical stuff in Outpatients. 'When?'

'Two weeks ago. I'm not stupid, and neither's Marnie,' she retorted. 'An appendix is easy to miss, so you can stop looking like it's anyone's fault. It seemed to be set-tling—until today. I was feeling a bit odd on the way up the mountain. By the time I reached the farm I thought I was relapsing with gastro. Tom put me to bed and then I rang Patty.'

'Tom put you… And then you rang Patty…'

'I was ill,' she said evenly. 'Why wouldn't I? Anyway, Patty came over to help. I couldn't keep anything down. Patty's Bill had just decided he'd drive me back here when I started feeling rebound.'

Rebound. It was an almost sure sign of ruptured appendix. If you pressed on the appendix site, there'd be little extra pain as you pressed down, but excruciating pain when you released the pressure.

That she'd coped...that she'd recognised it...

'Patty and Tom already had things in hand,' she said. 'When I said rebound we thought ambulance and then I thought of the chopper guys and got greedy. Jack was at the party—he was on my speed dial.'

'You didn't think to ring me first?'

'Your phone,' she said with remarkable asperity from someone who'd just come out of anaesthetic, 'was on message bank. The thought of leaving things till you'd finished was unappealing. And I rang you second. So here I am.' She smiled weakly. 'And Brian's fixed me. At least, I assumed he's fixed me. I assume I no longer have an appendix.'

'No,' he said grimly. 'You don't.'

'Then you can stop looking like that,' she said. 'If I'm happy, you should be happy. You can't think how good it feels to finally know what was wrong. It's been a worry, having cramps for all that time.'

'You should have told me!'

'And had you worry as well? I had it covered, Dr Williams. I did everything I could. If you're going to feel guilty that I and my doctor didn't pick up on the appendix then you can go put your head in a bucket.'

And then her voice faltered. She was weaker than she was letting on, he thought. He looked down into her eyes and they were moistening.

She was feeling anger, he thought. She was distressed.

'Don't do this,' she whispered. 'I'm not wearing your guilt. If you think that my appendix is down to you then your ego's more massive than every surgeon I've ever met. I don't depend on you, Luke Williams. I'm me, and if you don't let me be me then I don't want anything to do with you. Period.'

And finally, finally, she started to cry.

All this… All she'd gone through, and now she started to cry.

He'd let her down.

And then he thought…

He *had* let her down, but it wasn't because he hadn't diagnosed her appendicitis. He'd let her down because he hadn't reacted as he should have reacted.

It was like waking from a nightmare. Walking from darkness to light. He looked down at the woman he loved with all his heart and he knew what he had to do.

He knew that he could do it. It was line-in-the-sand time. Right here. Right now.

With love comes trust. And faith.

And joy.

He wiped away her tears, and then, very carefully, very tenderly, he gathered her into his arms.

'Lily, I'm sorry,' he said, holding her close. 'I am so, so sorry. Can we start again?'

'Wh-why would we want to?'

'Because there're things I need to say,' he whispered. 'I need to say how much I love you. I need to say how proud I am of you, how much I love that you did what you needed to do with courage and plain good sense.'

'Luke—'

'Hush,' he told her, kissing her hair. Kissing her eyelids. Tasting the salt of her tears. 'Lily, I'm ashamed of myself that my first reaction was that it was my fault; and that my second was anger that you hadn't referred everything to me. I need to know—and I do know—that I'm in love with a woman who knows how to stand on her own two feet. I know you're the woman I love most in the entire world, and I wouldn't change you for anything. I need to hold you, but I also need to let you go.'

She sniffed. She sniffed again into his shoulder and she wound her arms around his neck and held.

'Ouch,' she said.

'You push this button for pain,' he said, withdrawing in an instant and showing her the plunger for self-administering morphine. 'One push and the pain will subside.'

'Codswallop,' she said weakly.

'Codswallop?'

'Codswallop,' she repeated, and she held him tighter still. 'No drug's giving me what I want. If you want to be a really, really effective doctor, Dr Williams, you need to kiss me now, because absolutely nothing else is going to solve my problems.'

'I love you,' he said.

'That'll do nicely,' she whispered, pushing her plunger because a girl had to be sensible. If she was to hold him as tightly as she intended holding him, she needed to be very sensible. 'For a start.'

Spring was the very best time for a wedding. Everyone said so, from the Harbour janitors to Erich the medical director himself. The weather forecast was watched with anxiety by practically the entire hospital, because practically the entire hospital was on the guest list.

'It's like Christmas.' Evie chuckled. 'We're trying to get every patient home because the staff has better things to do than play doctors and nurses.'

Of course the hospital couldn't be emptied entirely and some staff needed to be left behind. For them, the IT guys organised a video link, so the wedding could be seen in every ward in the hospital.

The linking cameras were set up by a rippling creek on a beautiful little homestead at Tarrawalla, just underneath Tom's house—on the farm they intended staying on for the rest of their lives.

Ginnie was chief wedding planner. This was a job after her own heart. Teo planned the feast afterwards; his aunts cooked their hearts out. Half the district cooked their heart out. The rest… Ginnie had them hanging heart-shaped lanterns from every tree, stringing streamers, setting out chairs, tables, sunshades, candles that doubled as mosquito repellent—no mosquito was going to get within half a mile of this ceremony, Ginnie decreed, and who was to argue with Ginnie?

Finn was best man. He'd gone on leave, and his arm seemed better. There were still problems, Luke thought, but even taking leave had been a big concession. Evie still worried about him.

Evie could do the worrying, Luke decided. He'd stopped worrying. It was forbidden in Lily's code.

He was especially forbidden to worry about Lily.

'If you worry about me, I'll worry about you,' she'd told him. 'You want my stomach to be tied in knots every time you leave home? No? Then cut it out with your own knot-tying.'

He had a handle on it. One appendix…one capable woman surrounded by an army of friends… He wasn't alone and worrying was stupid.

He had a wedding to focus on, and a bride. How could a man worry with that to look forward to?

Tom was giving the bride away. 'I know being given away by the groom's uncle is different,' Lily had told him.

'But my alternative's my mum or Harold and I'm not going there. I love Tom to bits and he loves me, so it's perfect.'

He did. Tom was surrounded, astonished, by the direction his life was taking. All these people… Friends… Family.

Luke's parents were there, trying to disapprove, trying to look superior. Ginnie had them in hand. Two champagne cocktails one after the other the moment they arrived, and they were already unbending. There'd be no miracles, Luke thought, but he was pleased they were there.

And Gloria and Harold were there as well.

'You can come if you don't drink and you wear something respectable,' Lily had told her mother. 'Luke and I will pay for two nights at the Tarrawalla pub and for your air fares. No, you're not staying at the house, but we'd love you to join us for the day.'

Luke was pleased about that, too. Boundaries had been set, but Lily still felt she had her mother.

More, she had an entire family. A hospital and a farming community.

He was standing under the towering gums waiting for his bride. It was five minutes past the appointed hour. Where was she?

'Brides are always late,' Finn growled. 'They do it on purpose to put a man in his place.'

'Quoth the authority on weddings.'

'I've watched my share,' Finn said. They're like watching train wrecks—a man can't look away.'

'Finn…'

Finn gave a rueful chuckle. 'Okay, sorry. I know this isn't a train wreck. Even I, misogynist old bachelor that I am, concede it's right for you. Lily has you wrapped round her little finger and you're going to love it.'

They went back to waiting. Ten minutes late. 'This is killing me,' he said.

About three hundred people were gathered round the clearing by the creek. Three hundred people were waiting for one slip of a girl.

For Lily.

'I'm guessing this is her,' Finn said, grinning at his friend as the music from Teo's mate's band overrode the sound of the kookaburras in the trees overhead. 'I'm guessing. I'm not sure an orchestra would play a wedding march for the arrival of a door-to-door salesman.'

Luke had already turned to see.

The outdoor seating was separated into two sections, with an aisle between for the bride to approach. He could see her now. She was coming down the hill from the house, Tom by her side.

Tom was looking dapper in a suit he'd bought specially—'I'm not hiring any suit for our Lily's wedding,' he'd told them.

He was on Zelda.

Lily was riding Glenfiddich.

The onlookers gasped as one, and so did Luke.

She was…exquisite.

Her dress was simple, white damask silk, with tiny capped sleeves and a sweetheart neckline. Her curls were loose and free. She was wearing simple diamond drops in her ears—Luke's wedding gift—and no other jewellery. She needed no other jewellery.

Woman and horse. The combination was more than breathtaking.

She was using a sidesaddle. Her gown clung to her

breasts and waist and then flared out in a lovely sweeping skirt that draped over Glenfiddich's glossy black flanks.

Glenfiddich was looking like butter wouldn't melt in his mouth. If ever a horse could be said to be proud, it was Glenfiddich. Zelda trotted beside him and her eyes gleamed as well. They tossed their heads and practically pranced. These were horses on parade and loving it.

Once upon a time, Luke thought, seeing this woman on this horse had filled him with dread. Now he knew his Lily. She hadn't told him she was doing this but he knew her way with horses. She smiled at him as she neared and he smiled back, and his heart swelled with pride. His gorgeous, courageous, independent bride was on her way to marry him, and she could travel any way she liked.

The horses halted where the seating began. Luke started forward, involuntarily, to lift Lily down, but Finn took his arm and held.

'This is Tom's role,' he said, and it was. His uncle lifted Lily down from her horse as if he were thirty-five instead of seventy-five.

Then he tucked her hand into his arm, and proudly walked Lily to her husband-to-be.

The music swelled and died.

Lily reached him, smiled at Tom, released Tom's hand and tucked her hand into his instead. She smiled and he smiled.

'Hi,' she said.

'You're… There are no words to describe you.'

She chuckled and loved him with her eyes. 'Try.'

'I love you,' he said, simply and surely, and her eyes misted with tears.

'That'll do for now,' she whispered as they turned together to commence their wedding vows.

'Come to think of it,' she added as he held her tighter. 'That'll do for ever.'

* * * * *

SYDNEY HARBOUR HOSPITAL: HOSPITAL: ZOE'S BABY

BY
ALISON ROBERTS

Alison Roberts lives in Christchurch, New Zealand. She began her working career as a primary school teacher, but now juggles available working hours between writing and active duty as an ambulance officer. Throwing in a large dose of parenting, housework, gardening and pet-minding keeps life busy, and teenage daughter Becky is responsible for an increasing number of days spent on equestrian pursuits. Finding time for everything can be a challenge, but the rewards make the effort more than worthwhile.

For Linda, with much love. And Queenscliff.
The combination that made this story a joy
I will never forget.

CHAPTER ONE

NOTHING had changed.

Zoe Harper released the breath she hadn't realised she'd been holding, in a sigh of pure relief. The sound went unheard thanks to the wail of the siren outside the vehicle she was in.

It could have been yesterday she'd done her last shift as an intensive care paramedic instead of…goodness, how many months ago was it?

Too many.

Enough to have made her afraid that it would feel different. Be impossible, even, given the changes in her life since then. That what had seemed a brave decision could turn out to be disastrous and that it might even send her life tumbling back into a place so awful it was too terrifying to contemplate.

But this was good.

Better than good.

'Traffic's a nightmare.' Her crew partner for the day, Tom, leaned on the air horn and tried to manoeuvre the ambulance through a narrow gap. 'Bet you wish you'd stayed home with the baby a bit longer, eh?'

Being at home with five-month-old Emma instead of heading towards a multi-vehicle pile-up on the south entrance to the Grafton Bridge?

'No way.' Zoe grinned at Tom. 'Bring it on.'

She meant every word.

There was more than relief to be found here.

There was hope.

This was an opportunity to step back into the life she'd always chosen for herself. To shut the door, albeit temporarily, on what had become her new life. But it was about more than simply a job. This was the chance to find out if the person she'd always believed herself to be still existed.

Working at Australia's premier teaching hospital on the shores of Sydney harbour might be a dream come true but the hospital's central location didn't help when it came to traffic hassles after a consult at one of the suburban hospitals.

And while this new car was superb to handle and its leather upholstery supremely comfortable, no sports car on earth was designed for somebody who was six feet four with the build of a well-conditioned rugby player.

Teo Tuala flexed his shoulders and neck as the traffic inched forward and then came to another complete halt. He could see the flashing lights of emergency vehicles up near the bridge and now he could hear the chop of rotors from an approaching helicopter getting steadily louder.

If they were calling for air transport, it must be a fairly serious accident. Maybe they could use some assistance. Being in the left lane, Teo was able to nudge his sleek car out of the queue of vehicles and onto the motorway shoulder. He flicked his hazard lights on and got out of the confined space. A police officer, edging his way through the traffic jam on a motorbike, swerved into the space he'd created.

He was shaking his head. 'You can't park there, mate.'

'I'm a doctor,' Teo responded. 'Thought they might be able to use a hand up there.'

The young officer's expression changed. 'Hop on,' he offered. 'I'll get you on scene.'

Teo could see why the traffic was so disrupted as he got closer. Three vehicles were involved. One was upside down and partially crushed. Another was wedged between the upside-down car and the bridge supports. The third car was being towed from where it was blocking another two lanes of the highway.

Firemen were using pneumatic equipment to cut into the vehicles. The helicopter was hovering directly overhead, looking for a place to land. There was a background wail of additional emergency service vehicles approaching the scene from the opposite direction. The noise was overwhelming and yet Teo could still hear the shrieks of a terrified person who seemed to be trapped in one of those cars.

And it sounded like a small person.

A quick visual scan of the scene revealed the most senior ambulance officer amongst the knot of police and fire service personnel. The fluorescent vest with 'Scene Commander' on the back was being worn by a woman.

Teo stepped closer. 'Hey, there…'

The woman ignored his greeting. Her attention was still directed to a young, far more junior ambulance officer.

'Have you got access to the back seat?'

'The firies are working on that. That door's jammed as well.'

'And she's trapped?'

'Yes. Her leg's caught under the dash.'

'Get a C collar on her and keep her still until we can extricate her. Stay in the back seat and keep her head immobilised.'

'Zoe?'

The scene commander's head swivelled even further from where Teo was standing as another male paramedic approached. The movement, under the early morning sunshine, sent flickers of colour like small flames through her hair. She had pale skin, he noted, with a scattering of freckles on her nose and the top of her cheeks.

'What's up, Tom?'

'We need you. Oxygen saturation levels on the driver are dropping and there's a kid in a car seat in there as well that we can't get to. Too tight a squeeze for me. The firies reckon they've got the wreck stable. Thought you might be game to crawl underneath.'

The nod came without the slightest hesitation that Teo could detect. 'What status is the child?'

'Can't tell. The seat's upside down and the roof is badly dented on that side. I can see an arm. I reckon it's a toddler more than a baby.'

'I'm a paediatrician,' Teo cut in. 'Can I be of any assistance?'

She looked at him now. Green eyes were assessing him rapidly but with keen attention. He had the impression that he'd passed some kind of test. Pulling off her vest, she handed it to Tom. 'Take over scene control,' she told him. 'There're two more trucks responding and we should be able to start transporting using the northern lanes. The police are clearing an area for the chopper to get down but we'll keep them on standby until we know what's happening with the rolled car.'

She pulled another vest from a container labelled 'Major Incident' and handed it to Teo. 'Put this on,' she ordered. 'And come with me.'

This vest had 'Doctor' on the back. It was a tight squeeze for his large frame but Teo got it on as he followed Zoe. It took only seconds to get amongst the knot of fire officers working on the vehicle. Teo had to watch his feet as he stepped over the thick black cables that connected the cutting gear to the power generators. A blanket marked a patch of ground where a paramedic kit was opened beside a life pack and an oxygen cylinder. Tubing from the cylinder was attached to a bag mask unit being held over the face of the driver by another ambulance officer. A policewoman was holding a bag of IV fluid aloft, its tubing snaking in through the broken window.

'Any change?' Zoe queried.

'Sats down to 95. BP's still dropping. Ninety-five on 60 now. We should be able to get her out any minute.'

Zoe's nod was curt. 'I'll assess her for intubation as soon as she's clear.' She turned to Teo. 'Stay here,' she commanded. 'I'm going to take a few seconds to see if I can get to the child. If it's alive, we'll get it out and I'll hand over to you. The driver's status 1 and I'll need to focus on her.'

Teo knew that meant the victim was in a life-threatening situation. Was it the child's mother? Was the child badly hurt as well? Teo normally saw his patients in the well-controlled environment of a paediatric ward or sometimes the emergency department. This was the first time he'd been on scene in a situation like this. The tension was palpable. The working conditions were astonishing—so many people, so much noise, the smell of fuel and hot metal. How hard would it be to focus?

He watched the redheaded paramedic having a short but intense conversation with a fire officer. She jammed a hard hat onto her head and then lay down, edging herself beneath the wreck of the car's chassis.

Teo felt his breath leave his body in a silent whistle. Not only was it a challenge to focus in this kind of environment but these people were clearly willing to put themselves at considerable physical risk as well. This would be impressive at any time but the actions of this woman called Zoe were positively mind-blowing.

Because she was female?

Teo was ashamed to have to admit that was partly true but there was more to it in this case. Maybe it had something to do with this particular woman. With her striking colouring and those unusually obvious freckles on her skin that made her seem…younger? More vulnerable?

It wasn't a word he should even think of associating with a person who was clearly in command of such an intense situation but, oddly, it stuck somewhere in the back of his head as he stood there, his gaze fixed on the steel-capped black boots he could see protruding from this side of the vehicle. They were moving. Turning as Zoe was positioning herself inside what had to be an impossibly small space to work in. He could hear the muffled, shouted conversation she was having with firemen on the other side of the wreck.

They repositioned their equipment. The 'jaws of life' were used to cut through a central pillar on that side of the car and metal was being peeled back like the top of a spaghetti can. Teo's view was obstructed by the wheels of the wreck and then by the surge of rescuers that moved in. There was more shouting, the wreck rocked a little and then, less than a minute after Zoe had disappeared beneath the wreck, he saw the car seat being lifted clear and passed from one set of arms to another. It was carried towards him and suddenly Teo realised that it was actually easy to focus in the messy, dangerous environment. All you needed was a patient who needed you. This car seat had a small body strapped inside it. A baby about twelve months old. A boy who was not only alive but fully conscious. His eyes were wide open and frightened as he looked right back at Teo.

'Put him down here,' Teo said. He crouched beside the car seat and reached for the central buckle. 'Hey, there, little one…'

The driver of the car was freed from the wreckage moments after the baby seat had been extricated.

What a stroke of luck, having a paediatrician on scene. Not that Zoe would have had trouble coping but it was an undeniable relief not to have to deal with a baby just yet. That might well blur the comforting demarcation she was establishing between her private and professional life.

She would far rather attend to the female driver and deal with the life-threatening injuries that were immediately apparent as they transferred her from the back board onto a stretcher. She had a collarbone and ribs that had shattered and caused major lung damage on one side. Zoe had to intubate the woman to secure her airway and then do a needle decompression to relieve the increasing pressure from air and blood accumulating in her chest, which could stop her breathing altogether.

Even then, Zoe wasn't happy with how well the woman was breathing. Her blood pressure was still dropping as well and that might indicate further internal injuries.

'I'd like to go with her in the chopper,' she informed Tom when he joined the team assisting her in stabilising this patient for transport. 'I'd prefer to monitor that tension pneumothorax myself if the air rescue team don't mind.'

'We don't mind,' one of the helicopter paramedics said over his shoulder. 'You can party with us any time, Red.'

Zoe had never liked the nickname, earned thanks to her bright auburn hair colour, but the way it pulled her back in time was welcome. She still belonged in this world. It was Tom who would be most affected, however. 'Would you be OK to meet me at the hospital?' Zoe checked.

'Shouldn't be a problem. I'll let Control know, borrow a crew member from one of the other trucks and we'll transport the baby.'

'Oh…' It was the first moment Zoe had had to think about the child since her relief in finding it, hanging upside down in the car seat, but conscious and alert. 'How's he doing?'

'Teo's happy.'

'Teo?' The name was unusual.

'The paediatrician from the Harbour. Nice guy.'

'Mmm.' Zoe shifted her gaze. So his name was Teo? She had noticed the dark olive skin, of course, and the broad features that suggested he was Polynesian.

Right now, he had the baby, wrapped in a blanket, in his arms. He didn't notice Zoe's glance because he was looking down at the child. And…he was smiling. He was also radiating an aura of calmness. As if it was nothing out of the ordinary to be holding a baby at the scene of a major accident. As if he was actually *enjoying* it.

She was close enough to be able to hear if the baby was crying and she couldn't hear even a whimper. Zoe wouldn't have been the least bit surprised if she'd walked over there to find that the baby was smiling back up at him and, for some inexplicable reason that was irritating.

'What's the baby's status?' It came out almost as a snap.

OK, maybe the reason wasn't that inexplicable. How was it that this guy—who looked as if he was a rugby star or a bouncer at some night club or something—could make it look as if caring for a baby was easy. *Fun*, even, when she was a mother, for heaven's sake, and that kind of calmness or pleasure was…unimaginable.

It took an effort to tune in to what Tom was saying in response to her terse query.

'All checked out fine. Totally protected by the car seat, probably, but he'll need observing for a while. Teo says he'll drop into ED as soon as he gets his car clear of this traffic jam and make sure he gets a thorough assessment.'

Zoe turned away from the sight of the big man cuddling an uninjured child. She should thank him for his assistance but she had more important things to do for the moment and maybe she'd catch him later in the ED anyway. She checked the monitor display on the life pack as the helicopter crew secured it to the stretcher her patient was now strapped onto.

'Let's get moving,' she said.

'Hold up…' A police officer was hurrying towards them. 'This is her handbag. You might want her details. Her name's Michelle Drew, aged 34.'

'Thanks.' Zoe took the bag. 'Any next-of-kin details?'

'We're trying to contact her husband. We'll direct him to the hospital. You going to the Harbour?'

Zoe nodded, already moving to follow the crew. The stretcher was rolled swiftly to the back of the waiting chopper and then smoothly loaded. The doors were pulled shut and the rotor speed picked up until they lifted clear of the scene for the short run to the central city hospital.

Zoe had to suppress a smile at the adrenaline rush of being airborne as she moved to help monitor this critically ill patient. The smile was still there inside, though, as she took a quick glance down at the scene they were leaving.

She was more than ready for this kind of a party. She had missed this life *so* much.

The mass of vehicles and people grew rapidly smaller as they gained height but one figure stood out from the rest. The big man with the baby still in his arms. He was looking up, she noticed, watching them take off.

'Pressure's still dropping,' The voice came through the earphones in her helmet. 'Zoe, can you see if you can get another line in?'

By the time Teo walked back to where he'd parked his car on the motorway shoulder, the traffic was moving again. It took less than thirty minutes for him to get to a parking space at Sydney Harbour Hospital and walk into the state-of-the-art emergency department via the ambulance bay.

The triage nurse, wearing a headset with earphones and a microphone, looked up from directing the latest ambulance arrival to smile at Teo. There were more smiles as he went into the department. He'd learned a long time ago that the medical staff on the front line appreciated that a head of department took an interest in patients from the moment they arrived and, whenever possible, Teo would answer a call for a consult from the paediatric department instead of sending a junior doctor.

He went towards the glass board that had the ever-changing details of what patient was where. A glance to his left showed that the major trauma resuscitation area was crowded with staff. The bright red overalls of the helicopter rescue medics were on one side of the room as they observed what was happening with the patient that had to be the woman from the crushed car. His patient's mother.

Did that mean that the intensive care paramedic was still here as well? Zoe? He'd seen her leap into the helicopter. Superwoman. Directing a major incident one minute, crawling into a wrecked vehicle the next and then winging her way to the helipad here. Teo hadn't missed what she'd been doing in between either. The intubation and chest decompression on that woman couldn't have been easy procedures but they'd been done well and had undoubtedly saved a life.

Zoe wasn't in the resus area, however. He could see her standing quietly on one side of the huge glass board, scanning it for information. On the other side of the board, at the other end, were two other people, intently in conversation.

Teo knew both of them. Finn Kennedy was a neighbour, of sorts. He had the penthouse in the Kirribilli View Apartments, a nearby complex that many of the staff, including Teo, lived in. Finn was also the director of surgery here at the Harbour and was probably as frequent a visitor to this department as Teo was, but he knew that Finn's visits were far less welcome. No one could deny Finn's brilliance but it came with a price. Only the ignorant or very confident would attempt to stand up to this man and the person talking to him right now was definitely in the latter category.

Evie Lockheart, reputedly a rising star amongst the ED doctors, was also a resident at Kirribilli View, where she shared an apartment with another junior doctor, Mia McKenzie. Teo would have known about her anyway, however, because her family had the status of royalty around this place. Evie was the great-granddaughter of the man who had founded this hospital and, according to the rumour mill, it was now her father's generous contributions that kept the Harbour amongst the most prestigious teaching hospitals in Australia. Teo had heard that there was no love lost between Finn and Evie but what he was seeing right now made him pause.

'Send her to CT first,' Finn was saying. 'I'll have a theatre free in thirty minutes. It'll take that long to see what you're dealing with.'

'It'll take less time than that for her to crash. She's got

a haemothorax that's barely under control. We're losing fluid as fast as we can load it. There's an arterial bleed going on in there. She's lost the pulse in her right arm and she could lose the limb if we can't get in and deal with the damaged artery. *Now*, Mr Kennedy, not in thirty minutes.'

'And what is it, exactly, that you want from me, Dr Lockheart?'

What indeed? It wasn't the conversation that was piquing Teo's interest. It was more the way they were standing.

Too close?

Or maybe it was the way they were looking at each other. If he didn't know better, he'd think that that kind of eye contact was about something a lot less professional than juggling a theatre queue. It was ridiculous but it was making him feel like he was eavesdropping on a private conversation. Maybe he should step away. But Zoe was here. Was she listening too? A sideways glance seemed to coincide with exactly the same movement from the paramedic. For a split second they held the eye contact and he knew they were on the same wavelength. Teo stepped closer.

'I've just come in to check on the baby,' he said quietly. 'Do you know where he is?'

They both turned back to scanning the board. The department was clearly very busy. Dozens of boxes were filled with the scrawl of marker pen.

The voices on the other side of the board were fainter now.

'But didn't one of your recent edicts stipulate that there would always be a theatre kept free for emergencies from this department?'

Evie Lockheart wasn't a short woman. In the heels she was wearing now, she was only a few inches shorter than

Finn's six feet or so. And the way she was holding herself at this moment made her seem even taller.

'There is. You're using it. Plus one of mine for that ruptured spleen you sent up ten minutes ago.'

'You've got a patient in Theatre 5 who's about to go in for an elective procedure that could easily wait. They haven't started the anaesthetic and they're standing by for a green light from you to set up for Michelle Drew.' To her credit, Evie wasn't sounding smug. In fact, she seemed to have just the right note of reason and deference in her voice. She also sounded extremely persuasive.

Finn wasn't about to be a soft touch for anyone, especially a pretty young woman. His body language was defensive, to say the least. Was Evie about to have her head bitten off in public for interfering with his job? It hadn't been that long ago, in the wake of a discussion about funding cuts, that Teo had heard Finn make some disparaging comment about applying for a few more of the Lockheart millions seeing as their princess was currently a member of staff. But while Finn was giving Evie a glare that could have shrivelled steel, he was far too professional to lose his temper in here.

'Fine,' he snapped. 'I'll sort it.'

Evie's smile lit up her face. 'Fantastic. Thank you so much, Dr Kennedy.' She whirled away from him, heading back to the trauma resus area.

Finn stared at her back for a moment longer before swinging away himself, to head for the nearest telephone.

'Um…' Zoe cleared her throat beside Teo. 'I think your patient's in cubicle 4. Look…eleven-month-old boy from MVA. His name is Harry.'

'Cool. I'll go and see what they've found.' He lowered his voice. 'I might need to pull a few strings and get the little guy admitted.'

'Why would you do that?'

Teo didn't have a chance to answer as a nurse came up to the board with an eraser and a pen. She filled in an empty slot to show that a patient had just come back from CT.

'That was the woman from your scene,' she told Zoe. 'Good job you immobilised her. She's got cracked vertebrae C4 and 5. Could have ended up quadriplegic if they'd been displaced.' Then she smiled. 'Hi, Teo. We heard you were involved in a bit of action. Your baby's in cubicle 4 if you want to go and see him.'

'Thanks.' Teo returned the smile. 'And it's only a rumour, Louise. I'm not really the father.'

Louise giggled. Zoe didn't even smile. In fact, she was staring at him as if that tiny bit of flirting was just as unprofessional as the spat they'd overheard between Finn and Evie.

Suddenly, it seemed important to do some damage control. 'You're Zoe, aren't you?'

'Yes. Zoe Harper.'

'We didn't get the chance for a proper introduction, did we?' He held out his hand and gave her his best smile. 'I'm Teo Tuala.'

Her expression softened. 'And I didn't get the chance to thank you for your assistance.' Her hand was surprisingly soft. And small. It disappeared completely within his huge, brown paw. Teo gave it a gentle, friendly squeeze and let go.

Behind them, a team of people was swiftly manoeuvring the bed that Michelle Drew lay on towards the internal doors and the lift that would take her up to Theatre.

'How's she doing?' Teo asked.

'Touch and go. She really does need to get into surgery.' Zoe was watching his face. 'Why did you say that you'd find a way of admitting the baby even if he didn't need it?'

Teo rubbed the side of his nose. 'That's not what I said.'

'It sounded like it was what you meant.'

He smiled at her again. 'OK, I confess. I want to make sure he's got family to go to while his mum's in here. It's no secret that I'm not a fan of foster-care.'

Zoe's gaze flicked away. She was looking over his shoulder. 'Tom. You ready to hit the road?'

'Absolutely. Hi, Teo. You'll be happy to know that little Harry's been cleared. His dad's on the way here now. And his grandma, apparently.'

'Couldn't be happier,' Teo nodded. 'I'll go and see him now before I get any later for my rounds. Good to meet you both.'

Zoe watched him walk away, heading for cubicle 4.

She was trying very hard to suppress a niggly sensation in her gut that had the potential to undermine how good her first day back at work had been promising to be.

She recognised the niggle all too well.

Guilt, that's what it was.

Good grief... Teo Tuala was prepared to cross professional boundaries if necessary to prevent a child going into temporary foster-care.

What would he think if he knew that *she* had considered foster-care as an option for her own child?

That she'd gone even further than that and considered giving up her child for adoption?

He'd think she wasn't fit to be a mother.

And maybe she'd have to agree with him.

CHAPTER TWO

'Oh...*no!*'

The baby's face puckered in dismay at the tone of Zoe's voice. Hastily, she picked her up and held her, patting the tiny back. 'It's OK, Emma. Don't cry. *Please* don't cry.' She alternated the pats with some soothing circles. 'Come on, we'll find a clean suit for you and we can still be on time for our appointments.'

It took no time at all to find what she needed in Emma's room. Stretchy suits and singlets were folded and sorted according to size and colour in the dresser drawers. The change table was clean to the point of sterility with the wipes, creams and disposable nappies neatly encased in the plastic partitions of the slide-out drawer.

'No more spit-ups,' Zoe commanded, snapping the fasteners on the clean, pink suit.

Emma waved chubby fists and grinned up at her mother. Zoe sighed but stretched out to smooth back wisps of golden hair from the baby's forehead. 'At least you look like someone really loves you.'

Zoe loved her. She *did*. The only problem was that the realisation was in her head and not in her heart. She knew she loved her daughter. She just couldn't *feel* it.

There was no time to change her own shirt. Zoe dabbed at the milky stain with a wet cloth and then abandoned the attempt. Emma had an appointment at the paediatric clinic for a routine check-up. Zoe had an appointment with her psychologist, John Allen, which was hopefully also routine but being late for either appointment was not an option. She had to convince everybody that things were going brilliantly on the home front otherwise John might change his mind about it being a good idea for her to be back at work part time.

And it might have been only a few days since she'd started work again but Zoe already knew that it was the way forward for both herself and Emma. She wouldn't survive being a full-time mother on her own. Not now, when she'd been reminded of the person she'd once been. Not while the memories were still so fresh of how hard it had been in the mothering unit when she'd had support available 24/7.

With the confidence that stepping back into her old life for limited periods was providing, she was getting stronger. She could leave her failures behind her when she was on the road and, when she was at home, she could go through the motions of being a perfect mother and only she knew that she was counting the hours until she could be away from her child again.

Besides, she wanted to be a mother that someone could be proud of. There was nothing wrong with that, was there?

Emma's car seat had a handle with several brightly coloured toys attached by elastic cords. When the soft toys were tugged they made noises. The yellow duck quacked and the lime-green frog croaked. The cow bell was proving popular this morning and it jingled at regular intervals as Zoe drove towards Sydney Harbour Hospital. The noise could have become irritating but Zoe had other things to worry about.

Pulling up at a set of traffic lights, she checked the

nappy bag on the passenger seat beside her. Had she remembered the bottle of formula? After spitting up half her breakfast, Emma could well be hungry again by the time they got to the paediatric clinic's waiting room. The last thing Zoe needed was having to try and cope with a fractious baby under the watchful gaze of all the other mothers who would be there.

Mothers who would probably all be like that dreadful support group John had talked her into going to on one occasion. Women who adored their babies and knew what they were doing. Women who never ever felt an inkling of the panic and despair that Zoe had lived with every day since Emma's birth five months ago.

Before that, even. Well before that. Right back in the earliest stages of this whole nightmare when she had agonised over whether even to continue with the pregnancy or not. And when it had all become too much and James had simply walked away. Not that she could blame him. They'd been doing no more than dating casually when she'd become pregnant and while they'd tried to make a go of a relationship, there had been no way James was cut out to deal with the emotional wreck Zoe had morphed into.

Just like her mother.

Oh…rubbish. Zoe parked the car and made a determined effort to park that train of thought at the same time. If she didn't she might blurt something out in her session with John and that would be worse than having Emma screaming inconsolably in the waiting room. She wasn't going to discuss her mother with anyone. She wasn't even going to allow herself to think about her.

The waiting area was packed to the gills this morning. The place was cluttered with prams and strollers, toddlers fighting over the rather sad collection of toys available and babies crying. One distressed infant was pacified quickly by the offer of a breastfeed and Teo smiled at the mother.

Another baby was crying more loudly. Teo took a glance over his shoulder before he disappeared into the examination room.

And then he paused with his hand halfway to pushing the door open and took another look.

It couldn't be.

But it was.

Zoe Harper was in the waiting area and it was her baby who was distressed. Zoe was pacing back and forth, with the infant upright in her arms, tucked against her shoulder. Her head was bent, almost as if she was shielding the baby from view but Teo could see the way Zoe was scanning the area in an oddly furtive manner. She seemed embarrassed that her baby was crying but why? That's what babies did. It was part of their job description.

Maybe Zoe wasn't, in fact, the mother.

Teo dismissed the thought as he entered the examination room. Either the woman he'd seen in total command of a major incident the other day had an identical twin or Zoe had been left in charge of someone else's baby. Her sister, or a friend perhaps, who'd ducked off to go to the loo. That would explain the total lack of confidence he had sensed.

It took only a minute or two to confirm that his registrar had, indeed, picked up an abnormal murmur in a toddler's heart sounds. It took several more to reassure the parents that it wasn't necessarily anything to panic about but then Teo was able to leave the room, confident that his registrar could arrange the urgent tests needed so they would know exactly what they were dealing with. He knew he'd been a little abrupt compared to the time he would normally have spent on a consult like this but he would see the parents again as soon as the results came in.

And he had the strongest desire to check the waiting room again on his way back up to the ward.

This was Zoe's worst nightmare.

The clinic appointments were running late, the area was getting more and more crowded and she just couldn't stop Emma crying. It felt like it had been going on for hours now and the looks she was getting from other mothers had gone from sympathetic to pitying to frankly annoyed. Emma's shrieks had changed as well and the wails were now interspersed with that hiccupping sort of sound that advertised pure misery.

She'd changed her nappy, cuddled her, walked her up and down and now she was trying to feed her with the bottle of formula she'd mixed before leaving. Emma was having none of it. Her tiny hands were shoving at the bottle containing milk that had a totally unacceptable lack of warmth and small legs were kicking in outrage. Zoe could feel herself being watched. She could feel her face flushing and her shoulders hunching.

'*Please*, Emma,' she whispered. 'Please have a drink.'

Her baby's face took on a deeper crimson hue as Emma went rigid in her arms, arching her little back to produce the loudest crying Zoe had ever heard. What was wrong with her? What was *she* doing that was so wrong? Despair was enveloping her now and, to her horror, Zoe felt tears slipping down her own cheeks. She squeezed her eyes shut as she sensed someone approaching. A staff member, probably, coming to take her child away and give it to someone who could be a better mother.

The touch of a hand on her shoulder was so unexpected that Zoe's eyes snapped open. And then she blinked.

Crouched in front of her, so that he was on the same eye level, was Teo Tuala. He wasn't looking at her as if she was some kind of a monster mother either. He was smiling.

'Someone's not happy,' he said. 'Maybe I can help?'

Zoe had noticed what a big man Teo was but having him hunched in front of her like this made him seem like a huge, solid rock of a man. And he had the most extraordinarily dark brown eyes. Eyes that reflected his smile but with a depth that told her he understood that it wasn't just the baby that was so unhappy.

And he wanted to help. Zoe's brain provided a snapshot of the day she'd met Teo. When he had been standing in the middle of a chaotic accident scene holding a stranger's baby and looking as if it was nothing out of the ordinary. As if there was nothing about babies he couldn't cope with. Enjoy, even.

Something else came with that flash of memory. An instinctive sureness that she could trust him. And he was a paediatrician. Something had to be wrong with Emma for her to be crying like this. Without giving herself any time to think of the possible consequences, Zoe pushed her baby towards him. She didn't say a word. She couldn't. If she opened her mouth she would probably start sobbing as hard as her tiny daughter was.

Teo didn't even blink. He took Emma and made her look as tiny as a newborn in his big arms. He got to his feet and peered down at the baby as he rocked her.

'What's the story, little one?' he asked casually. 'It's not so bad around here, really.'

Emma hiccupped, staring up at this new person. And then, miraculously, she stopped howling.

Zoe could hear the sigh of relief coming from more than one of the other mothers around her.

And she had never felt more of a failure. She'd been doing her very best here for so long and it had taken less than thirty seconds for someone else to soothe her baby. A man.

She couldn't look at Teo. She stared down at the bottle of unwanted milk in her hands, her vision blurred by tears.

'Hey…'

Teo was still smiling, she could hear it in his voice. It was a gentle, soothing word that meant nothing but managed to contain an entire message. A 'here we are and it's not really all that bad, is it?' kind of message.

Emma was probably smiling back at him by now.

'Zoe?'

Looking up, Zoe knew instantly that the 'Hey' had been directed at her and not Emma. But she couldn't respond. He might think things weren't so bad because Emma had stopped crying but, for her, things were even worse.

And he knew that. Holding Emma securely with one arm, he reached down and picked up the handle of the car seat. 'Come with us,' he invited softly. 'You can bring the bag.'

Zoe still felt she could explode with the emotion she was trying to contain but she had no choice. She had to follow because 'us' was this paediatrician and *her* baby. And everybody, absolutely everybody in this waiting room, was watching. All the mothers, a sprinkling of fathers, the receptionists and nursing staff behind the desk. Even the older children present were all staring.

But not at her, Zoe realised. They were all watching Teo and the majority of watchers had smiles on their faces.

Because Emma was finally quiet?

Because the sight of such a masculine figure holding a small baby was guaranteed to tug at heartstrings?

Or did it have something to do with the fact that this

particular masculine figure was so good looking? It was more than the combination of even features and glossy black hair. There was something about the way Teo handled his size. The grace that came from not only confidence but a relaxed way of looking at life. And it was about the way he smiled so easily and the way he could see solutions rather than problems.

Zoe wasn't the only person following Teo. A little boy had abandoned the toy he'd been playing with and was trotting purposefully in the wake of the big man. His mother had to jump up and catch him before they reached the door.

Teo led her out of the waiting room and along a corridor. Then he opened the door of a room marked 'Private'. There were comfortable chairs in here, a change table, a big basket of toys and a tiny kitchenette. The coffee table had a large box of tissues on it.

'This is a room reserved for families who need a bit of time out or a special consultation,' Teo told her. 'It was a bit crowded out there, wasn't it?'

Zoe's nod was jerky. Her tears had stopped for the moment but she heard herself sniff. She pulled a few tissues from the box, blew her nose and then dabbed at her eyes, hoping Teo wouldn't notice.

He didn't appear to. He was looking down at Emma. 'So who's this little sweetheart?' he asked.

'Her name's Emma.'

'She's, what, about six months old?'

'Nearly.'

'And…she's yours?'

'Yes.' Zoe had noticed the hesitation and it made her feel ashamed. Was the lack of a normal mother-child bond so obvious?

Emma chose that moment to start grizzling, too, as if the confirmation that Zoe was her mother was disturbing. Zoe stared down at the bottle of milk she was still carrying.

'You could heat that up a bit,' Teo suggested. 'There's a microwave over there beside the coffee-making stuff.'

'We can't stay.'

'Why not?'

'Emma's got an appointment at the clinic. We've been waiting for ages so it must be nearly her turn.'

'That's not a problem. I can make sure she gets seen. Is there something you're worried about?'

'No. It's just a routine check-up.'

'So it's not urgent.'

'Well, no…except…'

'Except what?' Teo prompted.

'I…um…I've got an appointment myself. At 10.30.'

'Obstetric?'

'No.' Zoe didn't want to tell him. She could feel the flush of embarrassment colouring her cheeks. It was one of the worst things about being a redhead, the way blushes came so quickly.

'Sit down, just for a minute,' Teo said. 'Please. You won't be late. This clinic goes on for hours and you can always bring her back after you've been…wherever it is you need to go.'

He could see a solution for everything. And it didn't matter if she didn't want to tell him anything. In the short silence that followed, Teo sat down in one of the chairs. Emma was quiet again. She looked as if she'd fallen asleep in his arms, too exhausted by her misery to remember she was hungry. Zoe sank down onto the edge of another armchair, feeling defeated. There was no point in denying she had a problem. Teo had seen it for himself. He had been prepared to help her in what had been her worst moment for a very long time. He deserved some honesty.

'I have an appointment with John Allen,' she admitted. 'He's a—'

'Clinical psychologist,' Teo nodded. 'I know John well. He's a good friend. He and his wife Susie live in the apartment next to mine.'

Oh…help. Zoe took in a shaky gulp of air. 'I'd rather he didn't know about what you saw in the waiting room.'

Teo looked curious. 'What did I see?'

'Someone who was being a miserable failure trying to look after her baby,' Zoe muttered.

Teo shook his head. 'I saw a mother doing her best in difficult circumstances. Babies are very good at picking up vibes. What I didn't see was anyone offering you any kind of assistance and I have to say that was disappointing. This is my department and I'm going to have something to say about that at the next staff meeting. You know what?'

'No…' Zoe's response was cautious. She couldn't believe he was being so non-judgmental. Giving her credit, even, for the meltdown he'd rescued them from.

'I think I'll send out a memo. I can do that, cos I'm head of department here. Someone might even read it and take some notice.' Teo's smile was fading and his tone became a lot more serious. 'I saw something else, too,' he added.

Oh, no…*he* was the head of the paediatric department? If he did say something to his friend John, her psychologist would certainly take some notice. Zoe gnawed on her bottom lip, hoping she didn't look as anxious as she was now feeling. What else had he noticed?

'I saw someone who lacked confidence in what she was doing,' Teo said gently. 'And while there's nothing unusual in that when it comes to first-time mothers, in your case it astonished me.'

Zoe wished the floor would just open up and swallow her. This was unbearable.

'You want to know why?'

Not really, Zoe wanted to say. She didn't want to hear about just how inept she had looked.

Teo took her silence for assent. 'Because I saw you for the first time only a few days ago and you know what?'

'No…' Zoe almost smiled. She could play this conversational game, especially if he was going to say something nice after getting her to admit her ignorance about what he was going to say.

'I thought you were Superwoman.'

Zoe blinked. *'What?'*

'Superwoman,' Teo repeated. 'There you were, directing that accident scene, hurling yourself into a mangled wreck of a car, showing off some not inconsiderable skills in getting that woman's airway and breathing sorted, and then you jumped into a helicopter and took off. All in all, it was a breathtaking performance. You should be proud of yourself.'

It was more than a nice thing to say. Zoe could feel an unfamiliar glow happening inside. She *was* feeling proud of herself. For the first time in *so* long. She ducked her head, embarrassed by the sincere praise. Or maybe it was the frank admiration she could see in those dark eyes that was so disconcerting.

'You made it look easy,' Teo continued. 'Just another day at work.'

'It was. Kind of…'

'Kind of?'

'It was my first day back since…oh, since I was about six months pregnant and I was beginning to think I'd never be allowed to go back.'

'Why not?'

'Because…um…I got postnatal depression after Emma was born.' There. She'd said it. She risked a quick glance at his face. The admiration would be gone, for sure. Probably replaced with that wary look people got at the mere whiff of mental illness.

But Teo's face hadn't changed. 'Badly?'

Zoe stared down at her hands. 'Yeah…I got hospitalised and given some pretty heavy-duty drugs. And then I went into a mothering unit for a while. I'm back home now but…it's still hard.'

'Of course it is. Being a mother is hard enough without the extra challenge of PND.'

Zoe just nodded, glancing at her watch. If she left now, she could still make her appointment with John in time, but she didn't want to leave Teo with this negative image of her. It would be far better if he continued thinking of her as Superwoman.

'When I'm at work,' she confided shyly, 'I'm me. The me I used to be. The me I recognise. It's when I'm at home that it's different and it's in places like this when I know the other mothers are watching me and judging me that it's the hardest of all.'

She looked up at smiled. 'Thank you for helping,' she said quietly. 'I don't think you know how much it means.'

'It was a pleasure, Zoe. I'm sure you've got a ton of friends supporting you but if you ever need an extra, I'll be here.'

'Thanks.' Zoe wasn't about to tell him that all her friends were in the ambulance service, mostly younger than her, and being in the company of a baby was only marginally less attractive than being in the company of a depressed woman. Let him think she was popular and well supported—in between her stints as Superwoman.

The fantasy was so far from the truth it was amusing enough to bring a genuine smile to her face as she took Emma and tucked her back into her car seat. Emma, bless her, didn't wake up. Then she shoved the things threatening to spill from the pockets of the nappy bag back into place and she was ready to go.

'Can you manage all that?' Teo asked. 'I could wander up with you, if you like.'

'No, thanks.' The last thing Zoe wanted was for John to realise she had a connection to someone he knew on a personal basis. Professional confidentiality was all very well but it didn't apply between doctors, did it? 'I can manage.'

'Of course you can.' Teo smiled again as he held the door open for her. 'What I will do is have a word with the receptionist. They'll slot you in for Emma's appointment as soon as you get back from seeing John.'

Teo was busy for the rest of the morning and all afternoon that day.

A three-year-old boy, Timmy, who'd been burnt by climbing into a bath of scaldingly hot water was in the paediatric intensive care unit. Teo was part of the team led by Luke Williams that was having to deal with the complications of hypovolaemic shock caused by fluid loss from the burns. It was the child's kidney function that was causing concern today and haemodialysis had to be added to the plethora of procedures that was keeping the small boy alive.

Timmy's mother was beside herself with guilt and fear.

'I had to feed the baby,' she sobbed. 'I had no idea that Timmy was trying to be helpful and run his own bath. I always, always run the cold tap first and then add hot water. I thought he was watching TV in the lounge room. The baby's got colic and she's really hard work after a feed.'

Teo could only listen and imagine how hard this had

to be for her. There was no point in laying blame when it could only make things worse for everyone.

'His dad walked out on us when I got pregnant again. One kid was bad enough, he said. He couldn't handle having two.'

Teo made a sympathetic sound but part of his mind was wandering. Where was Emma's dad? Zoe hadn't mentioned a partner and he'd heard what sounded like a fierce determination to cope with her own situation. On her own. Had she been wearing a ring? He made a mental note to have a look next time he saw her.

Except he had no reason to see her again, had he?

The realisation was curiously disappointing and it stayed with him for the rest of the day as he did his rounds, checking on his small patients and comforting distressed parents. Zoe intrigued him. That she could be so competent in one area of her life and so lost in another made it seem like there had to be a key to unlocking the barrier dividing the areas. And it was sad that it was the home and family side that she was struggling with because Teo knew that was, by far, the most important part of anybody's life. If Zoe could find it, she might not feel the need to be at work at all during this crucial stage of bonding with her baby and then, later, she could have the best of both worlds.

The final task of his day took him back to the paediatric outpatient clinic. Empty of patients now, there was only a cleaner pushing a vacuum cleaner around the chairs and a weary-looking receptionist filing paperwork at the desk.

'Busy day, huh?' He smiled at the receptionist. This wasn't the time to take anybody to task for leaving a distressed mother and child without assistance while they had been waiting.

'It was a nightmare,' the receptionist said. 'One registrar got called away for something on the ward and another had to deal with a kid who had an epileptic seizure in the toilets and we were running *so* late.'

'Did Zoe Harper come back again with Emma?'

'Yes.' The girl gave him a curious glance. 'Is she a friend of yours?'

Teo didn't have time to respond. The cleaner was coming towards the desk.

'I found this under the chair over there,' the older woman said, holding out a leather wallet.

'Oh, my goodness.' The receptionist took the wallet. 'Thank you so much. Someone's probably worried sick about this.' She opened the wallet. It had a pocket at the back for notes and slots for credit cards on the other side. In the middle was a plastic-covered pocket for a driver's licence. 'Zoe Harper,' she said in astonishment. 'Good thing *you're* here, Dr Tuala.'

'Is it?'

'Well, she's a friend of yours. You could take it back to her.'

'I could.' Teo's tone was confident. Surely there'd be something in the wallet that would have her address on it? He could drop it off on his way home. He would get to see Zoe again. Even better, he could find out whether she had some support at home in the form of a partner.

He held out his hand for the wallet. 'I'm on my way home right now,' he said. 'Consider it sorted.'

CHAPTER THREE

THE knock on the door couldn't have come at a worse time.

Zoe was sitting in the tiny living room of her terraced cottage in one of Sydney's older suburbs. Emma had been bathed and changed and had just started her final feed for the evening. And, for once, it was going well. Sucking on her bottle, she lay in the crook of Zoe's arm, staring up at her mother. The memories of the awful morning they'd had in that waiting room were finally beginning to ebb away.

Zoe couldn't help jumping at the sound of the knock. Nobody came visiting at this time of day.

Her first thought was that it could be James and she didn't want to see him. There'd been undeniable relief on both sides when they'd decided to call it quits on their relationship. James had generously gifted her his share of the hefty deposit they'd put down on this cottage.

'Consider it child support,' he'd suggested. 'That way, we can go our own ways with no hard feelings.'

The gesture had been very generous, considering that Zoe had inherited a piece of land from her grandmother that was probably worth a lot now. Not that she'd had a chance to think about what to do with it with everything else that was happening in her life.

Even worse than it being James, there was the faint

possibility it could be one of her parents, given that she had finally written to them to inform them that they were grandparents. But she hadn't expected a reply to the letter, let alone a personal appearance. They would see the fact that she was unmarried with a baby as further evidence of the trouble she'd caused from the moment she'd been born. Besides, how many years had it been since her mother had even left the house?

Zoe didn't know because she hadn't been in contact with them since she'd come to Sydney at the age of eighteen to start her training as a paramedic. That had been nearly ten years ago.

The possibilities flashed through her head so fast, she had considered them both by the time the knocking stopped. Both were enough to make her feel incredibly tense. Emma was still staring up at her but her contented sucking had stopped. She jerked her head back and the teat of the bottle sprang free and sent a spray of milk onto Zoe's face. Emma's face was crumpling ominously as a second knock came. Louder and more commanding than the first.

Her heart sinking, Zoe got to her feet. Emma would be howling by the time she got to the door. If someone was going to try and sell her an encyclopaedia or something, it could very well be the final straw.

It wasn't James. It wasn't her father and, thank goodness, it wasn't her mother.

That it was Teo Tuala rendered Zoe completely speechless. He had something in his hand that he was holding out towards her.

'The cleaner found this in the waiting room,' he said. 'Good thing you had your driver's licence in it. Even better that it had your address on it too.'

'Good grief… I thought I'd left it in the car. I was going to go and look for it when I got Emma off to sleep.'

Which wouldn't be any time soon. Emma was rubbing her nose against Zoe's shoulder and her wails were increasing in strength.

'I was just feeding her.' Zoe couldn't help sounding defensive. 'She was perfectly happy a moment ago.'

'And I interrupted by pounding on the door. Sorry.'

Teo really did have the most glorious smile. It radiated charm with a good helping of contrition this time.

'I'll get back to it, then.' Zoe had Emma in her arms. She also still had the bottle in her hand. She hesitated for a second, wondering how to take hold of the wallet. 'Would you mind putting it on the hall table?'

'Not at all.' Teo followed her in. He closed the door behind him. He looked around. 'Nice place,' he said. 'I love these cottages. I live in a modern apartment block but only because it's handy for the hospital. I've got a house in Samoa, right by the beach.'

'Oh…' Zoe had an instant image of a tropical paradise. 'Do you get back there often?'

'I go back for a week every couple of months. I like to help out at the local hospital as much as I can.' His smile had a wry curl. 'It used to be to see all my relatives as well but a whole bunch of them live over here now and the others all come to visit. I've got my favourite cousin and her brood arriving tomorrow.'

He had a voice that was just like his personality, Zoe thought. Deep and rich and warm. It was relaxing to listen to. Even Emma seemed to like it. She was still grizzling but the head rubbing was slower. Suddenly, the awkward thought in the back of her head that she would have to usher Teo out when he seemed happy to stay and talk just melted away.

'Would you like a coffee or something?' she asked. 'It's the least I can do to thank you for coming all this way with my wallet.'

'That would be great.'

'I'll just need to finish feeding Emma first.'

'No worries.' Teo followed her into the living area. There was only the one couch in here. Zoe sat on one end, feeling the tilt of the cushions as Teo took the other end. He was so big, it meant that they were sitting very close together. Zoe pushed the awareness away. She tipped Emma back and offered her the bottle again.

Emma pulled away from the teat, turning her head one way and then the other. Her face got steadily redder as she gathered strength to let Zoe know that this was not going to work.

'I could have a go at that, if you'd like.' Teo's tone said it didn't matter in the least if she didn't like the idea. 'Seeing as it was my fault her supper got interrupted.'

He was offering to rescue her again. Because he thought she was pathetic?

'That way, you could make the coffee.' She could see a hint of mischief in his smile now. 'I haven't had one since about nine o'clock this morning and I'm having serious caffeine withdrawal.'

Not only was he offering to help, he was making it seem like she was doing *him* a favour. And did it matter if he thought she was pathetic? Judging by the way he'd handled Emma that morning, Teo was more likely to be successful in getting her fed and settled for the night. And if Emma settled, she would have a good sleep and be easier to look after tomorrow. Zoe would get a good sleep herself. She stamped on the pride or the need to prove herself or whatever it was preventing her from accepting her visitor's help.

'That would be great,' she said, deliberately echoing Teo's acceptance of her offer of coffee. She handed over her baby and then the bottle. 'How do you like your coffee?'

'Dash of milk and two sugars.'

Zoe grinned. 'Good to see a medical professional setting such a healthy example.'

'My aunties think I'm fading away. They give me six sugars. I'm in a programme to wean myself of the addiction.' The skin around the corners of his eyes was crinkling into well-worn smile lines. 'Hello, my name is Teo Tuala and I'm a sugarholic.'

A snort of laughter escaped Zoe, which made Emma's head turn. She looked surprised enough to have forgotten why she was crying. Teo eased the teat of the bottle into her open mouth and she turned back, sucking vigorously and reaching up with her hands to help hold the bottle.

'That's the ticket,' Teo said approvingly. 'Good girl, Emma.'

It didn't take Zoe long to make the coffee but by the time she brought two steaming mugs back from the adjacent kitchen, Emma had finished her milk. Teo had her upright on his shoulder, and was rubbing her back. Seconds later, Emma burped loudly.

Zoe shook her head at the ease with which Teo was going through the routine.

'How do you know so much about babies?'

'I'm a paediatrician.' Teo grinned. 'There was a class or two about babies, as I recall. I might have even read a book.'

Zoe didn't return the smile. 'I'm a mother,' she said. 'And I've read every book there is. I can't handle Emma that well.'

'I'm Samoan,' Teo said, as if that explained everything. Maybe it did. Maybe there was some cultural secret to knowing what to do with babies. If Zoe could find out what it was, it might be the answer to all her problems. Searching his face for a clue, she suddenly realised how long she had been staring at him. She sat down hurriedly, feeling herself blushing.

The way Zoe blushed was a dead give-away that something had emotional importance. The way she had been looking at him gave Teo a good clue as to what it was. She was lost in her position as a mother. She thought he might be able to help. There was a touch of desperation there that made him want to help. And maybe he *did* have the answer.

'I didn't come to Australia until I was eight or nine,' Teo said, his tone much more sober. 'In the islands, as soon as you're old enough, you get to carry around the little kids and feed the babies and so on. Everybody has lots of brothers and sisters, or, in my case, an unlimited number of cousins. Family is everything at home.'

Not just at home in the islands. Family was everything, end of story. For a mother to be going out to work wasn't the answer. Especially to a job like the one Zoe had. She was putting herself in danger out there. Maybe it was none of his business but if he could do anything to persuade her there might be another way to regain her self-confidence, he had to try.

He knew, far too well, just how bad it could be for a child to lose his or her mother.

'I think the secret is just learning to relax. Be confident that you're doing the right thing because you love them. That's all that really matters in the end.'

'I do love Emma.' Zoe was nodding. 'I *do*.' The last words were a whisper, almost as though she was talking to herself. Convincing herself?

Emma was a heavy, limp bundle on his chest now. 'I think she's asleep,' he told Zoe. 'Want me to put her down?'

She nodded. 'Would you mind? If I take her, she'll probably wake up again.'

'Show me where her bed is.'

Zoe led him further down the narrow hallway of the cottage. There was a bathroom at the end of the hallway and two bedrooms on either side before that. He could see a double bed in the room on the right. It had a smooth, white cover and some cushions arranged very symmetrically. The one on the left was beautifully decorated with a teddy-bear theme. The bassinette had a white cover as pristine as the one on the adult bed and Teo could see baby supplies and toys arranged with absolute precision all around him. It looked like an advertisement for the perfect baby's bedroom.

It didn't look as if anyone actually lived in it.

Zoe turned back the cover on the bassinette and he laid Emma down carefully, on her side. She pulled the cover back up and tucked the edges in carefully. She smoothed the wrinkles on the top, stood back and then bent down. Teo expected to see her kiss her baby goodnight but, instead, she gently stroked the wisps of hair that were curling on her forehead, patting them back to sit in line with the rest of her hair.

Teo was deep in thought as he went back to the living area. He could see it all around him now. The attention to detail. The effort for everything to be perfect. No wonder Zoe was finding it hard to bond with her baby and be relaxed in her role of a mother. She was attempting the impossible here.

He knew exactly how he could help her. He also knew it was going to take some careful persuasion.

'How did your session with John go?' he asked, as they sat down to drink their coffee.

'Good. He's happy that my being back at work is going well.' Zoe wouldn't meet his gaze and Teo knew why. They both knew how concerned John would be if he'd seen how distressed both Zoe and Emma had been that morning. That could well be the key but Teo needed a little time to think about it. He changed tack.

'You're an amazing housekeeper. I don't think I've ever seen a house that has a baby in it looking this clean and tidy.'

Zoe flashed him a sideways glance. 'Is it *too* tidy? I get the occasional visit from one of the outworkers at the mothering unit. I wouldn't want them to think I was OCD or anything.'

'They might think you employed a very efficient house-keeper.'

'As if! Paramedic salaries, especially when you're on maternity leave, don't run to flash housekeepers.'

'You do get some help, though, don't you?'

'What do you mean?' Zoe was eyeing him warily. She had the most amazing eyes, Teo realised. Quite a light green, but they had a circle of darker colour around the irises and tiny shards of gold that radiated out from the pupils like sun rays. He'd never seen anything quite like them.

The expression in her eyes was more than wary now. He could see a flash of fear. Did she think he was imply-ing that she needed help? That social services might swoop in and remove her baby if she was deemed to be coping either so well it seemed pathological or not well enough? He might be getting into deeper waters than he'd intended to here.

Teo did what he always did when faced with something

potentially stressful. He took a deep breath and consciously relaxed. That way, he could get a good look at the bigger picture.

'I meant a partner,' he said casually. 'Emma's dad?'

'Long gone,' Zoe told him. 'We were only casually dating when I got pregnant. It was a disaster, really. I thought I was safe being on the Pill and it was that "maybe it's time to go to bed to see if there's any real chemistry going on here" kind of sex.'

'And there wasn't? Any real chemistry?'

Zoe sighed. 'Not enough. We had a go of trying to make it work but it wasn't going to happen. He helped me buy this house in lieu of having to remember he was a father by paying years of child support and that was that. We shook hands and went our separate ways when I was about seven months pregnant.'

'And you haven't heard from him since?'

'No. I did have the horrible thought it might be him when I heard you knocking at the door, though, and it made me realise that I really don't want to see him again.'

Teo wasn't surprised. Didn't the man want to know if he'd had a son or a daughter? That everything had gone well? How could any man go off and pretend it had never happened? Babies were so precious. On some level it was satisfying to know that this James was out of Zoe's life. He wasn't good enough for her *or* Emma.

Somewhere, in the back of his head, was a buzz that suggested the idea of sex with Zoe would be a very attractive prospect. He needed to distract himself, fast. The last thing Zoe Harper needed was another casual relationship that would probably only serve to strengthen whatever barriers were in place to stop her bonding completely with her baby.

'What about family?' he asked. 'They must be thrilled to have Emma around.'

'No family,' was all that Zoe said.

Even if Teo couldn't recognise an untruth, the way the colour flooded Zoe's cheeks made it clear that this was another emotional minefield. The way her shoulders had hunched indicated a boundary that he had no trouble recognising.

But he could sense that this was it. The hub of the problem.

'You need a family,' he told Zoe. 'And it's very lucky that you've met me.'

'Sorry?'

'I have more family than any one person could ever need. You'd be most welcome to borrow it.'

Zoe's stare told him that she thought he was crazy but Teo wasn't deterred.

'I told you my cousin's coming to visit. Alisi. She's got a little girl—Kali—who's not much older than Emma. And a couple of older boys. We're having a family barbecue next weekend at Coogee beach. Come and join us.'

'Oh, no…I couldn't possibly.'

Teo pulled out the big guns. 'You know what?'

Zoe wasn't playing. She was setting her coffee cup down on the table with great care. She even turned it around until she was happy with the angle of the handle. Her lips were pressed together resolutely. She wasn't going to encourage him by saying no.

'I reckon John would think it was a great idea, too,' Teo said.

That made her look up. 'Why?'

'He's helping you through your PND, isn't he?'

'Yes.'

'A big part of getting through it is to do with being confident about being with your baby, wouldn't you say?'

'I guess.'

'You asked me how I knew what I was doing and I said it was because I was Samoan. If you came and spent an afternoon with my tribe you'd understand. You might find a new way of looking at things.'

He could see the moment that a ray of hope shone through the wariness and determination to keep to herself. The hope that there was a key out there to unlock a door and let her step into the place she really wanted to be.

Teo believed he had that key.

'I'll pick you up,' he said. 'And if you aren't enjoying yourself, I'll take you home again, I promise.'

Zoe was gnawing her bottom lip so hard it hurt.

The invitation was pulling her in opposite directions. She desperately wanted to go because, if Teo was so good with babies, imagine what she might learn by watching how the women handled their children?

But what if it just came naturally because they were Samoan? They'd look at her and think she was some kind of freak. A mother who didn't know how to love her baby. Teo might be embarrassed that he'd even suggested including her.

And why was he issuing the invitation? This was a family gathering and she was a total stranger. What could he possibly be getting out of this? He must know that she wasn't remotely interested in getting involved with any man. Interest in sex had been wiped from her life even before James had disappeared. She hadn't even been touched by a man with anything other than a medical procedure in mind for well over a year.

Except for when Teo had touched her shoulder in the waiting room that morning. And that had been simply a way of getting her attention. Connecting. A touch of friendship.

Was it possible that she could have this gentle giant of a man as a friend? Someone who accepted her PND as well as her baby as simply being a part of who she was at the moment? Someone who didn't judge her and find her a miserable failure?

He wasn't saying anything. He seemed to be enjoying the last of his coffee, just letting the invitation float there in the air between them.

Zoe had a flash of something like panic. If she didn't catch it, it might disappear and she would be left wondering if she'd lost the most important opportunity she might ever have.

'I…um… What would I need to bring?'

'Just you and Emma,' Teo said promptly. 'No food, please. My family could cater for an army.' His smile carried a warmth that enfolded Zoe completely. 'And whatever you do, don't eat any breakfast. My aunties will take one look at you and think you need a lot more meat on your bones.'

Zoe made a face. 'Are you kidding? I'm two dress sizes bigger than I was before Emma.'

Teo's smile left his lips but it was still there in his eyes. 'The Samoan way of thinking is different. I think you might like it.'

If Teo was a typical representative, Zoe was quite prepared to believe that. The bubble of hope inside her was growing. It was almost a trickle of excitement and that was something Zoe hadn't felt for anything other than her job in longer than she could remember.

'So you'll keep next Saturday free? You'll come to our barbecue?'

Zoe nodded shyly. 'Thank you. I'd love to.'

CHAPTER FOUR

IT WAS just as well Zoe hadn't needed to think about bringing food.

A beach outing with a baby was enough of a mission in itself. She had to pack a supply of clean nappies and wipes, bottles and premixed formula, sunscreen and hats and toys to entertain her with and two changes of clothes. The car seat could double as a place for Emma to take a nap but she had to find a muslin cloth that could provide shade and protection from insects.

April was the second month of autumn in Australia but there were still days that felt like summer and this was one of them. A clear, blue sky and not a breath of wind. The surf was picture perfect, rolling up the white sandy beach, but Teo didn't lead Zoe down the steps to the sand. He headed for the large grassed area dotted with trees and some permanent barbecue sites. Every one of them was being used today by groups of families and friends but Zoe could spot the gathering they were heading towards well before they got there.

It was the most crowded. The most colourful. And by far the noisiest. She could see women of generous proportions wearing brightly coloured floral dresses and men wearing board shorts and T-shirts like Teo was. And there were children. It seemed like there were dozens of children running around and the younger they got, the less in the way of clothing they were wearing. Two tots weren't even wearing nappies.

Zoe felt completely overdressed in her jeans and singlet top. She also felt intimidated by the shouting and laughter she could hear. And they were all Samoan people, which made her feel pale and out of place. Her steps slowed.

'I'm not at all sure about this,' she confessed. 'I had no idea your family was so big.'

Teo let her catch up. He was carrying Emma while Zoe had the overstuffed nappy bag. 'I wasn't expecting this many either,' he said. 'Word gets around the community, though, and I expect everybody wanted to welcome Alisi and the kids. Come on, I'll introduce you to Alisi. I think you two will get on just fine.'

Amazingly, they did. After a series of introductions that made Zoe's head swim and hugs that felt as warm and squashy as the most comfortable couch in the world from all the 'aunties', Zoe found herself sitting on the grass beside Teo's favourite cousin.

'I love your jeans,' Alisi said. 'You'll have to tell me where I can go shopping.'

'Bondi Junction's good.' Zoe unstrapped Emma and picked her up from the car seat. Far more effort had gone into dressing her daughter than herself and Emma was wearing a pretty, smocked pink dress, white socks and tiny sandals.

'Oh…isn't she gorgeous?' Alisi's face lit up with a wide smile that reminded Zoe of Teo's grin. She reached out to touch Emma's face with her forefinger. '*Lalelei pepe,*' she crooned.

Inexplicably, Zoe felt the prickle of tears at such effusive admiration of her baby. Emma *was* beautiful. She felt proud of her.

'Yours is a darling, too. Her name's Kali, yes?'

'Ai.' Alisi nodded. 'And those two ragamuffins plaguing Teo are my *ui*, Maru and Sefa.'

Teo didn't look like he was being plagued. He had half a dozen small boys in bright board shorts and nothing else dancing around him as he dribbled a football across the grass. There was a whoop of excitement when he kicked it and the boys competed hard to be the first to reach the ball. Except for one, who clung to Teo's hand.

'That's Sefa.' Alisi smiled. 'His uncle Teo is his favourite person in the world.'

Alisi's baby was enjoying a breastfeed. All Zoe could see were chubby brown limbs and nothing more than a singlet and nappy for clothing. Emma was even more overdressed for this outing than she herself was. In an attempt to cover her sudden awkwardness, she found a bottle of sunscreen and began smoothing it over her daughter's equally chubby limbs.

She was fitting a frilled, white sunhat on her head when one of the aunties spotted Emma.

'Oh…' she cried. 'The *lalelei pepe*. Please…' She held out her arms and Zoe didn't have time to even consider refusing to share her child. Emma was scooped into strong brown arms and carried away to be shown off. Zoe watched in astonishment as Emma was passed from one woman to another, often after what was obviously a difference in opinion over how long someone's turn should be. What was even more astonishing was that Emma seemed to be loving it.

Teo must have been keeping half an eye on her while playing football with the boys. Maybe he could sense her astonishment and took it for concern because he eventually called in one of his cousins to take over supervising the children and went to rescue Emma. He plucked her from the arms of a woman who had the most beautiful long black hair and a frangipangi bloom tucked behind an ear.

'My turn,' Zoe heard him say with authority. 'I'm her honorary uncle, after all.'

He held Emma with his two huge hands around her middle. Zoe's breath caught in horror as he suddenly swooped her skywards so that she was balanced in his hands looking down at his head. Then he bounced her. Emma's face split into the biggest grin ever and the gurgling sound of her laughter could be clearly heard.

Everybody watching beamed approvingly.

'*Ua fiafia le teine.*' Alisi smiled. 'She's happy.'

And Zoe wanted to cry. It was the first time she had heard her baby laugh.

Teo brought Emma back to her then.

'Don't know about her,' he said, 'but I'm starving. I'll help with the cooking and then it's time for a swim.'

Zoe found a bottle of formula and Emma didn't object to having cold milk. She saw Alisi glance at the bottle and cringed inwardly but she couldn't detect the slightest judgement in the glance. In fact, Alisi sighed with something that sounded like envy.

'Her hair is so lovely. Like the first kiss of sunset. We get the most beautiful sunsets in the world in the islands.'

'I'll bet.'

'Have you ever been to Samoa?'

'No. I've never been out of Australia.'

'You'll have to come and visit.' The statement held as much authority as Teo's had when he'd reclaimed Emma and announced his position as her honorary uncle.

Did he mean that? Would that make him an honorary cousin for her? Someone with the kind of bond that was palpable amongst this big group of happy people? The notion was more than appealing. It gave Zoe an ache of long-ing. She'd never had any siblings. Or cousins. Or even a family in the true sense of the word.

'We would love to have you,' Alisi added. And then she laughed. 'My husband, Rangi, refuses to leave the islands. He expects the world to come to him. I said I had to go and visit Teo and he couldn't understand why. Teo comes here every few weeks, he said. Why go all that way to a smelly city?'

'Does he? Go home every few weeks?'

'He has a house near the beach. He says it's the home of his heart. He works for a week at the local hospital at least once every three months or so.'

'Really?' Zoe was impressed. 'That's a wonderful thing for him to do.'

Alisi nodded. 'Everybody loves Teo. He has the respect of a chief.'

The two young women were sitting on a rug beneath the shade of one of the trees close to the barbecue area. Everyone else seemed to have something to do around them, either playing with the children or preparing the food. Delicious aromas of garlic and lemon, seafood and roasting meat were drifting over the area, bringing the children to crowd around the picnic tables.

Zoe found herself watching Teo. There was a lot of laughter happening around the hot grills of the barbecues, the group of men clearly good friends.

'How many of you are Teo's family?' she asked.

Alisi laughed again. She had her baby lying in her lap now and she was holding Kali's hands, gently making her dance with her arms.

'All of us,' she said. 'And none of us, in a way.'

'What do you mean?'

'Teo was an only child. His father died in a fishing

accident when he was a tiny baby. His mother met an Australian tourist and came here to be with him but she was sick and didn't realise it. By the time they found the cancer it was too late to treat it. I think that's why Teo works at our hospital so often. He doesn't want that to happen to anybody else. Anyway, her man left her and she was too ashamed to come back home. Teo cared for her and he was too young to know how to come home when she died. He ended up in foster-care until Hina found him one day, in trouble on the streets. He was about thirteen then.'

'Hina?'

'Over there. In the blue and white *lavalava*. Sarong, I mean. She took him into her family. Adopted him, in the end, because there were a lot of papers to sign. That wouldn't happen in the islands. Our families can be blended without any of that fuss. Anyway, she's his first auntie and she has a lot of family here.'

Zoe was curious now. To be alone as a child and watch his mother die of cancer would have been appalling. And Alisi's tone when she'd mentioned foster-care had been one of enough disgust to suggest that the care hadn't been acceptable. Something clicked in the back of her head. No wonder he was prepared to bend rules and keep children in hospital with their mothers if the alternative was a foster-care system he didn't trust.

Something else shone through as well. Teo had been found in trouble. On the streets. How awful had that time been for him? And how could someone end up radiating the generosity of spirit and laid-back charm that Teo had if he'd had such an unhappy childhood?

He was the most extraordinary man.

Emma had finished her lunch as everybody else began eating what was, to Zoe, the most extraordinary feast. The aunties insisted on cuddling both Emma and Kali, clearly well practised in juggling babies and eating their meals one-handed. Alisi was happy to hand Kali over and Zoe felt relaxed enough by now to do the same with Emma.

'You've got to try this,' Alisi said, reaching for a huge, plastic bowl on the table. 'It's called *okai'a*. It's lime-marinated tuna. Delicious. Sefa! Put that back. You only need *one* coconut bun.'

'And this is my favourite.' Teo appeared by Zoe's side, and put some meat fresh from the grill onto her plate. 'Honey-glazed chicken.'

'Thank you. It smells wonderful.'

He hesitated for a moment. 'You OK?' he asked quietly. 'Enjoying yourself?'

Zoe nodded. 'They're very kind people.'

'You coming for a swim later?'

Zoe shook her head this time. 'I didn't bring my bathing suit.'

'I could lend you a sarong,' Alisi offered. 'No good for swimming but we could take the babies paddling.'

'Great idea,' Teo said. 'When the tide goes out a bit further, there'll be some lovely shallow pools down there near the swimming pool.'

The rock pool was set into the cliff side and was large enough for any swimmers who wanted to stay out of the surf. At high tide, the waves broke over the edge of the pool but it was far enough out now for the pool to look as clear and calm as a mountain lake. Inviting enough for Zoe to wish she had brought her bathing suit. It had occurred to her to do so but the new curves of her post-pregnancy body were not something she had any desire to put on display. Anywhere. Her concerns seemed a bit silly now, in the company of so many women who were obviously completely at ease with their larger figures.

There were platters of fresh fruit offered for dessert

and a taro bread pudding that Hina had made. And then, by tacit consent, the whole group settled for a rest period. Someone produced a guitar and started singing softly. Several small children went to sleep on the laps of adults, including Emma, who was tucked into the folds of Hina's blue and white sarong. When Zoe offered to take her back to put her in her car seat, Hina waved her away with a smile.

So Zoe sat with Alisi in the shade of the tree, listening to the music and watching the waves breaking on the beach and the crowd of people out enjoying the gorgeous day. Coogee beach was a very popular place on a day like this and Zoe wouldn't have been surprised if she knew some of the people out there, swimming and sunbathing, but she had no desire to move away from this group of Teo's people.

She might be overdressed and the only pale person amongst them but somehow, in a very short space of time, they had made her feel as if she belonged.

The rest period appeared to be over with the same kind of unspoken agreement with which it had begun. Children woke up. Some of the women began clearing the table. Teo stood up and stretched.

'Time for a swim,' he announced. He stripped off his T-shirt, rolled it into a ball and threw it like a football to one of Alisi's sons.

'But I want to swim *with* you, Uncle Teo.'

'Later. I'm going out past the waves. Too deep for you, Sefa.' He turned away to head for the beach and Zoe caught her breath.

Teo's left arm, from above the elbow to the top of his shoulder, was covered with an intricate tattoo. The skin was almost black. It was the lines of uninked skin that made the patterns.

Alisi had noticed her involuntary gasp.

'Nice, isn't it?' she murmured.

Zoe didn't know what to say. Tattoos were not something she had ever associated with the kind of man she knew Teo to be.

Alisi smiled. 'It's a *pe'a*,' she told Zoe. 'Tattoo in Samoa is an art form. It's been practised for two thousand years. Originally, it was only meant for women of rank but now it's become a mark of manhood.'

It was certainly masculine. Zoe couldn't her take her eyes off Teo. She watched him run towards the surf, splash through the shallows and dive through a bigger wave. And then he was swimming, parallel to the shore, with a powerful overarm stroke that made his body move at an impressive speed.

She was still watching as he came out of the water and she was close enough to see the water dripping from the thick waves of his hair. The way his big, brown body glistened and the wet board shorts clung, leaving very little to the imagination.

The tribal tattoo *was* a work of art, she realised. As much a part of Teo as the rest of his rich, vibrant culture. And it was ultimately masculine. The mark of a warrior.

And from somewhere so deep within Zoe it took some moments to recognise what it was came the unfurling of physical desire.

An attraction more powerful than anything she had ever experienced. Or was it just because she'd been totally incapable of feeling the slightest interest in men since her life had been turned upside down by her pregnancy and then the depression?

Maybe it had something to do with the feeling of belonging to this group of people. This extended family. And it was more to do with something waking up inside her. A joyful thing that had not only been buried under the hopelessness of depression but had never really been there in the first place.

It wasn't as if it could go anywhere. This wasn't even any kind of a date, Zoe reminded herself, trying to drag her gaze away from Teo as he strode steadily closer and her heart rate picked up noticeably. He had offered to let her borrow his family, nothing more than that. Distraction was probably needed here.

'I think I'll take you up on that offer of the sarong,' she said to Alisi. 'I'd love to see what Emma thinks of getting her feet wet.'

The swim had been both relaxing and energising but it always left Teo with a poignant sense of homesickness.

He had seawater in his blood but it was never the same here. The water was so much colder and the surf wilder. The lagoons and gentle, sometimes barely there, waves of his boyhood beaches were central to his happiest memories of a time when life had been perfect.

When his mother had still been there, happy and healthy and waiting to enfold him in her love whenever life was difficult to cope with. His closest family. His strength.

Teo shook the sadness off, along with more water from his hair. He caught drips on his chin with his tongue and tasted the salt. At least he could get to the sea here. Finn Kennedy swam every day in a pool near the Kirribilli View apartments. He had invited Teo to join him more than once but for Teo, swimming in such an artificial environment would be soul destroying. Pools were akin to growing bonsai trees or something. A kind of travesty of the real thing.

The pools built into the sides of the cliffs along this coastline were different. The edges were carved from the same wild rocks that surrounded the manmade area. The waves filled them and kept them fresh and clear and salty. He could see people in the closest pool with their young children, teaching them to swim. The tide was well out now, exposing other rocks down on the sand and filling hollows to make shallow pools that would be warm from the sun.

He could also see Zoe and Alisi down there with their babies. Zoe had changed into a *lavalava*. She had it knotted just above her breasts and had tucked the ends up into her knickers. Her legs were long and pale and…very eye catching. Teo caught himself smiling. Good grief…was he feeling attracted to Zoe? That wouldn't do at all, considering he'd offered her a family outing as nothing more than a friend. Maybe his pleasure in watching her was simply because his idea had been so successful. It looked as though Zoe and his favourite cousin were becoming fast friends and, while she had looked a bit tense and shy to start with today, she was certainly far more relaxed now.

Emma was wearing her sunhat but nothing else. Little Kali was completely naked. Zoe seemed to be following Alisi's example, holding Emma upright under her arms and letting her feet catch the very last curl of surf as the long, low waves rolled in. He heard the shriek of an excited baby and the soft sound of feminine laughter and both the sight of the women and the sound of their pleasure was another nostalgic tug.

'Come on, Sefa. Maru? You want to come for a paddle?'

'Yes! Piggyback, Uncle Teo,' demanded Maru.

'Me too! Me too!' cried Sefa.

Teo grinned. '*E leai se popole*. No worries. You can both climb on board.'

He took both small boys out into deeper water and made his body into a raft for them to cling to. Maru, at four years old, could already swim like a little fish in calm water but he wasn't ready for the kind of rogue wave Coogee could throw in. Or the rips that lurked like an undersea monster, waiting to drag people away. Sefa was only two and Teo kept an arm loosely around the small, brown body at all times. There was a lot of splashing and laughter and Teo knew that both Alisi and Zoe were watching them.

And he liked that. He especially liked that Zoe was watching him. It could have contributed to how short the swim with the boys was because when he led them out of the waves, with one small hand in each of his, he took them to where the women were, in the rocks that extended out from the walls of the pool.

The tide was on the way back in now. Soon it would be time to pack up and head home but there were more moments of pleasure to be found. Like this one, where Alisi and Zoe were sitting beside the rocks with their babies on the sand beside them. They were protected by the rocks but these were wild rocks and there was no concrete to fill the gaps. When the waves came in and curled up against the barrier, there were gaps that let the sea water through, like fat hoses being turned on. The small, new waves rushed over the sand where they all sat, soaking sarongs and foaming over fat little baby legs.

Kali was giggling every time. So was Emma. And there was the occasional shriek of laughter if the gap between the waves was a little longer than the one before. Emma and Kali would look at each other while they were waiting and grin. Zoe looked up at Teo and smiled.

It was the first *real* smile he had seen her give. One that reached those astonishing green eyes and lit her whole face up with joy. She was loving this time with her baby. Loving being alive.

The idea that he'd found two such different personalities in the same woman had intrigued him. He'd seen the competent professional paramedic and the scared, lonely young mother. This was a third personality. Someone joyful and vibrant and…absolutely gorgeous.

Teo could feel a bubble of something warm and soft getting bigger in his chest. A combination of nostalgia and longing and…*hope*?

Whatever it was, it was cut off abruptly by the scream of a child in pain.

'*Sefa.*'

The small boy had been happily climbing over the rocks surrounding Alisi and Zoe but now he was hunched into a ball, shrieking with agony. His foot was covered in blood. Teo scooped him up and ran to deeper water to wash the blood away so that he could see what he was dealing with. A stubbed toe, probably.

It was. But it was such a bad stub that the big toenail had been almost ripped off. Teo knew that the best thing to do would be to get it off completely. He also knew it would hurt. He loved this little boy. The thought of hurting him made him feel sick.

Lessons well learned from the past were there to draw on. You couldn't help the people you loved if you couldn't keep enough distance to remain professional. Yes, it would hurt to rip the nail off but only for a split second. If he gave in to what his heart told him instead of his brain, Sefa would be in pain for hours and then have the terror of a doctor's surgery or the ED and the pain of a local anaesthetic that would be just as bad as what he was about to do.

Because he had to.

Teo waited for the next wave, so he could hold Sefa's foot under the cold, rushing water. He took a good grip on the edge of the toenail.

'Sorry, buddy,' he murmured.

And then it was done. The sea water cleaned the wound and Sefa had stopped sobbing by the time he carried the child back to his mother. He clung to Teo, his head buried against his shoulder, and even his whimpers had almost stopped by the time he reached Alisi.

'His toenail had to come off,' he explained. 'I did it then, rather than making him wait. We need to dress it but it'll stop hurting soon.'

Alisi nodded, gathering her youngest son into her arms. Teo picked up Kali for her. He could sense that Zoe was watching him carefully. Maybe she thought it was cruel that he hadn't waited until the toe could be anaesthetised to make the procedure painless.

He didn't want to talk about it.

'I think it might be time to go home,' he said. When he looked up, Zoe wasn't watching him any longer. She was wrapping Emma in a towel.

'Yes,' she said, without turning her head. 'I think it is.'

CHAPTER FIVE

THE knocking had started.

Sharply staccato. A sound that came from nowhere in the dark and Finn Kennedy knew there was no escape.

He was trapped.

The nightmare was here yet again.

It always began like this. The crescendo of knocking that was the sound of anti-aircraft fire. The blessed darkness that deep sleep brought was punctured by streaks of bright, white light. The red fireball of a mortally wounded fighter jet spiralling down from on high was merely a background because now the buildings of the army base were shaking. The ground was shaking.

He had to find Isaac.

His younger brother was here somewhere in the army base. The all-consuming urgency with which he had to find and protect his brother was bone deep, honed by so many years of watching out for the only person he truly loved as they'd survived a childhood and adolescence of care homes and trouble.

Thank goodness he was here now. Becoming one of the stooped figures running through the base as the bombs exploded and shrapnel ricocheted from every direction. Finn knew it was only by chance he could save Isaac. This was his last tour of duty and he would soon be a civilian. Safe.

Free to follow his dreams of medicine that wasn't being practised in a war zone.

The nightmare had the cruellest twists, however. Even as he ran now, with the desperate hope of finding Isaac and keeping him safe, he knew that at any moment he would become a victim himself. The blow on his head that was coming would knock him out briefly. The pain from the shrapnel in his body would almost incapacitate him when he regained consciousness.

That wasn't the worst layer of awareness, though. At an even deeper level he also knew that he would get through that pain and fear and be able to struggle on.

To find Isaac.

To hold his beloved brother in his arms as he died.

The grief would always wake him. In sleep, as in life, he could never get past that moment when his ability to feel any kind of emotion died along with Isaac.

Waking never ended the nightmare completely either. The layers were all still there in his head. The sounds and sights and smells. The fear. The grief. They swirled and tormented and there was only one way to try and escape.

An agonised groan escaped Finn as he raised his head from his hands. Throwing the covers off and swinging his legs so he was sitting on the side of his bed was so automatic he hadn't even been aware of the movement. Looking at his bedside clock was always the next step but it was only 3 a.m.

Far too early to go swimming and wash away the remnants of the nightmare with the combination of gruelling exercise and clean, cold water.

But neither could he stay in the confines of this apartment where the nightmare still filled the air and made him feel like he was breathing treacle. Just as well he had a plan B. One that he had used before with good effect.

Kirribilli View apartments had fire-escape stairs. A narrow column on a corner of the building. Flight after flight of bare, concrete steps, lit well enough on each landing to ensure people wouldn't fall and break their necks.

Nobody else used this access by preference, especially at 3 a.m. It was there for emergencies. And nobody else would be crazy enough to run down from the penthouse to the ground-floor exit, turn and take the steps two at a time to get back to the top. A minute or less to catch his breath and he could do it again.

And again.

It always took a while because it wasn't just a matter of shoving the memories dredged up by the nightmare back where they belonged. All the negative effects of the tragedy that had coloured the last ten years of his life tended to surface as well. It was a process that was becoming a habit. The self-recrimination for things he did. The justification for them. They never changed. Finn had learned to live with them.

The first run up and down the unforgiving steps—like the first few laps of the pool—were about burying the bombing raid that had killed Isaac. The second run was always about Lydia—Isaac's wife. The only link left to his brother. The self-recrimination was that he'd used that link. He'd used Lydia until she'd been strong enough to break off their half-hearted relationship.

You only want me because I remind you of Isaac. I need to move on, Finn. I need to start living again.

He'd used a lot of women since Lydia. Who knew why they found him attractive? But he took advantage of that when he needed a reprieve from being so alone. When he needed the release that only sex could bring.

He couldn't even remember all of their names. That recrimination took care of the next uphill slog. Finn was tiring now. Mariette had been a couple of months ago and she'd been happy to break up with him, moving on to better things with that young paediatric doctor. The latest one hadn't been so happy. He'd only broken that off last week and there'd been tears. He'd been unkind to her but he just couldn't stand tears. Such a visible display of weakness. What was he supposed to do about them? Feel sorry for what he'd done or said? Sympathetic for the way someone else felt? Not going to happen. *Couldn't* happen.

Even with Evie?

The rebellious whisper in the back of his head was easy to dismiss. *Especially* with Evie.

Personal relationships of any kind were unacceptable. His interactions with people were based on science and you could only do the greatest good for the greatest number by shutting out the annoying influence of emotional complications.

Finn needed to catch his breath before he reached the top this time. Concrete wasn't a good surface to run on. It jarred his neck and the pain was starting to bite now, radiating into his shoulder. That was good. This was the point he always needed to get to because physical pain was infinitely preferable to mental distress. He'd pushed himself so hard this time he couldn't make it back to the top. He actually needed to lean against the wall for support.

It was then he heard the sound of footsteps approaching from below.

Who the hell would be coming into the apartments at this time of night? By this stairwell?

Teo Tuala, that's who.

'Hey…' To his credit, Teo didn't sound at all disturbed by the sight of Sydney Harbour Hospital's director of surgery in an unlikely place, completely out of breath, at 4 a.m. 'Did you get called in for that nasty MVA, too?'

Wearing his running shorts and an ancient T-shirt? Hardly likely he'd head out looking like this. Still, it was an easy excuse to use.

'I'll go in soon. I was just getting my exercise out of the way.' Finn knew he sounded out of breath. Teo might be looking as laid back as he always did but there was something about the way he was watching Finn right now that made him feel uncomfortable. Breaking eye contact, he tilted his head and rubbed at the back of his neck, turning to make his way up to the next landing.

'Me, too.' Teo was following him. 'I've taken a pledge to use the stairs instead of the lifts.'

When they reached the landing, Teo got to the fire stop door first. He held it open. 'You OK?' he asked quietly.

Finn gave him the look anybody got if they asked a personal question like that but Teo didn't seem cowed.

'You look a bit sore, that's all,' he said. 'You were rubbing your neck a minute ago and now it's your arm.'

God…it was becoming a habit. Maybe he needed to bump up the painkillers.

'It's nothing,' he said dismissively.

'Old war wound?'

'Something like that.' Finn turned away sharply enough to twist something that made him wince. He walked away. 'It's nothing,' he snapped again. 'Get some sleep, Teo. You'll need it if you want to be on top of your game tomorrow.'

'You look like you had a hard night.'

'Yeah…' Teo pushed the button that controlled the pedestrian crossing on this main intersection. 'I should have been a psychologist, shouldn't I?'

'There's certainly something to be said for a nine-to-five job.' John Allen's smile for his neighbour was sympathetic. 'Hope it wasn't anything too traumatic that kept you up.'

'Car crash at midnight. Pregnant woman and three kids involved. Woman ended up going into labour so I hung around to make sure the baby was OK.'

'Was it?'

'Fortunately, yes. Few weeks prem but he should be fine. Hey…Luke…' He turned to greet the man who'd joined them. 'Did you get any sleep?'

'Not enough.'

He didn't look too bothered by it but Luke didn't look bothered by much these days. Still on cloud nine, obviously, thanks to the effects of being so much in love with Lily. Teo didn't see either of them much these days. They stayed out on Luke's farm unless the traffic was too awful or Luke was kept too late, as he had been last night.

The buzzing sound and green signal to cross propelled the men into movement. 'What time did you get in?' John asked Teo.

''Bout 4 a.m. Would you believe I found Finn Kennedy on the fire escape stairs? Looked like he'd been doing a circuit class or something.'

'He likes keeping fit.'

'I like keeping fit, too, but not at that time of night.'

They walked in silence for half a block. The grey sky seemed to be pressing down on Teo and if it rained, it would get cold. Not like in the islands. Alisi had gone home again yesterday and had made him promise to persuade Zoe to go to Samoa for a visit. Would John think that was a good idea? Should he even be talking to a colleague about a patient he had a personal interest in? Certainly not when Luke was there, even if he was a good mate. The interest he had in John's patient was confusing enough, without helpful mates pushing him in a direction he knew it would be unwise to go.

He'd had other things on his mind this morning, anyway.

'What is it with Finn?' he found himself asking. 'How can he handle his patients so well when his interpersonal relationships with everybody else are so bad?'

'You want a professional opinion?'

'Absolutely.'

John grinned. 'I think he has issues.'

'Hey...I could have told *you* that and I'm just a paediatrician.'

'I could have told you that, too,' Luke put in. 'He walked out in the middle of surgery a few weeks ago and left me to carry on. And Evie said something, too.'

'Oh?' Teo was well distracted from thinking about Zoe now and that had to be a good thing. Maybe he was going to find out what that odd undercurrent he'd sensed in Emergency between Finn and Evie was all about.

'She was worried about him.'

'Evie doesn't strike me as a worrying type,' John put in.

'No. That's what I thought, too.'

'What did she say?'

'She had some story about him dropping a clipboard. His hand being shaky. I wasn't listening that carefully, I have to admit. I had something else on my mind.'

'I'll bet.' Teo knew exactly what that 'something else' had probably been—a very attractive, blue-eyed blonde nurse by the name of Lily Ellis.

'She seemed to think we were more than drinking buddies but Finn doesn't let anybody that close, does he?'

'No.' The agreement from the other men was heartfelt.

'He certainly shut me out pretty fast last night,' Teo added.

'I didn't do anything about it,' Luke said. 'Maybe I should have.'

'Maybe you hit the nail on the head by saying you were drinking buddies,' Teo suggested. 'We all know he drinks a lot. Everybody who goes to Pete's knows how hard he can hit the whisky at times. The question is, why?'

'PTSD?' Luke offered.

Both Luke and Teo glanced at John but the psychologist only shrugged.

'He's never talked to me. I doubt that he'd be willing to talk to anyone.'

'No...' Teo could feel himself frowning. 'He looked like he was in pain last night but he wouldn't tell me anything. According to the grapevine, he got injured quite badly just before he left his army post.'

'A grapevine? At the Harbour?' John was grinning again. 'No-o...'

'His last conquest was a paediatric nurse,' Teo told him. 'I found her sobbing in the sluice room and had to hear all about it. Seems she's the latest in a long string of heartbroken females who find our director of surgery very appealing, despite the fact that he's so grumpy and never seems to bother shaving.'

'Very macho.'

'It's no wonder they call our place of work Sydney Scandal Central.' Luke grinned.

Teo chuckled. 'And what's the deal between him and Evie Lockheart?'

'What do you mean?'

'I saw them talking to each other in ED last week and I got the oddest impression that there was something going on. Something personal that didn't fit with what I've heard about the scraps they have.'

'Maybe it's familiar territory for her,' John mused. 'Not that I'm one to gossip but it's common knowledge that she had to battle her father to be able to do medicine in the first place and Richard Lockheart can be a difficult character, by all accounts.'

'Maybe she's attracted to a father figure.' Teo regretted the quip as soon as it left his lips. It was none of his business whether there was any kind of potential relationship going on between a pair of the Harbour's better-known staff members. He didn't want to go down the track of discussing such a possibility, either, because if he did, he might be steered into considering a far more personal attraction that was creating ripples in his own life right now. Good grief…he just couldn't stop thinking about Zoe for more than five minutes, could he?

'If Finn Kennedy's her choice, then good luck to her,' John said.

'Professional opinion?' Another joke seemed a good way to lighten the sudden tension Teo was aware of.

'Could be the making of the man,' Luke said, with the slightly smug air of a man who'd found exactly what he hadn't even been looking for.

'Of course.' But John didn't seem to be paying any real attention to the conversation now. He was looking beyond Teo. Towards an apartment block that was far older and more rundown than the Kirribilli View apartments.

'Oh, my God!' he said, the tone of dismay increasing with each word. 'Is that *smoke*?'

CHAPTER SIX

SYDNEY'S Kangaroo Day Care centre was one of the best.

The facility catered for babies and children aged from six weeks to five years and it had a great carer to child ratio. Zoe had never had the slightest qualms about leaving Emma there. It had, in fact, been a relief to start handing her child over on a regular basis when she'd gone back to part-time work. It meant that Emma was frequently in the care of these devoted professionals who knew far more about it all than she did. Not only did she get a reprieve from the difficult task of being a single parent, she got to go back to her old job for a good stretch of time. Back to being the old Zoe.

But something had changed.

Today, as she'd left Emma in another woman's arms and turned to leave, she'd felt a distinct qualm.

A small niggle, maybe, but enough for Zoe to turn and take another look at her daughter before going out through the rainbow-painted doors of the day-care centre with their round porthole windows.

It was guilt, she decided, driving towards the start of her shift at the Harbourside ambulance station. It wasn't as if Emma was crying or anything. On the contrary, she'd been smiling at the woman giving her a cuddle. And that background buzz of guilt should be something that Zoe was more than used to by now.

She'd felt guilty about getting pregnant in the first place. How stupid had she been to let that happen in this day and age? She felt even more guilty for considering the option of terminating the pregnancy but, most of all, she'd felt guilty for not feeling the way a mother should feel when her baby was born.

For not loving her child with all her heart and soul.

So, yes…Zoe was used to feeling guilty. So why did that pang on leaving Emma behind this morning feel different somehow?

Not that she wanted to waste time at work pondering something that was no part of her professional life but the day started by conspiring against her. It was unusually quiet and Tom wanted to chat as they went through the normal routine of making sure their ambulance was fully equipped and operational.

'We need more lancets for the blood glucose kit,' he noted. 'Did you have a good weekend?'

'It was great.'

'What'd you get up to?'

'I got invited to a barbecue at Coogee.'

'Nice weather for it.'

'It was. Fabulous.' Zoe went to the storeroom to get a handful of the tiny plastic devices that held needles for pricking fingers and testing drops of blood for sugar levels.

It *had* been a fabulous day, even though it had ended on a vaguely disturbing note with poor little Sefa having that toe-stubbing incident. Teo had seemed slightly distant on the way home, too. Still perfectly relaxed and friendly but Zoe had had the definite impression that a shutter or two had gone up. The horrible thought occurred to her that he might have somehow sensed her attraction to him and was letting her know that it was pointless. The thought was enough to ensure that she probably seemed equally distant.

In any case, it couldn't spoil what the day had given her. She'd heard her baby laugh for the first time. Such an amazing sound of undiluted joy—as if it didn't matter how hard Zoe was finding it to be a parent or that Emma was missing out on what every other mother seemed to be able to give their child naturally. It was impossible to hear the sound of baby laughter and not feel an echo of that joy yourself. And it was an echo that had stayed with her for the few days until she'd been rostered back on at work. The last of it had probably only gone this morning, when she'd had that odd qualm.

Even now, when she remembered Emma smiling at the woman from Kangaroo's, the qualm came back. Maybe it had something to do with the fact that it was someone else that Emma was smiling at, not her. Jealousy?

How ridiculous. Her baby had beamed at everyone on the day of the barbecue. She'd even giggled when Alisi had been tickling her toes the day the two women had gone shopping for jeans at Bondi Junction together. She hadn't felt jealous then. She'd felt…good grief…*happy*?

She was happy now, Zoe reminded herself firmly. At work. Able to do the things she'd trained so hard to be able to do. She had the next twelve hours to be professional. Ready for anything. In control.

A mental note was called for here, Zoe decided as she turned her attention to making good use of their quiet time by cleaning the ambulance thoroughly. Heavens…look at the way dust could accumulate so fast around the regulators on the big oxygen cylinders.

Yes. She made a note to tell John Allen in her next session how well everything was going. She could tell him with absolute honesty that she was experiencing moments of real happiness again for the first time since this whole nightmare had started. That she could see light at the end of the tunnel and knew that, one day, she would be well again.

She wouldn't tell him about that confusing little qualm, though. Zoe didn't want anybody telling her that the road to happiness lay with being a mother and not getting back to being the person she'd been before she'd got pregnant. She couldn't be a full-time mother. She'd just get sucked back into that dark place and it would be far, far worse for Emma than being left in the lovely, caring environment of Kangaroo Day Care.

Zoe stopped wiping and polishing surfaces and decided to take out all of the towels from their locker and refold them. She was saved from this mindless task, however, by the sound of her pager. She'd only started reading the message when Tom appeared at a run.

'Local job,' he called. 'Standby for the fire service. There's an apartment block on fire.'

It was her turn to drive. Zoe slid into the seat, pushed the remote to open the huge roller door to the station and started the engine. She activated the beacons as they cleared the door and hit the siren as soon as she turned onto the road.

No qualms now. This might not be a moment of pure joy but the satisfaction of heading towards a challenging job was just as good. Better, in fact, because she'd know exactly what to do when she got there.

There were still people trapped.

Three fire engines were on site now and there were police cordoning off streets, controlling traffic and bystanders. A police helicopter was hovering overhead as well, or was it a news crew filming the incident? It wouldn't be a rescue chopper because they were so close to the Harbour. There were ambulances here anyway, off to one side and well away from the danger of smoke inhalation or falling debris.

Was Zoe here? Part of Teo hoped she was because he wanted to see her again but a bigger part of him hoped she was safely at home. With Emma. Teo headed in the direction of the burning apartment block anyway, in case extra medical assistance was needed. Luke was beside him and had almost tripped on a coil of black hose unfurling beside a fire truck.

'Watch out for the hoses.'

Teo could only nod. If he tried to say anything, he'd start coughing again.

It had been John who'd alerted the emergency services when he'd spotted smoke curling from a window on one of the building's upper floors. Teo and Luke had rushed into the apartment block, going in different directions to bang on doors and yell to raise the alarm.

Teo had been driven by something like fury when he'd run upstairs to the second floor. The building might be too old and rundown to have any kind of sprinkler system but there was no excuse for it not to have smoke detectors and an efficient alarm sounding to warn goodness only knew how many people who needed to escape.

He'd sent a young mother and her pyjama-clad children running downstairs to safety. Then he'd found some foreign students who were confused and frightened but could at least get out by themselves. The elderly man he'd come across next had needed help to get down the stairs. Teo had turned back to get to the third floor but he couldn't get very far. There was smoke billowing down the staircase by now and he could hear the crackle of flames from above and Luke yelling from below.

'The fire service is here. They're getting ladders to the top floors. They said to get out.' He could hear Luke coughing harshly. '*Now*, Teo.'

Teo had no choice. He'd covered his mouth and nose with his arm but he could already feel the smoke biting into his lungs and his eyes were stinging. He passed firemen wearing breathing apparatus and carrying axes as he made his way outside. The right people were on the job now. He'd done all he could inside.

They might be needed outside, anyway. The area around the ambulances was busy.

And Zoe *was* here. In charge of the scene. Why did that surprise him when she'd been wearing that scene commander's vest the first time he'd seen her? Maybe it was because he'd met the other Zoes since then. The unhappy young mother. The beautiful young woman wearing a sarong on the beach…

'We'll treat it as cardiac,' he heard her saying to another paramedic. 'Usual protocol and transport immediately.'

The elderly man he'd helped down the stairs was on a stretcher, clearly short of breath. He had an oxygen mask on his face and the leads from a life pack attached to his chest. They were about to load him into one of the ambulances but he saw Teo and stretched out his hand. He pulled his oxygen mask off with his other hand.

'Thank you,' he croaked. 'Wouldn't have…got out… without you.'

'No worries.' Teo grasped the man's hand and smiled. He could feel Zoe pause and turn to stare.

'Teo! What are you doing here?'

'I was on my way to work. We spotted the fire.'

'And you went *inside*?'

'He got me out,' the elderly man said. 'Carried me... down the stairs.' His face twisted in pain and Zoe's gaze flicked instantly to the life pack.

'ST depression,' she snapped. 'Give him some more GTN and get a line in. He needs some morphine. Has he had aspirin?'

Teo stepped back as ambulance staff moved quickly to follow directions. He could see one of the students sitting on the back steps of an ambulance, crying. Someone was checking her ankle, which looked swollen. Turning his head, Teo could see a high ladder close to where the worst of the flames were. The shadowy figure of a fireman appeared in the closest window and something was shoved into the arms of the fireman still on the tiny platform at the top of the ladder. A bundle that looked like a baby.

Despite overseeing the management of the cardiac chest pain the old man was having, Zoe had seen it as well. She looked away from where the fireman was descending the ladder swiftly and caught Teo's gaze.

'You planning on hanging around for a bit?'

'You want me to?'

Her gaze clung to his for a heartbeat. She smiled. 'Please.'

She could manage perfectly well without him but she wanted him to stay. It was a little disturbing how good that made Teo feel but he didn't get much time to think about it. The fireman was on the ground now, running towards them. Zoe pointed to the open back of an ambulance and seconds later Teo was crowded in there, with Zoe and her partner and the firemen looking on as they tried to resuscitate a baby who was probably about the same age as Zoe's Emma.

The baby didn't appear to be burned but had inhaled enough smoke to go into respiratory and then cardiac arrest. Teo was given the task of finding a vein in the tiny hand as Tom and Zoe worked flat out, doing CPR and readying the defibrillator to try and shock a small heart back into action. The first attempt wasn't successful but they all knew this was just the beginning. No way would they give up on trying to save such a young life.

'We think we've got everybody accounted for,' a fireman said from the door. 'And the fire's almost under control. The baby's mother was downstairs, putting the rubbish out. She's pretty hysterical. There's a guy who says he's a psychologist looking after her. Want me to bring her over?'

'Not yet,' Zoe said. 'Maybe she could meet us at the hospital instead.'

'It'll be John Allen who's with her,' Teo said. 'He was walking to work with me and Luke. He'll take care of her.'

'If the scene's under control, I can step down. Find someone to drive us,' Zoe ordered the fireman. 'We'll transport under CPR. Teo—any luck finding a vein?'

'Still working on it.' Teo had the baby's hand bent over his fingers, stretching the skin on the back of it. He slid the needle in carefully and was rewarded with the flash of blood in the chamber that told him he was in the right place. He slid the cannula home. 'Got it.'

'Good. Stand clear. Shocking again.'

Zoe swapped places with Tom as extra crew members joined them. One climbed into the driver's seat to take the ambulance to the emergency department. Another was there to take over chest compressions. Zoe was preparing to intubate the baby now and Tom was drawing up drugs. It was crowded in there but Teo stayed where he was near the door. Zoe looked pale. Was it his imagination or did her hand shake just a little as she positioned the laryngoscope and the tube she needed to get into place?

Teo edged closer. 'How's it looking?' he asked quietly. It would be no easy task intubating a young child who might well have an airway swollen from heat damage and smoke.

'Can't see a thing,' Zoe said tersely. 'I'll have to go blind.'

The attempt was unsuccessful. Zoe looked up and Teo could see that this might very well be too much for her to handle. Of course it was. She was a mother and with the age of this child it had to feel like she was working on her own daughter. Unthinkably difficult.

'Let me try.' He didn't give her time to protest. He was, after all, the most qualified person here to be doing this and Zoe didn't need to know it was because he understood that she couldn't handle it emotionally—not that she was incompetent professionally. He'd be exactly the same if he had a baby of his own.

Just as well he didn't. And never would.

Zoe hesitated, though. Teo actually had to push her hand out of the way to take hold of the laryngoscope. He could feel how tense she was but this was a tense situation. He still managed to keep his voice perfectly calm.

'A guide wire would be good, if you've got one.'

She did. The tube slipped into place. By the time he'd checked the position of the tube and given the baby a couple of good squirts of oxygen with the bag mask, it was time to try defibrillating the infant again. They were also by this time pulling into the emergency department of the Harbour.

They got a rhythm. They took a few minutes before opening the doors to make sure the baby's condition was reasonably stable. It appeared to be, so as they unloaded the stretcher Teo stepped back. There were plenty of expert hands waiting to take over management inside the doors of the ED. He felt a hand grip his shoulder.

'You're a mess,' Luke said. 'Covered in soot. And have you seen what your clothes look like?'

Teo looked at his colleague and had to smile. 'Hey, you're not looking any better, mate.'

'Shall we find a shower and some scrubs?'

'Good idea. And then I want to check on how that little guy is doing.'

'I heard about him from one of the fire guys. Also heard that you and that cute paramedic made a good team. Going to follow up?'

'You mean on the kid? Already said that, didn't I?'

'No, you idiot.' Luke was grinning. 'I meant the cute paramedic. She's still in there now, isn't she?'

'Probably.' Teo wasn't going to let Luke know just how much he was tempted to muscle in on the team that would be at work in one of the resus rooms. To find a moment to let Zoe know that he understood how difficult the case must have been for her and tell her what a good job she had done. 'Might clean myself up first.'

He left it too late. By the time he went back into the emergency department, the only familiar face from that morning's incident he could see was that of John. He was with a white-faced young woman who had her arms wrapped tightly around her body, as if she were afraid something might break if she let go.

'This is Chloe,' John told Teo. 'Matthew's mum. Mattie's the baby who got rescued from the fire.'

Teo stilled as he heard Chloe suck in a very shaky breath.

'Teo's the doctor who was working with the paramedics to save Matthew,' he told Chloe.

One paramedic in particular, Teo thought. Only one

came to mind, anyway... A hint of a smile tugged at his lips. And they'd saved Mattie? He was doing OK?

'Thank you,' Chloe whispered. 'I...don't know what I would have done if...' Her voice trailed into a stifled sob.

'We're just going in to see how well he's doing.' John's raised eyebrow invited Teo to join them.

The doctor on duty was Mia McKenzie. Her long blonde hair was tied in a neat ponytail and she was listening to the baby's chest with a stethoscope. An anaesthetist was beside her, checking the settings on a ventilator.

Mia unhooked her stethoscope as she straightened and smiled at Chloe. 'I know this still looks scary but we're keeping Matthew asleep for a little while, until we know that he'd going to be able to manage his breathing on his own.'

Chloe nodded, her lips trembling. 'Is he...will he be...?'

'Babies are remarkably resilient,' Mia said. 'I'm confident he's on the road to recovery. He's going to go up to the intensive care unit now and they'll want to keep him there at least overnight so they can give him the best possible care.'

'Can I go with him?'

'Of course.' It was Teo who spoke. He turned to Mia. 'My team's on take today. I'll go up with him if he's ready?'

They both took another look at the readings on the monitors. Things were looking stable and Mia had every reason to sound as confident as she had.

'He's good to go.' She nodded. 'Thanks, Teo.'

'What's wrong?'

'What do you mean, what's wrong?' Zoe gave Tom a sideways glance. 'Isn't it enough that we're stuck in rush-hour traffic, going to what's probably a non-urgent medical job that'll we'll most likely have to transport when we're due to get off shift in exactly...' she checked her watch '...three minutes?'

'It's sure been a crazy day. Should have known things would turn to custard after such a quiet start.'

It had been one job after another ever since the callout to that apartment block fire. Barely any down time for lunch or replenishing supplies. There shouldn't have been any time or energy available for anything else but Tom was right. Zoe had things on her mind.

Disturbing things.

Like when she'd seen Teo at that first job today. It had been so unexpected and it had caught her unawares; her body had reacted a split second before her head had. That tiny curl of sensation in her belly had come with a clear image of seeing Teo emerge from the surf the other day, sun gleaming on warm, brown skin. Wet board shorts clinging to impressively muscular thighs. That hint of a wild edge that his tattoo bestowed.

The shaft of desire was even stronger than the qualm she'd had on leaving Emma that morning. It was a sensation that demanded recognition in the same way that those other feelings had for days, now, when an echo of her baby's laughter captured her. Feelings that were like pinpricks of light coming through holes in a dark curtain. Zoe was accustomed to being in that dark place and the light was full of swirling dust motes.

Unwelcome? No.

Confusing? Definitely.

Part of her wished she could turn the clock back a year or more and that she could have met Teo when her life had been...normal. But she wouldn't have really met him, then, would she? He might have been present at that car accident but he hadn't stepped into her life until he'd rescued her in the waiting room that day. He'd rescued her again today, come to that. When she'd been faced with a task that had suddenly been overwhelming.

'I'm just a bit peeved, that's all,' she muttered aloud.

More like frustrated. Frightened, even. OK, trying to intubate that baby that morning would have been a challenge and, yes, she'd had a bit of a wobble when she'd looked down at the little face and imagined that it was Emma instead of a stranger's child, but she would have got over it if she'd been given half a chance. She would have had to because the prospect of failing was terrifying. If she couldn't do her job properly, what did she have to hang onto that was still the person she remembered herself being? And now she couldn't know if she would have coped because Teo had stepped in and taken over. Shown her how it was done.

'What about?'

'I could have done that intubation this morning. Why do doctors think they can just take over like that?'

'Hey, the guy's a paediatric consultant, isn't he?'

'Yes.'

'So he was the best person for the job. What's the problem…you had something to prove?'

He *had* been the best person for the job and of course Zoe had wanted the best outcome for her patient but…how did he do it? Keeping a professional distance so easily? Did it come with the territory when you had to deal with small, sick children all the time? Kids were clearly a huge part of his life, both at work and at home. He wouldn't get a whole bunch of them following him around as if he was the Pied Piper or something, like he had at that barbecue, unless the love went both ways. And Emma had been the reason he'd stepped into her life in the waiting room. Not her. She needed to remember that, when her stupid reawakening hormones were making her feel things she wasn't ready to feel.

'Yeah…I guess.' Zoe pushed her thoughts away with a sigh. 'I still feel a bit rusty. And paeds cases are always that bit more intense.'

'Must be even more intense when you're a parent yourself.'

Maybe that was it. The reason why Teo could cope so well with children. This was just a wobble because it was the first paediatric case Zoe had had since she'd had her own child. Teo didn't have kids of his own and didn't seem to want any. Alisi had told her that.

'He won't even keep a girlfriend for more than a few weeks,' she'd confided sadly. 'I think my *ui* are going to be the closest thing to his own children that that cousin of mine will ever get.'

'*Ui?*'

'Piglets.' Alisi had dissolved into laughter at Zoe's expression. 'But in a nice way.'

'Here we are.' Tom's announcement was a welcome dead end for the intrusion of personal thoughts. 'Let's hope this isn't another paeds case for you.'

It wasn't. It was an eighty-seven-year-old woman called Agnes who'd had 'a bit of a turn' but had no intention of being taken to hospital.

'Your blood pressure's a bit low,' Zoe told her. 'And your heart rate's a bit too fast. You really need to get checked properly at the hospital.'

'I stay away from doctors, dear. Don't like them.'

'She went a horrible colour,' the neighbour who'd called the ambulance told them. 'All grey and pasty. I'm sure she would have fainted if I hadn't made her lie down.'

'I don't faint,' Agnes said firmly. 'Never have.'

'I think you came pretty close,' Zoe said. She was

watching the screen of the life pack. 'You sure you don't have any pain anywhere?'

'I'm a bit short of puff, that's all.'

Zoe caught Tom's eye as he handed her the nasal cannulae so they could give Agnes some oxygen. It was probably only a mild heart attack that Agnes was suffering but there was no way they could leave her at home, and it could take some time to persuade her to come with them.

They were going to be late home tonight.

It was lucky that the Kangaroo Day Care centre was so accommodating. Zoe gave them a quick call when they were finally transporting Agnes to hospital.

'Emma's fine,' someone told her. 'There's no rush. We're open till 8 p.m., remember.'

Which gave Zoe an opportunity she'd been waiting for all day.

'I just want to pop up to the PICU,' she told Tom, when they'd handed the care of Agnes to the team in the emergency department. 'I want to check on what's happening to that baby we resuscitated this morning.'

'I'd like to know too.' Tom was more than happy to hang around a bit longer. 'We're off shift. I can grab a coffee in the staffroom.'

'Wouldn't have anything to do with that cute blonde nurse I saw you watching today, would it?'

Tom grinned. 'Go away, Zoe.'

'You'd better work fast. I won't be long.'

Teo was in the unit.

Zoe should have been prepared for that. Prepared for that swirl of conflicting emotions that were clearly going to happen every time she saw him. Only…she'd never seen him wearing scrubs before. The pale blue tunic top left most of his arms bare. The tattoo was hidden but Zoe knew it was there and knowing that made it feel oddly intimate. As if she had a small part of him that no one else around here did. The pleasure that came with the notion was another one of those disturbing feelings. Maybe she shouldn't have come here but it was too late to slip away. Teo had noticed her arrival as he looked away from the conversation he was having with another doctor near the central desk.

'Zoe…good grief, are you *still* on duty?'

'Just finished. I wanted to find out how our case from this morning is doing.'

'Good timing. We were reviewing him just now. Wendy, this is Zoe Harper. She was in charge of the resus on scene for Matthew.'

'I can't take the credit,' Zoe said, avoiding Teo's gaze. 'It was lucky Teo was there.'

Wendy's gaze travelled swiftly from Zoe to Teo and then back again. She smiled. 'Good team effort, then,' she said. 'He's doing well. We've got him sedated and ventilated to monitor his gas exchange closely overnight but we're pretty happy, aren't we, Teo?'

'Yes…I'd like to see a bit more movement on that end tidal CO_2, though. Do you think—?'

Zoe turned away as the doctors began discussing the technicalities of the respiratory support the baby was getting. She could see him, through the clear glass of one of the partitions. A tiny figure, lost on the expanse of crisp, white sheet. Naked, except for a nappy and a spaghetti junction of monitor wires and IV lines.

His mother was sitting beside the bed, holding one of the baby's hands. She didn't see Zoe staring because her gaze was fixed on her child and Zoe could understand why. If that had been Emma lying there, she'd be doing the same thing. Touching her child. Willing her to get through this and survive.

A sudden tightness in her chest moved up to constrict her throat and, to her horror, Zoe could feel the prickle of tears behind her eyes. She blinked and cleared her throat. That made Teo look at her again.

'Did you want to go and say hello to Matthew's mother? I'm sure Chloe would love to be able to thank you.'

Zoe shook her head. 'Not right now. I have to get going. It's way past time for me to be collecting Emma from day care. We had a late job.'

'I'll walk down with you. It's time I was heading home myself.'

Zoe found herself feeling more and more tense as they walked in silence to the elevators. She punched the button.

'Thanks for your help today,' she said, finally breaking what had become an awkward silence, her tone cool.

She could feel the surprised glance Teo sent in her direction. 'No worries,' he murmured. 'It was a tricky intubation.'

'I could have done it, you know.' Zoe stared at the light above the elevator, waiting for it to glow. 'I was about to use a guide wire myself.'

'Would you rather I hadn't offered to help?'

The puzzled note in Teo's voice made her turn her head. Dark, dark brown eyes were watching her. Pulling her in.

'No, of course not.' Zoe swallowed. 'You were the most qualified person there. I just…didn't want you thinking that I was…incapable or something.'

'I would never think that.' The sincerity was palpable. 'In fact, I probably think you're capable of more than *you* think you're capable of.'

She was staring at him as the lift arrived with a 'ping'

and the doors opened. They stepped in. The doors closed, shutting them into a small space. Alone. Together.

Zoe sucked in a breath. 'I don't understand.'

'You're a skilled paramedic,' Teo said calmly. 'That's not what I'm talking about.'

'So what did you mean?' Zoe knew her tone was sharp. 'That I'm not a capable mother? Or…that because I'm a mother I'm less capable of doing my job or something? Is *that* why you took over this morning?'

Teo's breath came out in something like a sigh. 'OK, I did think you might be finding it tough dealing with a baby who was Emma's age. That it might be a bit close to home.'

'That baby was Kali's age, too. Did that bother *you*?'

'I'm used to it.' There was a curious shuttered appearance to Teo's face now. A barrier was up. It was an expression Zoe had seen before. On the beach, when he had dealt with the unpleasant task of causing pain to little Sefa by pulling off the damaged toenail.

And Zoe recognised that barrier. It was the way she felt about Emma. As though she was looking through a clear wall. Dealing with a baby that wasn't really hers. But she had no choice about that barrier being there. If she knew how to get rid of it, she would. Why would anybody want to keep it up?

Because that way they could do the kind of job that Teo did. They could have done Zoe's job this morning without the slightest wobble.

Was that what Teo meant by saying she was capable of more than she thought? Did he think she could take control of that barrier so that she could put it up at will?

Zoe wasn't sure she wanted to. That flash of feeling an empathy with both the baby and his mother had been… real. One of those pinpricks of light coming into the dark place. She couldn't pick and choose, could she? If she wanted to get mentally healthy and back to being who she wanted to be, she couldn't just choose to feel the good stuff. Like physical desire. Or baby laughter.

Dammit. It had been a long day and Teo was making her feel more confused than ever. Zoe didn't like it.

'You've got something against working mothers, haven't you?'

Teo shrugged. 'Doesn't seem ideal but maybe that's just because of the way I was brought up.'

'Emma loves day care.'

'And you're happy leaving her there?'

The elevator had stopped again. They got out and both walked in the same direction, towards the emergency department.

'I'm happy to be back at my job. Six months' maternity leave was enough.'

Teo shook his head. 'I don't think you've had maternity leave,' he said quietly. 'Maybe that's the problem.'

'What?' He thought she still had a problem? That made her feel…small in some way. Undesirable.

'You had sick leave,' he said carefully. 'Maybe maternity leave is exactly what you need now.'

Zoe's breath left her in an incredulous huff. Being told she still had a problem stung. She wanted to tell him to butt out. That it wasn't any of his business.

But she'd made it his business, hadn't she? The moment she'd shoved Emma into his arms in the waiting room that day. When she'd agreed to go to his family gathering in case there was a secret of some kind that Samoans instinctively knew when it came to caring for and loving babies.

She couldn't say anything in the end so she just glared at Teo instead.

He simply smiled. 'Alisi was practically in tears at the

airport yesterday, begging me to persuade you to come and visit.'

Zoe believed him. It had been the main topic of conversation on the shopping trip and she'd already had a text message from Alisi when she'd got home, to say that people were expecting her. Looking forward to meeting Teo's friend Zoe and her baby. Had it been at Teo's instigation?

'You're a lot better now,' Teo continued. 'If you had some real time with your baby, you might find the bond is a lot stronger than you think. That's what I meant.' His tone was gentle now. 'I think you're capable of being a fantastic mother but I think you're trying too hard at the moment. To be the best at everything. A few days in the sun with Alisi and you could really relax. You might even find that it's all a lot easier than you think.'

With a curl to his smile that made it almost a wink, Teo turned away, heading for the staff locker rooms. 'Think about it,' he called over his shoulder. 'There're some cheap flights going at the moment. I've just booked a few for myself.'

Zoe was left staring after him.

He made it sound so *easy*. As if there were no problems, only solutions.

And maybe he was right.

Things had changed for her since the barbecue. That was when the new feelings had begun to filter though into the numb place that was her soul.

Unbidden, an image of a tropical island came to mind. White sand beaches and palm trees. The sound of singing and laughter. A glorious sunset with the silhouette of two people walking hand-in-hand on the beach.

Lovers.

She and Teo?

This yearning was a new feeling, too. Powerful. Disturbing.

Think about it? Dream about it, more likely.

And Zoe knew she was going to find it impossible not to.

CHAPTER SEVEN

It was coincidence that both Teo and Zoe ended up on the island at the same time.

Or was it?

Zoe had known that he visited regularly to help out at the hospital. She had known that he'd taken advantage of those cheap flights and they were only available for narrow windows of time. She hadn't asked him if he'd be there when she'd impulsively booked tickets of her own the next day. How could she have, when she hadn't even seen him? She hadn't been at work and she'd been far too busy, anyway, organising a passport for Emma and getting packed. It seemed a huge effort to go to for just a few days away but Zoe had checked in with John to ask if he thought it was a good idea.

John had been enthusiastic. John was a friend of Teo's. Alisi was Teo's favourite cousin. There was no way he couldn't have known that Zoe was here in his homeland. If he'd wanted to avoid her, he could have done so very easily.

But here he was, walking towards where she was sitting under the shade of a palm tree on the beach. A good percentage of the village seemed to be accompanying him. Everybody aged under ten, anyway. He was wearing his board shorts and nothing else but that gorgeous smile of his.

Zoe's breath caught in her throat and her heart rate picked up with a thump. The fantasy of being on a tropical island with this man had been just that. A fantasy.

Until now.

'Hey… *Talofa*, Zoe. The kids told me I'd find you down here somewhere.'

The children were all staring at her with big brown eyes and wide, triumphant smiles.

Even a simple greeting failed Zoe. She could only nod and smile back. She was basking in Teo's gaze. What did he see? One of her own new sarongs—a lovely dark green one with huge, white frangipani flowers on it. Bare, sandy feet. Skin that had taken on a hint of a tan but not without paying the price of far too many new freckles. Hair that was wildly curly thanks to sea salt and soft breezes. A hibiscus flower tucked behind her ear.

Teo was grinning broadly now. Leaning down towards her. His hand brushed her hair and Zoe could swear her heart actually stopped beating.

'Didn't anybody tell you which ear to put this in? The left side says you're married.' He pulled the stalk of the flower from her hair. 'The right side says you're single.' He threaded the stalk into the curls over her right ear. 'Available, even,' he added in a wicked murmur.

Zoe's mouth had gone very, very dry.

Was she available? For Teo?

Oh…yes…

Did he want her?

She had absolutely no idea. He was here, on the island, where he must have known he could find her, but there didn't seem to be any intimate message hidden in his gaze right now. He was relaxed and friendly and so…solid. So…

Teo. A human rock. Just being close to him made Zoe feel safe. As if she could take on the world and succeed.

'It's great you could get here,' he said. 'Do you like it?'

'I love it.'

Simple words that didn't begin to say how much these few days had given her. A new way of life. A new family. Paradise.

Maybe the words hadn't said that much but something in her face or tone must have told Teo much more. His smile softened.

'I knew you would.'

The children had got over that shyness that Zoe always seemed to instil for a minute or two. Now she was one of them again and their attention was on Teo. They were talking. Clamouring. Tugging at Teo's hands and legs.

'We're going for a swim,' he said. 'Want to join us?'

The thought of shedding her sarong to reveal her bikini made Zoe feel as shy as the children had been a moment ago. She ducked her head.

'I should get back to the village. Emma's probably awake again by now.'

'From what I saw, a fight will probably break out amongst the woman over who gets the privilege of looking after her this time.'

It was true. Zoe almost had to beg to get a turn with her daughter. Except for night-time, when they lay cuddled together on their soft mat to sleep.

'Alisi said you were staying in the *fale*. She did tell you that you were welcome to use my house, didn't she?' Teo was being swept away by a small sea of children. 'It has walls, you know.'

Zoe smiled. 'I'm right at home in the *fale*, thanks. I like being with everybody else.'

At home in the traditional, thatched roof dwelling that

Alisi shared with her husband and children and extended family.

At home on this beautiful island.

At home. At peace.

'Come swimming with us,' Teo called.

She wanted to. She even got to her feet but something was holding her back. Had Teo expected her to stay alone in the house he had here, tucked amongst the tropical forest on a private beach? To be there, alone, when he came to visit?

Hope was the most delicious sensation. Exciting.

Dangerous because it could be trampled on and broken.

Zoe shook her head. 'I need to go and help with the *umu*,' she called back. 'They must have forgotten to tell me it's for your "welcome home" party.'

The village feast wasn't a 'welcome home' party for him. Preparations had begun well before Teo had arrived and no one had been expecting him today. Why would they, when one of his routine visits to help out at the hospital was only a week or two away? Not that they weren't used to him juggling tickets at the last minute when roster changes or something cropped up.

The impetus for this trip had sneaked up on him rather more slowly than the kind of things that usually prompted travel rearrangements. The excited text from Alisi the very day after he'd suggested that Zoe visit the islands had been more than satisfying. Zoe would love this place and a holiday, even if it was apparently only for a few days, would do both her and Emma the world of good.

It had been a couple of days later, when he'd known they'd arrived safely, that Teo had found himself becoming more and more distracted from his work. Thinking, way too often, about the Zoe he'd seen that day on the beach in Coogee. Imagining her with the backdrop of his beloved homeland. Walking barefoot on a white, sandy beach. Watching one of the sunsets that had to be the greatest show on earth.

Alone.

If he hadn't given in to the impulse to check the 'grab-a-seat' website the next day, only to find a ridiculously cheap airfare available, he probably wouldn't have even considered the extravagance of popping over for a weekend.

He wouldn't be here now, with the smell of slow-roasting pig on its spit, watching Zoe learn how to wrap food in plaited coconut fronds and banana leaves before it went on the *umu*. The stone oven was good and ready now. He'd helped to prepare the glowing hot lava rocks before he'd gone down to the beach to find Zoe.

Now he was having a beer with the men of the village, trying not to make it obvious that his attention was firmly caught by how Zoe seemed to fit in so well with this part of his life. With his people. She stood out, of course, with her pale skin and flame-touched hair, just like Emma did where she was sitting in a group of babies being watched over by the grandmothers. But even alone on the beach, in that *lavalava* that deepened the colour of her eyes to something he might find amongst the tropical greenery around them, Zoe had looked as if she belonged here.

He watched her helping the other women prepare the food. Then she went off arm in arm with Alisi and the two young women came back laughing, their arms laden with flowers they would use to make necklaces and crowns for this evening, and it was then that Teo realised he was seeing yet another side to this extraordinary woman.

Happy Zoe.

Absolutely, irresistibly gorgeous, *desirable* Zoe.

It became increasingly difficult not to set the old women's tongues wagging because Teo found himself drawn closer and closer to Zoe when the celebrations began. Finally, he gave in. With his plate laden with the wonderful roast pig and seafood, he went to sit beside her on a fallen log to eat, just outside the main group of people gathered around the bonfire.

Teo had been glancing at her plate often enough to notice how little she'd eaten.

'You don't like the food?'

'I do. It's delicious.'

'But you're not eating much.'

'I'm too…happy to feel hungry.' The statement sounded weird as soon as she uttered it but Teo merely tilted his head in acknowledgment.

'Contentment can be like that.'

What would he say if he knew that part of her contentment right now was due to the fact that *he* was here? Sitting beside her. Close enough for her to feel the warmth and strength of the hard muscles of his thigh through the thin cotton of her sarong.

'You're very lucky,' she told Teo. 'To have this place to call home. To have family that seems unlimited.' She couldn't help sounding wistful.

Teo gave her a searching glance as he swallowed his food. 'What's the story with your family, Zoe? I know you said you didn't have any but I got the impression that you said that only because you didn't want to talk about it.'

Zoe could feel herself blushing. 'You see too much,' she murmured. 'It doesn't leave me anywhere to hide.'

'Why would you want to?'

She couldn't look away from him. Why? Because she

didn't want to stop feeling this happy. This safe. What would happen if she told him the truth?

But he'd given her so much already. He deserved the truth. His gentle smile told her that she didn't have to hide. That he didn't want her to.

'My mother had several miscarriages before she had me,' Zoe said quietly. 'And then, when I was born, she... didn't want me.'

Teo sucked in a breath. 'Did she have postnatal depression?'

'It probably started with that but she went on to have full-blown psychotic episodes. She was in and out of a psychiatric hospital and on drugs for what seemed like my whole life. My father blamed me. My birth, anyway. My grandmother did most of the bringing up but she died when I was seventeen.'

'How is your mother now?'

'I don't know.' Zoe was ashamed to admit it. 'I left home when I was eighteen and I haven't had any contact with them since.'

'So they don't know about Emma?'

'I don't know. I wrote to them.'

'Are you going to call them?'

'I wasn't planning to.'

Teo turned his attention back to his meal, eating in silence for a minute or two, looking around at the crowd of people they were amongst. People who all seemed to be related in some way. Teo might not have his own parents any longer or any brothers or sisters but there were countless aunts and uncles and cousins and nephews and nieces. Real or honorary, it didn't matter.

'Family's family,' he said finally. Quietly.

And then he was silent again.

Zoe picked at her food, her appetite truly gone now. Teo

thought less of her for abandoning her family but she still hadn't told him the worst of it.

'I'm scared,' she whispered.

He stopped eating. Zoe was staring down at her plate but she knew his attention was completely on her.

'What are you scared of?' he asked softly.

'Being…being the same as my mother.' There, it was out. The thing that terrified her the most about everything that had happened since she'd become pregnant. Longer, even. Maybe ever since she'd been old enough to know that her mother was different. Brittle and sad.

'Zoe?' Teo's voice broke into the darkening swirl of her thoughts. She looked up.

'You're not your mother,' he said softly. 'You're *you*. I understand now why you're so hard on yourself and I can see why it was almost inevitable that becoming a mother was going to be tough, but you're going to be fine. You're clever and talented and beautiful and Emma is going to grow up being very proud of who her mother is.'

His hand brushed her arm, tracing it with the backs of his fingers until he reached her hand lying beside her plate on her lap. It felt tiny and fragile as he curled his fingers around it and squeezed gently.

'You don't have to have the perfect house and an amazing job and pretend to be happy if you're not.' Teo's voice was just a whisper now. 'You just have to be you and Emma will love you, I promise.'

With another squeeze he let go of her hand. Zoe blinked tears from her eyes and sat very still for a long moment, trying to catch every word he'd spoken as it floated around her. They were precious, those words, and she wanted to keep every one of them.

She could hear the smile in Teo's voice now. 'How 'bout we go and get some of my Aunty Moana's banana pancakes? Don't tell anybody but they're what I really come home for, every time.'

She'd told him the worst about herself. Zoe would never forget James's horror at discovering she had a mad mother. Even if everything else had been perfect about their relationship, which it hadn't, that revelation would have been more than enough to have him running for the hills. But Teo had simply listened and accepted it and suggested they have dessert, as though…as though it didn't even matter.

It was bewildering. But wonderful.

Zoe let herself get drawn back into the group and found she was hungry after all. She finished her meal and then the sweet treats and then went with Alisi and the other mothers to settle the younger children in the *fale*. As she tucked a sleepy Emma under the handmade quilt, Zoe could hear the sound of drumming start up. By the time she went back, a group of young men was crouched close to the dying fire, intent on their music.

It was Alisi's husband, Rangi, who started the fire dancing. Traditional grass skirts were produced from somewhere for the men to put on and Teo was one of them. Holding sticks that were flaming at one end, he joined others to dance in front of the glowing embers of the fire to the intense tribal rhythms of the drums.

There were several men dancing but Zoe couldn't take her eyes off Teo. He'd stripped off his T-shirt and put the grass skirt over his shorts and the image was timeless. Primitive. Erotic. The grace of his movements. The thrill of the streaks of fire against the dark night sky. The sheer, raw masculinity of it all.

The party finished with the dancing.

Or maybe it hadn't.

Back in his T-shirt and shorts, Teo came to where Zoe and Alisi were sitting.

'Tired?'

Zoe shook her head. How could she be tired when she'd never felt this…*alive*? The drumming was still there. Coursing through her veins.

'Come for a walk? There's something I'd like you to see.' He held out his hand.

Alisi gave her a nudge. 'Go,' she urged in a whisper. 'I think he wants to show you the moon on the beach.'

'But—'

'I'll look after Emma.' Alisi's expression was curiously solemn. 'You should go with Teo.'

He led her along a forest track. It smelled warm and damp and there were occasional drifts of some deliciously scented flowers. There were scuttles of unidentified creatures and insects as well but Zoe wasn't bothered. Her hand was in Teo's and she would have happily gone wherever he was leading her.

It turned out to be a beach that she hadn't seen before. A small curve of sand that was ghostly white in the moonlight. The sea was so calm there were virtually no waves, the moonlight reflected in a path that led to the curl of soft foam caressing the sand.

'My beach,' Teo said.

They discarded their sandals and walked the length of it, hand in hand, letting the water wash over their feet, deliciously cool. When they got to the end of the tiny bay, they stopped and looked out to sea, soaking in the sheer beauty of it all and the warmth of the tropical night. At least, that was what Zoe was doing. Finally, she drew in a deep breath of utter happiness and turned to thank Teo for showing it to her, only to find that he wasn't looking at the moon and the way it was reflected on the sea.

He was looking down at her.

His head dipped. Slowly. Slowly enough for Zoe to know that he was going to kiss her. Slowly enough for her to have ducked her head and let him know that she didn't want that to happen and no offence would have been taken.

But Zoe did want it to happen. More than she had ever wanted anything in her entire life. The magnetic pull towards him was so strong she could feel her toes sink into the sand as her weight shifted, her body lifting to close the distance a fraction faster, her head tilting at the last moment so that his mouth could find hers more easily.

The first brush of his lips was so gentle. A soft touch that was barely there, and then he raised his head again to look at her. Zoe's lips were still parted. She had to run her tongue across them. To taste him. To make herself believe it had really happened.

He was watching her. His breath left his lungs in a low groan and Teo gathered her into his arms properly. And this time, when his lips touched hers, Zoe knew they weren't going to be taken away any time soon. They moved over hers, the pressure a dance all of its own, and when she felt the slide of his tongue Zoe could swear something inside her body started to melt.

It had to be her bones. That would explain why they both sank into a kneeling position on the sand, the kiss unbroken and gaining intensity so quickly Zoe wanted to cry out, but the sound was lost inside his mouth. Teo's hands found the knot on her sarong and it fluttered against her body as it fell. He stripped off his T-shirt and dropped it and Zoe saw the moonlight bathing his glorious, dark skin. She could still hear the echo of those tribal drums as he unclipped her bikini top and discarded it. She arched back as his hands covered her breasts, the sharp sensations in her nipples so intense they were painful.

She lay back as his lips salved the pain into pleasure like nothing she had ever felt before. She lifted her hips so that Teo could drag her last piece of clothing away and she reached for his shorts to help him. Her desire was a living thing now, the urgency overwhelming, but Teo stayed her hand and stifled her whimper with his mouth. He soothed and stroked her and made the pace more fitting to the slow rhythm of the waves beside them. Gentle and sure and… relentless.

Zoe had no choice but to be carried along, totally lost in the sensations. The exquisite pleasure. The sheer wonder that this was Teo making love to her on a private beach bathed in moonlight. When she cried out for the last time, Teo's cry joined hers. A sound of triumph and ultimate satisfaction. Two sounds that became one and were swallowed by the vastness of the tropical night.

Zoe had no idea how long they stayed like that, entwined on the sand. Still joined. Finally Teo eased himself away from her but they were still touching as he took her hand again. He led her into a milky-warm sea and they swam together.

The silence didn't worry Zoe at all. Talking aloud might have broken the magic of being here. She'd never swum naked before and the delight of it was like a dessert after the feast of Teo's lovemaking.

Even then, the pleasure hadn't ended. Teo dried them both with his T-shirt and spread Zoe's sarong so they could lie together on the sand again. This time they simply held each other and talked quietly. About nothing important, like what Zoe wanted to do on her last day tomorrow. About everything important, like what Zoe wanted for Emma as she grew up. And every so often, when they caught each other's gaze, they would kiss. Softly. With a tenderness that wasn't going to ignite renewed passion.

This was Zoe's last night on the island and she knew she would remember it for ever. Whatever happened back home, she wouldn't regret what they had just done. How could she, when it had been so perfect? Propping herself on one elbow, Zoe took a moment to simply look at Teo. To imprint the memory of this night in her head. She had to touch him then. She traced the marks of his tattoo with her fingers.

'Did it hurt?'

'Yes.'

'I understand why you have it.' Zoe leaned over to press her lips against the skin she was touching. 'It's a mark of who you are.'

'A chosen mark,' Teo agreed, his voice a soft rumble in his chest that Zoe rested her head against. 'It tells a story of the people I come from. My roots.'

His arms came around Zoe.

'Life leaves all sorts of marks on us,' he said. 'Frown lines, smile lines, stretch marks.' His hand left her back to touch her head. To stroke her hair. 'Sometimes the marks can't be seen because they're hidden inside but they're all important because they're the story of who *we* are.'

Zoe could feel tears slipping down her cheeks. He was talking about her history. The things that scared her. He was accepting her for what she was. Scars and all.

And in that moment, Zoe fell in love with Teo. So hard and so deeply that she knew there would never be any turning back. She *had* never, *would* never, love anybody as much as she loved him. She was his, heart and soul.

He just didn't know it yet.

CHAPTER EIGHT

Zoe looked...radiant.

That was the only word Teo could think of when he saw her again the next day. She was on the beach with Emma and she was holding her baby close and cuddling her and looking at her like all the mothers he knew looked at their babies. With *love*.

Whatever barrier Zoe thought she had that had stopped her bonding with Emma was obviously gone, and Teo's heart squeezed from the joy of it.

He couldn't take the credit. The bond had been there all along but Zoe hadn't been well enough to recognise it. He had helped, certainly, by showing her how to relax again and what family could be like. He had encouraged her to come here, to a place where it was hard not to find what was real. And maybe their lovemaking on the beach last night had also had something to do with it. Zoe had let go and allowed herself to feel.

She had been his for the taking.

Maybe she could even be his for the keeping?

His heart had been captured by this woman and her child even before the magic of last night. He'd stayed awake for a long time after he'd taken Zoe back to the *fale*. Pacing his house, alone and...lonely. But he'd done what he'd hoped to do that day he'd been so astonished at seeing the sad, frightened side of Zoe. She was on the right track now.

Happy.

This was when he needed to step back. To be her friend but nothing more because that's all he could ever be to any woman.

But it was so hard this time.

Zoe had seen him arrive.

'How do you do it?' she demanded. 'How do you make babies laugh?'

'Like this.' He scooped Emma from her arms and held her up, a chubby baby wearing nothing but her nappy. He blew a raspberry onto the soft, bare skin of her tummy.

Emma waved her fists in the air and shrieked with laughter. He handed her back to Zoe.

'You try it.'

Her eyes widened. She took Emma onto her lap. She bent her head and blew a very creditable raspberry onto her daughter's tummy. Emma's eyes widened even more than her mother's had. She didn't shriek this time but she giggled, a delicious gurgle that made Zoe laugh as well.

Teo's gaze was caught by the back of Zoe's neck. Pale, pale skin that hadn't been kissed by the sun yet. He wanted to kiss it himself. Then Zoe's head swung up and she was smiling at him. Right into his eyes. He could feel it, all the way into his bones. And he knew what that feeling was.

Love.

'Got your camera with you?'

'In my bag.'

'I'll get a shot of you and Emma.' He found the camera in the side pocket of the beach bag. 'Make her laugh again.'

'There might not be much room on the memory stick

left cos I've taken so many photos.' But Zoe blew more raspberries and Teo captured the images.

'I'd like one of these,' he said. 'Man, I take some good photos.'

'I've taken some awesome ones myself. I can't wait to get them onto a computer and have a proper look.'

'That could be arranged. I'd like you to see my house before you go, anyway. That way you'll know what it's like if you ever want to come back and use it for a holiday.'

'Me too, Uncle Teo.' Alisi's little boy Sefa had come running from the surf. 'I want to see your house.'

'You've seen it before.' But Teo lifted Sefa into his arms for a bear hug. 'Of course you can come. Everybody can come. After lunch. Before we take Zoe to the airport.'

But the babies needed a nap after lunch and everybody else declared it was too hot to walk all the way to Teo's house so, in the end, it was just Zoe and Teo and Sefa who went. Sefa's little legs got tired before they got to the end of the forest track so Teo carried him piggyback until they got to the beach, where the little boy's energy suddenly returned and he had to run in and out of the waves at top speed as the adults walked on the damp curve of sand the receding tide had left.

Teo held Zoe's hand and, when he turned to share a smile at Sefa's glee, he knew they were both thinking about being here last night.

Being together.

The wave of longing caught him unawares. Desire he could deal with but this was much deeper. He wanted to be with this woman for ever. To see that smile every day. To feel her hand in his as they journeyed through life.

Maybe he was wrong to have cut himself off from that kind of love. That devotion that could be the heart and soul of one's life and give it the meaning and joy that nothing else could replace.

He opened his mouth, to say something to Zoe. To tell her he loved her?

He didn't know. And he didn't find out because Sefa chose that moment to come barrelling towards him and cling to his leg like a large, damp limpet. Teo had to pick him up again. He was still carrying the small child as he led Zoe into his house.

'Oh…Teo…' Zoe was standing in the living area of the house tucked into the edge of the forest. The wall's massive folding doors were open and the room and the wide deck beyond seemed to be a part of the beach. 'This is… gorgeous. Do you sit here to watch the sunsets?'

'Always.' The word came out with a curious gruff edge. Maybe it was seeing Zoe here, in the home of his heart, obviously loving it. Or maybe it was the feel of the child still in his arms. Teo could imagine it was one of their own children he was holding. Part of a family of his very own that lived in this house.

And it felt…perfect.

Blindingly perfect but, for just a few precious minutes, that didn't seem to matter.

It mattered a lot when Zoe was scrolling through the full-screen images of all the photographs she'd taken. Teo was fixing cold drinks for them all in his kitchen and he'd been listening to Zoe's excited exclamations.

'Oh…here's a gorgeous one of all the children swimming.'

'This sunset is incredible. I think I'll have it blown up to make a poster for my bedroom.'

'Here's Kali and Emma asleep together. They look so cute…like puppies in a basket.'

'Ooh…wait till you see this one of you with the fire dancing.'

And then Zoe went oddly silent. Teo added ice cubes to the lemonade and peeled the wrapper off an ice block for Sefa.

'Sit out on the deck,' he told the little boy. 'That way it won't matter when it drips.'

'Teo?' Something in Zoe's voice made Teo leave the glasses of lemonade where they were and walk towards her empty-handed.

'What's up?'

She was sitting in front of the computer and there was an odd stillness about her.

'Probably nothing but…'

'But what?' Teo was right behind her now. He put his hand on her shoulder as he leaned forward to look at the picture on the screen. He caught a whiff of Zoe's scent and lowered his head so that it was touching hers. They were both looking ahead at the photograph. It was a shot from last night, at the barbecue. One of the table, groaning with food, with the children crowded around filling their plates. Zoe clicked the mouse and there was another picture of the children. This time it was Sefa standing beside his big brother, Maru, beneath a tree. And then a closer shot of Sefa's wide grin and tousled mop of black curls.

Such a happy kid. Teo could feel himself smiling. He looked away from the screen to nuzzle Zoe's neck. Man… if Sefa wasn't sitting right outside, he'd just scoop Zoe up and carry her to his bedroom and make love to her. He'd—

'Do you see it?' Zoe whispered. The way she swallowed was audible. Or maybe Teo was only just becoming aware of the tension in her body. He blinked and looked again. And then his hand covered hers on the mouse and he clicked through all the images he could find that had

Sefa in them. Back and forth until he got to that close-up of the little face.

How could he not have seen it? The flash from the camera was reflected in Sefa's eyes. One eye looked normal. The other eye had a distinct white circle in its centre.

It could mean nothing.

It could also be an obvious sign of a retinoblastoma, a rapidly developing cancer that affected the cells of the retina. And maybe it did have one of the best cure rates of any form of cancer but this was *Sefa*—a child who had a place in his heart like no other.

He'd been playing with this child only minutes ago. Giving him a treat. Having some stupid fantasy about him being part of a nuclear family of his own. And seconds ago, he was thinking of nothing but making love to Zoe.

Blinded by love.

For one mercifully brief but horrible moment Teo was taken back to when he was no more than a child himself. When his love had blinded him to what he had to do to protect the person he loved the most. His hand slipped from Zoe's shoulder as he straightened. He shouldn't even be touching her. He'd known the danger all along but he'd let himself ignore the warning bells.

There was no ignoring this.

'Sefa?' He walked slowly to where his beloved nephew was sitting on the edge of the deck, chubby legs dangling and swinging, his tongue out to catch the drips of his ice block. 'You nearly finished?' Teo ruffled the black curls on Sefa's head. 'We're going to take you for another visit. Would you like to go and see the hospital where I work?'

The flight back to Sydney was the first chance Zoe got to try and put the pieces of her day back together again.

The way it had started, with the glow of her love for Teo

somehow spilling over or melting that barrier so that she was also, gloriously, in love with Emma as well seemed like a dream now.

With a sigh of pure relief Zoe realised those feelings were still there as they sped through the night sky into the small hours of a new day. She could see the back of Teo's head as he sat, two rows up and on the other side of the aisle. The last time she had walked past to go to the toilet Teo had had his arm around Alisi, who was sitting beside him, sobbing silently against his shoulder. Was Alisi asleep now? She had to be exhausted after the nightmare her day had turned into.

Just the sight of Teo's head…the memory of how it felt to bury her fingers in his hair as she helped bring their heads close enough for their lips to touch was enough to start that melting sensation in the pit of Zoe's stomach. And it wasn't just that she wanted to touch him again. To *be* touched by him. This was so deep there was no end to the love she felt for him.

He'd been amazing today. From that first, horrible moment of recognising the threat in that photograph, he'd been *so* strong. Sefa wouldn't have had any idea of the fear dogging their footsteps as they'd raced back to the village because Teo had kept him laughing. He'd sent him to play with his big brother while he'd talked to Alisi and Rangi and the senior members of the family. And then there'd been the car ride to the local hospital where a simple ophthalmoscope had been all the equipment a doctor had needed to confirm the possibility of a potentially deadly disease. Even then, Teo hadn't faltered.

'We'll take him back to Sydney tonight,' he told Alisi. 'We can't be sure until he has an examination under general anaesthetic and I don't want to do that here. He needs someone far more qualified than me to make a final diagnosis and start treatment.'

'*Treatment*?' Alisi had clearly been terrified. 'What kind of treatment?'

'I've been on the phone to Finn Kennedy, the director of surgery at my hospital. He's going to find the best ophthalmologist available in Sydney. In Australia, if necessary.'

Alisi was sobbing already. 'But what's going to happen?'

'If it is what I think it might be, there are several courses of action. Chemotherapy, radiotherapy, laser therapy or surgery. That's not for me to decide, though, Lisi. There are people who know exactly what they're doing. The cure rate is very, very high. Nine out of ten kids make it through this.'

'But I can't just send him to Sydney with you.'

'Of course not. You'll come as well. And Kali.'

'I'll help,' Zoe had put in then. 'I'll help you look after Kali and, if you're not at the hospital with Sefa, you can stay with me.'

Teo's nod and smile had been approving. Distant, perhaps, but Zoe could understand why he needed to pull the mantle of his profession around him like a cloak right now. He had dealt with Sefa's toenail like this, hadn't he? Putting the barrier up so that he could do what had to be done without having decisions and actions undermined because the patient happened to be someone very special.

He was being a tower of strength and Alisi certainly needed that.

And Zoe loved him for it.

When she tore her gaze away from Teo's head, it travelled only as far as the row of seats behind him. There were three children in that row, tucked up with the airline's pillows and blankets and all of them sound asleep. Sefa had been so excited at the prospect of an extra holiday with his Uncle Teo.

'Can we go to the beach again?' he begged. 'And play football?'

Such a dear little boy. Zoe stood up and leaned over the seats to check that the children were all fine. Very gently, she smoothed a corner of blanket away from where it was half covering Sefa's face. Her heart ached at the thought of what he might have ahead of him in the next few weeks.

Kali was flat on her back, her lips a cherub's bow and slightly parted as she snuffled in her sleep. Emma was curled up on her side, with one hand tucked under her cheek. The ache in Zoe's heart intensified and morphed into something new. Something so wonderful she could hardly believe she was experiencing it.

Mother love. The feeling that this tiny person was the absolute centre of her universe. That she would—and could—do anything it would take to protect her.

There was so much love to be found in this small space of a few rows of seats. Teo and Emma, of course, but also Sefa and Alisi and Kali. These people were her family now and she loved them all.

She could draw strength from that love.

It was the new anchor in her life and Zoe knew she would need it in the days to come.

When was it that the way Teo could distance himself and be so utterly professional started ringing alarm bells for Zoe?

Maybe it had been there, right from the very beginning. When he had been standing behind her to look at the pictures on the computer. He'd been touching her. Nuzzling her, even, and then he had simply stepped away and he hadn't touched her since. Certainly not with his hands or his lips. Not even with a look that held any kind of special connection.

They'd arrived in the middle of the night and, of course, she would have expected Teo to take his cousin and the children back to his apartment. It wasn't as if there weren't any number of other places Alisi could use as a base given the amount of family they had in the city. At least Alisi was desperately keen for Zoe to stay involved.

'That would be wonderful,' she said, when Zoe offered to be with her when they took Sefa into the hospital later. 'If you're sure it won't interfere with your job?'

'I'm only casual. Doing holiday relief and sickness cover. I can just tell them I'm unavailable at the moment.'

Surely Teo would approve of her dismissing work in favour of being there for her adopted family? Or was it reminding him of her own dysfunctional family relationships? Out of kilter with her sleeping patterns now, Zoe found herself awake for a long time when she reached her own house. She even found herself with a pad of paper and a pen in her hand. Maybe Teo was right in the importance he placed on families. It was up to her to try and build a bridge and see if there was any chance of making a connection to her own roots again. She'd received a card in response to her letter to her parents telling them they were grandparents. Maybe she could take the next step and invite them to visit.

She wanted to tell Teo about the invitation she'd sent when she saw him the next day but it wasn't the time or place. Alisi needed her as an interpreter. It wasn't that her English wasn't perfectly fluent but Zoe could understand the medical jargon better and that way Alisi didn't feel stupid when she had to keep asking the same things over and over, to try and get her head around everything that was happening.

And Finn Kennedy was a scary person for someone like Alisi. Zoe would have been just as terrified, listening to the way he put things straight out there, without hesitation. Not that he was so forthright in front of Sefa but the little boy was already in the paediatric ward, being spoilt rotten by every nurse he smiled at.

At one point during those first couple of days Zoe went with Alisi for an appointment in Finn's office. The director of surgery had been behind his desk. Alisi and Zoe sat in chairs in front of it. Teo stood to one side.

'We've ruled out things like Coat's disease and toxocaracanis,' Finn announced. 'And the abnormalities are strongly suggestive of retinoblastoma. We're not sure yet if there's any optic nerve involvement so the next step is to do an MRI. I've also contacted a friend of mine in Brisbane, who's prepared to fly down for the surgery. He's a world-renowned expert in the field.'

'S-surgery?' Alisi stammered. 'What kind of surgery?'

'It may be possible to remove the tumour. It may be necessary to remove the eye.'

Alisi gasped and grabbed Zoe's hand.

'We'll know more after the MRI,' Teo put in. 'It may also be possible to start treatment with chemotherapy and if it shrinks the tumour there's another kind of procedure where it can be frozen. It's still possible that we can save not only the eye but the eyesight as well.'

He sounded as calm as Finn, Zoe thought. This was *Sefa* he was talking about. It just didn't seem right.

'We need you to sign consent forms for a lumbar puncture and a bone-marrow examination,' Finn continued.

Zoe's mouth went dry. So far, the worst Sefa had had to endure had been blood tests, an ultrasound and a general anaesthetic. She couldn't imagine how she'd feel if she had to sign forms giving permission to have a sample of Emma's bone marrow or spinal fluid taken. No wonder Alisi was crying quietly now. She squeezed her hand.

'They're needed to check for any spread of cancer cells,' Teo told Alisi. 'We'll know more when the paediatric oncology team has reviewed the case later today.'

The case. It's *Sefa*, she wanted to shout at Teo but she couldn't because her throat had closed up in sympathy with Alisi. Tears were forming in her eyes and threatening to spill over at any moment.

'The odds are excellent.' Finn looked away from the distressed women. 'Isn't that right, Teo?'

'It is.' The affirmation was confident. Calm and steady.

So much so that Zoe looked up to see that Teo had stepped closer to Finn's side of the desk. The two men couldn't look any more different, Zoe thought. Finn was angular and rugged. He looked like he hadn't shaved for days and there was an intensity about him that was great if he was your doctor and was determined to cure you but there was no warmth of any kind of empathy there.

Teo was big and solid and…so much softer. She had seen this man play with children and cuddle babies. She had been made love to by him so she *knew* how gentle he was. How caring.

And yet, at this moment, the expression on his face was almost an exact match of the one on Finn Kennedy's face.

Determined.

And detached.

Chemotherapy for Sefa was started the next day. It was a major procedure because the cancer-fighting drugs were administered by a tiny tube that was put into a big artery and then threaded up into the optic vessels. Everybody hoped that the treatment would start getting results quickly but now that the initial rush of diagnosis and treatment decisions had been made, it was a matter of getting on with it and waiting.

It was hard on everybody and Zoe knew she was being selfish in letting it affect her so much but, with every passing day, she was feeling worse. She knew, without a shadow of a doubt, that however good a front Teo was capable of putting up, he was having to deal with something very difficult and personal. Maybe it was unreasonable to expect him to make time to spend alone with her but… she *loved* him. She desperately wanted to be allowed close enough to offer some comfort. Just to be there for him.

But he didn't seem to want or need her.

His department was only too keen to bend over backwards to help and he allowed that to happen. Sefa had a private room and there was a bed for Alisi in there as well. She was allowed to keep Kali with her most of the time and there was always someone available to help when she needed to be with Sefa for his treatment.

Word had got out amongst the Samoan community too and there was an endless stream of visitors and rules about the numbers allowed in a room at one time were often broken. These people brought gifts for Sefa and food for Alisi and they brought their love and laughter and prayers. While the friendship between Zoe and Alisi had deepened markedly over this period, Zoe's company was needed less often and that meant not even catching a glimpse of Teo when he was on the ward, tending to his small patients.

'You could go back to work,' Alisi told her. 'I'm fine, honestly. They seem to think that this treatment is working and I have Aunty Hina and everybody to help now. It's not that I don't love having you around but I'd hate it if we were making your life too difficult.'

It wasn't Alisi making her life too difficult. It was Teo.

What was happening between them felt like rejection and…it hurt. OK, life had happened and disrupted what had begun on the island but *something* had begun, hadn't it? Surely it wasn't just her imagination that had made her feel that it had been far more than some kind of one-night stand? If this was Teo's way of letting her down gently, it was unkind. It simply didn't fit with the man she was so sure he was, but if that was the case and she was going to have any chance of dealing with it and getting on with her life, she needed to know.

When she saw Teo out near the lifts as she left that day, Zoe took a huge breath, summoned her courage and walked straight up to him.

'We need to talk,' she said quietly.

There was a haunted look in Teo's eyes. 'I know,' he said. 'Look, I'm sorry. Things have been…'

'Difficult, I know.' Zoe wanted to reach out and touch Teo's arm but something held her back. 'But please don't shut me out, Teo. I want to help.'

He was shaking his head slowly. As if there was nothing she would be able to do to help him.

Zoe swallowed hard. Found some more courage. 'I don't understand,' she said softly, taking a swift look around to make sure no one was within earshot. 'I thought we were… On the island…'

Teo's gaze slid away. He actually shut his eyes for a heartbeat. 'That shouldn't have happened.' He opened his eyes again. 'I'm sorry, Zoe.'

'I'm not.' Zoe's heart was breaking but she could still feel the connection between them. Teo might not want it but it was *there*. Strong. Pulsing with life.

'Teo, I…I…'

I love you.

But the words caught. The connection might still be there but this wasn't the Teo she knew and loved, was it? There was a barrier between them that was as wide as an ocean. Unanswered questions about how and why he felt the need to treat Sefa as if he was just another patient. The child of a complete stranger.

'I just don't understand,' she whispered.

'Don't get me wrong.' A flash of something she recognised came into Teo's dark gaze and Zoe felt her heart lift. 'I think you're an amazing person, Zoe, and you're going to be a wonderful mother. You *are* already. Always have been, only you couldn't recognise it.' He sucked in a breath. 'You need a partner who can be everything you need him to be. Someone who can love you the way you deserve to be loved. I'm not that man. I can't be.'

The words came out before Zoe could salvage any pride. 'Why not?'

'It's not you. I can't love anybody like that.'

But he could. He did. He loved his family. And, just for a night, she had been so sure he loved *her*.

He must have seen the denial in her face. 'I won't *let* myself love anybody like that,' he said fiercely. 'It's a luxury I can't afford.'

Zoe had to take a step back from that vehemence. She shook her head in disbelief. Teo had shown her what love really was. She had opened her heart and, to her amazement, had become the mother she'd wanted to be, as well as this man's lover. And now he was pushing her away? What had she done that was so wrong?

Been estranged from her family? Well, she was trying to fix that, wasn't she?

Was it because she'd been the one to spot the sign that something was wrong with Sefa? No. They all knew it was lucky to have been found at this early stage.

Zoe tried to swallow the lump in her throat. 'We all need that kind of love,' she whispered.

'No.' Teo was rubbing his forehead so that she couldn't see his eyes. 'It makes you blind. You can't look after people.' He was actually moving away from her now. Towards the ward. Towards people he could look after?

Zoe fought the tears she knew would come. She opened her mouth to say something but Teo didn't give her the chance. He looked back at her and his words were very quiet and utterly final.

'I loved my mother like that,' he said. 'And that's the reason she died.'

CHAPTER NINE

SOMEONE had once told Zoe that people get sent into your life for a particular reason.

Remembering that gave her something to think about while she waited for the kettle to boil to make tea for her unexpected visitors.

If it was true, then Teo had clearly been sent into *her* life so that she could fall in love with her own baby.

There were moments of such joy to be found now.

The soft, silky feel of Emma's skin when Zoe stroked a finger down a chubby little arm or leg. The miracle of those tiny fingers and toes and nails. The way her baby's gaze locked onto hers when she was being fed. Her *smile* and, even better, the gurgle of her laughter. Zoe was getting very good at blowing raspberries.

Those moments would always be here from now on. Zoe knew that now her love had been unlocked, it would never go away, it would only get stronger. Of course there would be times of frustration and sadness, anger and probably fear, but that love would be there as an undercurrent. Something she could tap into for strength whenever she needed it.

She had Teo Tuala to thank for that.

But the price she now had to pay was *so* high.

Yes, there was joy to be found in hearing Emma laugh

but there was pain as well. Would she ever be able to hear that sound without seeing Teo on the beach that day? The way he had swooped her up into the air and bounced her, showing Zoe the real joy of being alive for the first time?

Her love for her daughter would always be there.

But so would her love for Teo.

And she simply didn't understand why he was pushing her away. What on earth had he meant by saying that his love for his mother had been the reason she'd died?

Zoe could remember the conversation she'd had with Alisi that day on the beach. Every moment she'd been with Teo and every conversation with, or about, him seemed to be etched into her memory with startling clarity. Alisi had told her that his mother had already been sick when she'd come to Australia but she hadn't realised it. That by the time they'd found the cancer it had been too late to treat it. He'd still been a child then. Did he think that it was somehow his fault that the disease hadn't been picked up early enough to provide a cure?

No. There was more to it than that. It had more to do with his other strange statement about love making you blind so you couldn't look after people. Somewhere there was the key to the way he could distance himself and be so completely professional when he was dealing with a member of his own family, like Sefa.

Zoe could understand why he felt he needed to be distant to provide medical care but she still couldn't get a handle on *how*. She could have done it herself, in the early days with Emma, when her love had been in her head and not her heart, but now…there was no way she could distance herself. Just thinking about what Alisi had had to go through, being with Sefa while he had a lumbar puncture and bone-marrow aspiration, was enough to bring tears to her eyes. If it had been Emma, she'd have felt everything herself and it would have been infinitely worse, seeing it happen to her precious baby.

Finally experiencing the kind of love a parent could have for a child had changed Zoe for ever.

Being close to Teo, even for such a short period of time, had also changed her. His pride in where he came from and the way his family was such an important part of his life had been the catalyst for writing that letter to her parents.

And now, here she was, making a pot of tea to take back into her living room where her parents were sitting, taking turns holding their granddaughter.

Had they been sent back into her life for a particular reason?

No. Zoe had summoned them back, hadn't she, with that letter she'd written inviting them to come? And when her father had rung today to say that they were in a motel in Sydney, having come all this way to meet Emma, her first reaction had been one of horror.

What had she done?

The plea in her father's voice had been unmistakable, however, and a habit that had become ingrained ever since she'd come back from her brief holiday in Samoa kicked in. She could imagine that Teo was standing right beside her. Watching her. The desire to see approval warm that dark gaze was still a powerful influence, even now, when it appeared that the reason he'd come into her life was no longer valid. That the task had been accomplished and her life had to move on.

Did her future include her immediate family?

Taking the tray of tea, Zoe went back to the living room. Her mother was holding Emma and smiling brightly.

Too brightly?

Her father sat very close to her mother on the couch.

He was leaning over Emma as he made faces, trying to make her smile. Emma obliged. She even reached up with a small fist and managed to knock his glasses off his nose.

John Harper laughed, sitting back as he pushed his glasses back into place.

'I think she might end up being a boxer.'

'No-o-o.' Celia Harper planted a kiss on Emma's head. 'She's far too darling to want to do something so violent. I think she might be a ballet dancer.'

'What do you think, Zoe?' John asked.

The stream of tea coming from the pot wobbled slightly. Zoe put it down. 'I just want her to be happy,' she said quietly.

The atmosphere became instantly strained. Her father cleared his throat. 'Of course,' he said. After another heavy silence, he spoke again. A little tentatively. 'Are you happy, Zoe?'

She nodded. Talking about her postnatal depression to her parents was not an option because it would open a vast can of worms she was nowhere near ready to deal with. And she was happy. So far, she was even coping with the fear of a future that didn't include Teo. It hurt, of course, but it hadn't sent her plunging into depression and that, in itself, was giving her more strength.

'I have a beautiful daughter,' she said aloud. 'And a great job.'

She told her parents about her job as they drank the tea. She told them about her holiday in Samoa. When it came time for them to leave, she told them she was happy that they'd come to meet Emma.

'We're here tomorrow, too,' her mother said. 'We'd love to spend some more time getting to know her.'

'I'm working tomorrow,' Zoe said apologetically. 'Emma goes into day care.'

'Oh…does she have to? We could look after her.'

'No…' Zoe's headshake was definite. She found herself tightening her grip on her baby. 'I don't think so.'

Her mother bit her lip. Her eyes filled with tears but she managed to smile. 'I…understand, love. It's…all right.'

But it wasn't all right. Her parents went out to their rental car but her father came back to the door.

'This means so much to her,' he said. 'She's OK now. She hasn't been in hospital for years and she's even come off her medication, but her life has been…a bit empty, I guess. When your letter came, it was like the light came back on. She's so excited about Emma. So…*happy*.'

It was a shock to see that there were tears in her father's eyes. He loved her mother. They both wanted to love Emma. Was it possible there was still family to be found?

'I don't know when we'll be able to get back to Sydney. You did ask us to come and meet Emma. Is there really no way we could spend some time with her tomorrow?'

Zoe hesitated. She hadn't had the slightest doubt about leaving Emma to be cared for by Alisi or the aunties. And she *had* invited her parents to come and spend time with their granddaughter. What would Teo say if he could see her refusing to trust her own family?

'I'd be there every minute,' her father added quietly. 'I'd make sure she was safe, if that's what you're worried about.'

It was, but saying it aloud was too awful and might mean that she could never find a way of having her own family in her life. After an agonising silence Zoe found herself nodding slowly instead. Making the arrangements so that her parents could come and spend the whole day here with Emma.

Trusting them.

* * *

He knew she was in the department even before he saw her.

He had to glance up, of course, to see if that odd feeling of alertness was justified and there she was. Zoe was pushing one end of a stretcher into the emergency department, having been cleared by triage. Her patient seemed to have been assigned a bed close to where he was standing and Teo had to suck in a deep breath to steady himself.

It had been a couple of days since he'd told her he couldn't be the partner she deserved to have and it had been the hardest thing he'd ever done. It had been the right thing to do, he knew that, so why did it have to feel as though he'd ripped off one of his own limbs or something?

It hurt.

The whimper of the child on the bed beside him was like an echo of his own suffering but it also served to bring him back instantly into a professional space. He was standing beside Evie Lockheart, who was doing an ultrasound examination on the abdomen of a small girl.

Ruby was one of the Harbour's well-known patients. The surviving conjoined twin had been an inpatient not very long ago, having extensive skin grafts to her hip area as a final repair after the separation from her twin, Amy. She had been doing very well but had been brought in this afternoon with a worrying history of severe pain and frequent vomiting.

She whimpered again now, even though Evie was being very gentle with the ultrasound probe.

'Hey, little one…' Teo tried to distract Ruby. Maybe he was distracting himself at the same time, because he could hear Zoe's voice in the background, reassuring her own patient as they prepared to transfer him to a bed. 'Did I hear your mummy say that you're going to school soon?'

Ruby sniffled loudly but nodded at the same time. 'I've got a pencil case,' she informed Teo tearfully.

'Awesome. What colour is it?'

'Pink.'

'Of course it is. That's your favourite colour, isn't it?'

'Mmm.'

'Teo?' Evie's voice was carefully neutral. 'Look at this.'

With another smile for Ruby, Teo turned his head to look at the shifting, shades-of-grey shapes on the screen as Evie angled the probe again.

'Definite obstruction,' he said quietly a moment later.

'Oh, no…' Ruby's mother groaned. 'Will she need surgery?'

Teo nodded. 'As soon as possible. We'll get her up to the ward very soon. She hasn't had anything to eat or drink in the last four hours, has she?'

'No…she's been vomiting since first thing this morning.' Ruby's mother looked close to tears. 'I can't understand why this has happened. I thought the grafts were the last procedure she'd need.'

'It could be scar tissue from the separation that's causing the obstruction,' Teo told her. 'The surgeon will be able to tell you more later.'

'Who's going to be doing the surgery?'

'I'll get hold of Finn,' Evie said. She smiled at Ruby's mother. 'I'm sure Mr Kennedy won't want anybody else in charge of our Ruby.'

The young mother looked relieved. 'I wouldn't want anybody else either. He might be grumpy but he's the best, isn't he?'

'He certainly is.' Evie flicked a glance at Teo that looked…oddly defensive? 'I'll call him now, if you're happy?'

Teo gave a single nod. 'And I'll get a line in. She's very dehydrated already.'

The nurse had to go into the adjoining area to get the IV trolley and Teo saw Zoe look up and smile at her. Then her gaze shifted a fraction and she saw him and her smile faltered visibly before she turned away.

Teo was aware of a constriction in his throat that made it hard to swallow. He'd hurt her, he knew that.

How could he have let things go as far as they had on the island? Getting that close. Making love to her had been a huge mistake.

But how could he not have let things go as far as they had? He'd been pulled closer at a relentless pace. It was astonishing how many images could be present in his head at the same time.

The fear in her eyes when he'd seen her in the paediatric outpatient waiting room.

The look on her face when she'd heard Emma laugh that day on the beach at Coogee.

Moonlight on her naked skin...

Teo had to look somewhere else. Fast. Evie was on the phone, presumably to Finn Kennedy, and something about her stance, or maybe the tilt of her head, made him remember that odd impression he'd had weeks ago that there was something going on between Evie and Finn that had nothing to do with their strained and frosty professional relationship.

Then again, maybe it had everything to do with it.

Maybe he and Evie had something in common. Perhaps they both wanted something they couldn't have because it would be wrong. Dangerous, even.

Evie hung up the phone but didn't move for a long moment. When she looked up, she saw that Teo was watching her and she held his gaze for a heartbeat.

Yes. There was something going on there and it wasn't something happy. Evie seemed to feel his empathy. Her smile was wry.

'He's going to meet us up on the ward. He's not very happy about being interrupted, mind you.'

'I guess he's tired too. We all had a hard night and it's been a long day already.'

'It's part of the job.' Evie straightened her shoulders. 'You can't have a career like this without that kind of commitment.'

'Especially when you've had to work so hard to get it in the first place.'

'Yeah…'

The look acknowledged another kind of connection Teo had with Evie. OK, she hadn't had the kind of financial struggle he'd had to get through medical school and become a doctor but he'd heard that her father had been pretty obstructive. And he'd also heard that Evie had a very sick sister.

He'd lost his mother.

Maybe their reasons for letting a career like this become their lives weren't so different.

Maybe they could draw strength from each other.

Teo smiled at Evie. 'Let's get Ruby sorted and up to the ward.'

Teo was in the department.

Zoe had spotted him instantly, as though her gaze had automatically been drawn in that direction. He had his back to where she was, apparently intent on watching an ultrasound that Evie was performing. Zoe turned her attention quickly back to her patient. She certainly wouldn't want Teo to catch her staring at him.

It wouldn't always be this hard, would it?

Could she get used to seeing him? Get to a point where it wouldn't fill her with longing and regret and this awful, dull ache that felt horribly like despair? It was bad luck that they were taking their patient into an area so close to where Teo was working but he hadn't noticed her. Either that, or he was ignoring her.

That hurt.

'Ready to lift?' Tom was on the other end of the stretcher. They seesawed the load higher until their patient would be able to slide across onto the bed. An emergency consultant came in with a registrar.

'This our SVT?'

'Yes.' Zoe nodded. She finished raising the back of the bed so that the man could sit up, which would help him breathe more easily. 'This is Colin Jeffries. Thirty-nine years old. No cardiac history. He's got a narrow complex tachycardia with a rate of 200. Oxygen saturation down to 96 per cent.'

The consultant was smiling at her. Zoe smiled back. Luca di Angelo was new to the department but it was no wonder the gorgeous Italian doctor was turning heads in here. And judging by the sexual wattage in that smile, Zoe wasn't at all surprised by the rumours she'd heard of his womanising tendencies.

Luca had introduced himself to the patient and was talking to the registrar as a nurse hooked up the ECG leads.

'What do you think?'

'Valsalva manoeuvre?'

Tom caught Zoe's gaze. They had already tried that without success.

'If that doesn't work, we could sedate him and defibrillate. Or we could use adenosine.'

Tom nudged Zoe. 'Ever seen adenosine used?'

'Yeah...' The drug gave the chemical equivalent of

the jolt of electricity a defibrillator delivered. 'Dramatic, isn't it?'

'I've never seen it,' Tom said wistfully. He checked his pager and then edged closer to the doctors. 'Mind if we hang around and watch?'

'Watch what?' The patient was looking alarmed. 'What are you going to do to me?'

'Nothing scary,' the registrar assured him. 'The first thing we're going to do is to get you to blow through this straw. As hard as you can for as long as you can.'

'Why?'

'Sometimes it's enough to fix whatever it is that's making your heart go too fast.'

A nurse came in, looking apologetic. 'Can I borrow the IV trolley for a minute? We haven't got one.'

Zoe smiled at her and stood back to let her pass. She looked up at the same time, only to find that Teo was no longer ignoring her. His face had that kind of detached, professional expression she had seen before. Like when he'd been with her and Alisi in Finn's office while they'd discussed Sefa's prognosis. The kind of look that said he was uninvolved enough on an emotional level to be able to deliver the medical care needed. The way he intended to stay uninvolved with anyone. Especially *her*.

Zoe tore her gaze away and turned back to watch the next stage of the management of Colin's SVT. She hoped her pager would go off. Tom would get another opportunity to watch the powerful effects of adenosine. Surely things wouldn't stay this quiet for much longer? She wanted to get back to the station in any case, in the hope of not being deployed on a late job.

Not that things didn't seem to be going well for her parents and Emma. She'd rung several times already today only to hear that Emma had had a nap and been taken for a walk to the park in her pram and that her parents had had no trouble in getting her to have her lunchtime bottle. Her father had sounded more relaxed with every call. Had he been expecting problems too? All Zoe wanted was for the day to be successful and…over. She wanted to get home and care for her baby herself. Maybe trying to have a career like this and be the kind of mother she knew she could be now was not going to work.

Colin had had two attempts with the straw to no effect. The ECG screen showed his heart rate to have increased if anything and he was even more short of breath now after blowing so hard into a tiny space. They were getting ready to use the adenosine, which was a procedure that needed careful management. The drug had to be injected into the right arm to get to the heart as fast as possible and it had to be flushed with a good dose of saline. It required two people because it took two hands to push the plunger on the large syringe of saline fast enough.

Zoe found herself as caught up as Tom as she watched the medical team position themselves and then count down to administering the drug.

And, right at the critical moment, her pager sounded.

No…it was her mobile phone.

Horrified, Zoe slipped out of the resus area. She'd need to get outside to take the call because cellphones could disrupt things like IV pumps.

She couldn't help looking at the screen on her phone, however, and when she saw that it was her own home number, she had to answer it. Her father wouldn't be calling her mobile unless it was some kind of emergency.

'Dad? What's wrong?'

'Zoe…I …. Oh, God…I don't know how to tell you this…'

Zoe was near the glass board now. The place where

Teo had introduced himself all those weeks ago. Where he had touched her for the first time when he'd taken her hand. The memory had no chance of making any kind of impact right now, however.

'Just tell me,' she breathed.

'Your mother's disappeared.' There was a catch in his voice that sounded almost like a sob. 'The car's gone too.'

Zoe could feel the blood draining from her face. She knew the answer to the question she was going to ask but she had to ask it anyway.

'Where's Emma?'

'Not here… I think…no, I know that Celia's taken her with her.'

'How do you know?'

'She rang. She said…she said…don't worry, I've got Zoe. I'm going to take good care of her.'

I've got *Zoe*?

Just how off the planet was her mother?

'Call the police,' Zoe said with icy calm. 'I'm on my way.'

Except she wasn't. Not yet. A curious buzzing sound was already filling her head so that her voice sounded like it was coming from a long way away. It was quite possible that she was going to faint, she realised. She held her hand out, groping for something solid to hang onto.

Something solid got hold of her first. Strong, solid arms. A face that was close to her own. A voice that sounded horrified.

'Zoe. What's wrong? What's happened?'

The buzzing in her head receded a little. Zoe used both her hands to push Teo away from her. Her breath came in short, sharp puffs as she backed away.

'Emma's gone,' she gasped. She stared at Teo, a maelstrom of emotion sweeping through her. She wanted to scream. She wanted to collapse on the floor and sob. She wanted none of this to have happened because she had no idea how she was going to be able to cope with it.

And she was angry, too. Angry with herself for having agreed to put her precious daughter at risk. Angry with her mother for being unstable. Angry with Teo because if it hadn't been for him, she'd never have invited her parents back into her life.

She was still staring at Teo. Her voice came out sounding nothing like it ever had before. It had all her anger and anguish and fear in her words.

'This is all *your* fault.'

CHAPTER TEN

WHAT was more shocking—the anguish in Zoe's voice or the thought that something terrible had happened to Emma?

At some level, Teo knew there was something else that was shocking. The knowledge that there was no way he could push Zoe and her baby far enough from his life to keep them safe. How could you push something away when it had become a part of who you were? The part that was responsible for keeping life going, in fact.

His heart.

He didn't question Zoe's accusation that it was his fault. Had something happened because he'd even considered letting himself love someone the way he loved Zoe? And Emma? Of course it had. He'd known the danger was there all along.

Except…it didn't make sense.

'What's happened?' He kept his voice low and calm, knowing that people all over the emergency department of Sydney Harbour Hospital were watching them both. Like Evie and her friend Mia. Luca di Angelo and Zoe's crew partner, Tom. Zoe wouldn't let him touch her, that much was obvious from the way she'd backed away from him, but he held her with his eye contact, willing her to let him closer. To let him touch her with his mind and heart, if not his body.

'I believed you…' Zoe's voice was a broken whisper. 'I thought, if I didn't have you, at least I could have my family again.'

'Your family? You mean your parents?'

'I believed you,' Zoe repeated. 'About how important family was. I let my parents visit. I gave them my trust and…'

'And *what*?' Teo took a step closer. The suspense was killing him. '*What's* happened, Zoe?'

'My mother's taken Emma. She's disappeared.'

'Oh, my God!' There was no stopping Teo from pulling Zoe into his arms now. He could feel the fear that was making her body rigid. She felt as brittle as a pane of glass that could shatter at any moment. 'What do the police say?'

'I…don't know. I don't even know if my father's called them yet.'

'That's the first step, then. Come on, I'll take you home.'

Zoe shook her head wildly. 'You can't… I…' She pulled away, looking around her.

Tom was nearby now, looking as horrified as everybody else. 'You go,' he told Zoe. 'I'll let Control know.'

Evie was there, too. 'You go too, Teo. I'll take Ruby up to the ward and hand over to Finn. Go,' she repeated decisively, as she turned away. 'Zoe needs you.'

Did she? Teo still had his hands resting on her shoulders even though she'd pulled clear of his embrace. He could still feel that terrible tension in her body. She had nodded her thanks to Tom, with a jerk of her head, and was looking at him again.

There was desperation in that look. She needed him all right. But there was an edge of something even darker there as well. Hopelessness? Did she think he wasn't available for her?

There was no way he could even think of anything or anybody else right now. He was hers, a thousand per cent. His hands gripped her more tightly, drawing her closer.

'I'm here,' he said quietly. 'I'm here for you. We'll get through this together.'

His hand was her anchor.

Warm and strong, it cradled her hand as she sat beside Teo on her couch. She was close enough for the muscles of his thigh to be pressed against hers as well but it was his hand that was keeping her sane. The tiny movements of his thumb as it stroked her palm were a constant message of reassurance. He might not be saying very much but he was here. Totally here. As tense as she was about the whole situation but focused on protecting *her*.

They weren't alone in her living room. Her father sat on an armchair, his hand clutching his mobile phone and his head bowed as he stared at it, willing it to ring. Two police officers, a man and a woman, were also in the room. Daylight was fading now but Zoe couldn't bring herself to move and turn on any lights because that would mean letting go of Teo's hand and if she did that, she was afraid she would shatter into a million pieces.

The silence was unnerving. It made the house feel like an empty shell. Zoe could feel every inch of the space inside this cottage and how empty it felt because Emma was not there.

This silence had come after so many questions that had gone round and round.

'When did Celia disappear?'

'How did it happen?'

Her father had fallen asleep, that's how it had happened. On this couch.

'I didn't mean to,' John had said. 'It had been a long day what with the early start to get her so that Zoe could get to work on time. And we'd had that long walk in the park when we went to feed the ducks. I…I'm getting old, I guess.' He sounded old. Unutterable weary. Defeated, even.

'Celia said she was going to change Emma's nappy and I was sitting here waiting for her to come back and…and it just happened. I fell asleep. I'm sorry, Zoe. I can't tell you how sorry I am.'

'Why would she have taken off with Emma?' the police wanted to know.

'Because she's crazy,' Zoe had told them, not caring that she saw her father flinch.

'She's not crazy,' he'd defended his wife. 'She's had a long history of bipolar disease that has been difficult to control but…we thought we'd finally beaten it. She's been so good recently. You can talk to her psychiatrist…look, I have his number right here.'

Who would carry around a phone number for a psychiatrist if they weren't with someone they thought could tip over the edge at any moment? Seeing him take that card from his wallet had been a dark moment in this nightmare. Maybe John could sense that Zoe was thinking about it again now. He looked up and caught her gaze. Zoe saw him swallow hard and press the redial button on his phone. He held it to his ear but then looked away as he shook his head, killed the call and lowered the phone to his lap again.

Her mother's phone had been turned off. Hours ago now.

'Are there any friends or relatives she could have gone to?'

No. None. How sad was that?

'Where do you think she's gone?' The police had asked.

Home, was all John could come up with.

'She thinks that Emma is Zoe. She wants to take care of her. Where else would she go but home?'

It had taken far too long for the police to get to the key question. 'Do you really think that Emma is in danger?'

'*No*,' John said desperately.

'*Yes*,' Zoe said, with even more desperation.

People were out there, searching for the rental car. The police helicopter had been alerted and would be circling the vast city of Sydney until daylight had gone completely. Which would be all too soon.

The silence was getting heavier by the minute. This sitting around, waiting, was getting unbearable.

'I want to do something,' Zoe whispered. 'I can't just *sit* here.'

'There's no point in just driving around,' Teo said quietly. 'Not until we have some idea of where they are.'

There would be a point, Zoe thought. She would feel as if she was trying. She would be away from this room. From the uniforms of the police and the broken-looking figure of her father that made her angry and sad. So angry. He'd promised he would keep Emma safe. He'd been with her mother for so many years, surely he could have recognised that some trigger had been set off? She was angry with herself, too. For trusting them. Her anger at Teo had faded, however. Yes, he'd made her believe in the importance of family but that was because he lived with the truth of it.

She wanted to be with *his* family right now. With Alisi and all the aunties. With that human raft of love and faith and unconditional acceptance that would surely keep any member afloat. At least she had Teo. She could only pray that that would be enough. Her love for her daughter was woven into her love for Teo and it felt like they were one unit. A family unit. She knew that Teo was finding this unbearable too. She knew that if heading out and taking on the world would bring Emma back safely, he would have been long gone. She could feel the waves of frustration coming from him in the way his hand tightened on hers occasionally. The way his face was set in such uncharacteristically grim lines.

'She won't hurt her, Zoe.' John's low voice broke the new silence. 'I'm sure of that.'

'How can you be so sure? She's off her head, Dad. She thinks that Emma is *me*. That somehow the clock's gone backwards and she's got her own baby again.'

'That's why I'm so sure. She loves you, Zoe. She always has. She was terribly afraid that she might hurt you when you were a baby and she couldn't bear the thought of anything happening to you. That was why she had herself admitted to the hospital that first time. To keep you safe.'

'And what if she feels like that again? What if she just abandons Emma somewhere to keep *her* safe?'

'An abandoned baby would be spotted quickly,' the female police officer said. 'People might not take a second glance at a grandmother caring for a baby but they would notice something that's not right like a shot. We'd have calls coming in instantly if she left Emma somewhere.'

'I wish she would, then,' Zoe said, bitterness making her words harsh.

The crackle of one of the officer's radios made her jump and Teo's grip tightened convulsively until it was strong enough to be painful. The senior police officer unhooked the radio from his shoulder and spoke into it. They could all hear the message that was relayed to him.

'The vehicle's been located.'

'Where?'

'Parking lot at Strathfield train station.'

'Any sign of the occupants?'

'No. Engine's cold. It's been parked there for some time.'

'Anyone remember selling a ticket to an older woman with a baby?'

'Not yet. Trains are being checked. We'll keep you posted.'

'Roger.'

The police officers seemed more confident now. 'If she's on a train, there'll be plenty of people around her. She'll be on board for a couple of hours to get home. We'll find her.'

The female officer got up and turned on a light. 'Any chance of a coffee?' she asked Zoe. 'I can make it.'

'No, I'll do it.' At least it was something she could occupy herself with for a few minutes. She let go of Teo's hand and stood up. He shot to his feet as well.

'I'll help,' he said.

Teo closed the door of the kitchen as they went through it. He kept going towards where the electric kettle sat on the bench but then swung back, brushing past Zoe as he made for the door again.

He felt like a caged animal.

This was, potentially, a life-and-death situation and he was powerless to do anything about it.

Powerless to help the people he loved so much.

Zoe.

And Emma.

He could feel Zoe staring at him, wide-eyed. Was he scaring her, unleashing this tiny fraction of his frustration?

'Sorry,' he growled. 'It's killing me, not being able to *do* something to help.'

'You are doing something,' Zoe said quietly. 'I'd be a total mess if you weren't here, Teo. Or I'd be attacking my father and blaming him for everything.' Zoe's face crumpled. 'And what good would that do? He already looks so...*broken*.'

'He's exhausted. Worried about his family. He probably wants to be out there doing something too. Searching... *somewhere*.' Teo had reached the door again with his pacing. He raised his fist as though about to pound on the wood but controlled the movement with a supreme effort so that it made no sound when it finally made contact. 'Oh...God,' he ground out. 'I shouldn't be here.'

'*No*.' Zoe's voice sounded as agonised as his had. 'You shouldn't.'

He swung around to face her. 'Why did you say that? How do *you* know?'

'Know what?'

'That...that I've been here before.'

Zoe's face clouded with bewilderment. 'What are you talking about?'

'Sitting...waiting. Holding someone's hand instead of doing something. Not knowing what it is I should be doing.' Teo closed his eyes and rubbed at his forehead with his knuckles. His chest was heaving with the effort of sucking in air. He wanted to run. To hit something. To—

He felt Zoe's hand on his, pulling it down from his face.

'Is this about your mother?'

'*No*.' How could she think that he would try and make this nightmare about *him* instead of her and Emma? He shook his head to emphasise his denial.

'What happened to her, Teo?'

'She had cancer. She didn't get treatment.'

'Why not?'

'Because...because...she was ashamed of herself, I

think. She'd gone against the family to come to Australia with her boyfriend and then he left her and we were alone. If she'd gone for treatment, they would have put her in hospital. They would have put me in foster-care.'

'But what happened?' Zoe was still hanging onto his hand and she gave it a tiny shake.

'She got very sick one night. I wanted to go and get help. Find a doctor or call an ambulance or something but she wouldn't let me. She wanted me to stay with her. She wanted to hold me. For me to hold her.' Teo dragged in a breath and the air seemed to burn his lungs. 'When she started having real trouble breathing, I tried to get away but...I was just a kid and my mum was a big lady.' Teo could feel his lips wobble as he tried to smile. 'You've seen my Aunty Hina? Well, Mum could have flattened her.' He tried to swallow past the lump in his throat. 'She only let go of me when she drew her last breath. And then I ran and yelled for help but...'

'But it was too late,' Zoe finished for him. 'Oh...*Teo*...'

'They told me it wouldn't have made any difference. That she would have died that night anyway, but how could I believe that? It wasn't true.'

'No...' Zoe had tears in her eyes. 'It wasn't true.'

Her agreement was so shocking Teo froze.

'It wasn't true because it would have made a difference,' Zoe said softly. 'Don't you see, Teo? Your mum died holding the person she loved the most. *Being* held. If you'd gone and called an ambulance, she might have died in an emergency department, surrounded by strangers. They wouldn't have let a little boy go in and cuddle his mum, would they?'

Teo couldn't say anything. He'd never thought of it like that. Never.

'And I told you that all this was your fault,' Zoe groaned.

'I'm so sorry, Teo. It's *not* your fault,' she added fiercely. 'And…you went for help for me. But this is completely different, don't you see? There's nothing you *can* do except wait and…and hold my hand.'

Teo was still stunned. Still hearing the echo of Zoe's words about his mother. And about something else.

'But you don't want me here,' he said slowly.

'That's not true.'

'You said I shouldn't be here.'

He could see the way Zoe struggled to collect herself as he reminded her of those agonised words. He felt her body stiffen as she let go of his hand and pulled away, nodding.

'For your sake, not mine.' She turned and reached for the kettle, tugging the lid off with one hand as she turned on the tap with the other. But she didn't fill the kettle. Instead, she put it down and turned back to face Teo.

'Look at what's happening here. How broken my father is. That's what happens when you love someone who has a mental illness. It breaks you. It breaks families. You don't…' Zoe drew in a shaky breath. 'I care about you too much to want that to happen to you. You were right. And it's a good thing that you don't let yourself love anybody like that.'

'No. I was wrong.' Teo reached behind Zoe and turned off the tap. Then he put his hands on her shoulders and held her gaze with his own. 'I thought I was right and I thought I was protecting you by thinking like that, but now I know how wrong I was. And I knew how wrong I was the moment I saw you looking like you did when you got that phone call in the emergency department today.'

'Like what?'

'So frightened. I know how strong and brave you are, Zoe, but right then you needed someone to stand beside you and do whatever it would take to protect you. And there's only one person who can do that.'

Just for a moment, it seemed that Zoe had forgotten what was happening around them here. He knew they would focus on Emma again within seconds but this moment was about *them* and only them. Zoe was listening to every word and the fear in her eyes had a glimmer of what looked like…hope?

'The person who loves you,' Teo continued softly. 'I was so wrong when I said I couldn't love anybody like that because I can. I already *do*. And…and you are *not* your mother. You're well now. You'll stay well but even if you don't, I'm not going anywhere.'

Of course he wasn't. Because how could he leave his heart behind?

'I'm here,' he added softly, 'because there's nowhere else I could be right now. *Ou te alofa ia te oe*. I love you. I love Emma. I'm not going anywhere. *Ever*.'

Yes, there was hope in Zoe's eyes but it was snuffed out in a heartbeat as the door to the kitchen opened behind them and the senior police officer stepped into the room.

'We've had reports in from all the northbound trains,' he told them. 'I'm sorry, Zoe, but there's no sign of your mother. We don't think she got on a train. Not to go home, anyway.'

'Where…? What…?' Zoe whispered. She felt Teo's arms tighten around her.

'So what are you doing about it?' Teo asked.

'We're widening the search. Checking other trains. We've got an APB out so all stations and patrol cars are aware of the situation. It's a matter of waiting. Hoping that Celia will get in touch.'

Teo could feel the frustration clawing at him again.

'Not good enough,' he growled. 'For God's sake, man.

There's a baby out there who needs her mother. I'll get out there and start searching myself.'

'Let us do our job, son. You do yours.'

'What…sitting here and *waiting* while nothing happens?'

'No.' The police officer smiled gently. 'Looking after Zoe. That's your job and you're doing it well.' He raised an eyebrow as he backed out of the room again. 'That coffee would be great when you're ready.'

Teo was staring at the door as it closed again.

He'd just been given permission to do nothing but care for Zoe. To hold her and comfort her and…*love* her.

It was the right thing to do.

And maybe Zoe was right and it had been the right thing to do for his beloved mother as well?

The thoughts were confusing. They were washing up against years of deeply buried guilt and sorrow. But they were wonderful, too, because it felt like absolutely the right thing to do to gather Zoe into his arms and hold her against his chest. To rock her gently.

'We'll get through this,' he murmured. 'Together.'

Zoe could feel the steady thump of Teo's heart against her cheek. She could feel the unwavering strength of the arms that held her. And she could hear the echo of his words, telling her that he loved her and he wasn't going anywhere.

Somewhere, amongst the new despair of the bad news of not finding her mother and Emma on a northbound train, there was something warm deep inside her.

Teo loved her. He didn't believe she was going to end up like her mother but even if the possibility was there, he wasn't going anywhere.

'I'd better make that coffee,' she murmured finally.

'I'll do the kettle,' Teo said. 'You find the mugs.'

It was when Teo snapped the lid back onto the kettle that he paused and looked at Zoe.

'Where would you go?' he asked suddenly.

'Home,' Zoe said.

'What if you didn't know where home was exactly? If you were confused?'

'What are you getting at?'

'I'm trying to think. Let's say your mother is confused and she really believes it's you she's looking after. That she's a young mother again with her new baby but it's all a bit weird. Where would you go?'

Zoe didn't have to use her imagination to conjure up the scenario. She'd been a new mother herself only recently and she'd been frightened and confused.

'I wanted my family,' she whispered. 'My mum.' She had to blink back tears. 'But I was too scared even to think about her. Too scared that I might see what I was becoming.'

'You weren't,' Teo said gently. 'You aren't. You're *you*, Zoe, not your mother.'

Zoe nodded. But she was thinking about something else. She was using her imagination now. Thinking of her mother nearly thirty years ago. With her own baby. Wanting her own mother?

She licked suddenly dry lips as she caught Teo's gaze again.

'I think I know where she might have gone.'

CHAPTER ELEVEN

'WHERE are we going?'

Teo was driving his car. They had made coffee for the police officers and her father and then said they needed to get out of the house for a bit. A change of scene. Some fresh air. They would have their mobile phones and would come back instantly if they needed to.

'Watsons Bay. I own a piece of land up there.' Zoe's hands were trembling in her lap. This was such a long shot and what if she was way off base? They'd be back to square one. Worse than square one because maybe this was the only possibility that offered some hope.

There was an astonished silence as Teo absorbed the information. 'You own two properties?'

'Only one house. There used to be a house on this land. It was my gran's.'

'Your dad's mother?'

'No. My mother's mother. That's why it only occurred to me after you asked me where I might go with a baby.'

'Why didn't you say anything to the police?'

'Because it might waste valuable time when they could be looking somewhere else. It's totally on the wrong side of the city from where she left the car. It would be quite a mission to get trains and buses from there with a baby but at least it's an idea. A place I *can* look.'

'*We* can look,' Teo corrected, taking his eyes off the road long enough to smile at Zoe. Then he frowned. 'Why didn't your dad say anything about it?'

'He's probably forgotten. It got left to me when Gran died and we weren't allowed to talk about it again. Mum said she didn't want it. She'd never set foot on the place again. It's not as if there's a house there any more. It's a few years since I went to look at it and there was nothing more than a burnt-out shell then. It's probably fallen down completely by now.'

'What happened to the house?'

'It was left empty for too long. It got vandalised. And then it was a target for an arsonist. I was at the point of trying very hard to leave my family and all the memories behind so I could start a new life. It felt…I don't know… cursed or something. I've barely thought about it again until tonight.'

Another silence as memories crowded back on Zoe. Her grandmother's protection had been wonderful but she hadn't understood her own daughter.

It's all in her head, for heaven's sake. If she had a bit of backbone, she'd get over it.

The acceptance of and treatment for mental illness of any kind was so different now. If her mother had had the kind of treatment and support Zoe had had, would that have made things better?

'Which way here?' Teo asked as they approached some traffic lights.

'Stay on Oxford Street. After Bondi, it'll lead onto the old South Head road. I could be wrong.' Zoe was twisting her hands together in her lap. 'It's only a possibility if it's really true that Mum's confused enough to think she's back in time. Before the fights.'

'What went wrong?'

'Gran was a wonderful woman but she was pretty old school and as tough as they came.' Zoe's smile was poignant. 'She told Mum she was being a drama queen and it was time she snapped out of it. That she didn't deserve a beautiful child if she couldn't pull herself together. She'd arrive and take me away to stay with her here in Sydney and then a few months later Dad would turn up and take me home again because Mum was out of hospital and couldn't stand the thought of her mother taking care of me. She stopped talking to Gran before I was old enough to really know what was going on.'

'And you got handed around like a parcel?' Teo sounded horrified.

'I loved Gran. She...*wanted* me. She loved me.'

'Your dad loves you. I'm sure your mum does, too.'

Zoe shook her head. 'Dad thought it was my fault that Mum went crazy in the first place.'

'What?' Teo took his eyes off the road again to flick an incredulous glance at Zoe. 'You are kidding, right?'

'No. I heard someone say it when I was about five or six. Some women from the church brought a casserole around when my mother had gone into hospital again. "It all started with her having that baby," one of them said. "That triggered the depression and it's been a downward slide ever since. No wonder John wishes it had never happened."'

'Malicious gossip,' Teo snorted. 'I've only just met your father but I can see how much he loves you. And Emma. He's desperate to look after his family. His whole family.'

'It didn't feel that way when I was growing up.'

'No.' Teo was silent for a minute. 'But we don't understand a lot of stuff when we're kids, do we?'

He sounded as though he had more on his mind than this mission. Of course he did.

Had he always carried the guilt that by loving his

mother he had somehow contributed to her death? He'd become a man who had devoted his life to saving people. He even factored in a long journey back to the land of his birth at regular intervals to try and make sure what had happened to his mother never happened to anybody else. He wanted to be the one to pick up the early signs of something like cancer and ensure that one of his own people got the treatment they needed.

Good grief…did he feel the same way about Sefa? That he'd missed something he should have picked up? There must have been a point there when he'd been afraid of losing the little boy he clearly loved so much. No wonder he'd pulled his professional role around himself like a cloak. She could understand now and it felt like the volume of her love for this man had just been turned up to full power. Her heart ached for him. She would be there for him from now on. She would give him all the love he'd never allowed himself to accept since he'd been that lost, guilty child.

'Did you see Sefa today?' she asked suddenly.

'Of course.'

'How is he?'

'Doing really well. It's a fast-growing tumour so it's responding fast to the chemotherapy. Finn said he'd bring the specialist in to look at doing the cryotherapy possibly as early as next week.'

'So he's going to be all right?'

'Yeah…' Teo's voice was gruff. 'He probably won't even lose his eyesight. We have you to thank for that, Zoe. You're not going to believe the kind of party you'll be having the next time you're back in the islands.'

Would she? Would she ever party again if something had happened to Emma?

'Take the next turn,' she told Teo. 'There's a sign there for The Gap.'

Zoe felt her blood run cold as the words left her mouth. She gasped.

'*What?*' Teo swerved the car towards the curb and slammed on the brakes. 'What is it, Zoe?'

'I didn't think. I… Oh, my God…Gran's house is so close to The Gap.'

'What difference does that make?'

'Don't you know? You *must* know. You've lived in Sydney for so long.'

Comprehension was dawning. 'It's the spit of land that makes it look like a harbour entrance. Where that ship got wrecked way back.' His voice was trailing away. 'The place with the cliffs.'

Where about fifty people a year went to commit suicide. Zoe couldn't bring herself to say the words aloud. She didn't need to. With a wrench Teo put the car back into gear and put his foot down on the accelerator. The engine of the little sports car growled in response and responded with a smooth burst of speed.

Apart from the terse directions Zoe gave Teo, nothing else was said for the rest of the journey.

Because there was nothing else to say, was there?

The garden had been her grandmother's pride and joy but the masses of trees were overgrown now and made a suburban jungle that covered a large piece of land. What had once been lawns and flowerbeds was now a knee-high tangle of weeds. A kind of track had been trampled through the growth. Vandals? Her mother?

Zoe followed Teo towards the blackened stump of the old house. Surprisingly, it still had most of its exterior walls. Steps to the veranda were broken and dangerous and Teo kept a firm grip on her hand. With his other hand, he angled the torch he'd brought from the car. The small spotlight roved over what was in front of them. A desolate ruin of a family home. The front door of the house hung on one hinge and every window was a gaping hole with a few shards of broken glass.

'We shouldn't go inside,' Teo said heavily. 'It's too dangerous.'

Zoe was shaking all over now. Shivering with both the chill of the night and an unspeakable fear. If her mother had come here, she couldn't help but be forced back into the present time, could she? She would feel the emptiness of this house and know that it had been a very long time since it had been lived in. She would know that she wouldn't find her mother here. She would remember why.

She would feel...desperate?

Zoe felt desperate. Her mother wasn't here. Emma wasn't here.

She sank down onto the edge of the bottom step. She buried her face in her hands. Teo paced, shining his torch over the house. Around the menacing darkness of the garden. He wasn't going to give up. Not yet.

'There,' he said. 'Where would that go?'

Zoe raised her head. The cobbles of an old path showed between flattened clumps of grass. 'There're steps further down the hill. There used to be a goldfish pond and a summer house. And there was a gate that opened onto the track to the reserve. If you go far enough, you get to the cliffs.'

They were so far away from any other house that she could hear the way Teo pulled in a breath. The night was so still at this moment. So dark. So quiet and...dead.

And then they heard it.

A tiny whimper being carried who knew how far in the still night.

Zoe was on her feet in a heartbeat. Her heart recognised that sound. *'Emma.'*

Teo had heard it too. He was already moving down that old path.

Zoe caught up with him as he went through the gate. Hand in hand, they ran along the track. A public place this, and it was clear and easy to navigate. It led to a lookout. There were signs here warning people not to go past the fences but everybody knew how dangerous these cliffs were. Nobody went out of the safe area—unless driven by a force so powerful it was greater than the will to survive.

The way it had driven her mother.

Celia Harper was standing on the other side of the safety barrier. Only a few feet away from the edge of one of those famous cliffs.

Zoe was dragging in a breath ready to scream at her mother. She was gathering her strength to leap over the fence but something stopped her.

Teo.

'Don't rush her,' he said, his voice low. 'Stay right where you are.' He put his fingers across her mouth. 'Don't even say anything.'

Zoe pressed her own hand to her mouth as Teo's grip pushed her into a crouch. She wrapped her other hand around her body and stayed there, hunched and frozen. She had no idea what to do.

Did Teo?

He seemed to. He stood there silently for a long moment and then he spoke.

'Hey…you're Celia, aren't you?'

Her mother's head whipped sideways. 'Who are you?'

'I'm Teo.' He didn't elaborate any further. Was he trying to find out if Celia was back in touch with reality yet?

Whether she knew that the baby she was holding was not Zoe?

Was he smiling at her mother? She was staring at him.

'Bit cold out here, isn't it?'

Celia nodded.

'Would you like to go somewhere warmer?'

She shook her head. 'I went to my mother's house but…' Another headshake, confused this time. 'But I don't think she's there.'

'I could help you find her, maybe.'

'No. She wouldn't want to see me anyway. She hates me.'

'Mothers never hate their children.'

'She thinks I'm weak. And she's right. I don't deserve to have a baby.'

Zoe's heart stopped as she saw her mother move but all she did was pull whatever was covering Emma into place.

'Nobody thinks you're weak, Celia. We understand.'

'No. Nobody understands.'

Maybe that was true, Zoe thought suddenly. Her mother had lived in a small community. She'd had her husband but the only other member of her family had been impatient with her and offered no compassion. Had her grandmother been afraid, as so many people were, that mental illness was somehow contagious?

How grim had life been for her?

Maybe her mother had never known what family could be like?

Zoe hadn't known, until Teo had opened that door into another world. He'd made her baby laugh. He'd taught her to relax. She'd been so afraid. Trying so hard to cope and be perfect and the stress had made it impossible to include joy in her life. *She* had it now, thanks to Teo. Joy and the love that created it.

What joy had her mother ever had?

Had Teo caught something of her thoughts? He was looking at her now. There was a depth of compassion in that look. A touch of helplessness but also a strength that Zoe could hang onto.

She stood up very slowly.

'I understand,' she said. 'I've been there.'

Celia's head turned as slowly as Zoe had moved.

'Who…? What…? I don't understand…'

'It's all right.' Teo's voice was gentle. 'Everything's all right, Celia.'

'No…' Celia looked agitated now. She moved again and this time it was her feet. She stepped backwards and then turned. Towards the cliff.

Maybe Emma could sense the danger. Her cry was loud and demanding.

'Shh…' Celia rocked the baby. 'Shh, darling.'

Zoe started moving. She felt Teo's hand catch her arm but then let go.

'Mum?'

Celia stopped.

'It's horrible, isn't it?' Zoe said softly. She was edging sideways. Trying to get herself between Celia and the edge of the cliff. She could see Teo poised, ready to leap but undecided about whether it was the best thing to do. 'Feeling lost. Feeling like nobody understands.'

The baby's cries were getting louder. Celia swung her head from side to side. 'I don't know what to do,' she moaned.

'You're doing the right thing,' Zoe said. 'You're helping to look after Emma. That's what grandmothers do. But Emma needs her mum now. She needs *me*.'

'You…?'

'I'm her mum. She needs me. You're my mum. I need *you*.'

'No…nobody needs me.'

'You're family.' Teo's voice came from closer than Zoe expected. He was right beside her. 'We all need our family.'

Celia was staring at Zoe again. 'Who is this, Zoe?'

'It's Teo, Mum,' Zoe said. 'He's family too.'

She stepped forward and took Emma from her mother's arms. The sheer relief of holding her baby was enough to make her knees buckle but it didn't matter because there was a strong arm to support her. And Teo had a free arm. He used it to gather Celia close.

'That's right,' he said. 'I'm family and families look after each other.' He was moving them all away from the edge of the cliff. Towards a safe place.

A phone call would be all that it would take and they would have all the help they needed. The police. An ambulance that could take Celia to where she needed to be to get the kind of help that even Teo couldn't provide.

She could take Emma home and look after her and know that her precious baby was safe again.

That she herself was safe because she wasn't about to lose her daughter.

Or the man she loved so much.

Zoe snuggled closer to Teo's body. Help would certainly come and very soon, but she didn't need to be anywhere else to feel safe. Teo's arms did that for her and she knew they always would.

Overwhelming relief gave way to gratitude.

Love.

Enough love for everybody. Even her mother.

'Teo's right, Mum,' she said softly. 'Everything's all right. Or it will be. You'll see.'

CHAPTER TWELVE

Teo had been so right about so many things.

About how she needed to relax and not stress so much.

About how she was not her mother and that she was in control of her own destiny.

About how she wouldn't believe the kind of party she'd be having the next time she was back in the islands.

A wedding party.

It was over now. The celebration and music and a feast. Emma was asleep, safely surrounded by what was now her own family. The couple at the centre of the celebrations had slipped away to have a quiet moment together.

Getting married on the same beach where she and Teo had first made love had been too perfect for words. In bare feet, with baby waves lapping at her toes and dampening the hem of the most beautiful white dress that had ever been created. Zoe still had the fragrance of frangipani coming from the flowers in her hair as they found themselves back on the beach. She had the warmth of a tropical night surrounding her and the colours of a glorious sunset painting the evening sky.

Best of all, she had the arms of the man she loved around her. His lips touching hers, his eyes holding the promise of everything she could ever want in her future.

'We'll have to do this again,' she said.

'What...this?' Teo kissed her again. Long and slow and so tenderly.

'Mmm.' Zoe smiled. 'Definitely. But I meant get married.'

'I don't think so.' Teo sounded very stern. 'I have no intention of getting *un*married, thanks very much.'

'Just another ceremony. Back in Sydney. So that everybody from the Harbour can be there. So that...Mum can be there, when she's well enough.'

Teo nodded. 'Did I rush you? So much has happened in a very short space of time.'

'It's perfect.' Zoe reached up to touch his face. 'When something feels this right, why wait? It would be special to share it with people back home, that's all.'

'But this is home, too? Will you be happy spending as much time in the islands as I'd like to?'

'Being with you is my home, Teo. It has been, since I first met you. Being here in the islands is a huge bonus. I love it.'

'We'll have to come often for the next year or so. To supervise building that new wing on the hospital.'

Zoe's smile was joyous. 'Won't it be wonderful? Who would have thought that Gran's property would be worth so much? *Millions*.'

'You're a very wealthy woman, Zoe.' Teo's smile was just as wide. 'Thank goodness you met me before you knew it.'

'Why?'

'Because with that kind of wealth I'd imagine you could get anything you want. Any*one* you want.'

'But I did.' Zoe stood on tiptoe to kiss Teo again. 'I want *you*, Teo Tuala. I was the richest woman on earth before I even knew about Gran's place. I will never stop wanting you. Loving you.'

A rogue wave swept in and washed around her ankles. Zoe squeaked and Teo scooped her into his arms. He didn't seem to mind that the trousers of his lovely dark suit were getting soaked. He stayed right where he was in the foam and looked down at the woman in his arms.

'For ever's not going to be long enough,' he said. 'For loving you.'

And then he kissed her. Again.

* * * * *

SYDNEY HARBOUR HOSPITAL: HOSPITAL: LUCA'S BAD GIRL

BY
AMY ANDREWS

Amy Andrews has always loved writing, and still can't quite believe that she gets to do it for a living. Creating wonderful heroines and gorgeous heroes and telling their stories is an amazing way to pass the day. Sometimes they don't always act as she'd like them to—but then neither do her kids, so she's kind of used to it. Amy lives in the very beautiful Samford Valley, with her husband and aforementioned children, along with six brown chooks and two black dogs. She loves to hear from her readers. Drop her a line at www.amyandrews.com.au.

To six Aussies and a Kiwi—thank you!
I had so much fun writing this continuity with you.
And to Meredith Webber, an amazing writer,
fabulous mentor and generous friend. Your
down-to-earth advice always keeps me grounded and
your encouragement has led me into new worlds.

CHAPTER ONE

DR MIA MCKENZIE didn't know it yet but her night was about to go from bad to worse.

And that was no mean feat.

A full moon didn't usually bode well for emergency departments and this clear, cold Saturday night was no different. Moonbeams sprinkled like fairy dust on the world-renowned surface of Sydney Harbour, lending a deceptive calm to the view from the windows of Sydney Harbour Hospital.

But inside the walls of the emergency department it was crazy town!

At two in the morning there had been no let up from the insanity. SHH, or The Harbour to those who worked there, was living up to its reputation as the busiest emergency department in the city.

'I could have been a dermatologist,' Mia grumbled to Dr Evie Lockheart, her best friend and flatmate, as she strode out of the resus cubical, turning her back on the torrent of abuse from a drug addict she'd just brought back from the brink of death.

'They don't get abused by patients at half past stupid o'clock. You know why? Because they're sleeping. No on-call, no such thing as a dermatological emergency in the middle of the night, no urgent consults required.'

Evie, clutching a portable ultrasound unit, grinned. 'You'd be bored to tears.'

Mia's long blonde ponytail swished against her shoulder blades as she made her way to the central nurses' station with the patient's chart in hand. 'I could do bored.'

Evie snorted. 'Yep, whatever you say.'

Mia ignored her friend's sarcasm. 'How much longer are you and George Clooney going to be with the MVA?'

Evie laughed. 'The name is Luca. Dr Luca di Angelo.'

As far as Mia was concerned, the hospital's new director of trauma looked more like the devil than an angel.

He certainly seemed to be having a devil of a time with every available female walking the halls of SHH in the very short time he'd been here.

Which was fine by her. It was his life. And in a way she admired him for it. She too liked to keep her liaisons short and sweet.

But maybe that's what caused an itch up her spine whenever he was around—besides his disturbing good looks apparently honed beneath a Sicilian sun. She recognised a kindred spirit.

And didn't like what she saw.

'And he really is quite dishy.'

'Yes,' Mia mused. 'That he is.'

Evie grinned. Now, why couldn't she be interested in a tall, dark, handsome Italian who was living up to the reputation of sex god that had preceded his arrival at The Harbour a few weeks ago? Why was it the infuriating, dictatorial Dr Finn Kennedy that her brain insisted on conjuring up with monotonous regularity?

'Anyway,' she said shaking the thought away. 'We're stabilising the patient at the moment. He needs to go to Theatre for a laparotomy.'

Mia nodded. 'Okay, but when he's gone, go home. You were supposed to have finished three hours ago.'

'Yeah, yeah.' Evie grinned as she departed.

Mia had ten minutes' respite to catch up on some charts before a stocky man with swarthy features and wild eyes burst through the ambulance bay doors. 'My wife…she's in labour. The baby's coming now!' And then turned around and raced out the door again.

Mia sprang to her feet as a shot of adrenaline surged into her system. She hurried after the man, followed by Caroline, the triage nurse. She didn't notice the chill in the air, just the beaten-up old car parked at a crazy angle near the doors and a woman's urgent cries.

'Hurry,' the man yelled, wringing his hands.

Mia was there in seconds. The woman was lying on the back seat yelling, 'It's coming, it's coming.'

'Hi, I'm Dr McKenzie,' Mia said over the din. 'What's your name?'

'Rh-Rhiannon,' the woman panted.

Mia smiled at her encouragingly. 'How far along are you?'

'Thirty weeks, she's thirty weeks, all right?' the husband barked.

The man seemed hostile and had his wife's needs not been so urgent she'd have told him to back off. The last thing she needed right now while having to deliver a ten-week premature baby was a man with some kind of chip on his shoulder.

'Caroline, page the neonatology team, please,' Mia said quietly as she reached for the endless supply of gloves she had stashed in her pockets. 'And get Arthur to bring out a gurney.

'Okay, let's have a look here,' Mia said calmly.

The woman groaned again and it took Mia two seconds to identify a crowning head, despite the poor light. 'Right, well, you're absolutely correct, Rhiannon, this baby is coming.'

'I have to push,' Rhiannon yelled.

'That's fine.' Mia nodded, her heart bonging in her chest like the bells of a clock tower. 'I'm here to catch.'

Thirty seconds later the scrawny bawling infant slipped into Mia's waiting hands. 'You have a boy.' Mia grinned, laying the baby on the cloth seat and hoping that Caroline thought to bring back something warm to protect the newborn from the brisk air.

'Let me see it,' the father demanded.

But Caroline arrived, blocking his view as she handed Mia a pre-packaged emergency birth pack and some blankets fresh out of the blanket warmer. 'Neonates are doing an emergency intubation in Labour ward,' she said quietly. 'They'll get here as soon as they can.'

Mia nodded as she quickly laid the babe on a warm soft blanket, unwrapped the birth pack and efficiently clamped and cut the cord. She bundled the still crying baby up and handed him to Caroline.

'Get him into Resus so we can give him a proper check over, although his lungs seem pretty fine to me.'

Caroline laughed as she turned to go.

'Where are you taking it?' the father demanded.

'Inside,' Caroline said calmly. 'You can come too if you like.'

The father stalked after Caroline while Mia and Arthur helped Rhiannon onto the gurney. They covered her in warm blankets and pushed her inside to the resus cube next to her baby. The little boy was quiet now as he basked beneath the warm rays of a cot's overhead heater.

The father was pacing the cubicle when they arrived and seemed agitated. 'Red hair. It's got red hair,' the father growled at Rhiannon as he approached her with a sneer on his face.

'Oh, for crying out loud, Stan. Your grandfather had red hair.'

'Whose is it?' he demanded, rattling the rail of the gurney. 'Who's the father?'

Mia felt the hairs rise on the back of her neck as the father's puzzling behaviour gained some context. But context or not, he didn't get to act like a bully in her ER.

Thoughts of her own father wormed their way into her head and she quashed them ruthlessly.

'Sir!' Mia stood between him and the exhausted Rhiannon. 'You will not raise your voice in here. Whatever the issue is, this is not the time or place for it. Now, why don't you go and shift your car from the ambulance bay? When you come back, you'd better have calmed down or I *will* call Security.'

Mia was used to dealing with emotionally charged situations. Also drunks, drug addicts and a whole bunch of other people who didn't respect the sanctity of a hospital.

But she was a doctor. And Rhiannon and the baby were her patients. It was her duty to protect them.

The man scowled at her and left, muttering to himself.

'I'm sorry,' Rhiannon apologised. 'He gets so paranoid sometimes but he's harmless.'

Mia smiled. 'It's fine.'

A midwife from the maternity ward chose that moment to arrive. 'The team's going to be another twenty minutes or so,' she apologised.

'That's all right,' Mia dismissed. 'I think this little tyke's going to be fine.'

The ugly incident with Stan was forgotten as the midwife tended to Rhiannon, delivering the placenta while Mia gave the baby a check over. 'They'll probably want to keep him for the night in Special Care, given his early arrival, just to be on the safe side,' Mia pronounced, 'but everything checks out so far.'

She stood aside for the midwife to wrap the little boy up in that special way they did with babies so they looked just like glowworms, with only their little faces showing. Then Mia picked up the precious little package and asked, 'Would you like to hold your son?'

Rhiannon nodded and Mia was walking the baby over to her when the curtain flicked back a little and Stan stood there, looking slightly mollified. The time away seemed to have helped. Mia changed tack. 'Would you like to hold him?' she asked.

In Mia's experience, babies melted even the hardest of hearts. What man could resist such a gorgeous package? Hopefully this little impatient cherub would help Stan focus on what was important in life.

He looked uncertain for a moment then looked at Rhiannon. 'Can I?'

She smiled at him and Mia could see the love shining in the other woman's eyes. 'Of course.'

Mia eased the little bundle into Stan's arms. He seemed more dazed than elated but Mia knew that for some new fathers it was a big adjustment. He walked up and down the length of the cubicle with the baby, rocking him as he went, his gaze fixed on his face.

'What are you going to call him?' Caroline asked.

'I like Michael,' Rhiannon murmured.

The tight swaddling had loosened a little from the rocking and the baby stirred, displacing the wrap covering his head. Stan stopped as he stared down at a shock of red hair. He whipped around to face his wife. 'Is that his name?' he demanded. The baby started to cry. 'Michael? The man you've been sleeping with?'

Rhiannon groaned. 'Stop it, Stan. I'm sick of these accusations. You know there's only ever been you.'

'I want a paternity test,' he yelled.

Mia looked at Caroline then at a near-to-tears Rhiannon. 'Stan—'

Stan swung wildly around to face her and the baby cried louder. 'I want you…' he jabbed the air with an index finger '…to do a paternity test.'

'Stan this is ridiculous,' Rhiannon wailed, a tear trekking down her face.

Stan swung back. 'Are you refusing?'

'Okay, Stan, enough,' Mia said firmly. Stan turned abruptly and faced her. 'That is no way to be talking and certainly no way to be flinging a baby around. Listen to him, you're making him cry.'

She walked briskly towards Stan, her arms extended. 'Give him to me.'

Stan leapt back, his eyes wild again as he pulled a pocket knife out of his back pocket, flicking the blade open with one hand while he clutched his son in the other.

'Stay back,' he screamed. Caroline gasped, Rhiannon wailed and Mia stopped in her tracks. 'Don't come near me.'

Stan swung wildly from side to side, brandishing the knife as he backed slowly away from Mia.

Oh, good Lord! Mia felt a spurt of annoyance. *She did not have time for this.*

'Okay, Stan.' Mia summoned her most placatory voice as she put her hands out to calm the situation. She didn't think that Stan would harm anyone but that wasn't the way to play it when he was holding a brand-new thirty weeker in one arm and a knife in the other.

'Okay, I can do that for you,' she soothed, deftly placing her own body between Stan and Caroline.

Caroline, bless her cotton socks, picked up on her cue and quietly crept out of the cubicle. Mia knew one push of the panic button located under the desk in the nurses' station and every security guard rostered for the shift would be here in under two minutes.

'But you're going to need to give me the baby first.' She took another step towards Stan, tuning out the lusty newborn's cries and Rhiannon's pleading.

Stan slashed the blade through the air. 'No! Get back,' he yelled.

Luca di Angelo, who was passing the resus bay, frowned at the raised voice, louder even than the squalling baby. He strode in through the partially open curtain, surveying the scene rapidly.

A man with a knife. A bawling baby being held to ransom. A crying woman. A terrified nurse. And gutsy Dr Mia McKenzie—aloof, frosty little Mia—standing in the thick of it.

'What the devil is going on here?' he demanded.

Stan swung around again, slashing the air in Luca's general direction. 'Stay back,' he yelled.

Luca stopped. 'Dr McKenzie?'

'It's fine, Dr di Angelo,' she said, a placid smile plastered to her face as she inched closer to Stan. Very soon there'd be maximum force at her disposal—she could do without the Lone Ranger potentially ramping the situation up in the mean time.

Even if he did look good enough to spread on toast.

Mia's stomach rumbled.

'Stan here just wants a paternity test so he's going to give me the baby and I'll draw some blood. Right, Stan?'

'No.' Stan looked wildly between the two of them. 'The baby stays,' he insisted.

Luca watched Mia in his peripheral vision as she crept forward at a snail's pace. 'But how can we take blood when you're holding a baby, Stan?' Luca reasoned, distracting the man.

Mia, grateful if a little surprised that Luca had caught on really fast, took another step closer.

'Stay back,' Stan bellowed. The baby's cries rose another octave.

'I can't take your blood from here, Stan,' Mia soothed.

The adrenaline flowing through her system brought

everything into sharp focus. The sweat on Stan's brow. The harsh suck of his breath as he heaved air in and out of his lungs. The white spittle forming at the corner of his mouth. The way he turned the knife over and over in his palm and constantly shifted his weight from one foot to the other as his gaze darted between the two doctors.

But she was probably even more aware of Luca. Somehow it was he who dominated the room, not Stan. He towered over the knife-wielding man, all lean and broad shouldered, in sharp contrast to Stan's stocky stature. And despite the deceptive casualness of his hands-in-pocket stance, Mia could see the hard clench of his jaw and sense the coiled rigidity in those muscles barely contained behind the snug-fitting polo shirt.

She reminded him of a taipan, ready to strike. Swift and deadly.

Just then there was a commotion behind them as several security staff arrived at once.

Stan looked over Mia's shoulder. 'What are they doing here?' he roared, his hold on the baby tightening and causing further lusty protest.

Luca held out his hand as Stan's agitation increased. 'It's standard hospital procedure,' Luca soothed, moving a little closer. 'It'll be all right, though. I'm going to ask them to stand back, okay?'

'I don't think that's a good idea, Doc,' the chief security officer said.

'Back! You heard him, get back!' Stan shouted, brandishing the knife a little too close to the baby's head.

The midwife gasped.

Luca turned to the security contingent. 'It's okay,'

he assured them. Then he turned back to Stan. 'They're going, see?' Luca said as he heard the guards shuffling away.

Mia kept her gaze focused on Stan and the baby. 'Okay, Stan, now we've done something for you, you've got to do something for us.' She covered up her next step closer by holding out her arms. 'Give me the baby. He's scared and hungry. Listen to him. I'm sure a nice feed will settle him down and we can talk about this without upsetting him any more.'

And, frankly, the infant's cries were getting on her last nerve. The situation was fraught enough without the distinct urgency of an escalating newborn baby's cries.

'She's right, Stan,' Luca agreed as he edged nearer too. 'This isn't something a baby should be part of.'

'It's not my fault.' Stan's voice cracked as his face beseeched them. 'I work hard all day and she repays me by sleeping with half the neighbourhood.'

Mia felt a chill as if a ghostly hand from the past had stroked down her spine. She ignored it.

Luca nodded. 'I know. Believe me, I know.' And he did. He understood the desperation that Stan was feeling, the sense of betrayal. *Intimately.*

Mia glanced sharply at Luca. There was empathy, real empathy, in his tone.

'We can talk about all that, Stan,' Luca continued. 'Just give the baby to Dr McKenzie.'

Stan looked from one to the other and Mia saw the uncertainty on his face, saw that even Stan in his crazed state had registered Luca's compassion. She took advantage and moved forward slowly, unsurprised to sense Luca doing the same.

'It's okay, Stan, you're doing the right thing,' Mia reassured him.

Stan shook his head from side to side. 'I just need to know.'

'Of course,' Luca murmured. 'Of course you do, Stan.'

They were close now and Mia could sense Stan weakening. His grip on the knife had slackened. But so had his hold on the baby. Everything inside her urged her to leap forward and snatch the bawling infant from him but she knew any sudden movements would be a bad idea.

'Give your little boy to me, Stan,' she implored quietly.

Stan looked down at the crying bundle, the red hair even more vivid against the white of the wrap. He shook his head, his grip tightening again.

'He's not my baby!' he roared, lunging the knife at her.

Everything slowed as Mia watched it come towards her chest. She wasn't conscious of anything else, just the hypnotic arc of the blade as its point drew closer to her heart.

'Mia!'

Luca reached out and grabbed her, pulling her towards him. The sweeping slash of the knife missed her torso completely but sliced into the flesh of her upper arm. Mia gasped as bright, piercing pain stole her breath.

Luca swore in his native tongue as his hand shot out and crushed Stan's wrist in a vice-like grip. Stan yelped and dropped the knife.

'Security!'

His voice cracked like a whip into the charged atmosphere and in an instant five burly guards had entered the fray. The fight instantly went out of Stan at the sight of overwhelming force.

'The baby,' Luca demanded, and the midwife leapt forward, snatching the squalling infant.

'Go easy,' Luca ordered as the guards hauled a now passive Stan away. 'Are you okay?' he asked switching his attention to Mia.

She nodded automatically as the baby, now safe in his mother's embrace, began to settle. 'I'm fine.' Even though the hand that had instinctively covered the wound to apply pressure was sticky with her own blood. It had quickly oozed through the material of her cotton shirt.

Luca looked at the dark red blood running down her arm and shook his head. Most women he knew would have been hysterical by now. But not Mia. She'd kept her head in the face of an emotionally overwrought father with a knife and had dismissed what looked like a substantial wound as if it were a paper cut.

'Go to the minor ops room, I'll take a look at it.'

'It's fine, just superficial,' she said dismissively.

Luca pointed. 'Blood is running down your arm.'

Mia looked down at the thick trickle, surprised to see it. 'I'll get Evie to look at it.'

'I sent her home.'

'Dr di Angelo?' Caroline interrupted them. 'The psych reg is on the phone. He wants to speak with you.'

Luca quirked an eyebrow at her. 'I can't have one of my staff expiring from blood loss. It wouldn't look very good. Minor ops. Now. I'll be along after the call.'

Mia watched him go, a well of resentment rising in

her. She'd been looking after herself for a lot of years, she didn't need Mr Tall Dark and Handsome pulling the boss card and she certainly didn't need him fussing over her.

No one had ever fussed over her. *And that was just the way she liked it.*

A couple of steri-strips and she'd be fine.

A few minutes later, Mia pushed into the on-call room and plonked herself down at the table in the kitchen area, spilling her supplies on the cluttered top. Her arm hurt like hell and all she wanted to do was crawl into one of the private rooms off to her left and collapse on one of the pull-out beds.

The adrenaline had worn off and her earlier tiredness had taken hold and intensified.

And if she was asleep, the memories that Stan's actions had unleashed tonight couldn't bother her.

It was quiet in the room as she fumbled one-handed with the buttons of her blouse. The sleeves had a firm cuff that sat snugly around her biceps and couldn't be rolled up enough to gain a good visual of the damage. She winced as she slipped the blouse off, every movement jarring though her lacerated deltoid.

She tossed it on the floor—that was going straight in the bin.

She inspected her spaghetti-strapped top, pleased to see that no blood had seeped into it. This kind of undergarment was a permanent fixture beneath whatever shirt she was wore on a night shift. The hospital air-conditioning seemed to reach freezing point at around four in the morning and, even in summer, the extra layer helped.

Mia was especially grateful for it tonight.

She looked down at the wound on her upper arm. The blood had dried and crusted, making it difficult to tell the extent of the laceration. It looked ugly, though, as she gently probed it with her index finger. It was quite long and for a moment she let herself think about what could have happened had Luca not pulled her out of the way.

She noticed her hand was trembling and she dropped it from the wound, clamping down on her thoughts.

She hadn't been stabbed in the chest. She hadn't died. *Luca had pulled her out of the way.*

But it didn't stop the trembling from spreading to all her limbs and then to her insides. She took a couple of deep breaths, desperately trying to quell the outbreak.

It was a reaction, that was all. It would settle.

But the longer she sat, trying to get control of her breathing and the shaking, the more vulnerable she was to her emotions and thoughts. And she hated that—she'd learned long ago they didn't get you anywhere.

But tonight she didn't seem to be able to stop them.

Was that how her own father had felt when he'd found out about the paternity of her stillborn sister? Like Stan? Desperate and enraged? If there'd been a knife or a gun handy, would he have used it on her mother?

He'd walked away from them that day but she hadn't known why until years later. Years of blaming him for abandoning them, years of hating him, only to find out that it had been her mother's infidelities that had driven her father away.

Mia shook her head. *Stop it. Stop it!*

This situation tonight had come too close to home but there was no need to fall apart. She wasn't ten years old any more. She was an adult.

Clean yourself up and get back out there again!

Mia forced herself to action. To tend to the wound. Open the dressing pack, pour in some antiseptic lotion, pick up the gauze, work away at the dried blood.

It was awkward and hurt like the blazes but she welcomed the distraction from her thoughts and her shaking hands settled with a familiar routine.

Two minutes later Luca strode through the door. Mia glanced up at him, feeling strangely naked with her blouse discarded. Which was ridiculous—she was more than adequately covered. She ignored him, returning to the task at hand.

Luca lounged against the table and smiled to himself as Mia barely acknowledged his arrival. 'You're making a mess of that,' he mused.

Mia glared at him. 'It's a little difficult.'

'I do believe I told you I would attend to your wound.' He folded his arms across his chest. 'But you don't like asking for help, do you, little Mia?'

His slight accent gave his deep baritone a very sexy edge as it rolled over her. 'It's Mia, or Dr McKenzie. Please refrain from addressing me any other way.'

Luca chuckled as he pushed off the bench. 'Okay, *Mia*.' He sat on the chair next to her. 'Allow me,' he said as he picked up some gauze and dabbed at the wound.

Mia didn't protest—she was making a hash of it anyway. His touch was gentle as he coaxed the dried blood from the cut and she shivered. His fingers were dark against her paler skin and long.

Her father had long fingers. A pianist's hands. He was tall too, like Luca. He'd told her he was her prince and she was his princess and they'd be together for ever.

And then he'd left.

She squeezed her eyes shut. *Stop it. Stop it.*

Luca watched her. It was the first time he'd spent any length of time in her company and he was curious. He'd already noticed on their brief acquaintance she was a good-looking woman with a cute mouth and a sassy swagger.

But up close she was really quite exquisite.

Her face was long, as were her eyelashes. A frown appeared between her brows and her lips parted. She looked in pain.

'Am I hurting you?' he murmured.

Mia's eyes fluttered open. *How had he got that close?* She could see the individual whiskers making up the smooth blue-black of his jaw and just make out the black pupil in the middle of his bottomless brown eyes. His hair, as dark as his eyes, was thick with a slight wave that brushed his forehead and the tops of his ears.

And his mouth. The full curve to that bottom lip was wicked.

His fingers stroked gently over her skin as he cleaned the wound and it reminded her it had been a while since a man had touched her.

She lowered her gaze to the column of his throat. 'No.'

Luca was captivated by the slide show of emotions in her large blue eyes as magnificent and as transparent as a stained-glass window. The husky timbre of her voice wove between the bands of steel around his heart. 'Are you okay?'

Mia nodded, keeping her gaze firmly fixed on his throat. The long tanned column of his neck was also shaded in blue-black smoothness. She remembered how she'd loved the sandpaper roughness of her father's neck as he'd cuddled her close to read to her at night.

Damn it! She gripped the back of the chair hard. 'I'm fine.'

'You've been through an ordeal tonight. That knife came very close to—'

'I said I'm fine,' Mia interrupted, raising her face to scowl at him. 'Just clean the damn wound.'

CHAPTER TWO

LUCA paused in his ministrations for a moment, the blue of her eyes frosty now. He'd only known her for a few short weeks and while he'd been impressed with her empathy for patients and her good rapport with her colleagues he'd also sensed she was a woman who preferred to keep herself pretty much to herself.

But she'd always been polite about it.

Something was definitely eating at Mia McKenzie tonight.

He shifted his attention back to the wound.

'It's borderline,' he mused, looking at the clean ten-centimetre laceration. 'It's deeper laterally, could probably do with a couple of sutures there.'

Mia nodded to the pile of medical supplies on the table. 'Steri-strips there somewhere.'

'Sutures would be better.'

'Steri-strips will be fine.'

'The scarring will be worse if we use steri-strips.'

Mia shrugged. 'I don't care about a scar.'

Luca looked at her for a moment then fished around for the strips. 'Most women would,' he murmured when he located them. He doubted he'd ever been with a single woman who didn't obsess over the slightest blemish.

'I'm not most women.'

Luca chuckled. 'Yes. I think you are right.'

Mia sat still as he opened the packet and secured the wound edges together, applying firm tension through each sticky strip. Then he applied an adhesive dressing over the top. She watched as he absently brushed the pad of his thumb back and forth over the dressing as if he were a parent, rubbing a boo-boo better.

Just like her father had done.

'You look like you've got a lot on your mind,' he murmured.

Unfortunately, he was right. She hadn't been able to stop thinking about her father since Stan's episode. It had probably been the first time ever she'd been confronted with how emotionally untenable it had been for him to stay.

'It's busy,' she said brusquely, rising from the chair and clearing away the detritus from her dressing and tossing it in the bin. 'We can't just skulk in here all night.'

'The team have got it covered. And you're not going back out there until you've had a break. Try and get some sleep.' She opened her mouth to protest and he stood. 'That's an order.'

Great! What in the hell was she going to do alone in here with a bunch of unwanted memories that wouldn't quit? *Things she just wanted to forget.*

'What if a bus crash comes in?'

Luca grinned. 'I'll come and wake you.'

Mia felt the grin right down to her toes. It twinkled

in his eyes and gave the devil a whole new degree of wicked.

The fact that she noticed his twinkling eyes rankled. 'Are you flirting with me?' she demanded, crossing her arms.

Luca chuckled. She didn't beat around the bush. 'Would it be a bad thing if I was?'

'Yes,' she said. Something told her he wouldn't be an easy man to walk away from. Not disposable, like the others. 'Stop it. I have no desire to become a notch on what I understand is your very crowded bedpost.'

Luca regarded her for a moment. In her top and jeans, arms crossed, a frown knitting her brows, she looked quite fierce. But Luca knew women. He knew them well.

And Mia McKenzie was definitely protesting too much.

His gaze slipped to her mouth. 'Are you sure?'

Mia felt her lips tingle beneath his heated stare and felt her resistance ebb. *Now, he was something that could make her forget for a little while.*

Luca grinned, pleased to have discomforted her. 'Goodnight, Mia. Don't let the bed bugs bite.'

By four a.m. Luca was ready to head home. The craziness had settled and things were quiet—for now anyway.

He'd checked on the MVA from earlier—the laparotomy had found a perforated bowel. Stan had been admitted to the psych unit on a ninety-six-hour hold. The baby was settled into the special care nursery for overnight monitoring.

And his paperwork was up to date.

Just one last thing to do—check on Mia.

He hesitated, his hand on the doorknob of the on-call room. Prickly little Mia probably wouldn't appreciate being checked up on.

Her prim *I have no desire to become a notch on what I understand is your very crowded bedpost,* had played on his mind ever since she'd uttered it.

She obviously disapproved.

What the hell was wrong with indulging in a little flirtation here and there? Spending an enjoyable few hours with a woman who was fully aware that one night was all he was interested in?

He was always open and honest about his intentions. And he never made the mistake of giving false hope by going back for seconds. He knew his limitations where relationships were concerned—had learned them at a very early age.

Best not to set expectations—that way you couldn't let anyone down.

He loved women—bronzed, natural, fun-loving Australian women in particular—and they loved him. And he was a healthy adult male.

Still, Mia intrigued him. Her resistance even more so. He'd be lying if he said he didn't want her.

He twisted the knob and opened the door. She wasn't around and the light had been turned out. Sleeping room one had its door shut and he padded over to it, knocking lightly when he reached his destination.

No reply was forthcoming. He hesitated again before gently twisting the knob and opening the door a crack—checking on her *was* the right thing to do.

The sight stopped him in his tracks.

She had fallen asleep in a semi-upright foetal position on the triple-seater couch. Her head was snuggled against the fat cushions of the sofa, her spine propped up against the squishy arm, her legs, tucked in close to her bottom, had fallen sideways to rest against the back of the couch.

She'd taken her hair out of its clasp and it fanned around her shoulders and the couch cushions. Her feet were bare. A medical journal lay open on her chest.

The lamp on the table beside the couch illuminated her relaxed profile in a warm yellow glow. His gaze tracked the outline of her nose, the slope of one cheekbone, the plump fullness of her mouth.

He was satisfied to see the journal on her chest rise and fell in a regular rhythm. His eyes dropped to the white dressing covering her upper arm and he absently noted there was no fresh ooze.

She was obviously fine.

As he watched, a little frown wrinkled her forehead and a soft mew escaped her mouth. He wondered what she was dreaming about. Her near-death experience? The flash of a blade? The bawling of a baby?

His question—*are you sure?*—from earlier?

She mewed again and he realised he was staring at a sleeping woman who would most definitely not appreciate the attention. He left the door ajar and turned away.

Mia was trapped in a dream she didn't seem able to fight her way out of. It was one she hadn't had since she'd been a little girl but it was disjointed, jumping back and forth between now and then. Between Stan and her father. Each slash of the knife through the air shunting the dream to the other person, to another time.

Her mother was there too somewhere, holding a

wrapped bundle that Mia knew was her stillborn sister. Her mother was sobbing those deep, gut-wrenching sobs that had been indelibly woven through the fabric of Mia's life.

She was holding her father's hand, her little ten-year-old fingers tugging at his long ones, asking him not to go. And then Stan would yell to get back, get back as the knifepoint came ever closer.

Daddy, don't go. Don't go.

Slash. Back, get back. Slash.

Please, Daddy, don't go.

Slash. Slash. Back! Get back!

Daddy!

'Daddy, come back!'

Luca was almost at the door when he heard her cry out. Without thinking, he hurried back to her, pushed open the door and strode over to the couch as Mia cried out again, flinging her head from side to side. The journal had already fallen to the floor.

Luca took her by the shoulders and gave her a gentle shake, mindful of her injury. 'Mia! Mia.'

Mia heard a voice. A different voice. And the urge to run towards it, to run away from the feelings of hopelessness, was overwhelming.

Luca? Luca?

'Mia.' He shook her again. 'It's Luca. Wake up. Wake up.'

Mia's eyes flew open. *Luca?* Luca was here?

The mellow lamplight bathed his strong masculine features, softening them—his jaw, his cheeks, his mouth—and he finally looked like that angel. She blinked away the crazy thought as tendrils of dread clung to every heartbeat.

Mia tried to sit up but her limbs wouldn't co-operate and her arm throbbed. 'Luca?'

'Shh,' he murmured, the pads of his thumbs absently stroking her shoulders. Her large blue eyes reflected her confusion. 'It's okay, you were having a bad dream.'

Mia nodded. 'It was…there was…'

'Your father?'

Mia blinked up at him. He pronounced the *th* softly, giving the word a gentleness it hadn't had in the dream. Her head was crowded with memories. One after the other, battering her brains and beating against the locked door to her heart.

Old and long forgotten. Supposedly.

She had to make them stop.

'Are you okay?' Luca asked.

She looked at him, into eyes so deep and brown it was like falling into a well.

He could make them stop.

'Mia?'

She shook her head. 'Not yet.' *But she would be.*

Then she leaned forward and pressed her lips to his.

Luca stilled at the tentative touch. He pulled back and searched her eyes. 'Mia?'

She shook her head and, supporting herself on her good arm, leant in close, locking her gaze with his. 'Kiss me,' she murmured, her mouth a whisper from his.

In fact, she was close enough that Luca could almost feel those two little words branding his lips from the sudden heat rising between their bodies. He dropped his gaze to her mouth—so near, so luscious—and he was instantly hard.

'What happened to not wanting to be a notch on my bedpost?'

'Stan,' she muttered.

After that Luca wasn't sure who closed the hair's-breadth between them. But he did seize control.

His mouth opened over hers and demanded she follow suit. And follow him she did, opening to him eagerly. He thrust his tongue into her mouth and the little whimper at the back of her throat implored him to keep going.

He tunnelled his hands into her hair, angling her head back to accommodate more, and the kiss escalated. Got deeper, wetter, hotter. His body moved over hers, forcing her knees down, crowding her back against the cushions, imprisoning her against the couch, her head falling back over the arm.

His hand brushed the side of her breast and she moaned deep and low. He drew it lower, to her waist, her hip as his mouth broke from hers to ravage her neck, stretched out before him, the pulse at the base beating as madly as his own.

Mia felt the memories disappear into the ether as a veritable storm of sensations swept through her body.

Yes, yes, yes.

'Yes,' she cried out as Luca licked along her collar bone. 'Yes,' as he nipped at the base of her neck. 'Yes,' as his hand squeezed the exact spot where, beneath her jeans, butt met thigh.

One-handed, she pulled his polo shirt out of his jeans and ruched it up his back, his skin hot and vibrant beneath her palm. She kept pulling till it was past his shoulders and gave a triumphant cry when Luca ducked his head through the opening and she pulled it off him entirely.

His smooth chest was totally bare to her touch and she pressed a kiss to a flat brown pec, then his collarbone, then the hollow at the base of his neck.

She breathed him in, his scent intoxicating. Potent. Virile. Male. It filled up her senses. Like a drug.

And left her wanting more.

He claimed her mouth again, pressing her deep into the cushions, and she revelled in his weight, in the tangle of his legs, in the oh-so-right angle of his pelvis.

Luca felt the agitated circling of her hips and ground himself against her. He swallowed her gasp, making her moan more deeply as his hand travelled back up her body, pushing beneath her top. He needed to touch her breasts. To see them. Taste them. To feel them rubbing against his chest.

He pushed the fabric up, his hand filling with soft, delectable female. Satin, lace and heaven all in one sweet handful. He rubbed the hard point with his thumb and she gasped.

Luca broke away from her mouth, his lips instinctively following the dictates of his body as his tongue stroked down her neck, over her collarbone, the slope of her breast then finally her nipple. The lace was rough against his tongue as he sucked the tip right through the material of the bra.

Mia's breath hissed out as her back arched involuntarily. It jarred painfully through her sore arm and she cried out in pain this time, her eyes squeezing shut.

'Mia?' Luca broke away. 'Oh, sorry, did I hurt your arm?'

Mia shook her head, her eyes still shut. 'It's okay, it's settling.'

Luca groaned, dropping his forehead onto her chest. Her heart beat frantically there as her ribcage heaved in and out. His own breathing was loud and ragged in the silence.

Mia's eyes slowly fluttered open as the pain ebbed. She looked down at his head, his thick wavy hair tousled from their ministrations. It was suddenly absurdly funny and she felt a bubble of laughter rise in her chest. She bit down on her lip to stop it from spilling out.

But her ribcage shook with the effort to keep it in and it bubbled up anyway.

Luca felt the vibration against his forehead and glanced up just as she laughed. Their breathing was still erratic, they were both half-undressed and thoroughly bedraggled, he had a raging hard-on—and she was laughing.

It was absurd. So he laughed too.

'You're crazy,' he said after their laughter had died down.

Mia shook her head. 'This is crazy.'

Luca had to agree. Even if his hard-on didn't. 'You want to stop?' he murmured.

His husky voice thickened his accent and a surge of lust welled deep down low in her. Mia shook her head. She couldn't have stopped now even if a bus had crashed right through the walls of the on-call room.

She was a healthy adult woman, and it had been a couple of weeks since her last liaison. 'That would be even crazier.'

Luca grinned, dropping his mouth to her chest, running his nose lightly along the slope of a breast and upwards to nuzzle her neck. 'Pure insanity.'

She stretched her neck to give him better access. 'Certifiable,' she agreed.

Luca laved the pulse half way up her neck with his tongue. 'Utter lunacy.'

'I think we should get the door, though,' she managed through the haze of lust descending on her.

Luca's head snapped to the doorway. He swore softly against her neck at its partially open state and was rewarded with another throaty laugh. He kissed her hard on the mouth.

'Take your clothes off,' he said, before pushing off her, padding over to the door and locking it.

'You do realise this is a one-off, right?' she said as she tried to wiggle out of her jeans essentially one-handed.

Luca turned and watched her. He could clearly see her nipples through the lace of her bra and it made him harder.

He undid his zip and peeled off his jeans. 'Of course. My bedpost is littered with one-offs. Or hadn't you heard?'

Mia went to grin but it died on her lips as the pure male beauty of his physique was fully exposed to her. Long, lean legs, dusted with black hair. Flat, flat belly. Broad in the shoulder, narrow in the hip.

And if the bulge in his snug cotton boxers was anything to go by, large, in all the right places.

She'd seen a marble statue just like him in Rome many years before. Luca di Angelo had *Made in Italy* stamped all over him.

Then he came to her, towering over her, snapping the

lamp off, helping her out of her jeans, kissing her everywhere, arching her back over the arm of the lounge, thrusting her breasts upwards towards his eager mouth. Making her sigh. Making her whimper. Making her come.

And, best of all, making her forget.

Three days later Dr Finn Kennedy, chief of Surgery, strode into the emergency department on what he was sure was going to be a fool's errand. He was tired. His upper arm had ached all night despite several shots of whisky, and he rubbed at it absently. His eyes felt scratchy and his damn nuisance thumb was numb and tingly.

He pulled up short as Evie approached him. Great, just what he needed. Dr Evie Lockheart. *Princess Evie.* Born with a silver spoon in her mouth, working in her granddaddy's hospital, a place still generously supported by the Lockheart family trust and her father in particular, who was treated like royalty by the boffins upstairs.

With absolutely no idea how hard ordinary people had it.

And the only woman in the entire hospital who seemed to be able to push his buttons. She didn't simper or cower. Just looked at him patiently with those damn hazel eyes.

'Dr Kennedy,' she greeted him.

'There's a consult for me?' he asked, not bothering to acknowledge her greeting. He had a feeling that she saw beyond his curt exterior and he didn't like it.

The only other woman to have done that had been

Lydia—his brother's widow—and that had been an un-mitigated disaster.

Evie refused to give Finn the satisfaction of seeing how his brusqueness grated. He wasn't in the army any more and she wasn't one of his soldiers to be ordered around. Instead, she launched straight into her spiel. Still, it didn't stop her heart from pounding like a run-away train in her chest—she'd made an amazing inci-dental find and despite his gruffness she was desperate for his approval.

'Twenty-two-year-old female, with a painful lump in her breast. Ultrasound identified a small benign cyst—'

'Are you kidding me?' Finn glared down at her, hands on hips. 'You do know I'm a cardiac surgeon, right? That means stuff to do with the heart.'

Evie held his gaze and her tongue and continued as if he hadn't just rudely interrupted her. 'She also com-plained of fatigue, shortness of breath and intermittent chest pains. Incidental finding reveals bicuspid aortic valve with associated ascending aortic aneurysm.'

Finn stared at her. Was in hell was she on about? 'Sure,' he said sarcastically as he held out his hand. 'Radiographer report?'

'There isn't one. Radiology was backlogged and the ultrasound was performed in the department.'

'I see. By who, exactly?' he demanded.

Evie's gaze didn't waver as his piercing blue eyes dared her to blink. 'By me.'

Finn snorted. 'You? You diagnosed a complex heart condition through a breast ultrasound?'

Evie crossed her arms too. 'Yes.'

'That's not even remotely possible,' he snapped.

Until right now, Evie would have agreed. 'It is if the woman in question has very small breasts.'

Finn glared at her. Princess Evie—her place at the prestigious SHH emergency department no doubt paid for by her father's huge donations—wasting his time. 'Where's the patient?'

'Cubicle fifteen,' she said calmly.

'What have you told her that I'm going to have to untell her?' he asked silkily.

'I told her I couldn't get a good enough angle and I was going to call for someone more experienced,' Evie bristled. 'I did *go* to medical school, Dr Kennedy,' she said frostily.

'Really? Daddy couldn't fast-track you, then?'

Evie ignored the dig. 'I graduated top of my year.'

'He gives to the university too, then?' Finn retorted, before turning on his heel and heading for the indicated cubicle.

Evie's heart tripped in her chest as she struggled to keep up with his long-legged stride. But even falling flat on her face would be worth it just to see the look on Finn's when her diagnosis was confirmed.

Finn snapped back the curtain and introduced himself to a petite young woman in a hospital gown who was chewing on her bottom lip. He smiled at her. 'Hello. Bethany, is it?' he asked, consulting her chart. 'I'm Dr Kennedy. Dr Lockheart's asked me to have a look at you.'

'Is something wrong?' Bethany asked, looking from one doctor to the other.

Finn patted her hand. 'Give me one minute and I'll be able to tell you.'

He turned away to the compact mobile ultrasound

machine and shot Evie an exasperated look. It was hardly the most sophisticated machine in their radiology arsenal. He found it hard to believe anyone could diagnose a potentially fatal heart problem on something so basic.

He picked up the transducer from its cradle fiddled with the pulse settings and the screen brightness and turned to back to Bethany, who'd already opened her gown and put her arm above her head.

Finn squeezed a blob of warmed gel on Bethany's chest, noting that she did indeed have practically non-existent breast tissue. 'Okay, here goes,' he murmured as he ploughed the transducer through the middle of the gel.

He ignored Evie, who was standing at his elbow, and concentrated on the small screen as the grainy grey and black image of Bethany's pumping heart came into view. It took him less than a minute to concur with Evie's very impressive diagnosis.

He flicked a glance at her and met her unwavering hazel gaze. There was no triumph or smugness there, just complete confidence in her diagnosis, and he felt a rather foreign feeling of grudging respect.

Maybe there was more to her than the Lockheart name.

'Is everything okay?' Bethany asked.

Finn shook his head. 'No. There's a problem,' he admitted. 'But it's okay,' he added quickly. 'I can fix it.'

Evie listened in awe while Finn sat with Bethany and explained how the small benign-looking cyst in her breast was nothing compared to the real problem, and what he could do about it. For such an arrogant, rude, human being he had amazing rapport with patients.

When they walked out of the curtain thirty minutes later Evie had seen an entirely different side to the infamous Dr Finn Kennedy. She'd known he must have had a heart in there somewhere but it was the first time she'd ever seen any evidence of it.

'Organise a bed for her in CCU,' Finn said briskly, handing Bethany's chart to her.

Evie nodded as she accepted it, trying not to feel discouraged. She hadn't really thought he'd congratulate her, had she?

'Good catch, Dr Lockheart,' he murmured. 'Maybe you're not Daddy's little girl after all.'

And then he turned in the opposite direction and strode away.

Evie blinked as the back-handed compliment sank in.

High praise indeed!

CHAPTER THREE

WHEN Mia came on duty later that afternoon the first person she spied was Luca. Which wasn't difficult, given that his very presence seemed to attract attention. She'd bet whoever had invented the term *chick magnet* had met Luca di Angelo.

Of course, she could also just have conjured him up—she couldn't deny she'd been thinking about him and their illicit liaison in the on-call room a little too often on her days off.

She squeezed her eyes shut tight for a few seconds then opened them again. Nope—still there.

And looking right at her.

Smiling at her, actually. Like he knew all her dirty secrets. And that he was one of them.

She graced him with an indifferent glare and a cool nod of the head as she slung her stethoscope around her neck and deliberately walked in the opposite direction.

Luca chuckled to himself as he watched the hypnotic swish of her blonde ponytail. She seemed all prim and neat, her dark grey tailored trousers classically elegant, her high-necked, capped-sleeve blouse in sapphire blue crisp and stylish.

Not a wrinkle. Or a hair out of place.

Very different from the Mia of the other night. Who had looked rumpled and disturbed and hadn't cared about either.

A hum coursed through his blood at the mere thought. It certainly hadn't been the way he had envisaged that night would turn out. In fact, if someone had asked him who'd be the woman least likely to sleep with him, he would have said Mia McKenzie.

But it had been pretty damn amazing. Once she'd made up her mind she hadn't held back. She hadn't done that irritating talking/fishing-for-compliments thing that a surprising amount of women did during sex. Or tried to twist herself into some uncomfortable position because she knew it was her best angle.

She hadn't even asked him what he liked in an effort to make it all about him.

No. She'd known exactly what she'd wanted and she'd taken it. But she'd given, too. She'd been confident and assured and had met him as an equal.

It was the most uncomplicated one-off he'd ever had.

Now, if he could just stop thinking about it…

Mia moved through the shift with her senses on high alert. Her skin prickled when he was near. The hairs on her nape stood to attention. Her nipples seemed to stay in a state of permanent erection. It seemed every cell in her body was well and truly tuned in to Luca.

And it didn't help that they kept running into each other.

The first time had been in the lift after she'd been on for half an hour. She'd just caught it before the doors had shut and squeezed in with several other people sharing the space with a transport bed. The patient had been almost lost amidst the equipment on the bed and the stuff hanging off the rails had made it an even tighter fit.

She'd smiled at the patient as the doors had shut and turned to stare at the opposite wall, only to be confronted by Luca's slow, sexy smile.

'Dr McKenzie,' he murmured.

'Dr di Angelo,' she replied, dropping her gaze to the knot of his tie rather than the knowing look in his eyes.

'How were your days off?' he asked innocently.

Mia couldn't believe how intimate it could feel between them in a lift full of onlookers. She kept her gaze firmly on the knot at his throat.

His long, tanned throat she'd licked every inch of.

'Fine, thank you.' *Apart from daydreaming about you.*

His grin broadened as if he could hear the words she hadn't said. 'I trust your arm is getting better?'

Mia had felt sure that if his voice could cure wounds hers would have miraculously healed on the spot. She kept her gaze resolute, trying not to think how erotic the smooth glide of his jaw had been against her breasts.

'Thank you, yes.'

'I can look at it later, if you like. I think there're still some dressings left in the on-call room.'

Mia's eyes flicked up before she could stop them and his smile gained a slight triumphant edge. A blast of heat arced between them and Mia was surprised that it hadn't incinerated everyone in the lift.

'Thank you Dr di Angelo. I can manage,' she murmured as the lift doors opened and she walked out on legs that felt like wobbly jelly.

The second time she'd worked with him on a fifty-two-year-old construction worker who had come in from an industrial accident, having sustained major chest and abdominal injuries. He'd placed a chest tube and done the intubation while she'd inserted a central line.

They'd worked in tandem, like a well-oiled machine, but she'd been aware of him and his every move every second. Their gazes had locked regularly. At one stage their heads had even bumped together, competing for the same line of sight. He'd apologised, but their faces had been very close. His gaze had dropped briefly to her mouth and her mind had strayed to exactly where she'd put it on his body.

The third time she'd been plastering a fifteen-year-old-boy's broken arm when he'd lounged in the doorway to the plaster room. He hadn't announced himself but something had alerted her and she'd looked up to find him propped against the doorframe.

'Haven't you got something better to be doing?' she asked testily, returning her attention to the job. How was she supposed to avoid him when he seemed to be wherever she was?

Luca shook his head. 'All quiet. I thought I'd *skulk* here for a while.'

She'd glanced up at his use of the word 'skulk' and he grinned at her. He advanced into the room and she tried not to notice how his beautifully cut trousers and khaki business shirt fitted him to perfection. He could easily have been strutting a Milan catwalk.

'You the boy who was having a light-sabre fight with your little sister?' he asked the teenager.

The boy nodded glumly. 'She's never going to let me live it down.'

'Sisters can be very unforgiving.'

'You've got sisters?'

Luca nodded. 'Three.'

'Man, that's harsh.'

Mia slid him a sly glance. His accent had thickened and his words had seemed tinged with something she hadn't been able to put her finger on. Then the two of them got into a conversation about *Star Wars* and Mia gritted her teeth and pretended Luca and his mouth were in a galaxy far, far away.

By the time he passed her in the hallway at ten o'clock she was walking a very fine line between homicidal mania and sexual frustration. The man was everywhere—in the department and in her head—and, heaven help her, she wanted to push him into the nearest available private space and tear his clothes off.

But it had been a one-off.

They'd agreed.

'Oh, Dr McKenzie, I meant to tell you earlier, I've arranged for a debrief session with John Allen from Psych for you.'

Mia slowed and turned. How could she want to kill him and kiss at the same time? 'Cos she did. *She wanted to kiss that smug Sicilian mouth so badly she could scream.*

'I don't need a damn debrief,' she snapped, tossing her head, daring him to push her. 'I'm fine.'

Luca smiled at the flash in her eyes—like sun shining on a cathedral window. He liked the way her chest rose and fell just a little bit too fast. And how it pulled at her blouse in all the right places.

He pushed back. 'I'm sure you are. But you're having one, anyway.'

That was it! Mia put her hands on her hips, barely

suppressing the juvenile urge to stamp her foot. 'Oh, no, I'm not.'

He nodded. 'Ten tomorrow morning.'

Her gaze locked on his mouth the same time his locked on hers. Something stirred deep in her belly. A primal recognition of attraction. A potent force.

She lifted her chin. 'You can't make me.'

Luca felt a subtle shift in the signals emanating from her. Had that challenge been sexual? A nurse bustled past and gave them a strange look.

Luca inclined his head to a nearby door. 'Shall we discuss this in private?'

Mia knew it was the on-call room. 'Fine,' she muttered, her heart rate suddenly trebling.

She followed him through the open doorway into the empty room. 'I'm not seeing a shrink, Luca. You can—'

Luca turned abruptly, cutting her off with a swift, hard kiss, crowding her back towards the door, shutting it with the combined weight of their two bodies.

Every cell in Mia's body leapt to life. She grabbed the knot of his tie, pulling him flush against her.

She groaned, or was it him?

Madness, it was madness.

She broke off. 'We said once,' she gasped.

Luca nodded. 'I know.' And then he went back for more.

Mia gave herself up to the urgent press of his mouth. The bold stroke of his hand against her breast. The hard thrust of his erection.

She whimpered as he ground his pelvis into hers and rubbed herself shamelessly against him. Her hands travelled to his butt, urging him closer, nearer, angling him just right.

She shut her eyes as he hit the spot, her head lolling back against the door. His mouth moved lower to the mad flutter at the side of her neck.

The flutter was everywhere. In her breasts and her belly and between her legs. It thrummed through her ears in a deafening thunder like the roar of the ocean or the call of the wild.

Luca. Luca. Luca.

Not even the peeling of an emergency beeper pierced it. It took two squealing beepers to manage that.

Mia pushed on Luca's chest as the sound finally penetrated. They were both gasping, their clothes askew as they automatically reached for their pagers.

Damn! 'Cardiac arrest two minutes out,' Mia panted.

Luca nodded as he read the same message on his beeper. 'Great timing,' he murmured.

Mia took a few seconds to straighten her clothes and clear the heavy fog of lust from her brain. Luca followed suit.

'How do I look?' she asked as she quickly retied her hair to its pristine smoothness.

Luca smiled. 'Like you've been thoroughly kissed.'

Mia glared at him.

That was exactly what she'd been afraid of!

The following night, Mia snuggled into her ancient duffle coat as she and Evie left The Harbour behind them and crossed over the road, heading for the flashing neon sign that read 'Pete's'. It was nearly ten o'clock but Wednesday was traditionally staff discount night— if you could produce an SHH badge, drinks were half-price—it was an ingrained part of The Harbour's culture.

Not that the majority of people letting their hair down at tables needed to produce ID. Pete, the owner, had been running the popular bar for the last twenty years and not only knew who was who but usually who was doing who as well.

Of course he would never have disclosed such information. Like every good barkeeper, discretion was his middle name. And it was definitely the reason why Pete's had been *the* hangout for SHH staff over the years.

Sure, proximity and comfy booths also helped but when down-time was limited, a cosy place nearby where a busy professional could talk and unwind and not be *on* for a while or worry about gossip, which was already rife enough in their work environment, was definitely appreciated.

He was also fiercely protective of the hard-working staff at Sydney's most prestigious hospital. He didn't tolerate customers who complained to him about bias or hassled his favourite clients in any way. After all, the good staff of The Harbour had been his bread and butter since he'd opened.

But it was more than that. The doctors and nurses of the SHH were special. Too many times he'd seen them walk through his door with weary, haunted expressions. They saw things on a day-to-day basis that were the stuff of most people's nightmares. And if a drink or two at his bar managed to take their minds off that then Pete considered he'd done a good day's work.

Mia welcomed the blast of heat as Evie opened the heavy wooden door to Pete's. They shrugged out of their coats and headed to the bar, greeting several people they knew along the way.

'It's freezing out there,' she said to Pete, thrusting out her hands. 'Just feel these.'

Pete smiled at them and dutifully folded Mia's chilly fingers in his big warm mitts. 'Cold hands, warm heart,' he quipped.

Mia grinned at him. 'You are a romantic.'

'Nothing wrong with that, love. Right, Evie?'

Evie, distracted by Finn chatting to a busty blonde further along the bar, answered automatically. 'Right.'

'Pete, Pete, Pete,' Mia tutted. 'Romance belongs in books.'

'Maybe you should read a couple,' he jested.

'Books? We don't have time for books, do we, Evie?' Mia asked.

'Nope,' Evie murmured, sliding a surreptitious gaze towards Finn.

'Journals are all I get a chance to read,' Mia lamented.

Pete sighed. 'No time for a man either, I suppose?'

'There are men,' she protested. Being happily married for thirty years had rendered Pete's vision permanently rose coloured.

Pete gave her a reproachful look. 'Men, sure. But one man, Mia? That's what you need.'

Mia rolled her eyes. 'If I were a man, would we be having this conversation?' She looked around and spied Finn with a vaguely familiar blonde—Suzy someone? One of the scrub nurses from the OT. 'Do you say this sort of stuff to Finn?'

Pete clutched his heart in a wounded fashion. He was

like the SHH fairy godfather, wanting happily-ever-afters for *all* his regulars.

'Of course. I say it to Finn most of all.' He deliberately looked at a distracted Evie. 'That man needs the love of a good woman more than anyone.'

Evie looked at Pete sharply and didn't say anything for a beat or two. 'I'll have a tequila shot followed by a bottle of lager, thank you, Peter.'

'Just the usual for me,' Mia added.

He grinned at them. 'Okay, okay. I can take a hint.'

Pete served Evie's shot first and she snatched it up and threw it straight down her throat, revelling in the burn. As she slammed it back on the bar she glanced Finn's way. He was looking at her with those piercing blue eyes and for a moment their gazes locked.

Was that disdain? Judgement? Disapproval?

Too bad, so sad.

'Orange juice for you,' Pete said, placing it on the bar in front of Mia. 'Beer for Evie.'

Evie picked up her drink. 'Let's go over there,' she said, moving off the bar stool in the opposite direction to Finn, before Mia even had a chance to lift her juice. She shrugged at Pete and followed.

Unfortunately, Evie was heading to a booth Mia would rather not be at but it was difficult to change direction now the occupants had spotted them and waved them over. And she didn't want to have to explain to her friend who would no doubt put two and two together and come up with five.

'Move over,' Evie announced. 'We're coming in.'

Mia tried not to look at Luca as she was forced to take the seat next to him. But she could feel his eyes on hers and the heat of him immediately enveloped her as her body responded in an almost Pavlovian fashion to his proximity.

The booth was spacious but with three bodies either side it was a cosy fit.

'Mia, long time no see.'

Mia smiled at John Allen, the psychologist she'd been forced to see that morning by Luca. Susie, his wife, was also there and greeted Mia warmly. Of course she saw them regularly enough anyway, given that they too lived at the nearby Kirribilli Views apartments where a lot of The Harbour staff resided.

'How did the debrief go?' Luca enquired.

'Mia's fine.' John winked.

She glared at him. 'I *am* fine.'

'Sure,' he soothed.

'You know, Mia, it's not a bad thing, to talk this kind of thing through.' Rupert Davidson, head of Neurology, entered the conversation.

'He's right,' Teo Tuala, SHH's head of Paediatrics, agreed.

Mia looked at all of them, exasperation bubbling inside her. She inclined her head towards Luca. 'He didn't. He was being threatened too.'

'Yes, but I wasn't lunged at with a knife. Neither did I have my arm slashed open by said knife.'

Mia took a long swig of her drink as his voice, so close to her ear, took her right back to the on-call room. 'I'm fine,' she repeated.

'Well, you know where I am if you want to talk any more,' John offered.

Mia couldn't help but think that a sweaty twenty minutes with Luca had helped more than an hour's conversation with John but it was a dangerous path for her thoughts to take given how aware she was of Luca right now.

'Absolutely.' She nodded. 'What's happening with Stan?' she asked, deftly moving the focus of the conversation off her. 'His ninety-six-hour hold must be up by now.'

John nodded. 'He's staying on voluntarily. He's had increasing paranoia episodes over the last few years apparently. We want to get his meds right and get him well supported before we discharge him.'

Mia nodded and soon the conversation drifted to other subjects.

Ten minutes later, Evie finished her beer and stood. 'Gotta go. I promised my father I'd drop by some hideous dinner party he's having. He's sending a car for me.'

Mia leapt at the opportunity to escape and stood as well. 'I'd better go too. I'm on in the morning.'

'Oh, Mia, no,' Susie objected. 'Don't leave me alone with all these men talking shop. Stay a bit longer.'

Mia looked at Susie's beseeching gaze and acquiesced. It had absolutely nothing to do with every cell suddenly crying out for Luca's heat to be squashed back up against her again. 'Okay, I guess I can stay for one more.'

'I'll get another round,' Luca said. He climbed out of the booth and watched bemused as Mia took a step back. 'Is that vodka and orange?'

Mia shook her head. 'Just orange.'

He frowned. 'You're not on call, are you?'

'Nope. Just not drinking.'

Luca slid a glance at the table, where the merits of a journal article were being debated. He looked back at

Mia. 'Are you worried you may lose your inhibitions?' he murmured, dropping his voice a little. 'I don't need alcohol to lose mine.'

Mia, aware of how close he was standing, felt the pronunciation of *inhibitions* slide right down her spine. His English was perfect but the occasional word leant towards his native Italian.

'I wasn't aware you had any,' she said, her voice steely.

Luca walked away chuckling, deep and low. Unfortunately, that was exactly where Mia felt it—deep and low.

Standing at the bar a couple of minutes later, Luca rattled off the drinks order and waited for Pete to return with them.

'Here you are, Luca,' Pete said, placing them on a round tray.

'Thanks.' Luca handed over the money.

'You're with Mia, I see,' Pete said casually. 'Great girl.'

Luca nodded, his gaze straying back to a smiling Mia. She was wearing a long skirt, a turtle-neck skivvy and black knee-high boots. He'd been fantasising about her in those boots, just the boots, all day.

'Yes,' he agreed. Except they weren't the words he'd have used. Sexy, feisty, prickly seemed to suit her so much better.

'Fantastic doctor,' Pete pressed, joining Luca in his observation of Mia.

Now, those were words Luca would use. 'Yes, she is,' he agreed.

'Hard to believe someone like that's still single,' Pete mused.

Luca looked back at the bartender. 'And why is that, do you think?'

Pete looked Luca direct in the eye. 'Men these days scare too easily. They buy into her *I'm fine* exterior.'

'And she's not?'

Pete shook his head. 'Of course she's not. She just doesn't know it yet.'

They watched her again for a moment or two. 'But don't tell her I told you that,' Pete added.

Luca laughed, picking up the tray. 'Deal.'

'So, Luca.' Susie, desperate for a topic change, watched Luca slip back in beside Mia. 'Sicily, huh?'

Luca nodded as the familiar feeling of dread and loss and yearning threatened to swamp him. He pushed them back. 'That's right.'

Mia glanced at Luca as she felt his thigh, jammed against hers, tense. This close to his delectable profile she could see the clench of his jaw.

'Where exactly?' Susie continued, unaware of Luca's reluctance to talk about his past. Especially his home.

Luca forced himself to breathe out, to loosen the suddenly tense muscles of his neck. 'Marsala.'

'Like the wine?' she asked.

Luca nodded. 'Yes. Like the wine.'

'We never got to Sicily,' Susie said. 'But we adored Italy, didn't we, John?'

John nodded. 'Europe as a whole. We're actually going skiing in France at the end of the year.'

Luca slowly relaxed each muscle group as conversation moved to travel but a pall had been cast over the evening. If it wasn't for the alluring press of Mia against his side, he'd have excused himself almost immediately.

But her nearness held him in check. He'd been aware of her since she'd first entered the bar and he could tell she was more than aware of him. There was a crackle between them that had nothing to do with the delicious rub of their thighs.

And after the way the conversation had turned tonight he couldn't think of a better way of keeping the memories of Marsala at bay than getting lost in Mia for a while.

To hell with their one-off pact.

Teo drained his cola and stood. 'I have to go back to The Harbour and check on a patient then I'd better head home. Emma's teething and keeping Zoe and me up most of the night.'

'Teething already?' Susie marvelled. 'Isn't six months a little early?'

Teo shook his head. 'Every baby is different.' And he grinned at them because even with the sleepless nights, Zoe and Emma had made him happier than he'd ever thought possible.

'Aw,' Rupert, also happily married, teased. 'Ain't love grand?'

Mia, barely able to suppress an eye roll at Teo's goofy expression, saw her second chance at escape. 'Yep, me too. Early start.'

'Same here,' Luca said, letting her out. 'I'll walk you to your car.'

Mia felt a thickening in the air between them as their gazes skittered past each other. Yep, like that's what she needed right now. *Sex-on-legs escorting her anywhere.*

But, sensing he was as desperate to get away as she was, she nodded her head graciously. They said their goodbyes and made their way through the throng to the coat stands by the front door.

'I'm not driving,' Mia said as she shrugged into her coat. 'I live just down at Kirribilli Views. I walk to work. I don't need an escort.'

Luca smiled as he adjusted the collar on his suit jacket. 'What a coincidence. So do I.'

Mia's fingers fumbled with the tie of her coat. *Of course he did.* 'Of course you do,' she said faintly. She hadn't seen him around but it was a big place populated with shift workers.

Luca chuckled as he opened the heavy wooden door and gestured for her to precede him. He looked back over his shoulder as he departed. Pete grinned and gave him a thumbs-up.

CHAPTER FOUR

MIA buried her hands in her coat pockets as her warm breath fogged into the night air. She glanced at Luca, who had only his suit jacket to fend off cold winter fingers. But he looked warm and vital—like a walking hot-water bottle. She shook the tempting image of her wrapped around him in bed from her head. It was disconcerting to say the least when the streets were dark and practically deserted and they kept passing interesting alcoves and alleyways where two people could warm up really quickly.

Mia clamped down on the direction of her thoughts and the strange undulation of her pelvic floor muscles. 'Aren't you cold in that?' she groused.

Luca shrugged. 'Two beers help.'

Mia nodded. 'I don't drink much,' she replied.

Why she felt the need to share that she had no idea, but she could feel his pull and knew she was on a slow march towards an inevitable ending. This wasn't how it was supposed to be between them and she felt suddenly nervous.

'You don't like it?' Luca enquired.

Mia shook her head. 'I went through a stage where I liked it a little too much.'

'Ah,' Luca said, intrigued by the nugget of information. Was this what Pete had alluded to? 'Care to elaborate?'

Not bloody likely! Mia couldn't believe she'd told him that much. Damn this man! But there was something about him, a recognition that they were the same, that seemed to loosen her lips around him. Still, she had absolutely no intention of reliving two years of booze and bad men with him.

The past was the past.

'No,' she said. He quirked an eyebrow at her and she said, 'It's complicated.'

They walked in silence for a few moments. 'I suppose a man from Marsala probably doesn't understand that.'

Luca tensed. He'd been enjoying the build-up between them as each footstep took them closer to their apartments. To their beds. The footpath had narrowed and their arms brushed; her body warmth mixed and flirted with his. Their footsteps matched, their breathing synchronised.

But suddenly that was forgotten.

Mia turned her head to face him. 'How long ago did you leave?'

Luca bit down on the urge to laugh at her choice of words. Leaving implied consent. He hadn't been given a whole lot of choice. 'I was sixteen.'

She whistled. 'That's a long time.'

Luca chuckled, trying to divert the conversation. 'Are you implying I'm old?'

Mia laughed too and let it peter out. 'You're a long way from home, Luca,' she mused.

Although she, more than anyone, knew that geographic proximity had nothing to do with that sense of 'home'. She'd grown up a twenty-minute drive from here and it may as well have been Italy for all the connection Mia felt to the brick and mortar house where her mother still resided. Mainly on the couch.

Luca kept his gaze firmly fixed on the illuminated arch of the Sydney Harbour Bridge he could just see through the treetops. 'Yes.'

Mia smiled. 'Care to elaborate?'

'No.'

'Word on the grapevine is you studied medicine in London. I thought Italian mamas liked to keep tabs on their sons. No decent universities in Italy?'

Luca saw his mother's broken face again on that horrible day that had changed everything. The sorrow and disappointment etched in lines that had seemed somehow instantly deeper. He schooled his expression as he looked at Mia and repeated her response.

'It's complicated.'

Mia nodded. If anyone understood that, she did. And she understood the underlying message—butt out. She got that too.

They lapsed into silence again but she was aware of him large and silent beside her. Aware of his tension and his potent, brooding masculinity.

'Here we are,' she announced unnecessarily as the doors to the ten-storey apartment complex loomed ahead.

Luca dragged himself out of the sticky web of his past. 'Yes,' he murmured. He looked down at her. 'Your place or mine?'

Mia swallowed. She should have been outraged at his assumption. But he was looking at her intently with that devil mouth and heat was flooding through her belly and tightening her breasts.

She didn't do repeat performances, that was her golden rule, but, heavens above, she wanted him.

'Yours,' she murmured huskily. 'I share with Evie.'

He held her gaze for a moment before opening the door for her and following her to the lift. They rode it to the ninth floor in silence, Luca propped against one wall, staring across at Mia propped against the opposite wall. The bold way she returned his gaze tugged at his groin and his whole body tightened in anticipation.

Mia felt utterly dominated as Luca lounged against the wall, arms crossed. His gaze raked her body lingering on her breasts, her thighs, her boots. Then travelled all the way back up again to rest on her mouth.

The seconds ticked by as his eyes locked on her lips. Her tongue darted out to moisten them, a nervous gesture.

His nostrils flared. She swallowed.

His arms dropped. Her heart skipped a beat.

He took a step towards her. She tensed.

The lift dinged. He stopped. She breathed again.

'Ladies first,' he murmured. 'Number nineteen.'

Mia walked on legs made of Plasticine to the indicated apartment, aware of his eyes on her the whole time. She could barely breathe by the time she pulled up in front of his door.

Absently she reached for the doorhandle the same time he did. He sucked in a breath. 'Your hands are freezing,' he murmured.

'Yes,' she agreed. That was because all her blood had drained to her belly and breasts. In fact, apart from her torso she felt cold right through to her bones. She even shivered involuntarily.

Luca grinned at her as he pushed open the door. 'I have the perfect solution.'

He tugged on her hand and she followed him into the toasty centrally heated apartment.

Luca strode into his bedroom, Mia in tow, flipping lights on as he went. He walked straight past his bed, turning right into a spacious en suite. He ushered her in, shut the door, flipped on a wall-mounted heater, opened the shower screen and turned the hot tap on full bore. Instant heat puffed into the air from the shower head.

He turned to look at Mia, shrugging out of his jacket. 'Get naked.'

Mia quirked an eyebrow at his imperious command. 'Boy, you sure know how to seduce a woman.'

Luca grabbed her by her coat lapels and hauled her up against him. He lowered his mouth and on a groan unleashed a truly devastating kiss.

Mia's response was instantaneous. His mouth was hot, hot, hot and it fanned the flames burning in her belly to the rest of her body. Raising herself on tiptoe, she tunnelled her hands into his hair, pressed her breasts hard against the solid warmth of his chest.

His hands cupped her bottom, dragging their hips into alignment. Mia rubbed herself against him, causing a delicious friction that spread more warmth to every part of her body.

Luca groped for the tie of her coat and yanked it loose, his hands invading the cocoon of heat around her belly and stroking down her sides and back. He felt for her zip and undid it, pushing the skirt off her hips.

Mia broke away from the drugging intensity of his

mouth, her rough breath almost as loud as the teeming shower that poured an endless supply of steam into the hothouse atmosphere.

She was hot now. Very, very hot.

She quickly stepped out of her skirt, removed her jacket and followed it with her skivvy.

Luca's breath caught in his throat as she stood before him in matching champagne-coloured underwear and a pair of black knee-high boots.

He breathed out reverentially. '*Mia bella*,' he murmured. Thoughts of the mess he'd left behind in Marsala were now a distant memory.

Mia blushed. She had no idea what that meant but it sounded pretty damn complimentary to her. Which spurred her on even more. Removing the clasp from her hair, she shook it free so it fell down her back and flowed over her shoulders in a golden stream.

Aware that Luca, hands on hips, was watching her every move between heavy eyelids, she lifted a booted foot and placed it on the edge of the bath. She leaned forward until her breasts were brushing her thigh and slowly—very, very slowly—undid the side zipper on her boots.

Luca heard every one of the zip teeth release as he watched Mia intently. She had her back to him and his gaze roved hungrily over the brief triangle of fabric encasing the enticing wiggle of her butt cheeks. He lifted it higher to the indentation that formed the small of her back. Higher still to the long delicate stretch of her spine partially obscured by her long blonde tresses.

Mia looked over her shoulder at him and smiled as she straightened and flicked the boot off. The steam was building in the bathroom and her face felt flushed, although the kick in her pulse told her it had more to do with Luca's smouldering look than the atmospheric conditions.

When she turned back to bend over the other boot, Luca couldn't hold back. He moved in close behind her, pushing her hair off one shoulder and leaning forward to drop a kiss. His hands gripped her hips and pulled her against him, snuggling her bottom into the heat of his groin.

Luca was consumed with the erotic image in front of him. He fully clothed, his erection straining for release, Mia scantily clad and bent provocatively in front of him. He wanted to tear her knickers off and take her right here and now.

He pulled her in tight.

Mia's hand faltered on the zip as Luca circled his hips against her. She shut her eyes as he created delicious havoc in just the right spot, her breath coming faster. The boot forgotten, one foot still propped on the bath edge, she straightened, arching her back against him, her arms snaking up behind her to clasp around his neck, gratified to feel both of his hands slide up from her hips, over her belly and higher.

'Mia,' he groaned into her ear as his hands found her satin-clad breasts.

Mia whimpered, biting her lip as he squeezed and flattened then peeled the cups aside and ran the pads of his thumbs against her tight, bare nipples.

'I want to be inside you,' he murmured, his lips finding her neck and licking all the sensitive areas.

Mia opened her mouth to answer but one of his hands moved lower and dipped beneath the band of her underwear, seeking the slick heat of her. He ploughed a finger through her aching sex and found just the right spot, causing her to lose all vocal ability.

'Mia,' he murmured as she bucked against him. 'You are hot here. Very, very hot.'

Mia couldn't speak as one hand teased a nipple and the other moved rhythmically between her thighs. Her knee buckled slightly and she was vaguely aware of Luca pulling her back against him.

Her hands, however, had a mind of their own and while she left one anchored around his neck the other one sought to touch him as intimately as he was touching her.

She reached behind her, grabbing for his belt as her brain liquefied. One-handed and on an inexorable march towards orgasm, she managed the buckle and the zip and finally she was freeing him, his hard length surging into her palm.

Luca threw his head back on a groan, squeezing his eyes shut as she gripped him firmly and ran her hand up and down the length of him. The urge to bury himself in her, ram into all that slick heat as far as he could go, roared through him as his fingers picked up their pace.

Mia could feel the edges of her world starting to fray and she gripped his neck hard as a wild heat started to boil out of control in the deepest part of her. Her hand clamped around his girth became dysfunctional and uncoordinated as the all-consuming urge to ride his finger, seek her own pleasure, became a blinding imperative.

She sagged against him as standing upright became impossible. 'Luca,' she moaned.

'Yes,' he whispered in her ear. 'Yes.'

'Luca-a-a-a!'

She bucked as the orgasm slammed into her. It picked her up, whirled her round and smashed her back down only to lift her again—higher. She gasped and jerked against him, rocking her pelvis in sync with his fingers, squeezing every last liquid drop of pleasure out of it.

'Yes, Mia, yes,' he urged, rubbing harder and faster, pushing a finger deep inside her, feeling her clamp hard around him.

Mia moaned loudly as her body automatically accepted his penetration. It was shockingly satisfying and she cried out as another finger filled her.

Luca held her tight against him as she whimpered and gyrated her pelvis, grinding herself against the hard intrusion of his fingers.

The orgasm began to fade and Mia felt as if she was walking through a rainbow. Cool mists of colour stroked her skin like sighs, caressing and cradling, bringing her down gently despite the frantic beat of her heart and the tortured sound of her breath.

Finally her feet touched the ground and she opened her eyes. Became aware that she was leaning heavily into Luca, his hands were cradling her hips and his erection still coursed hard and potent in her hand.

She moved against him. Dropped her leg to the floor, kicked off her boot and turned in his arms.

Luca brushed her hair off her shoulder. 'Warm now?' He grinned.

Mia laughed. A part of her was vaguely aware the floor tiles were warm underfoot and that he could obviously afford to fork out for one of the more luxuriously appointed apartments. And that he no doubt had Bridge and Opera house views too.

But none of that mattered as she plastered her lips

to his. It only mattered that she could make him groan just like that. And...she rubbed herself along the length of him...hard just like this.

'Shower,' she murmured, pulling back and quickly divesting herself of her underwear before stepping into the spacious cubicle.

She turned through the cloud of steam. 'Are you coming?' she asked.

Luca, captivated by the water running over her naked body and her hair turning dark gold as the spray doused it, didn't move for a moment.

'Luca,' Mia growled impatiently, taking in his partially undressed body and his very, very aroused state. 'Come here and do me against the tiles.'

Her provocative words galvanised him into action and he tore at his shirt, toeing off his shoes, grabbing for his wallet before he divested himself of his trousers, pulling out a foil packet, ripping it open and hastily donning the protection he never went without.

Two steps and he was in a cloud of steam, enveloped by hot water and her. He plastered her against the requested wall and plundered her lips and her neck and her breasts with his mouth. Then he boosted her up the tiles, positioned her slippery body at just the right height and plunged straight into her, his mouth swallowing her guttural cry.

Luca pounded into her relentlessly, satisfied to hear her gasps, to see the loll of her head as each thrust rocked her entire body. He tongued her breasts, her heat and her sweat and her essence in each drop of water sluicing over her nipples.

Pressure built strongly and relentlessly as each drive took him closer. In his veins, in his head, in his loins.

Pleasure, so intense it hurt, coiled low in his gut. She cried out and bucked in his arms and the coil whipped out, cracking like a lightning strike, zapping every erogenous zone, every cell.

She tightened around him and he came and he came and he came.

Luca was in the kitchen, percolating coffee in nothing but a low-slung towel, when Mia came out of the bathroom dressed in the clothes she'd arrived in half an hour earlier.

Minus her underwear.

And the earring she'd lost somewhere in the midst of the head-banging sex. Down the drainhole, she suspected. Her hair was hanging in wet strips down her back and her body ached all over.

In a good way.

'Coffee?' he asked.

Mia shook her head, distracted by the perfection of him. Broad shoulders, trim hips, flat belly. His damp hair curled around his nape and ears. She felt the slight ache inside her begin to throb in carnal recognition of him and the things he could do.

It'd be so easy to take four or five paces forward and whip that towel away. Drop to her knees. Show him she was a pretty dab hand at doling out pleasure too. Go again right there on the kitchen floor as her traitorous body was demanding.

But then what? Once more after that? Stay the night?

She wasn't a stay-the-night kind of girl. It was why she always went to the guy's place—easier to leave and never look back than to tell someone to go.

'No, thanks,' she murmured. 'I'm going to head home.'

Luca lounged against the bench and crossed his arms over his very impressive chest. 'You're not clingy. I like that.'

Mia nodded. 'Good. Looks like we'll get along just fine, then.'

'I think you're the first woman I've met who didn't want to be held afterwards.'

Mia shook her head. 'Not the cuddling type, I'm afraid.'

Luca regarded her silently for a few moments. He could almost buy into her act. Except he'd seen another side to her that first night. Sure, Mia McKenzie seemed feisty and tough but there was definitely a vulnerable side.

She was an intriguing woman.

'And why is that?' Luca mused.

Mia knew exactly why. She wasn't blind to the scars that growing up in an emotionally barren house had left. Sex was a quick, easy connection—she'd found that out at uni. But cuddling—staying?—was hard. Sex was physically intimate. Cuddles emotionally intimate. Certainly not something she'd had an awful lot of experience with from the main male role model in her life as she'd been growing up.

Cuddles called for a certain level of trust. And she'd been too scarred to trust anyone at any level—particularly men.

He was standing patiently, all big and solid, looking at her with expectation. She could have easily opened her mouth and told him the reasons.

But it was none of his damn business.

'It sends the wrong message,' she said.

Mia shifted slightly as Luca studied her with his big brown eyes. It was kind of unnerving.

She straightened her shoulders. 'Do you have a problem with that?'

Like she cared if he did.

Luca stayed very still. 'No. It just seems like something a—'

'What?' she interrupted, scorn lacing her voice as her blood pressure rose a couple of notches. 'A man? Like something a man would say?'

Why was it okay for men to use women for sex but not for women to use men?

'It's a new century, Luca. Gotta move with the times.'

Luca chuckled at the sudden glint of fire in her stained-glass eyes. Her whole body had become animated. His gaze drifted to the bounce of her unfettered breasts before it flicked back to her face. 'Sicilian men aren't known for their tendency to move with the times.'

Mia shoved her hands on her hips as her nipples responded to his blatant stare. 'You going to go all Neanderthal on me, Luca?'

Luca pushed off the bench and moved towards her. 'Not at all. I am a highly evolved Sicilian. I like a woman who knows what she wants.'

Mia watched him prowl closer and felt that ache intensify. How was it possible to look sexy and menacing all at the same time?

He stopped in front of her, close, nearly touching. But not. 'Especially one who appreciates the type of liaisons I also happen to favour.' He dropped his gaze to her mouth for long moments before returning it to her face. 'Where have you been all my life?' He grinned.

It took Mia a moment to reel her body in enough to respond. Kissing him seemed the best course of action but she needed to go home.

She. Must. Go. Home.

And never come back.

Mia took a step back. 'Goodnight, Luca. See you in the morning.'

Luca watched the sway of her hips as she made her way to the door and felt himself twitch beneath the towel. 'I'm having a party in a couple of weeks. Everyone from work is coming. You should too.'

Mia's hand paused on the doorknob. 'No,' she said, without looking back.

One thing she knew for sure was that Luca wasn't like any other man she'd known. In a brief time he'd got firmly under her skin and she wasn't about to lose the upper hand to him.

There wouldn't be a next time. Certainly not a party.

Luca's wicked chuckle mocked her as she turned the handle and slipped out of the apartment.

Evie bustled through the deserted outpatients department at seven o'clock the next evening. She'd begged a chart from Enid Kenny, the NUM of the department earlier, who'd relinquished it only after Evie had promised faithfully to personally return it before she left for the day.

Someone else might have sent a courier but not Evie. Sister Enid Kenny was an institution around The Harbour and not to be messed with! Hence the sweet note and box of chocolates she was also clutching in her hand.

She turned right, passing a row of examination rooms

on her way to Enid's office. She noticed a light on in the far office. Voices floated out. Male voices. She frowned. Who on earth was working this late?

Then, to her utter surprise, Finn stepped out, followed by Rupert Davidson. Evie faltered and dived into the nearest exam room. Recovering quickly, she cautiously peeked around the door. In the empty department their voices carried easily and she eavesdropped unashamedly.

She watched as they shook hands and Rupert said, 'You're entitled to a second opinion, Finn. But you know as well as I do that the conservative approach is only a sticky plaster and you can't keep going on like this. Surgery will have to happen at some stage.'

Then Finn nodded but even from a few metres away she could see that familiar set to his unshaven jaw. 'Thanks, Rupert. I'll think about it.'

And then he turned and walked away in the opposite direction.

Evie fell back against the wall of the examination room, her heart pounding. What the hell had that been about? She grappled with what she'd heard and seen, trying to make sense of it.

Finn was seeing Rupert? A neurologist? *You can't keep going on like this.* Was there something wrong?

She recalled the uneasy feelings she'd had for a while now that something was up with Finn, and the rumours that he'd been wounded on a tour in Afghanistan when he'd been in the army. Had he sustained injuries during his time there? Injuries that could affect his job?

Eric Frobisher, SHH's officious medical director, would be furious if that was the case. He and Finn already butted heads on a regular basis.

Evie drummed her fingers against the chart as curiosity and concern for Finn warred within her. She told herself it was pure collegial interest. One doctor looking out for another. Even if said doctor was the most surly and unappreciative man she'd ever met.

Making a decision, Evie waited for a couple of minutes before pushing herself off the wall and heading towards her original destination. She stopped in midstride as she passed the last office and blinked at Rupert with what she hoped was her very best round-eyed surprise.

'Rupert?' she asked. 'What are you still doing here? Burning the candle at both ends?'

Rupert, who was writing in a chart, laughed as he put down his pen. 'No such luck. Just a late appointment.'

Evie nodded, glancing at the chart trying to see a name. 'Gosh, that's dedication.' She smiled.

Rupert shrugged. 'It was a favour.' He nodded at the package in her hand. 'What about you? Those chocolates for me?'

She laughed. 'Oh, no, these are major sucking-up chocolates for Enid.'

Rupert laughed back. 'You're coming to Luca's party in a couple of weeks?' she asked.

Rupert nodded. 'Wouldn't miss it for the world.'

'Great,' she said as she backed out the door, her head still swimming with what she'd just witnessed.

What in the hell was wrong with Finn Kennedy?

CHAPTER FIVE

Two weeks later Mia was watching the clock, thinking that for once in her working life she might actually get off on time. Her shift, one of those rare short shifts, was due to finish at two and things were looking good. With Evie going off to Luca's party tonight—the one she was *not* going to attend, no matter how much Evie begged— she had a quiet night of reading planned.

The latest blockbuster novel had been sitting on her bedside table, gathering dust, for too long.

She glanced nervously over at the man in question as he spoke on the phone at the other end of the central monitoring station. She'd managed to keep her attraction at bay this past fortnight—until last night. A cluttered, semi-dark storeroom had seriously tried her resolve to keep away when they'd both ended up inside. His body had been big and close, his lips had kicked up into a frank smile, his gaze firmly fixed on her mouth.

How she hadn't pushed him against the wall and ravaged him she still wasn't sure.

But she hadn't. She'd caught herself at the last second. Remembered that she'd already broken her golden rule once and she wasn't going to do it again. Even if he was the most skilled, most exciting lover she'd ever known.

Unfortunately, the buzz from last night's near kiss was still vibrating through her system and they'd been trading furtive glances all morning. He'd looked at her with undiluted lust half an hour ago and she still could barely see straight.

His gaze met hers again, his brown eyes knowing, and her pulse picked up a notch.

'Ambulance two minutes out.'

The urgent note in Nola's voice dragged her attention back to reality and Mia looked down to where the efficient triage nurse sat, the red emergency phone to her ear, speaking out loud as she wrote the details down from the ambulance coms centre.

'Thirty-year-old male. Jumper. Two storeys. Bilateral comminuted fractured tib and fibs, right compound fractured femur, query fractured pelvis, query spinal injuries, fractured right ribs, GCS twelve, major internal injuries, query ruptured spleen, hypotensive and tachycardic.'

Luca joined them, all business now as he read the details again over Nola's shoulder.

'I'll page Ortho and General Surgery,' Mia said, grabbing the phone nearest her as the distant wail of a siren permeated the thick walls of the hospital.

Luca also picked up a phone. 'I'll alert blood bank that we might need to initiate the massive transfusion protocol.'

By the time the ambulance pulled up a minute later, everything was prepped and Luca and Mia were standing outside, ready to receive the patient.

Luca grabbed the ambulance doorhandle and pulled

it open as the paramedic driving the vehicle joined them, launching into a rapid-fire handover of injuries, actual and suspected.

He and the treating paramedic pulled the gurney out of the back of the ambulance. The patient was moaning, his face covered by an oxygen mask.

'Pupils equal and reacting,' the paramedica continued as they pushed the gurney towards the entrance, Mia and Luca keeping pace. 'BP ninety over sixty, pulse one hundred and forty, resps fifty and shallow. Right chest tube inserted on scene, two IV cannulae wide open.'

'Do we know what happened?' Mia asked, clinging to the gurney rail as they practically flew inside to the prepared trauma cubicle.

'Paternity test showed he wasn't the baby's daddy,' the paramedic stated dispassionately.

Mia felt a prickle up her spine as she and Luca shared a look. 'Is his name Stan?' she asked.

The paramedic nodded. 'Stanley James.'

Repeat customers—especially suicides attempts—were reasonably common in the department. As were frequent-flyer drug addicts and patients with chronic conditions. Mia treated them all with courtesy and professionalism, careful not to get emotionally invested in them.

But this man had held her at knifepoint. Had yanked her back into the convoluted emotions of her childhood. Had been the catalyst for what had happened later that night with Luca.

Mia felt sick as two nurses descended and between the four of them they quickly transferred Stan to the hospital gurney on the count of three. Whether she liked it or not, she and Stanley were connected.

And she really didn't want to have to deal with that.

Stan pulled his mask off and grabbed her hand. 'I told you,' he said. 'I told you she was cheating on me.'

Mia looked into his anguished face, trying not to see her father, trying only to see the man who had menaced her with a knife. But he looked…broken.

Just like her father.

'It's going to be okay, Stan,' she murmured, replacing his mask as people bustled around her. 'We're going to get you patched up.'

He pulled it off again. 'No. Just leave me. Just leave me to die.'

Mia and Luca's gazes met for a moment. She felt rage build inside as she looked back down at Stan. He'd taken the coward's way out, just like her father. Her father had walked, Stan had jumped—both ways showed very little regard for the people left behind.

For a tiny baby. For a bewildered ten-year-old girl.

'Please, just let me die,' Stan begged.

Mia bit down on the urge to tell Stan that if he'd really wanted to die he should have jumped from a higher building. The fact that he hadn't spoke volumes about the incident. She doubted it was a true attempt—more like a cry for help.

And she was damned if she was going to let him die on her watch.

She put the mask back. 'Can't do that, I'm afraid, Stan.'

'We need X-Ray,' Luca said. 'And get Psych down here. I want to consult with John Allen.'

Luca and Mia, their personal situation forgotten,

worked methodically over the next hour to stabilise Stan for Theatre. They intubated, placed lines and another chest tube, gave blood and plasma expanders, consulted with Ortho, General Surgery and Radiology.

And all the time Luca was chanting, *Come on, Stan, come on Stan, come on Stan. Don't die. Don't die. Don't die.* If it took everything he had, Luca was not going to let this man die.

Not that he'd ever been particularly emotional about life-and-death situations. Being a trauma specialist, he saw the struggle between the two on a regular basis. Like two powerfully competing forces pulling in opposite directions. He worked hard to save every patient but not even he was arrogant enough to assume that hard work was always enough.

Sometimes, no matter what he threw at a patient, they died.

He got that. People died.

Children, teenagers, athletes, mothers, forty-year-olds with everything to live for.

People died.

Hell…they were all dying.

But the truth was, Stan had struck a chord. And probably for the first time ever he actually felt personally invested in a patient. And not because Stan had threatened him with a knife but because Luca knew all about the demons that had driven him.

He knew how it felt to be betrayed by the person you loved. How it felt to have your whole world yanked out from under you. And how life-changing that could be.

He knew how it felt to be a father one moment and then suddenly not.

To feel powerless.

To feel alone.

It may have been a whole bunch of years ago but some things never left you.

He glanced at Mia as she took a phone call from the lab. Mia, who was working just as hard to pull Stan through. The man who had threatened to stab her, who had slashed her arm with a knife.

What was driving her?

The same things that had driven her to cry out in her sleep that night? That had spurred her to seek amnesia in his arms?

What were the things that haunted her? That made her tough and feisty and not the *cuddling* type?

Had Stan stirred them up for her as he had stirred things up from *his* past? *Daddy, come back.* That's what she'd cried out that night. Did Stan remind her of her father as he had reminded him of his sixteen-year-old self?

'Haemoglobin's eight,' Mia announced. She ordered another bag of blood to be hung and administered stat. 'Let's get him to Theatre for that laparotomy,' she said. 'He's bleeding from somewhere.'

As if by magic, an anaesthetist, a nurse and two orderlies arrived and Luca dragged himself out of his reverie to help with the handover.

Within ten minutes Stan had been whisked away and the two of them stood in an empty trauma bay. The floor was littered with packaging and discarded dressing material that had fallen short of the bin. And where there'd been frantic activity and the beeps and alarms of monitors seconds ago, there was now absolute quiet.

Luca glanced at Mia watching Stan disappear down

the corridor with a look on her face he couldn't quite work out.

He put his arm around her shoulder. 'He'll be okay,' he said, even though he had no earthly idea why he'd said it and absolutely no way of knowing how true it was.

Mia nodded. Physically, sure…maybe. After an extended recovery period and if they could control the bleeding and get him through about a hundred complications that could arise.

But mentally?

Would Stan ever be the same again? Was her father?

For a few insane seconds she leaned into the hug, soaking up the comfort, surprised to find that she needed it as a block of unexpected emotion lodged in her chest, invading her throat, threatening to choke her.

And she hated it.

She pulled away, stripped off her plastic gown and peeled off her gloves, disposing of them in an overflowing bin.

'I'll follow up with John,' she said.

And left Luca behind in the bay.

Later that evening, Mia accompanied Evie to the party. She'd finally caved to her friend's relentless insistence that she go. Stan's case had been playing on her mind all afternoon and she knew she wouldn't be able to settle to a book. She needed a distraction and there was no doubt Luca distracted the hell out of her.

That brief comforting hug had been playing on her mind too but she pushed it aside. The distraction she needed from Luca did not involve anything as nurturing as comfort. She needed hard and ready. Hot and sweaty. Down and dirty.

And since she knew he gave it better than anyone else—could obliterate everything else from her brain—only he would do.

The party was in full swing when they finally stepped inside two hours late. Familiar faces milled in groups all around Luca's apartment and greeted them enthusiastically, despite their tardiness. Shift workers accepted that shift times varied and punctuality was fluid.

Mia felt Luca's eyes on her instantly and looked directly at him. Neither of them smiled as music pulsed around them and their gazes ate each other up.

Luca, surprised to see her, devoured the sight of her as she shrugged out of her leather jacket and made her way over to Luke Williams, one of The Harbour's plastic surgeons specialising in burns, and his partner, Lily, a nurse at SHH.

Mia was wearing a tight denim skirt that didn't quite reach her knees, a pair of long rainbow-striped socks that ended in little bows just below her knees and a singlet-style shirt that did up snugly across her front with corset-style lacing.

Thank goodness his apartment was centrally heated.

Her hair hung loose around her shoulders and an image of him removing that lacing with his teeth surrounded by the curtain of her golden hair wreaked havoc in his groin.

His gaze drifted to the reddish-pink scar on her upper arm visible from all the way across the room. It reminded him of that night and what had happened.

It reminded him of today. Of anguish so familiar he

had recognised it immediately. Of those brief few seconds with Mia after Stan had left for Theatre when he'd felt a strange moment of solidarity, of connection.

He pushed the thought aside. Stan had made it out of surgery and was stable in Intensive Care. And Mia had stepped away from him.

Work was work.

This was a party.

He took a swig out of his long-necked beer, his eyes never leaving her. She laughed at something Luke said and shook her head, her hair swinging enticingly around the cleavage barely contained by the faux corset top.

She glanced at him and their gazes locked, the message in her eyes heating his loins. He took another pull from his beer, keeping up the eye contact, matching her frank, unwavering stare. If she wanted to play chicken, he was up for it. He smiled to himself as Lily said something to her and Mia was forced to break contact first.

Why had she come when she'd been so adamant she wouldn't?

Just for the sex she was patently up for? Or was there something more to it? Had Stan rattled her again? Or maybe that moment they'd shared had? Had she come to prove it hadn't? Or to explore if it had?

The thought alarmed him and Luca served himself up a mental slap. What the hell business was it of his? Her motivations? He knew what he wanted and it didn't involve second-guessing a gorgeous woman who had come here to have sex with him. Whatever she was offering, he was going to take it.

And have a damn fine time doing so.

* * *

Mia wandered around the different groups of people, stopping to chat, talk shop, laugh with her friends and colleagues. And all the time she was conscious of Luca tracking her around the room. He hadn't even said hello to her but she could sense his intense interest, feel the weight of his gaze, the heat of his laser-like focus trained squarely on her back.

Sure, he was playing the perfect host—attentive and charming as he moved around the apartment—but underneath that bronzed Latin skin she could sense the leashed desire he was just barely keeping a lid on. His glances may be smouldering with lust but she could also feel his impatience as they slowly circled each other.

She walked past a large bay window and stopped to admire the view. She knew he'd have one. A man with heated bathroom tiles would certainly have a view!

The iron arch of the illuminated Sydney Harbour Bridge and the floodlit white sails of the Opera House glowed like beacons in the night. Of course, these could also be seen from the upper floors of SHH but it was still a pretty amazing sight, no matter how many times she'd been privy to it.

The hairs on the back of her neck prickled and she was instantly aware he was zeroing in.

Luca sauntered up to her. 'I didn't think you were coming,' he murmured.

Mia didn't turn to look at him. She could see his reflection. Tall, broad shouldered, looking very fine in snug blue jeans and a close-fitting black T-shirt.

All he needed was *Security* emblazoned across the front. Or maybe *Italian Stallion*.

'Nice view.'

Luca, who hadn't taken his eyes of her said, 'Indeed.'

He took a sip of his beer. 'The view from my bedroom is even better.'

Mia smiled. 'Don't you have guests to entertain?'

Luca chuckled, turning so his back was to the window. Their arms brushed and he felt a kick in his groin. 'They seem to be amusing themselves just fine.'

Mia turned too just in time to see Finn entering with a stunning-looking redhead she'd not seen before.

'I didn't think Finn would come,' she mused. Evie had been sure of it but she herself hadn't been convinced.

'Why not?' Luca frowned.

'He's not really the social type.'

He shrugged. 'He is tonight.'

Apparently. Very social, if the redhead's relaxed intimacy was anything to go by. Mia flicked a glance towards Evie and watched her friend's face fall a little. She gave an inward sigh, wishing she understood Evie's attraction to the maverick surgeon.

Sure, his legendary status was alluring and he was sexy in a rumpled kind of way. And single. But that just-rolled-out-of-bed look didn't do it for her.

She preferred clean-shaven men.

Like the one standing beside her.

'So…' Luca dropped his head so his mouth was near her ear. 'About that view?'

Mia felt goose-bumps break out on her arms as her belly constricted. But Evie was looking around with an overly bright smile on her face and Mia knew that her friend needed her.

'Patience is a virtue,' she murmured.

She heard Luca chuckling as she slunk away.

* * *

Half an hour later Evie was standing in a circle, ostensibly talking to Mia, Luke Williams and a couple of nurses from the emergency department. But her gaze kept wandering to Finn, who was sitting on the wide windowsill of the bay window, talking to Rupert. He had dismissed the redhead when Rupert had approached and now they seemed to be having quite an intense discussion.

Finn was nursing his usual Scotch and it didn't look like he appreciated what Rupert had to say. After another minute Rupert shrugged and walked away.

'Excuse me, guys. I'll go and grab another drink.'

She felt Mia's concerned gaze on her as she slipped away but no one else paid any attention. Evie grabbed a beer out of the ice-filled sink then wended her way through to Finn.

Finn watched Evie approach through the prism of his glass. She lifted a beer bottle to her lips and tipped her head back as she drew close. When she was done her lips were moist and he found himself wondering what she tasted like.

He tensed at the errant thought, which cranked up the throb in his already aching arm. That, on top of Rupert's little chat, made him even crankier.

'Well, well, well. I thought the Lockheart heiress would be into champagne.'

Evie let the insult slide off her back. She'd learned to chug beer and drink shots at uni just to annoy her parents.

'Beer is better.'

She stood in front of him, one hand shoved into the front pocket of her skinny jeans, the other one wrapped around the bottle. She was wearing a floaty top that fell off her shoulder, which he studiously ignored.

He raised his glass to the light. 'Scotch is the only drink.' It smoothed out the edges and helped with the pain. Physical and mental.

Evie inspected him. Sprawled on the windowsill, his shaggy look was sexy as hell. Unlike other guys she knew, the stubble was real, hinting at disregard rather than fashion. It also lent authenticity to the boast she'd once overheard—apparently he only ever got three or four hours' sleep a night.

She shook her head. *Why?* Was it deliberate? Did his brilliant mind never shut off or was it involuntary? Was the mysterious injury responsible for Finn's chronic insomnia? Or had his time in the army left him with nightmares? It was rumoured he'd been to Afghanistan and Iraq.

Or was it just the redhead or any of the other women he was seen with, keeping him up all night?

She didn't understand why she felt so compelled to try and figure him out. But she did. 'What did Rupert want?'

Finn, the glass halfway to his mouth, paused slightly before lifting it to his lips and draining the entire glass.

'I need another drink,' he said.

'I heard you and Rupert talking a couple of weeks ago. It was in the evening…in the outpatients department.'

Finn felt his hackles rise. 'Spying for Daddy?' He knew how chummy the hospital's biggest benefactor was with pernickety Eric Frobisher.

Evie heard the low menace in his voice and watched as his piercing blue eyes practically bored into her.

'He mentioned surgery.' Evie paused and perused his hard, shuttered face for any signs of softening. 'Is there something wrong, Finn?'

Finn heard the quiet strength in her voice. As if it never occurred to her that he wouldn't confess. The kind of strength that came from growing up in a nurturing environment where a person's opinion, even a child's, mattered.

'I think you should stick with diagnosing complex heart conditions.'

She ploughed on despite his rigid jaw and frigid stare. 'There are rumours about you being wounded in the army. Do you have some residual effects from that?'

Finn's heart pounded in his chest. Only little Miss Rich Girl would dare to push him like this. He stood, instantly towering over her, and was gratified to see her take a step back, to see she wasn't so sure of herself after all. 'I need a drink.'

He brushed past her without looking back.

Conversation over.

At two am only Mia and Evie remained as Luca shut his door on the last of his guests. He caught Mia's eye. She'd been a walking, talking temptation all night and now it was time to pay the piper.

Mia grinned at him. 'I'm going to stay and help Luca clean up,' she said to Evie, carrying some glasses into the kitchen and setting them on the substantial granite bench top beside the sink.

Evie nodded, tired after her long day shift and distracted by thoughts of Finn, who had hastily downed a drink after their *chat* then left with the redhead clinging to his arm. 'I'll help.'

Luca, picking up some more glasses behind where Evie was located, shook his head and mouthed, 'No.'

Mia grinned some more. 'No, Evie. You're done in. Go to bed. I won't be far behind you.' She was so revved up she'd probably come in under a minute.

'Oh, but—'

'No buts,' Luca insisted. 'Go. We'll be fine.'

Evie *was* exhausted. 'Well…if you're sure…?'

Luca nodded, vigorously aware that Mia had turned on the tap and was leaning over the sink. 'Absolutely.'

He ushered Evie out the door and shut it with quiet determination then leant against it, hard. He watched Mia fill the sink with glassware through a haze of high-octane lust.

'Leave that,' he said as he slowly prowled towards her.

Mia looked at him and grinned. It faded in a flash at the naked intent in his gaze. 'It's just a few dishes,' she said lamely as her insides melted to the consistency of chocolate sauce.

Just like his lust-drunk eyes.

Luca reached her side, flicked off the tap, swept the remaining dirty dishes into the sink with a huge clatter, grabbed her around the waist and boosted her up onto the bench.

Mia opened her mouth to protest against the tinkling glass and chipping crockery but mostly the cold granite on the backs of her legs. But Luca didn't give her a chance. He stepped between her thighs, forcing them apart, and claimed her mouth in a kiss that silenced all her inane worries.

A kiss that lit a fuse that ignited a powder keg. After

two weeks of abstinence and an evening of sexual chess they devoured each other like a raging bushfire.

Luca slipped his hands under the hem of her skirt, pushing it up her thighs, exposing her flesh and her heat. He dragged her core hard against him, the bench top just the right height, moaning when Mia locked her ankles around his waist, wedging them together as intimately as they could be fully clothed. She gasped as he kissed down her neck—hard, biting kisses that stiffened her nipples to unbearable points.

Yes. This was what she needed.

This.

Something to forget the day.

She grabbed for the snap on his jeans as he squeezed a breast with his hand. She undid his zip, pushed his underwear aside and grasped his warm velvet girth.

His mouth slammed against hers on a full, throaty groan as he fumbled with the lacing of her shirt, half undoing, half tearing at the fabric until it succumbed to his will. He dragged his mouth from hers, down, down, down to her breasts, ripping aside the cups of her transparent bra and gorging on the ripeness of her nipples.

Mia's back arched, one hand automatically holding his head to her, the other squeezing his rampant erection, rubbing herself against it, whimpering as it caused the most wicked friction.

'Back pocket,' Luca whispered as he lifted his head to pay equal homage to her other breast.

Mia fumbled. His lips were creating havoc and she felt like she'd been to the dentist and been given a full body shot.

Limp with lust. Prostrate with pleasure.

Her fingers found the hard edges of foil and whipped

it out triumphantly as his hand pushed aside her undies and stroked against her so intimately she thought she was going to die.

Too much more of that and she'd be done.

It was bloody-mindedness alone that accomplished sheathing him as he sought and found where she was hottest. Where she was the most ready.

'Ah,' she cried as the friction hit just the right spot. 'Now,' she cried, tilting her pelvis in supplication. 'Now.'

Luca didn't need a translation. He ran his palms up her back, anchored both hands over her shoulders, leaned forward to suck hard on a ripe, plump, moist nipple and rammed into her in one quick decisive thrust of his hips.

Their combined groan no doubt caused a blip at some seismic centre somewhere.

And then they were moving and pounding together in unison, rocking and rocking, higher and higher, gasping and sighing and reaching for breath until it all coalesced in one magical moment and the stars shattered around them.

CHAPTER SIX

A WEEK later Mia was examining a severe case of cel-
lulitis around a ten-day-old calf laceration when Luca
entered the cubicle. He smiled at her and her breath
hitched.

'Can I help you, Dr di Angelo?'

'You don't happen to have an otoscope by any
chance? They all seem to have gone walking.'

Mia didn't register his words. Just the way his eyes
crinkled at the edges as he looked at her with a gaze that
paid way too much attention to the dip of her cleavage.
And the way his lips moved, all soft and full, exactly
the same as when they stroked down her neck.

Luca quirked an eyebrow as Mia's normally clear
blue gaze became a little heated. 'Mia?'

She blinked and her cheeks warmed as she realised
she had no idea what he'd asked for. 'Sorry?'

Luca grinned. It wasn't often he saw her blush and
he liked it. It seemed completely at odds with her
feisty, my-way-or-the-highway demeanour, softening
her. Cranking up the strong sense of attraction another
notch. 'Otoscope?'

'Oh. Yes.' she shook her head to clear it as she removed the equipment from the pocket she'd jammed it in earlier. 'Here.'

Their fingers brushed as he took it and Luca smiled again as he felt the pulse of awareness in his fingertips and knew she'd felt it too. 'Thank you.'

It took Mia a few seconds to realise he'd disappeared as her body recovered from just the faintest contact with his.

'He's a bit of a hottie, dear.'

Mia looked down absently at Mable Richardson, her eighty-six-year-old patient. She had snowy white hair and a wicked gleam in her eyes.

'He could park his slippers under my bed any day.' Mable sighed. 'If I was only forty years younger...'

Mia stared at her patient open-mouthed, shocked by such ribald frankness from an octogenarian.

Mable cackled. 'I'm old, deary, not dead.'

Mia laughed. From the twinkle in her eyes, Mable was obviously one of those lovely old ladies who loved to shock.

'Laugh all you want.' Mable patted Mia's hand. 'You blink one day and suddenly you're eighty-six. Mark my words, young lady—take your opportunities when you get them.' And then she winked.

'Mable, you're incorrigible.'

Mable cackled again, seemingly delighted by Mia's description. 'I hope so, deary.'

Mia returned her attention to Mable's gardening wound, which had developed an infection in the sub-cutaneous tissues. Had Mable seen something pass between her and Luca—something intangible—that had prompted such an observation, or was she just someone who appreciated good eye candy when she saw it?

Not for the first time she wondered what the hell she and Luca were doing. Okay, there'd been no more liaisons since the party and they'd only been together a few times anyway. But it was a few times more than she'd ever allowed any other man. And, if his rep was accurate, the same applied to him.

Why did this man, Luca di Angelo of all men, have this…pull, this sway over her?

No.

Mia smiled absently at Mable as she pulled the gurney rail up decisively and excused herself to arrange for Mable's admission for several days of intravenous antibiotics.

She wasn't going to analyse what had gone on.

She wasn't going to give it any importance by pontificating over it.

They were attracted to each other. They'd had a good time. And that was that.

Period.

A couple of hours later the red emergency phone rang and Luca picked it up. He scribbled notes as he listened to the ambulance comms officer on the other end.

Mia and Evie looked at him as he hung up and Mia quirked an eyebrow. 'Multiple casualties, first five minutes out, from the Douglas army base. Some sort of an explosion. Two critical. One with penetrating chest trauma, the other with a partially severed leg.'

Caroline, on triage, appeared at his elbow and said, 'On it.'

Luca thanked her. 'I'll page Finn,' he said.

Then everyone scattered to do their jobs, ensuring the trauma bays were fully stocked for the incoming wounded and other departments alerted, including Pathology, Radiology and the operating theatres. Luckily it was Sunday when demand for these services was reduced.

Finn, in his standard surgical uniform of blue scrubs, arrived just as the first ambulance was pulling in.

'You take the chest trauma,' Luca said to his colleague, donning a yellow paper gown. 'I'll take the leg.'

Finn nodded, accepting a gown from Evie and quickly securing it before snapping disposable gloves into place.

'Evie, you go with Finn. Mia, you're with me.'

Finn opened his mouth to protest but Mia and Luca had already split off and ultimately it didn't matter who worked with him as long as they were competent. And, as reluctant as he had been to believe it, Princess Evie knew her stuff.

'You ready for this?' he demanded as the paramedic opened the back door.

Evie nodded, determined not to show him how much his enquiry rankled. 'Of course.' She gave him a serene smile to hide her gritted teeth.

A cry of pain, like that of a wounded animal, penetrated Finn's cynicism and tore his attention away to the soldier on the gurney, his dusty boots and army fatigues eerily familiar.

It took him back a lot of years.

He knew all about cries like that. Had heard them too often to forget. Had held Isaac, rocked him, as the yelling had quietened and finally abated, leaving only silence as the life had drained from his brother's trusting eyes.

'Twenty-eighty-year-old sergeant, bomb disposal

officer at Douglas, took the full impact of an explosive device. Safety gear rendered some protection.'

Finn shook his head and blinked as the rapid-fire handover spat out at him like the rat-a-tat of a machine gun. He couldn't think about Isaac. About a distant battlefield.

This soldier needed him.

But *this* soldier was about Isaac's age and cried out in pain just like Isaac had.

Finn pushed it away, knocked it back as the gurney moved rapidly into the emergency department.

'Matthew! Matthew!' the soldier called, pulling the oxygen mask aside with bloodied hands.

The paramedic continued his handover above the soldier's increasingly frantic cries. Evie listened intently while Finn stared at the young man's bloody face.

'Matty!'

'Matthew is his brother,' the paramedic informed Finn and Evie quietly as he helped transfer the soldier to the hospital gurney. 'He's the second soldier. With the…leg.'

Finn gave a grim nod as he looked at the blood-soaked combat shirt that had been cut away from the bleeding chest wound. Isaac had cried out for him, too. He could still hear the panic in his brother's voice. *Finn! Finn!*

'Matthew. Are you okay, Matthew?'

Finn moved in close to the soldier's head while all around him nurses jumped into action. Tears had cut grimy streaks through his grisly war paint of dirt and blood.

'Oxygen saturations eighty-nine, tachy at one fifty-nine,' a nurse relayed.

Finn's heart thundered in his chest as he fought back a tide of memories he'd thought he'd long ago buried deep. 'What's your name, Sergeant?'

Finn's enquiry was quiet but held a note of authority not forgotten from his own time in the army. It seemed to settle the soldier's agitation. He looked at Finn, his eyes filled with pain and emotional anguish.

'Phillips, sir, Sergeant Damien Phillips.' Damien grabbed Finn's gown, yanking him close, jarring his already throbbing upper arm and neck. 'Don't let me die. I don't want to die.'

Finn suddenly felt the weight of the promise he'd made to his brother all those years ago. It burned as fiercely on his conscience at this moment as it had that day sprawled in the dirt of a land far away. A promise he'd known, crippled by his own injuries and with help too many precious minutes away, he couldn't keep.

A promise that had haunted him.

But he could make good on a promise to Damien. In this top-notch facility and with his top-notch skills.

And he'd be damned if he'd lose another soldier on his watch.

'I won't, Damien. I won't.'

Evie looked at him sharply as a nurse passed her a chest tube. The soldier and Finn were practically nose to nose but, still, the husky promise surprised her. And not just because of the raw emotion she could hear in it.

Had Finn gone mad? Why on earth would he make such a promise? Damien's injuries were extensive—no one could promise that. Not even someone with Finn's legendary skill!

'Blood pressure ninety systolic.'

Finn glanced at her and she sucked in a breath at the brief flash of anguish, like the sweep of a lighthouse beacon, she saw there. His piercing gaze clouded temporarily with something she couldn't put her finger on—pain, compassion, loss?—then cleared as he stood abruptly.

'Let's get him prepped for Theatre,' Finn ordered.

Two hours later, in the thick of the operating theatre after Finn had demanded she scrub in, Evie's shoulders ached and her neck was stiff as they battled to plug the holes in Damien's heart. They'd replaced his entire circulation with donated blood products twice over. And he was still bleeding.

No one was surprised when a life-threatening arrhythmia caused a sudden dangerous dip in his blood pressure.

But Finn didn't give up.

He had the young soldier's heart in his two bloodied hands and was squeezing it as if he could make the heart start beating again through sheer force of will.

He'd promised.

Too much death. Too many young men like Damien. Like Isaac.

Damn it! He'd promised.

But as the downtime extended, even he could see the futility of it. Finn found it hard to breathe as he gently removed his hands from around the soldier's heart and stepped back. He peeled off his gloves and glanced at the clock.

'Time of death fifteen thirty-one.'

No one spoke as they watched Finn walk out of the theatre. But a little bit of Evie went with him.

An hour later after attending to all the legalities, Evie felt drained, totally strung out from the after-effects of adrenaline and their exhaustive yet futile efforts to save Sergeant Damien Phillips's life.

Except it wasn't over because she had to find Finn, who wasn't answering his page. He had to sign some paperwork.

And she was worried about him...

Her fingers trembled as she pushed the change-room doors open. She needed to get out of these scrubs. They reminded her too much of the tragedy she'd just witnessed.

Of Finn's hands squeezing Damien's dying heart.

Her heart leapt in her chest as Finn came into view. He was sitting on the floor, staring at the wall, the lockers supporting his back. His knees were bent up and his hands were hanging between them, his surgical cap dangling from his fingers.

She swallowed. 'I've been paging you.'

Finn heard her voice as if from far away. He didn't want her there. He didn't want her to look at him with those calm hazel eyes of hers, eyes that saw too much, and mouth some horrible cliché.

He wanted to go home, pour himself a Scotch. And then another one. Drink until he could be sure he wouldn't dream about Isaac.

He kept his gaze firmly fixed on the wall. 'I've been ignoring you.'

Evie stared at him, dismayed at the return of his churlish tone. She should have expected it but for some reason, after their frantic efforts with Damien and the shared horror of losing him, she'd thought it'd be different.

He'd be different.

Irritated, she sauntered over to the patch of wall he was fixated on and deliberately parked her butt on it. Now he had no choice but to look at her. She folded her arms.

'There's some paperwork for the coroner you need to sign out in the office.'

Finn flicked his gaze up to her determined face. 'Fine.'

They stared at each other for a moment, the blue of Finn's eyes even more pronounced against the blue of his scrubs. Evie battled the urge to debrief, as she would normally with a colleague who had shared such an emotionally intense situation. Even a churlish one. But everything about Finn said, *Back off.*

But, then, when hadn't it?

'Damien's been taken to the morgue and—'

Finn pushed himself to his feet, interrupting her words. He bit down on a wince as a hot needle jabbed viciously into the nerves that ran down his right arm.

'We're not talking about Damien,' he said, turning to his locker, his back deliberately to her.

Evie took in the expanse of his back in his scrubs as she reeled from the vehemence in his words.

But I want to talk about him. I had my hand in his chest too, felt his heart pulsating. I need to talk about him.

She pushed off the wall and took a tentative step towards him and even though she knew she was overstepping the line, she didn't seem to be able to stop.

'Finn.'

His back stayed stubbornly turned away. Evie stared at it and let out the breath she'd been holding. She waited for a moment and stepped closer. 'Maybe it'd help...to talk about it?' she murmured.

His silence was absolute and out of pure frustration she tentatively placed her hand on his left shoulder. Despite the flinch she felt right down to her soul, Mia kept it there. His muscles were knotted with tension, practically vibrating beneath her hand, and she moved closer again until her body was almost touching his.

Finn shut his eyes as her scent and her warmth enveloped him. He could sense her right there behind him. Could hear the soft huff of her breath and the empathy oozing from every pore. A part of him wanted to unburden so badly it was shocking in its intensity.

Would it hurt to lean back a little, to have just a moment today that made sense?

Even if it didn't?

Evie held her breath as his body swayed a little and then seemed to slowly relax back against hers. His scrubs felt warm on her skin and she could sense the vitality of him as they stood in silence, cradled against each other, her cheek brushing his shoulder blade.

It was a magical moment and she shut her eyes to absorb every second. Everything suddenly seemed... right. Evie felt safe. She felt understood.

'You were brilliant today,' he whispered.

Evie eyes fluttered open at the barely discernible words. Had he said it or had she only imagined it? She opened her mouth to return the compliment but a beeping pager shattered the intimacy.

Finn's eyes opened instantly. His surroundings came

into sharp focus, the feel of Evie pressed against him suddenly too, too close for comfort.

What the hell was he doing?

He shrugged her away. 'I have to go,' he said gruffly.

Evie stepped back from him, reeling from the quick severing of the fragile emotional connection they'd just made.

He didn't even look back as he departed.

Mia headed straight for Pete's Bar after work later that evening. It had been a harrowing day for all of them, with Evie seeming particularly stressed when she'd finally returned to the department. They'd arranged to meet for a drink and a bit of a debrief session. Her friend was obviously taking the soldier's death hard.

Evie, however, was nowhere to be seen amidst the surprising Sunday night crowd as Mia made her way to the bar.

Luca, on the other hand, was easily spotted by her specially tuned senses and even if she'd been able to resist his devilish smile, she couldn't resist his I've-been-waiting-for-you stare.

Luca slid over as Mia approached, a sense of inevitability taking hold. What was it about this woman that made him want more? Her complete lack of sexual inhibitions or was she just a novelty, something familiar for a change instead of just another pick-up?

Or maybe it was her emotional unavailability? Knowing that she wanted the same thing he did—no commitments, nothing but a good time.

He watched the tame swish of her ponytail as she came closer, knowing what that hair looked like loose and wild and knowing from the heat in her gaze that tonight was going to get very wild indeed.

Mia refused to look at Luca as she slid in beside him. She didn't want to alert the two other occupants to what was going on between them. She and Luca were sex—just sex—and she didn't want the others to get the wrong impression.

She greeted Charlie Maxwell, the orthopaedic surgeon who had operated on the partially severed leg earlier, and Carl Todd, the anaesthetist. They were chatting about the bomb blast at Douglas and the two operations that had followed.

'He's not out of the woods yet,' Charlie said, taking a mouthful of his cola. He was on call and could well be called back to amputate the leg. 'We managed to save it but I'm not entirely convinced it'll be viable in the long term. There was extensive blood loss and a lengthy ischaemic time.'

Mia was always surprised whenever Charlie was serious. The lovable, laid-back, ex-pro surfer with his shaved head and wicked sense of humour gave new meaning to the Aussie word 'larrikin'. It was hard to tell at first glance that beneath it all he was a dedicated and committed professional.

'The trip from the army barracks isn't exactly short,' Mia mused. They were the nearest tertiary hospital to the barracks but in a situation where every second was vital, it was just a little too far away.

'Absolutely,' Charlie agreed. 'You guys did a great job getting him to me as quickly as you could.'

They chatted about the procedure for a while and Mia was pleased to hear that the patient was still stable in ICU with good pulses when Charlie rang to get an update.

Working on saving the leg today with Luca had been an exhilarating experience, and it was good to know that their efforts had contributed to the thus far positive operative outcome.

She glanced at Luca and felt her breath hitch as he chose that moment to glance at her. Heat surged up the side seam of her jeans where their legs touched. Under the table, his hand slid onto her thigh.

She felt her breath seize in her lungs. But, as his fingers started to smooth the fabric of her jeans in light patterns, she didn't remove it.

'Well, at least you had better luck than Finn,' Carl commented, dragging Mia's attention back to the conversation. He inclined his head to indicate the man in question, who was sitting at the bar by himself, staring into his Scotch.

'He worked like a demon, trying to save the other soldier. It was like he was possessed or something.'

Even knowing how much Carl liked to embellish things, Mia was startled by the anaesthetist's description of the frantic efforts in Finn's theatre that afternoon—no wonder Evie needed to debrief.

'Evie's pretty wrecked,' Mia commented when Carl finished.

'She's in the wrong specialty. She'd make a great surgeon,' Carl mused. 'Kept her head no matter how testy Finn got.'

Mia glanced at Finn again just as Suzy plonked herself down in the chair next to him. The theatre nurse was a regular at Pete's and Mia had seen her flirting with Finn here before, but a blind fool could see that Finn was not in the mood for company.

He gave her one of those polite frozen smiles she'd seen Finn give once too often to hapless medical students or to Eric Frobisher in particular, but Suzy seemed as oblivious or impervious to Finn's signals as Eric did.

Luca's signals, however, as his fingers continued to brush against her thigh, were loud and clear. Mia fought the urge to turn her body towards him, raise her mouth to his.

Carl looked over his shoulder again. 'Well, well, well. Looks like Finn's found a little distraction for the night.'

Mia just stopped the eye-roll. Carl was a top-class anaesthetist and still fancied himself as a bit of a ladies' man but he obviously wasn't a student of body language—he was way off the mark.

Luca winked at her. 'Oh, you think so?' he asked, watching an obviously distant Finn.

Carl took a swallow of his beer. 'Oh, yes.' He tapped his nose three times with his index finger. 'I've been around long enough to tell when there's hanky-panky going on between the staff.'

Luca felt Mia's thigh tense beneath his palm and he grinned. 'Really?' he murmured as he resisted Mia's sudden attempt to remove his hand from her thigh.

He easily won the necessarily subdued struggle.

Carl nodded. 'Of course. I picked Luke and Lily long before anyone else did. And this bloke...' he jerked his thumb towards Charlie. '...is virtually an open book.'

Charlie looked affronted. 'Me? What about him?' Charlie pointed to Luca. 'His reputation *preceded* him.'

'Ah, well.' Carl laughed. 'That's true.'

Luca laughed good-naturedly. 'And what about Mia?'

he enquired innocently, daring to stroke his fingers closer to the apex of her thighs. He didn't even wince when his ankle suffered a short, sharp jab from a hard pointy toe. 'Any gossip on her?'

Carl shook his head with a faux crestfallen look. 'Oh, no. Mia informed me a long time ago that fooling around with someone from work was a recipe for disaster. I think they were the words, right, Mia?'

Mia nodded her head graciously. She'd told Carl that most emphatically one day just after he'd tried to come on to her. And she meant it as much now as she had then.

So why the hell was she sitting at a booth with an Italian devil who was practically bringing her to orgasm in front of two oblivious colleagues?

Surely Carl could see the pheromones wafting off her body?

'What?' Luca feigned shock, looking down into Mia's face, gratified to see heat shimmering in her eyes like a mirage as his finger found her inner seam. He noticed her knuckles whiten as her grip on the edge of the table tightened. 'There's been no work flirtations?'

'Oh, no,' Carl answered for her. 'As far as I can tell, there's been no one. And I have a pretty good radar,' he added, tapping his nose again and smiling at Mia.

Luca flicked a finger across the seam that ran down from the bottom of her zip where it joined the two inner thigh seams. He felt her resistance melt to nothing as her legs eased apart a little and he thought, *Carl, you are a fool!*

Mia knew she shouldn't. They were in a public place, for crying out loud. A place that was crawling with staff from The Harbour. But his fingers were creating such delicious havoc…and no one could see…

She spread her legs a little further and smiled at Charlie as she changed the subject.

Evie was late to Pete's but that was the nature of the job. A last-minute patient had kept her involved for a while, which had been fine by her. Becoming absorbed in her work had helped keep her mind off Finn and what had happened between them today.

Because, whether he liked it or not—whether *she* liked it or not—something *had* happened. She'd had a glimpse of his humanity and no matter how many patients she'd seen since, she just couldn't banish that from her head.

And that brief moment when he'd leaned into her… It had felt like some kind of…surrender.

She'd never seen Finn emotionally vulnerable but today had been different. Today he'd leaned on her. Actually let himself go for once and trusted her enough to drop the cantankerous-but-brilliant-surgeon facade and just be a doctor who'd lost a patient. Be human. Be a man.

She could still feel the imprint of him against her. The flat of his shoulder blade against her cheek, the warm, solid roundness of his shoulder beneath her palm, the press of his broad back against her chest, their hearts beating almost as one.

She wasn't stupid enough to read anything into it. But she was intrigued. She wanted to know more. She wanted to know what had happened in his past to make Damien's case so personal to Finn. So personal that he'd let his guard down to her, of all people. Let her touch him. Let himself touch her back.

You were brilliant today, Evie.

Those words had meant more to her than any compliment she'd ever received-professional or personal. She hugged them to herself as she crossed the road to Pete's.

If Finn was at Pete's, she was going to repay the compliment. She was going to buy him a drink, tell him he was brilliant and badger him until he talked.

Staff at The Harbour always talked about what a maverick he was, what a legend. They held him in awe, hoisted him on high like some kind of trophy, made him untouchable. Like he was a machine, a robot. But they seemed to forget, underneath it all he was also a man.

But she hadn't. She'd seen the man today.

And men needed to be touched too.

Finn probably most of all.

Finn wasn't really listening to Suzy as she prattled on about some movie she'd just seen. He didn't want her there, he didn't want to talk or make light conversation.

He didn't want to hook up. Even if Suzy was extremely attractive and obviously up for it.

He came to Pete's for one reason only. To drink.

Sure, he could drink at home. And he'd do that too. But drinking a little in public tempered the urge to drink a lot when he got back to his apartment.

The Scotch helped with the pain from his injuries and it helped obliterate the events that had caused them.

Suzy couldn't do that. No woman could. Not even Lydia.

And then Evie's lovely face entered his vision and

for one crazy moment panic rose in him as he thought he'd conjured her up. But then she pushed the heavy door open wider and their gazes met.

For a moment there was a shimmer of recognition between them, a whisper of what they'd both endured together, and then she smiled at him, a smile that seemed to see right inside him. A smile that said, I know you're hurting; let me help you.

And for one mad instant he wanted that. He wanted to feel again what he'd felt that afternoon in the change room cocooned against her. That strange kind of peace—like nothing he'd ever known.

The panic intensified.

The sheer power of these strange, unwanted feelings Evie evoked overwhelmed him. He dragged his gaze away, his heart beating like that of a wild animal suddenly caged and fighting for his life. She didn't know him. She didn't know anything about him. How could she? Princess Evie couldn't even begin to comprehend where he'd come from, the things he'd seen, the promises he'd broken.

He turned to Suzy and dazzled her with a smile. 'Whaddya say we get out of here?'

Evie, her heart light as she spotted Finn, made a direct line for him. She stopped three paces later when she realised he wasn't alone. The smile he gave the blonde, one she'd seen him with here before, took her breath away and she struggled with the sudden urge to turn on her heel and run.

Or slap someone. *Back off!*

But he wasn't hers to make such an order. The realisation brought with it a sudden crushing sense of despair. Just because they'd shared a moment, that didn't make him hers.

Finn smiled down at Suzy as she leaned forward and whispered in his ear. Her cleavage was exposed to his view and he looked his fill.

It was an impressive cleavage and he was a man, damn it.

A man who appreciated a woman's body but did *not* get emotionally involved with them. And the sooner Evie got that through her head, the better.

He wasn't some wounded hero that needed saving. He was a cantankerous bastard beyond redemption.

'C'mon,' he said, sliding off the stool, putting his hand out to help Suzy off hers but looking directly over her head, meeting Evie's shocked look with practised indifference. 'Let's go back to my place.'

Evie couldn't move for a moment, the cold of Finn's piercing gaze freezing her to the spot. He seemed totally unreachable as his eyes told her things he couldn't say in a crowded bar.

Like, *what happened this afternoon meant nothing. You mean nothing.*

Suzy smiled up at Finn, disconcerted to find he wasn't looking at her. 'I thought you'd never ask.'

Finn dragged his gaze away from the emotions in Evie's hazel eyes. There was hurt and disgust and even a touch of scorn.

And he deserved every one of them.

He threw another dazzler Suzy's way before tucking her hand in his, straightening his back and making a beeline for the door.

Evie watched him go, a veritable storm of emotions raging inside. Anger, repulsion, despair.

Where was the Finn from earlier? The one who had leaned into her and told her she was brilliant?

She looked back to find Pete watching her. He was holding up a cold beer and a shot glass and his gaze radiated warmth and sympathy.

Thank God for Pete.

CHAPTER SEVEN

TWENTY minutes later Charlie drained his glass and stood. 'I'm going to go and check on my patient.'

'That's very dedicated of you,' Mia teased, wishing both he and Carl would leave so she could drag Luca into the nearest dark corner and have him finish what he started, instead of taunting her in secret with those very clever fingers.

But she'd soon learned that two could play at his game and Luca was looking decidedly uncomfortable himself.

'Of course the delectable Nurse Barry has nothing to do with it,' Carl added.

Charlie grinned. 'I'm affronted, Carl.' And grinned again.

Carl tossed back his beer. 'Hang on, then, I'll walk you out.'

They said their goodbyes and Luca and Mia were finally left alone. Luca dropped his mouth to her ear. 'You're going to pay for that. Let's go. Now.'

Mia smiled as his voice, thick with lust, emphasised his accent. A surge of anticipation tightened her pelvic floor. 'If you can't take it,' she murmured, sliding slowly out of the booth, 'you shouldn't be dishing it out.'

'Here you are, Mia. Sorry I'm late,' Evie said, plonking herself down on the opposite seat, pushing a tray of orange juice, beer and shot glasses onto the table. 'I'm warning you now, I plan on getting very, very drunk.'

Mia shut her eyes briefly. *Damn. Evie.*

Luca's caress had managed to erase all trace of the reason she'd come to Pete's tonight in the first place. She glanced at Luca, saw lust rippling through the dark chocolate pools of his eyes and felt everything clench. She forced herself to look away.

'I can see that,' Mia murmured, as Evie raised the shot glass to her lips.

'Oh, hello, Luca,' Evie said as she slammed down the first shot and lined up her second. 'So glad you're here. Maybe you can explain to me how the male mind works?'

Luca looked from Mia to Evie and back to Mia again. He'd had a vision of how the evening was going to pan out and this had not been part of it. He watched as Evie threw back her second shot and knew enough about women to know that he had one too many y chromosomes to be a part of this conversation.

He glanced at Mia, who shrugged an apology at him, a small smile playing on her lips. He stroked up the centre seam of her jeans and was gratified to see the smile disappear.

He patted her leg twice. 'I think I'll go and leave you lovely ladies to it.'

Mia scooted out and Luca followed her, her rear end at an enticing level before he stood and towered over her.

He nodded at Evie. 'Goodnight.'

Evie grunted something as she contemplated her

third shot and he turned to Mia. 'I'll see you...' he quirked an eyebrow at her '...soon?'

Mia watched as Evie downed another tequila. 'Later.' She grimaced.

Luca dropped his gaze to her mouth then sighed. 'Later.'

It was low and raw and whispered along her nerve endings and Mia felt decidedly wobbly as she slid back into the booth, her insides melting.

'Are you okay?' she asked Evie, refusing to turn and watch Luca walk out of the bar. Pete had already given her a speculative look as she'd sat—she didn't want anyone else in the bar wising up.

Evie shook her head. 'Nope. But I will be.' She slammed another shot back. 'Real soon.'

Mia sipped her orange juice. 'You won't be in the morning.'

'Well, I have two days until I'm back on shift to recover.'

Mia pushed the beer towards her friend and dragged the tray with three more shots on it out of reach. 'You may well need them.'

Evie didn't protest, just sipped at her beer.

'Carl was telling me you had a pretty harrowing time in Theatre with Finn. Tell me about it.'

Evie raised her eyes to her best friend. 'Oh, Mia, it was the most incredible thing I've ever witnessed. Finn was...he was...magnificent.' She sipped her beer again. 'And then he went and acted like a total jerk.'

Mia nodded. 'Okay, start at the beginning.'

Three hours later Evie had unburdened and Mia had managed to stagger home with her and put her to bed.

She left a jug of water, a glass and two tablets by Evie's bed for when she woke up feeling like someone was drilling for oil in her brain, her mouth as dry and putrid as the newspaper that lined a budgie cage.

She watched her friend sleep for a moment. Evie really had it bad. She didn't know it yet, of course, but a man who drove a girl that crazy was more than some nutty crush.

Which was why her way was much better. Give them your body but keep your heart and mind out of contention. Use them for sex then walk away.

Like her and Luca.

Except she hadn't walked away, had she?

She looked at Evie's face, troubled even in an alcohol-induced slumber. If this was what pining after a man got you then she wanted no part of it.

She had to end it with Luca.

After tonight.

Mia glanced at Evie's bedside clock—it was nearly one in the morning. Would Luca be awake?

She remembered how hard he'd been beneath his jeans as she'd fondled him under the table.

He'd be awake.

Her own body was still humming like an electrical substation generating enough heat to power the entire eastern seaboard.

She smiled to herself as she hurried to her bedroom, stripping off her clothes, pulling her hair out of its ponytail, opening her wardrobe, yanking her long winter coat off its hanger and stepping into its folds, the lining cool against her bare, heated flesh. She overlapped the edges and tied the cord securely around her waist—

there were buttons but they were going to take too long to undo for her purposes.

Mia inspected herself in the mirror. She looked very modest in the calf-length coat and heels. Should she, on the slim off chance at after one in the morning, happen to bump into someone in the lift, they couldn't possibly be aware she didn't have a stitch on under the coat.

Neither would Luca.

Mia smiled at her reflection. All she needed was a little eye make-up and some lippy and she'd be perfect for an early-morning booty call.

Hell, if this was going to be their last time, she might as well blow his mind.

Luca was brooding in front of his magnificent bay window when he heard the knock. He allowed himself a smile for the first time since arriving home alone with a raging hard-on over three hours ago.

Anticipation tightened his groin as he stalked to the door and yanked it open to find a rugged up Mia leaning casually against the jamb.

'Oh, good.' She smiled. 'You're awake.'

Luca sucked in a breath. Her hair was loose and her eyes were heavily kohled in shades of grey and black, emphasising their blueness. Her mouth was painted fire-engine red. He moved in close until their bodies were almost touching. 'It's hard to sleep in my condition,' he murmured.

Mia pouted. 'Poor darling. Can I come in? I could help you with that.'

Luca's gaze drifted to her mouth. 'Are you sure? I wouldn't want you entering into a recipe for disaster.'

Mia laughed as devilish memories from Pete's surfaced. Luca touching her under the table, stroking between her legs. She lifted a finger and traced his bottom lip, almost moaning out loud when he sucked it into his mouth. 'Carl's a sore loser,' she whispered.

Luca, his body taut with longing, swirled his tongue around her finger and gently released it. 'Come in, take your clothes off. You are way overdressed.'

He stepped back and Mia strode into the room. The heat enveloped her and she turned to find Luca watching her from the shut door. She untied the coat and shrugged out of it. It fell to the floor and she was standing before him in nothing but a pair of heels.

'Will this do?' she asked.

Luca's brain temporarily powered down as his hungry gaze ate up her body. Her long legs, the jut of her breasts, the flare of her hips, the shadow of her sex.

Mia's nipples hardened at the intensity of his scrutiny. It felt more intimate than if he'd touched her and she suddenly felt like he could see right inside her. She fought the urge to cover herself.

Luca swallowed. 'Spin around.'

His husky command spread tentacles of heat through her belly and she performed a slow teasing rotation, looking over her shoulder at him as she circled her hips like she'd seen once in a documentary on pole dancing.

Luca's belly clenched tight. He pushed away from the door and was in front of her, reaching for her in seconds, his hands sliding around her waist, his mouth descending.

And then he was kissing her and she was kissing him back. Long, deep, wet kisses that had her gasping and sighing and begging for more as she pulled at his clothes, desperate for some skin on skin.

Her nipples rubbed against his naked chest and Luca groaned deep in his throat. Then he swept her up into his arms and strode through the apartment, their mouths locked, their hearts beating to a rhythm that pulsed like a rock concert through the air around them.

Luca reached his bed and threw her on it. Mia was startled as she free-fell, landing softly but breathing hard. Somewhere along the way she'd lost her heels so she was one hundred per cent naked now.

She looked up at a half-undressed Luca. His lips were moist from their kissing, his shirt was half off, his zipper undone.

'You look good,' she murmured.

Luca grinned. 'You look better.'

Then he was stripping off his clothes, reaching for a condom, sheathing himself, then joining her, tangling his limbs with hers, kissing her mouth and her neck and her breasts, ignoring her entreaties to finish it as he licked lower. And lower.

It wasn't until she lay spent beneath him that he succumbed to his own body's dictates, entering her slowly, revelling in her exultant cry, rocking and pulsing, building her again until he was pounding and pounding, pushing them both to impossible heights and then pushing them both over into oblivion.

It was several minutes before either of them was physically able to speak. Luca, who was now lying on his back, recovered first.

'Do you realise this is the first time we've actually done it in a bed?'

Mia, her brain cells still reorganising themselves after a mass meltdown, just nodded. It took her another couple of minutes to process and for a spike of worry to register.

Somehow landing in Luca's bed made this whole thing seem more intimate. The other places had personified their relationship—the on-call room, the shower, the kitchen bench. Quick and impersonal.

Places to get off then move on.

They had spelled temporary, fleeting, momentary.

But to be in his bed, in his bedroom? What the hell did that spell?

Mia didn't think it was prudent to stick around and find out. Just as soon as she could move without her legs collapsing, she was out of here. The perfect opportunity arose when Luca went to the bathroom to relieve himself of the condom but her legs refused to co-operate so she was still lying stark naked on his bed when he returned.

'You look good there,' Luca murmured as he approached the bed.

Mia watched him draw nearer, unashamedly naked, his beautiful smooth face and body a sight to behold. Desire stirred in her belly.

Right, that was it! *Get up now, McKenzie!*

Except the phone beside Luca's bed chose that moment to ring, scaring the living daylights out of her. She glanced at the clock. 'Who on earth is ringing at this ungodly hour?'

Luca felt his heart rate accelerate. *People who lived in places where it wasn't an ungodly hour.*

He reached the phone in three purposeful strides and snatched it up. *'Ciao.'*

Mia saw another chance to escape but Luca talking in his native tongue was such a treat, even if she didn't understand a word, she just lay and listened to him. He sat on the side of the bed his back to her, and she resisted the urge to run her palm up and down the broad expanse of his ribs. To contrast the white of her skin with the tantalising copper of his.

The first sign that the phone call wasn't social was Luca raising his voice. He raked his hand through his hair and seemed to be demanding something of the caller. She heard the word '*nonna*' a lot. Wasn't that Italian for grandmother? Had something happened to his grandmother?

There was some more rapid-fire conversation before Luca hung up, tossing the hands-free receiver onto the bedside table with a clatter.

Mia pushed herself up on to her elbows, staring at the solid wall of his back. 'Is everything okay?' she asked tentatively.

Luca dragged himself back from the brink of the abyss the phone call had taken him to. For a moment he'd forgotten Mia was even there. He was inordinately pleased she was.

Which didn't sit well at all.

He rubbed the back of his neck. 'No. That was a cousin of mine. My grandmother is dead.'

Mia heard the husky rawness behind the blunt delivery and in that instant she forgot that she was naked, forgot that she was supposed to have already gone, forgot that she didn't get involved. The driving need to offer him comfort, as she would do anyone—a friend, a patient a colleague—overrode everything.

She sat and scooted over to him shunting in behind him, spreading her legs to accommodate him, his bottom fitting snugly into the cradle of her pelvis, her thighs bracketing his.

She leaned her torso into him, her breasts squashed against his back. Her hands found his arms, her palms running up and down the warm solid weight of his biceps.

'I'm sorry,' she murmured, her cheek resting against his shoulder blade. 'Were you close?'

Luca nodded. Regret, never far away, twisted the ever-present knife deep into his heart. He had been the apple of his nonna's eye. Even after that horrible day that had changed his family life for ever.

She'd been the only one who'd believed there was more to Luca than the irresponsible teenager who had let everyone down.

Turning his back on her had been a particular wrench.

'We spoke once a week.' It was how he knew his family still hadn't forgiven him.

Mia absently brushed her mouth against Luca's back once, twice, three times. His muscles seemed to be quivering beneath her lips and she knew she couldn't leave him like this.

'It's okay, Luca,' she murmured. 'C'mon, lie down for a while.'

She scooted back, until she was sitting propped up a little against the bedhead, and placed a hand on his shoulder. For a moment she thought he was going to resist but then he let her pull him down so the back of his head was cradled against her shoulder, her arm braced across his chest.

Luca lay still as Mia settled the sheet in around them. He turned his face and nuzzled her arm, inhaling her fragrance, letting the beat of her heart close to his ear soothe the ache in his chest.

'Do you want to talk about her?' she asked, trailing the fingers of her free hand up and down his arm.

Luca shook his head. He didn't want to talk, he didn't want to think. He just wanted to lie here next to her and forget the world.

'Okay. We'll just lie here for a bit, then.'

So they did.

She had absolutely no intention of staying. Absolutely no intention of falling asleep. No intention whatsoever other than to offer a little bit of comfort and companionship in Luca's time of need.

She really, really didn't mean to fall asleep.

Or stay the night…

Mia woke to the most delicious feeling of warmth. Of being wrapped in a cocoon of contentment. She stretched languorously against all that solid heat behind her then snuggled back into it again. A heaviness at her hip spanned her waist and curled around her breast. A delicious sensation buzzed her neck. A hardness nudged at the cleft of her bottom.

Hmm. Luca.

She sighed as sleep wrapped her in a sticky embrace. For five seconds.

Then panic set in.

Luca!

Damn! What time was it?

She cracked open one eye, then the other, squinting at the digital clock on the bedside table. Eight-fifteen.

In the morning.

Damn, damn, triple damn!

She lay very still for a long moment, listening to him breathe, not daring to do so herself. It was deep and even. Was he asleep? His lips had brushed her neck only seconds ago but had that been involuntary?

His hand at her breast, tantalising and erotic, seemed lax. Not that her nipple seemed to know the difference as it scrunched and scraped erotically against the flat of his palm.

Neither, for that matter, did his erection. She could feel it nestled against her, big and heavy.

Ready for action.

How the hell could he sleep with that thing? Surely his brain was being deprived of oxygen?

Mia waited a bit longer for signs of life. Other than his erection.

No. He was definitely asleep.

She took that as her cue to get the hell out. What had she been thinking? She didn't do this. She didn't stay the night. She didn't…spoon.

Hell, she didn't even cuddle.

And he knew that!

Okay, no one she'd ever been to bed with had received a phone call that their grandmother had died either—but that was beside the point. She was supposed to have left hours ago. She couldn't let one man's personal life alter years of self-discipline.

She'd very nearly failed medical school, thrown away her future, by letting men and booze rule her life for those couple of crazy years after she'd found out about her father, about her mother's deception. She'd made a promise to herself back then that it would never happen again.

And Luca was no exception.

Yes, he'd transcended her staunch one-night-stand policy. But he was still just a convenient body—hot, sexy, best she'd-ever-known body—and that was all.

Dead grandmother or not.

Her decision from last night—before she'd totally messed up and stayed—to end things with Luca suddenly just got a whole lot more urgent.

Mia didn't breathe again until she'd slunk very carefully out of his bed and tiptoed out of his room. Thankfully the central heating was still on because it looked like a frosty old day through those big bay windows as a stiff breeze blew across the harbour, rippling the surface like goose-bumps on flesh.

She strode to the centre of the room and scooped up her jacket, shrugging into it, again ignoring the buttons as she tied it at the waist.

Now, where the hell were her shoes?

She quickly scanned the shoeless route from the lounge to Luca's bedroom. Her gaze stopped at his doorway.

Please, don't make me go back there.

She didn't need the temptation of a sleeping Luca. She hadn't looked back as she'd fled the room and she didn't want to know now either. She needed to get out.

She'd leave her bloody shoes if she had to. Even if her feet would be half-frozen by the time she reached her apartment.

Yes, she needed to tell him this wouldn't be happening again. Especially now. Especially after last night.

But she could leave that for tomorrow. For now she needed to get out. And quickly.

Her panicked gaze backtracked, sweeping a broader area than before. It snagged on a partially obscured heel somehow under the bar stools that lined the central kitchen bench.

Wow. She must have kicked them off wildly—or had Luca pulled them off then tossed them across the room?

Her mind had been mush at the time.

Mia quickly retrieved it, trying not to think about just what she and Luca had done on that kitchen bench. How he'd swept aside the dirty dishes and taken her right there on the cold granite bench top.

Stop it! Don't go there!

Mia shook herself. One shoe down, one to go. She refined her search—if one had ended up near the kitchen, the other one could be anywhere. She dropped to her knees in front of the lounge suite and looked under the chairs.

Bingo!

She reached under for it but the lounge didn't have a lot of clearance and she had to get down lower to even get her fingers to it. She extended her arm further and finally dragged it out, giving a triumphant murmur as she sat back on her haunches.

'What are you doing?'

Mia lurched abruptly to her feet. Luca was leaning against the doorframe, in nothing but underpants, his arms crossed, a small frown making a harsh line out of his beautiful mouth. There was a shadow in his eyes that was a perfect foil for the one darkening his jaw and seemed to match his serious countenance.

'Luca.' Mia, excruciatingly aware of her nakedness beneath the coat, absently kicked first one foot up behind her and then the other as she slid the shoes in place, 'Sorry...couldn't find my shoes.'

Luca watched as she shimmied into her stilettos.

Usually he liked the way women did that. It was sexy. But this morning the death of his grandmother and the burden of guilt he felt over his absence in her life weighed heavily.

As did Mia being witness to it all.

This morning he was immune to sexy.

When he'd woken alone he'd been relieved. His vulnerability last night had shaken him. He wasn't used to being that emotionally exposed to anyone, least of all a woman. Marissa had burned him for life in that regard and he had no desire to repeat the experience.

The last thing he needed this morning was to see pity in Mia's eyes.

He needed to be alone.

'I need coffee,' he said abruptly, pushing away from the doorframe.

Mia watched him stride to the kitchen, a very different man from the post-coital Luca she'd come to know. No sexy smile, no lazy laugh, no knowing gaze. And certainly very different from the man she'd held last night, who'd fallen asleep in her arms.

He seemed to have erected a wall and was putting her firmly on the outside.

Which was great. *Exactly what she wanted.* Exactly what she'd been hoping for. No need for the big talk after all. Just slip out of his apartment and consider it over.

Perfect.

If only her body wasn't rebelling. The site of his strong, naked back, the way the muscles played beneath the fine moulding of copper flesh, the sexy indentation of the small of his back was causing a riot amongst her hormones. She ground her feet into the carpet to stop herself taking a step towards him.

When had her body started to crave his like this? It was so…base.

'I'm going to go,' she announced to his back. 'Check that Evie hasn't slipped into an alcoholic coma. And you have a lot to organise today.'

Luca frowned as he filled the percolator with water. 'Organise?'

'Flights, time off work, packing.'

'Flights?'

It was Mia's turn to frown. 'For the funeral? I'm sorry, I assumed your grandmother lived in Italy? Is she here in Sydney?'

He hadn't told her that. But, then, why would he? They didn't…chat. They'd had sex a few times. That's what they did. That's all they did.

Until last night.

And it was why they were over now. Now that their relationship had evolved to a level of emotional intimacy neither of them wanted.

Luca flipped the switch on the coffee machine and turned to face her, his hands gripping the bench behind him, his knuckles white. 'I'm not going to the funeral.'

Mia blinked. 'What?'

'I'm not going,' he repeated.

'But…I thought you said you were close to your grandmother?'

Her yearning for a grandmother of her own, someone who could have softened the harsh realities of her childhood, been a buffer even, returned as Mia struggled to understand what Luca was saying.

Luca nodded. 'I am.' He raked a hand through his

hair as he realised what he'd said. 'I was… I haven't been back to Italy since the day I left and, trust me, no one in my family wants me to return.'

The edge of bitterness in his voice surprised Mia and instead of turning and walking to the door, which would have been the wisest course of action, she wandered closer to the kitchen.

'No one?'

He nodded grimly. 'Sicilians have long memories.'

Mia slid onto one of the stools, the urge to comfort him as strong as it had been last night despite his *keep-out* expression. 'Look, I don't know what happened with you and your family—'

She held up a hand as he opened his mouth to interrupt. He looked like he was going to tell her to mind her own damn business, which was fine by her. Apart from knowing he'd left Marsala at the age of sixteen, he hadn't told her about his past or the fact that he'd never been back.

And she didn't want to know. That wasn't what they were about—it was nothing to do with her.

Except she understood. She understood how things could be so bad that you'd never go back. How many times had she visited her mother in the last five years? Half a dozen? And how long ago had she given up on trying to keep in contact with a father who had moved on to a new family after the woman he'd loved had totally destroyed his old one?

'I don't want to know, Luca, but it was a long time ago, yeah? Maybe things are better now?'

Out of habit or manners, Luca poured two coffees and pushed one towards her. Even though he didn't want her to stay. He could see empathy in her gaze and wanted no part of it. They were just about sex—nothing else. Sex was all he did. He'd lost his head for a little while, but not any more.

'They're not.'

Mia stared down into the thick dark coffee—the colour of Luca's eyes. 'I'm sorry,' she murmured.

He shrugged. 'It's the way it is.'

Mia looked up sharply. She could see regret in his espresso gaze and hear a slight rawness to his accent. And suddenly she was mad. *Damn it!* Why was it that way? Why was he still being made to suffer twenty odd years later—this was his family. What had he done that had been so bad? Why did she feel guilty about not keeping her family together, about not keeping in contact when neither of her parents bothered? Why should she give a damn when they didn't?

'You should go,' she said.

Luca saw something glittering in her stained-glass-window eyes. They shone with an intense brightness that for a second looked almost like tears. But then it crystallised into determination.

He shook his head. 'Some things are better left alone, Mia.'

Mia shook her head emphatically. 'No, damn it! She was your grandmother and you loved her. And you need to go to her funeral and to hell with what everyone else thinks. You need this for you, Luca. You deserve this. Don't let them take this from you because of some stupid ancient history.'

Luca wasn't entirely sure that this passion was all about him and his predicament but he appreciated the sentiment. It was surprisingly good to have someone on his side in this whole family mess, even though she had no clue of the facts.

Another spurt of guilt made him uneasy. Would she be this passionate about it if she knew the background? Was she only being this vehement because she thought she knew him well enough to surmise that he'd been wronged by his family?

'Don't think I'm the injured party here, *cara*. They had every right to ostracise me. To be angry with me.'

His voice sounded far away in another time and Mia paused. She hadn't expected any explanation but she had expected him to defend himself when offering one. They'd ostracised him and he just accepted it?

'Still?' she demanded, regrouping. 'After all these years? Doesn't that make you angry?'

Luca shook his head. He'd given up being angry about it a long time ago. Regret was a constant companion—if he could go back and change things he would—but he'd worked through his anger.

'No. Not any more,' he said.

Mia couldn't believe how calm he was. She could feel a burning in her chest at his ostracism and hers. Her father leaving physically and her mother leaving emotionally had completely excluded her from the possibility of a normal life.

How could people who supposedly loved you act so callously? Even in grief? Her heart pounded, there was a ringing in her ears, her hands shook as she clasped them around the coffee cup.

It would be so easy to lose it. Just lose it. She hadn't been this stirred up in years. Maybe not since the day she'd discovered her stillborn baby sister hadn't been her father's child and that's why he'd left. That her mother had been lying to her for years.

She had a sudden insane urge to cry, which both scared and horrified her in equal measure. What the hell was wrong with her?

Mia McKenzie did not cry. Not in front of friends or colleagues and most certainly not lovers.

Not ever!

Luca was a man she'd had sex with a few times and slept with once. She shouldn't care about any of this.

She pulled herself back from the edge. Just. 'Well, I think you're wrong, but…' she shrugged with as much nonchalance as she could muster when her brain was melting down '…it's none of my business.'

She stood. She had to get out of there. The intensity of her feelings was scaring the hell out of her. He plainly didn't want her hanging around and she'd been trying to leave since the moment she'd woken with his hand on her breast.

Luca nodded, gripping the bench harder as the foolish urge to reach for her took hold. To put a hand on her shoulder, tug her into his arms. She looked a little wan and frankly he'd rather spend the day putting some colour back into her cheeks than thinking about his grandmother and the mess he'd left behind in Sicily.

But she'd turned away and was walking rapidly towards the door. Do not pass Go. Do not collect two hundred dollars.

'*Ciao*, Mia,' he called out.

Mia heard the finality in his voice and knew it was goodbye.

CHAPTER EIGHT

Evie woke at ten-thirty feeling as if the New Year's Eve fireworks, for which Sydney was famous, had been let off in her head. All at once. She groaned out loud and stuffed the pillow over her head to quell the racket.

Not that it helped, given that the noise was coming from inside her skull, not from the outside.

The previous momentous day with Finn and then the bitter disappointment of the night came back in a rush and she groaned again. *Damn the man to hell*. It was his fault she felt this way.

She could only hope he'd been blessed with a hangover of equal proportion. But, of course, he wouldn't have. Because the man could drink whisky like water. And because little Miss Suzy Happy Ending had been draped all over him when he'd left.

She didn't even want to think about why that bugged her so much. The man could sleep with whomever he liked. And quite often did. In the years they'd co-existed at The Harbour, he'd slept with a string of women.

It was no skin off her nose.

Just because Stuart's devastating betrayal had made her more selective with men, it didn't mean the entire world had to follow suit. If Finn wanted to sleep with every floozy Suzy that came along, more power to him.

Evie pulled the pillow off her head—damn it, now he'd made her think of Stuart. She'd been such a fool for that man, believing that he'd loved her when he'd been using her all along for her family connections.

She'd been humiliated and heartbroken and had endured the rather cruel twist of fate that had seen the hospital rumour mill peg her as the bitch of the piece. Apparently Dr Evie Lockheart had considered herself too good for the lowly Stuart.

It had taken her a long time to win back people's respect after that.

She was damned if she was going to lose that hard-won respect by making a fool of herself over another doctor. Especially one as arrogant and infuriating as Finn Kennedy.

The apartment was quiet when she entered the open-plan living area, pulling on a thick woolly dressing gown over the clothes she'd worn all day yesterday and apparently to bed too. She had a vague memory of Mia getting her home and helping her into bed but she must have drawn the line at undressing her.

She flicked on the jug and waited impatiently for it whistle. The aroma of coffee infused her senses as the boiling water hit the granules and Evie's stomach grumbled. She opened the fridge to grab the milk, only to find there was none.

Her stomach revolted. The fireworks in her head popped louder.

Oh, hell—she couldn't do black coffee. She just couldn't.

Without giving any thought to her appearance, she

shrugged out of her gown, grabbed a mug, pushed her feet into some discarded shoes by the door and was standing outside the lift in under thirty seconds.

Susie and John were bound to have milk.

Finally the lift arrived on her floor and for a second Evie almost wept. It was a short-lived emotion as the doors opened to reveal Suzy, also in the same clothes as last night, looking like she hadn't slept a wink. And not in that horrible bed-hair, bleary-eyed way that Evie was sporting. Oh, no. In that loose, relaxed, I've-had-all-my-kinks-ironed-out way.

Suzy smiled a bright, peppy smile. 'Hi, Dr Lockheart,' she chirped.

Evie cracked a small smile and gave what she hoped was a gracious nod because the alternative—launching herself at young, peppy, cute Suzy—was just not physically possible with a headache the size of Sydney Harbour.

Finn stared at the ceiling, absently massaging his right thumb to relieve the painful tingling, and wished he felt better after a very pleasant night with a gorgeous athletic young woman. But he didn't. And it had nothing to do with his physical injuries.

He kept seeing the look in Evie's eyes at Pete's last night. Those twin hazel pools had been like a damn open book as she'd telescoped her disapproval. The disgust and scorn he'd seen there he could live with. He saw them in the mirror every morning and he was pretty immune to them by now.

The hurt had been a lot harder to get past.

It reminded him a lot of Lydia and those horrible few years. Trying to make things better for her—easier—but only making them worse. His brother's widow had turned to him in a dark moment of grief and it had begun a long-drawn-out, complicated affair that he'd needed yet resented all at the same time.

Lydia had needed something that he hadn't been able to give—comfort. After a childhood in institutions and the horror of losing his brother, Finn just hadn't been capable of it. He hadn't known how to comfort himself let alone a grief-stricken widow.

It had been a relief when she'd finally moved on enough to end it. And yet, strangely, he'd also felt bereft. His one link to his little brother, the little brother he'd defended and protected from one care home to the next, the only constant in his childhood, had no longer been there.

The fact that he hadn't loved Lydia, or she him, hadn't mattered so much after she'd walked away.

So he knew exactly how a woman looked when she was hurt. And there'd been no doubt about it—Dr Evie Lockheart had been hurt last night. And he'd been responsible.

But, damn it all, could he help it if she'd read too much into a fleeting moment?

A temporary weakness?

Princess Evie could keep her goo-goo eyes to herself. He was fine. *Just fine.*

Mia was shocked to see Luca standing on her doorstep later that night. Between her morning-after regrets and Evie's monster hangover the day had dragged more slowly and become more depressing than a wet week.

She had been in her pyjamas and ready for bed when the knock had sounded. The cold air from the hallway rushed around her and she pulled her hot-pink polar fleece dressing gown closer.

'Luca?'

'Who is it?' Evie called from the couch, where she'd been watching old sitcom reruns all day.

'It's just Luca,' Mia threw over her shoulder as casually as she could. Because it could never be *just* Luca. The man was dressed in a suit and looked like a matinee idol, even with his face set grimly.

She really, really shouldn't want to drag him to her bedroom. But, heaven help her, she did.

Evie, her face fixed on the screen, laughed. 'Does he want to borrow a cup of milk?' And she laughed again.

Luca frowned. 'Huh?'

Mia shook her head. 'Long story.' She noticed a suitcase standing nearby in the hall. She raised an eyebrow. 'Going somewhere?'

He nodded. 'I decided to follow your advice.'

'You're going back to Italy?'

'Yes.' He gave her a ghost of a smile. 'To hell with them, right?'

Mia searched his face for a moment, pleased that he was doing the right thing but puzzled as to why he'd bothered to stop by and tell her.

The man was about to fly halfway around the world to go to his beloved grandmother's funeral against the wishes of a family he wasn't on good terms with and hadn't seen in over two decades—he probably didn't need her questions.

'Right,' she said awkwardly.

'I'll be back in five days,' he said.

'Five days? Hell, Luca, you're going to be next to useless when you return.' She saw something flit through his eyes and quickly added, 'Professionally,' in case he thought she'd meant it any other way.

She had no doubt that his *other* functions would be in *fine* working order.

Not that she cared or would be thinking about his other functions at all.

'I've arranged cover at work for seven days and business class helps.'

Mia nodded. 'I'll bet.'

'John said his housekeeper, Gladys someone…'

'Henderson,' Mia supplied. The spritely sixty-year-old cleaned their apartment too.

'Yes, that's her. She's going to keep an eye on the apartment for me.'

'Okay.' Mia waited for him to say more. Or to pick up his bags and leave. He didn't. She frowned. 'Why are you here, Luca?' she asked wearily.

Luca put his hand in his pocket. 'To thank you.' He looked at her intently, her fluffy pink dressing gown somehow just as sexy as the winter coat from last night. 'You were right. I needed to do this.'

Mia shrugged. 'No worries.'

He chose his next words carefully. Normally he didn't have to give 'the speech' but Mia was different. Somehow she'd got past the barriers that he'd erected since Marissa and she deserved him to be straight with her.

He wanted her to know that it wasn't her—it was him.

He just didn't do emotional connections and he especially didn't need that baggage now, heading off to face some pretty big demons.

He was surprised, though, at how hard the words were to say. At his reticence.

'I know I wasn't good company this morning and—'

'It's okay, Luca,' Mia interrupted, knowing from his eyes what he was going to say and suddenly not wanting to hear the words come from his mouth. 'I get it. You and I were always just a one-time thing that went on for longer than it should have. Neither of us do this sort of thing. I think we can just walk away and chalk it up to experience.'

Luca pursed his lips. It was an easy out for him but, still, her even easier acceptance rankled. It shouldn't have. It should have been a relief.

But it wasn't.

'I think it's best,' he murmured.

It was. It had to be.

'Of course,' she assured him. So why didn't it feel like it? Why did she feel worse than she had all day?

They stood in the doorway, looking at each other for a moment, not speaking. *It was for the best. It was.*

'I'm sorry.' Luca grimaced, checking his watch. 'I have to go, I have a taxi waiting.'

Mia nodded, her heart hammering in her chest. 'Sure. I'll see you when you get back,' she said. 'At work.'

'Yes,' he agreed, fighting the urge to seize her in his arms and kiss her and the even more bizarre urge to ask her to go with him.

To complicate it much more than it already was.

'At work,' he repeated. Then he turned away, picked up his bag and strode down the corridor to the lift, not daring to look back.

Mia stared after him, watching until he disappeared.

It—whatever *it* was—was over. She should be over the moon.

She wasn't.

'That seemed pretty intense. What was it about?' Evie asked.

Mia swivelled her head to find her friend walking towards her. At least she finally looked interested in something else other than overdosing on salt and vinegar chips and Boston pub life.

'Nothing,' Mia said, recovering sufficiently to withdraw into the warm apartment and shut the door.

'Didn't look like nothing to me,' Evie mused.

'It is now,' Mia assured her.

For five days and nights, despite her every effort not to, Mia thought of Luca constantly. Her feelings fluctuated wildly from complete understanding and agreement with their decision to walk away from each other, to worry about how it was all panning out in Marsala, to an uncharacteristic yearning for something she couldn't even put her finger on.

Add to that a healthy dose of sexual frustration from vivid dreams and Mia was a wreck.

The dreams were the worst.

Happily-ever-after fantasies—erotic one moment, white-wedding poignant the next. They woke her often, rendering her perpetually tired. And cranky. The staff avoided her. Her patients asked the nurses their questions. Even Evie stayed out of her way.

In fact, by day five her best friend was suggesting she burn off some of the bitch with a good old-fashioned bar pick-up somewhere.

Then, on the sixth night, Luca came striding into the

department at almost midnight. His luscious wavy hair, speckled with raindrops from the stormy weather outside, looked like it had hadn't seen a comb in a while and it was the first time she'd seen him unshaven.

He looked like hell.

And her body responded with a primal lurch.

If anything, with the heavy growth of blue-black stubble and the wicked way he filled out a pair of jeans, he looked more like the devil she'd first pegged him as than ever before.

But she knew him much better now.

Well…better than she had, anyway.

'Luca?' Her heart pounded in her chest. Damn it, this wasn't how she'd planned on greeting him on his return. Where was her polite smile and cool nod? 'You're not due back until tomorrow!'

Luca ran a hand through his already unruly hair. She was a sight for sore eyes. It had been a harrowing time in Sicily and even though they weren't together—had never really been together—he wanted to drag her to the on-call room and get lost in her for a little while.

Just one more time.

'I couldn't sleep and I heard the ambulances.' He shrugged. 'Thought I'd drop by and see if you guys needed a hand.'

Mia saw the flash of desire in his deep dark eyes, like a candle in a well, and felt it slug her right in the belly. She was grateful for the bustle of the department around them. If he'd come to her door, she'd have been lost in a look like that. Their parting conversation from six days ago smothered by a fierce surge of lust and a strong urge for privacy.

She blinked, taking a mental step backwards. 'You look tired. Are you up to it?'

'I'm fine.'

Mia raised an eyebrow. 'You don't look it.'

Luca waved a dismissive hand. 'I'm exhausted and my body clock's screwed up but I'm not sleepy. In fact, I'm buzzing. I'm good to work.'

Mia scrutinised him for a moment but that was just plain dangerous. Besides, she understood how jet-lag could mess with your body but have the opposite effect on your brain. And they were pretty slammed at the moment.

'Okay, sure. There was an industrial fire with several burn victims, we're down a couple of nurses and Evie's attending an arrest on one of the wards. It's bedlam.'

He nodded. 'Okay.'

She waited for him to move on, brush past her, leap into action, but he didn't. He just stood looking at her, weary and subdued. 'How...how was it?'

Not that she cared. Not that she wanted to know.

Luca rubbed at his stubble. 'Bad.' A nurse bustled past them.

Mia heard the low accented rumble right down to her toes. 'Do you want to talk about it?'

What the hell?

She didn't want him to talk about it. She didn't want to listen. She didn't want to know. The only thing she was interested in was the magic he could wreak on her body.

And even that was now off limits.

His life was none of her damn business and she liked it that way!

Luca shook his head. He didn't. He really, really

didn't. Three days of dealing with family history had been enough to bear, without rehashing it. What he wanted was to forget it. Lay her down and let their magic take him somewhere else.

A place where he wasn't a hormone-driven, starry-eyed sixteen-year-old. Where he hadn't got his brother's girlfriend—now wife—pregnant. A place where there were no toxic family relationships, where he hadn't let anyone down, where no one disapproved.

And Mia was the perfect woman for that. Gorgeous, sexually uninhibited and emotionally unavailable.

That's what he needed. Talking—not so much.

'I just need to work.'

Mia nodded. 'Cubicle two.' And held her breath as Luca brushed past her.

Two hours later the department had quietened down. The minor burn victims had been triaged, assessed and transferred to the burns unit. Of the two more serious burns, one had gone to Theatre, the other to ICU.

Mia was able to breathe again. To think of something other than ABCs and burns percentages and fluid requirements. She glanced at Luca, who was writing in a chart. He glanced up at the same time and the heat flaring between them could have lit the Sydney Harbour Bridge for all eternity.

Okay. *Enough.* They'd been lovers—briefly. That was all and now it was over. They'd agreed. This... sexual ESP stuff couldn't go on.

It just couldn't.

She stood. 'Can I speak with you please, Dr di Angelo?' she asked quietly, looking around her at the completely disinterested staff going about their own business.

Luca looked up at her, the quiet steel in her voice at odds with the heat in her eyes. 'On-call room?'

Mia felt the kick in her pulse. *The things they'd done in that on-call room...* But the fact was that their privacy was absolute there—the perfect place to tell him this couldn't go on.

'Sure.'

Mia turned and led the way on very shaky legs, hyper-aware of his gaze glued to her back. When she finally reached her destination she headed straight for the kitchenette and grabbed two mugs, absently going about the business of fixing them coffee. She heard the door shut behind her. Then lock. She was conscious of Luca leaning against it, watching her.

Mia turned to face him, her butt resting against the sink. He looked dark and wild and every fibre of her being wanted to melt into his arms. 'We agreed not to do this any more.'

Luca hung onto the doorknob. She was right. They had. But he'd thought of nothing else for the last few hours. Since returning home. Hell, since leaving. And he'd happily walk away. But he needed tonight.

He didn't know why. He just knew he did.

'I know.'

Mia shook her head emphatically. 'I don't do this, Luca. We,' she wagged her finger back and forth between the two of them. 'We don't do this.'

Luca pushed away from the door and prowled over, halting in front of her. Close enough to see the frantic flicker of the pulse at the base of her throat, the flare of her nostrils, the dilation of her pupils.

'I know.'

Mia felt the rumble of his voice curl her toes. Lust, full and throaty and undisguised, thickened his accent. He crowded her against the sink and her fingers automatically curled into the sleeves of his shirt. Their bodies touched from hip to shoulder and it felt so good she almost whimpered.

Mia swallowed and clawed desperately for some self-control. 'We're alike, you and I, Luca. We have scars… trust issues. We guard our hearts. We don't get involved. It's why we're emergency doctors—patch 'em up and ship 'em out, right? No time to get involved. It's who we are.'

Luca looked deep into her eyes. 'Who are you trying to convince Mia—me or yourself?'

Mia glared at him. Damn it, she was trying to walk this thing back. *Why wasn't he meeting her halfway?* Why was he trying to change the boundaries he'd set before he'd left? Damn it all, the boundaries he lived by.

They both lived by.

'Am I wrong?' she challenged.

Luca shook his head. 'No.' In fact, she was one hundred per cent accurate. But that didn't stop the primal beat of a jungle drum thrumming through his blood. His gaze brushed her mouth. 'But I need this. I wish I didn't. But I do.'

He placed a hand on the cold stainless-steel of the sink either side of her and dropped his head, claiming her mouth on a muffled groan. She opened for him instantly, her tongue seeking his, and his barely leashed desire blazed to life with all the heat and intensity of a solar flare.

His hands skimmed up her body and buried themselves in her hair, pulling at the band tying it back, releasing it in a tumble of blonde, his fingers seeking the spot where nape met scalp. Her corresponding moan went straight to his groin.

Yes, yes, yes. This was what he needed. A place to feel good, to feel like a successful, virile man again instead of a home-wrecking boy. A place to forget.

He pulled away from the softness of her mouth to explore the delights of her neck. 'I missed you,' he murmured against the pulse fluttering in her throat.

Because he had. Thoughts of her had been his constant companion while he'd been away. Had often been his only relief from what had been a tense and stilted time.

His hands left her hair, travelled to her hips, gripping them hard as he lifted her onto the narrow edge of the sink, stepped between her legs, forcing them apart, grinding his monster erection against the place where he knew it fitted perfectly.

Mia gasped as her hips responded to the blatant invitation. She wanted him inside her so badly she could practically feel his hardness stretching her.

Here on the sink. In the on-call room. With the bustle of an entire emergency department just outside the door.

This was madness!

'Luca, stop, no, please, stop.'

She pushed at his shoulders as his tongue laved a wet track from her ear to her collarbone. Her heart pounded in her ears and for an insane moment she thought it was someone pounding against the door. 'We really need to stop this.'

Luca pulled away, his chest heaving. 'If you want me to stop, I'll stop.' His breath sawed in and out of his chest as he stared into blue eyes that were hazy with lust. He pulled her in tight to his hips. 'But I don't think you really want me to.'

Mia's head was spinning, her chest was bursting, her belly was clenched in a tight knot. Common sense warred with primal craving. He rotated his hips against hers and she bit down a moan.

To hell with it. She wanted it, needed it—needed him—too much to deny it.

'This is it, Luca. After this, there is no more.'

The words were barely out before Luca was whispering, 'Done,' and reclaiming her mouth.

Mia welcomed the sweep of his tongue and the triumphant noise at the back of his throat when she opened to his long, deep, hot kiss. She especially welcomed his harsh intake of breath as her hands found his zipper and tugged it down.

'Wrap your legs around me,' he murmured, scooping her hips off the edge and grasping her buttocks firmly in his hands as he hauled her off the sink and headed for one of the rooms. Her ankles locked around his waist and he almost stumbled as her hands continued their quest to get behind his zip while her tongue flicked at the pulse thudding at the base of his throat.

He kicked the door shut behind them and tumbled them onto the couch her legs wide, her knees bent, his hips perfectly aligned with hers. His shirt was off in five seconds. Hers followed closely after.

And then a pager beeped.

Mia froze. Luca cursed in his mother tongue.

They both lay there for a few seconds, not moving,

their frantic breath and the trilling of a pager the only sound in the room.

Mia pushed against Luca's shoulders. 'Let me up,' she requested, hating how husky her voice sounded.

Luca pushed off her, sitting back on the couch, his chest naked, his fly gaping open. He raked a hand through his hair while Mia ripped the pager off her waistband and read the liquid crystal display. 'Chopper retrieval,' she relayed. 'MVA near the Blue Mountains.'

She swung herself into a sitting position, her scrambled thoughts sluggish as she tried to switch into medical mode. Luca handed over her shirt and she looked at it absently for a moment before realising she was sitting there in her bra and a pair of jeans.

Too close to Luca for comfort, she stood and fixed her clothing. She straightened her shoulders, pulled her hair back, cleared her throat. She headed for the door and paused with her hand on the knob. 'I'd better go.'

Luca watched her from the sofa. 'This isn't over, Mia.'

Mia knew they couldn't keep doing this. Whatever the two of them were doing had overstepped both their boundaries and all this sexual gratification was doing was prolonging the inevitable. If they'd been meant to be together one last time, they wouldn't have been interrupted.

The pager was a sign from the universe.

'Yes, it is,' she said without looking back, and then swept from the room.

Luca watched her disappear and knew in his bones that there would be no changing her mind. It shouldn't have mattered. He'd done this dozens of times with dozens of women. Had had a good time for a while then walked away without looking back.

No harm, no foul.

Except it did matter. Somehow these past weeks with Mia had come to mean more than a sexual pressure valve.

Mia mattered.

CHAPTER NINE

TWENTY minutes later Mia and Luca were sitting opposite each other strapped into the rescue helicopter, watching the rooftop helipad lights bend and twist as they refracted through the raindrops clinging to the chopper's windows. Luca had volunteered to go with her due to the shortage of nurses in the department and the ICU retrieval team also being out on a call.

'Okay, folks, welcome to Brian Air. Please ensure your tray tables are in an upright position and your seat belts are fastened low and tight. It's going to be an interesting ride.'

Mia grinned at the amplified patter in her earphones despite the tension she felt at sitting opposite a man she'd been mere minutes away from feeling deep inside her. Brian was one of the pilots who had been flying rescue choppers for ever and his skill and experience were much appreciated on a stormy night.

Even his sense of humour.

'Please don't tell me we're heading into a storm, Brian.'

'Would I do that to you, Mia, my lovely?'

Luca gritted his teeth at the easy banter. He had a sudden urge to break something of Brian's. Something non-essential, of course. He still had to be able to fly the damn chopper.

'There is some storm activity but I'll be skirting around it. Safe as houses. Cross my heart. Would I lie to you?'

Mia laughed. 'You? Never.'

Brian laughed back. 'Got yourself a man yet?'

Mia's smile died, her gaze locking with Luca's. 'I'm too busy for a man.'

Brian tsked into his headset. 'Now, if only I was twenty years younger. What's wrong with men these days, Luca? Are they blind?'

Mia tried to look away from him but Luca's brooding gaze held her captive.

'Not all of us,' Luca murmured.

Mia pursed her lips. 'You know me, Brian—don't like to be tied down.'

Luca had no doubt the words were for his benefit and he switched off to the patter as he shifted his gaze from Mia to the now far-away lights of Sydney. The steady beat of the rotors above him echoed the thud of his heart beat as he tried to catalogue the swirl of alien feelings churning in his gut.

In less than two months Dr Mia McKenzie had taken over his life. And he wasn't sure exactly when it had happened. All he knew *for sure* was that the thought of never being with her again was not one he relished.

She'd been the one he'd thought of while he'd been away. Not the air hostess in business class who'd slipped him her card. Not the many beautiful Sicilian women who had smiled at him with frank interest on the streets of Marsala. Not even Marissa, his brother's wife, the woman he'd foolishly thought himself in love with all those years ago.

Mia. It had been Mia who he'd thought of. Mia he'd picked up the phone to ring after his brother had paid him a visit at his hotel and told him to go home. *And then put down again.* Mia who he'd credited as he'd talked to his grandmother standing by her fresh grave after the other mourners had left. Mia who had got him through a killer flight as he'd fantasised about their reunion.

He stole a glance at her as she flicked through the retrieval paperwork balanced on a clipboard on her lap. She was gorgeous even in a big yellow helmet that made her look as if she was trapped inside a giant insect eye and flight overalls that seemed two sizes too big for her.

He looked away again as the insanity of it all hit him. He'd always been able to walk away. Always. None of this made sense.

And none of it made him happy.

It was official—he was having a truly hellish week.

'So the ambulance crew on scene have the patient stabilised and ready for transport,' Mia said, conscious of his eyes on her and desperate to get back to a professional footing after their *coitus interruptus.*

Their patient had suspected spinal injuries requiring rapid air evacuation for maximum treatment success and that's what she needed to focus on.

Luca nodded. 'Should just be able to scoop and run.'

Mia hoped so. The rain had picked up and the chopper seemed to be being buffeted by some decent wind. She could see lightning in the distance and guessed that was the storm they were skirting around. At the best of times Mia wasn't the greatest flyer in the world and she knew that Brian wouldn't be flying if he didn't think it was safe but the sooner they were back at The Harbour in one piece, the better. And then there was Luca, sitting opposite her, watching her with brooding eyes and causing another kind of storm. Inside her. She'd never met a man she couldn't handle and she hated it that she couldn't shake him. From her thoughts. Her dreams.

Her daydreams!

'Think I might get a bit of shut-eye,' she said into her mike. It was, after all, nearly three in the morning and she'd long ago learned the value of power-napping.

She didn't wait for anyone's permission, just closed her eyes. And dreamed of Luca.

A loud bang woke her with a start fifteen minutes later. The chopper spun wildly and her head was filled with Brian swearing and putting out a mayday call. Her eyes flew to the man opposite her. 'Luca?'

Luca saw alarm and fear in her eyes and felt his own pulse leap as the helicopter seemed to be losing altitude as it spun. 'Brian?' He spoke into his headphones. 'What's happening?'

'Lightning took out the tail rotor,' Brian said calmly, while desperately trying to regain control of the spiralling chopper.

'I thought you said you were skirting around the storm?' Mia said above the noise of her pistoning heart and the whine of the labouring engine. She braced one hand against the stretcher beside her and the other against the aircraft shell to steady herself in the midst of the crazy spinning.

'I am. Mother nature can be a bitch like that sometimes.'

How was it possible that Brian could even sound upbeat during a mid-air emergency?

'Are we going to crash?' she asked.

'Hell, yeah,' Brian said matter-of-factly. 'Brace yourselves, guys, we're over national park and there're a lot of trees down there.'

Mia tamped down on the rather alien urge to become hysterical. It wasn't what she usually did in a crisis but, hell, they were going to crash. She was twenty-nine and she was going to die. She hadn't witnessed the northern lights. She hadn't bought herself that cute little retro convertible. She hadn't been to the ballet.

She hadn't been in love.

Except she had, of course.

And the man she loved was going to die with her.

Her gaze locked with Luca's. What a really, really horrible time for such a profound revelation. No time to hug it to herself like a delicious little secret.

'Oh, God,' Mia whispered, her throat suddenly as dry as ash, her eyes trying to take in every detail of Luca's face.

'It's going to be okay, Mia,' Luca said.

He reached out his hand, hoping his grandmother was out there somewhere watching over them. He was damned if he was going to die before telling Mia how he felt about her.

Whatever the hell that was.

If he'd learned anything this past week it was that life was short and you couldn't live in the past.

Mia slipped her hand into his and gripped tight. It was cold and she was trembling and he'd have given anything to erase the glimpse of mortality he could see in her eyes.

'Just because we crash it doesn't mean we're going to die. Does it, Brian?' Luca queried.

He was calm, so bloody calm. How could Luca be this calm as the helicopter spiralled out of control in a death plunge? Her brain was spinning just as wildly. Desperately trying to remember helicopter crash statistics while grappling with regret that she wasn't closer to her parents and sorrow that her fledgling love for Luca was going to be snuffed out before she'd even had the chance to explore it.

'Not on my watch,' Brian chirped. 'Okay, guys, hold tight. Prepare for impact.'

Mia squeezed Luca's hand hard. 'I've never seen *Swan Lake*.'

Luca smiled at her. 'When this is over, we'll go and see it together.'

There was no time for her to smile back. The crippled chopper hit trees with a violent jolt, halting the rapid downward spiral most effectively. Mia squeezed her eyes shut as the impact raced through her body like a giant shock wave. She vaguely heard cracking glass, a loud expletive followed by a guttural cry from Brian and then nothing other than the screech and grind of the rotors could be heard as they sliced through the canopy. Mia, eyes still shut, hit her head several times against the shell of the cabin and she was grateful for her helmet as the chopper lurched and listed, dropping a little then stopping then dropping again as the branches beneath buckled beneath its weight before it finally came to a shuddering halt.

After a good twenty seconds of no movement, Mia cracked open an eye. She could hear Brian talking to Air Control, she could smell rain and fuel and eucalyptus, she could feel the wind buffeting the chopper and hear it whistling inside the cabin. Her eyes adjusted to the sudden darkness and she could see Luca sitting opposite, wonderfully intact.

She was alive. *They were all alive!*

'You okay?' Luca asked.

Mia thought about it for a moment. Everything felt fine. She nodded. 'Yes…I think. You?'

Luca nodded back. 'Yes.' And then he grinned. '*Swan Lake,* here we come.'

Mia grinned back. Her first instinct, to throw herself at him, was pulled up short by a moan coming from the front.

'Brian? Are you okay?' Luca asked.

'Leg's busted,' the pilot panted as he killed the engine.

Luca glanced at Mia. The pain in Brian's voice was obvious. 'Is that a guess or can you see it?'

Brian swore again. 'Tree branch breached the cab, drove into my leg. I can see the bones.'

They exchanged glances again. Luca felt a moment of guilt at his earlier wish that Brian would break something. 'Any other injuries?'

'Nope. Don't think so.'

Luca wasn't totally reassured. Often people could have wounds they weren't even aware of if there was one overriding painful injury.

'Okay, so we need to get you out of there onto the stretcher so we can splint your leg and give you something for the pain. Lucky for you, you crashlanded a mini emergency ward, they have all the best drugs.'

Brian gave a half laugh, half snort at Luca's attempt

to keep things light. 'Ah. You cottoned onto my dastardly plan.'

Luca unbuckled. Mia followed.

'Wait,' Brian called out. 'We need to assess how this bird's being supported. I don't know how precarious it is and moving around could dislodge it. I'd hate to survive the first crash only to be killed on impact with the ground.'

Luca paused. He could tell that Brian was trying to make light of the situation but he also knew that Brian was still thinking like a pilot. Which, given his horrific injury, was amazing.

'Okay,' Luca said. 'How do we do that?'

'If you can open your door safely, grab the torch and have a look out, see if you can see what's supporting us. But move carefully until we know. The crash would have activated our emergency locator transmitter so Air Control will know where we are but they'll want a sit rep—once we know what we're up against, I'll let them know.'

Luca glanced at Mia. The chopper had come to a stop in a reasonably level position with a slight tilt to the left so he was pretty certain that movement wouldn't be an issue but that all depended on what was beneath them.

'Buckle up,' he said as he reached for the torch strapped to the cabin above his head and gently removed it.

Mia felt a trickle of dread drip down her spine. 'Be careful.'

Luca nodded, aware that they might well be precariously balanced and not keen to be the one that upset the apple cart. It was good to know that their ELT had been activated and that help would no doubt soon be on its way. But Brian, while he was being very stoic, needed urgent medical attention, so they couldn't just sit around and wait.

He swivelled in his seat and shone the torch out the window. Through the now driving rain he could see that the door appeared to be free of any vegetation so he gingerly reached for the handle and gently eased it open. The freezing rain assaulted him almost immediately as he carefully lowered himself to the floor of the cabin, hung his head out and shone the torch under the chopper.

They appeared to be wedged between three massive looking tree trunks huddled together. The bottom of the cabin was supported by sturdy interwoven branches which appeared knotted. The tail also seemed wedged between two trunks further back.

Luca shone the torch down towards the forest floor. Whether it was the rain or the dark or the sheer distance, he couldn't make it out. It was nothing but a swirling abyss of cloud and night.

He crawled back in and gently shut the door. His overalls were soaked around the shoulders and the part of his face not protected by the helmet was as wet as if he'd just stepped out of the shower.

He scrambled to his feet and gave a very slight experimental bounce. When the chopper stayed firm he gave another bigger one. 'I think it's fine.'

He relayed the info to Brian who spoke with Air Control. Luca experimented some more, shifting slowly and carefully around the cramped confines of the chopper, which was hardly made for ease of movement anyway.

It seemed stable and he let out a little sigh of relief.

'Bad news.' Brian's voice interrupted Luca. 'The weather has worsened. High winds and driving rain are going to make rescue impossible for a while. It's too dangerous to send another chopper and a winch crew. Meteorology think the system's going to hang around for quite a few more hours so we're stuck up this tree until daylight. Like the bloody Swiss Family Robinson.'

Mia heard Brian laugh at his own joke then suck in a breath on a deep guttural groan.

'We've got to see to him,' she said.

Luca nodded. 'I think the chopper's stable enough to drag him out of his seat and onto the stretcher. It's going to hurt, though.'

Mia nodded grimly. Hell, yeah. 'We could get him to splint his leg first—we carry vacuum splints—it might help a bit.'

Luca nodded. 'Okay. Let's do it. Unbuckle, but slowly. And leave your helmet on. Let's make sure this bird can take both of us moving around before we get too carried away.'

Mia unbuckled and stood slowly. Luca held out his hand and she glanced at him as she took it.

'You're freezing,' he murmured, enclosing her hand within his.

Mia was surprised to realise she was—she'd been in survival mode and hadn't realised it. 'The wind's getting in somewhere,' she said absently, caught up in the warmth of his hand.

Despite how soaked his shoulders and arms were, his hands were like a toasty pair of gloves. In fact, his mere presence was like a beacon of light in this cold, dark, scary scenario they'd landed in.

Luca was here and he was warm and solid and one hundred per cent in control.

'Near Brian, I think,' Luca murmured, steadying her. 'Grab the splint,' he said. 'Slow and easy. I don't know how much weight distribution is aiding stability.'

Mia nodded and reluctantly let go of Luca's hand. She'd felt safe under the influence of his touch. Which made no sense. They were still stuck up a tree. In a helicopter. In the middle of a storm.

Which just went to prove what she'd always thought— love was crazy!

She took a tentative step and then another towards the storage cupboard. Like boats, helicopters made excellent use of space and Mia knew what was in every nook and cranny. The floor felt solid beneath her as she inched her way closer.

She grabbed the splint and the pump and turned to face Luca. 'What now?'

He held out his hand and she passed him the gear. He gestured her close. 'I'm going to drag him out from behind. You stand by at the stretcher for when he's out. Let's get an IV going and give him some morph.'

Mia looked at the cramped confines of the single pilot's seat. The end of the stretcher protruded into the front cab area where in most commercial choppers there would have been a second seat.

'Are you going to be able to manoeuvre him out from behind?'

Luca grimaced. 'I hope so. I'm not sure how stable the chopper will be if I have to climb up onto the stretcher and pull him from there. The tail's wedged fairly solidly so I doubt it'll tip backwards. I'm not so sure it won't tip forward.'

Mia swallowed. So this was the meaning of being stuck between a rock and a hard place. But Luca seemed so confident—like GI Joe, Action Man and Inspector Gadget all rolled into one.

'It's going to be fine, Mia.' He smiled. She returned his smile with one that was suddenly wobbly and thanked any and all deities out there that if she'd had to be in a helicopter crash, at least Luca had been with her.

'Okay. Let's do it.'

Twenty minutes later, after a lot of effort and pain, Brian was on the stretcher, an IV had been inserted, fluids were running, nasal prongs with a trickle of oxygen had been applied and, because they could, he was being monitored. His badly fractured leg had been left in the splint and he'd drifted off to sleep on a morphine cloud.

Finally they both settled back into their seats. The wind howled around the chopper and whistled through the shattered glass at the front. She could feel the slight shuddering of the aircraft as the wind buffeted it from what seemed like all directions. The steady beep, beep, beep of the monitor seemed alien amidst the wild brutality of Mother Nature.

'How long do you think the oxygen will last?' Mia asked into the growing silence.

She knew that Brian didn't really need it but she was aware it was a finite commodity and that they had no idea how long they'd be there. They'd completed a thorough primary and secondary survey of Brian's injuries but what if they'd missed something? What if his condition worsened?

'Quite a few hours, I expect. It's only running at one litre.'

Mia nodded. Would that be enough? How long would it be before they were rescued? The way the wind howled and the rain beat incessantly against the window, it didn't look like any time soon.

She tried really hard not to think about the precariousness of the situation. Their position might feel stable enough but that didn't alter the fact that they were still in a great deal of danger.

'So, now what?' Mia asked.

'We should get some sleep too,' Luca said into the silence.

Mia shook her head, reaching across to feel once again for the pulses in Brian's foot. They were there but feeble and Mia guessed the injury was compromising the blood flow lower. 'I'm worried about the circulation,' Mia murmured. 'It'd be awful to survive a crash like this then go on to lose your leg.'

Luca, who was worried too, gave her a reassuring smile. 'Hopefully we'll be out of here before it comes to that.'

Mia nodded. Suddenly aware she was still wearing her helmet, she pulled it off.

Luca placed a stilling hand on her forearm. 'You should leave it on,' he said.

Mia shook her hair free and finger-combed it. 'I'll feel ridiculous sitting here for the next who knows how long in this stupid helmet.'

Luca sought her gaze. 'If whatever's supporting us gives way, that helmet could be your lifeline.'

Mia glanced away from the stark reality she saw in his deep, dark eyes. 'Well, I doubt very much it'll prevent my neck from being broken, which is the most likely outcome if this thing plummets to the ground.'

Luca knew she was right. Spinal compression injury would be the true killer. That and the many other possibilities in between flitted through his mind as he watched Mia with a growing sense of helplessness.

He hated being powerless to affect change in this situation. That all three of them were dependent on things outside his control—the weather, branch structure, the expertise of others.

He'd been taking care of himself for a long time now. So, he suspected, had she. This kind of impotence was reminiscent of his past. And he'd had a little too much of that already this last week.

He took off his own helmet and ruffled his hair.

'We're going to be fine,' he murmured. If he had to hold this helicopter in place through sheer force of will, he would. *He wouldn't let Mia down.* He tapped the top of her helmet. 'Keep it close.'

Mia nodded. 'I don't suppose Air Control said what was happening with the patient we're supposed to be evac'ing?' Luca had talked with Air Control while she'd been inserting the IV.

'They're coming in by road. No choice now.'

Mia knew that would be an hour or so's drive in these treacherous weather conditions, even with lights and sirens. The mountain roads were dangerous when wet and low cloud would further inhibit speed.

'Hopefully the patient's spinal condition is minor,' Mia commented, rubbing absently at her arms. Although she doubted very much they would have been sent out on such a night for a chipped vertebra.

'You cold?' Luca asked.

'A little,' she admitted. The breached cabin was a perfect conduit for the freezing wind and the temperature inside the crippled aircraft had dropped considerably.

They'd covered Brian in a space blanket but now her adrenaline had settled and their activity had ceased she was starting to feel cold gnawing at her arms. 'You must be too,' Mia said. 'Your overalls are wet around your shoulders and chest.'

Luca wasn't really. His body was still on high alert, his metabolic rate steaming along like a whistling kettle. But they were probably going to be there for a while…

He leaned across and dragged a pack out from under the stretcher, locating the stash of space blankets folded neatly into playing-card-sized packaging.

'Here,' he said, passing her one. Then he opened another and unfolded it. The thin, metallic, foil material crinkled noisily, like a chocolate wrapper, as he proceeded to scrunch it up.

'What are you doing?' Mia asked as she unfolded hers and stood so she could wrap it around her entire body.

'I'm going to plug the hole with it,' Luca murmured.

'Ah…good thinking,' she said as she moved aside to give him more room to manoeuvre.

Luca carefully leaned over Brian's seat and gingerly stuffed the whistling hole with the scrunched-up foil blanket. 'That should do it,' he said, standing back to admire his handiwork.

'Sounds like it,' Mia agreed as the whistling magically stopped.

He smiled down at her and in the confines of the helicopter a hunched Luca seemed to take up all the space.

She hadn't had time to think about her startling revelation from earlier, but now it was all she could think
about.

She was in love with Luca di Angelo.

For better or worse. And surely this *had* to be the
worst?

'It's going to be okay,' Luca murmured, lifting his
hand to cup her cheek. 'You're going to be okay.'

Mia wasn't sure if she'd ever be okay again. She'd
gone and done something she'd sworn she never
would—fallen in love. How could life ever be okay?
How could it ever be the same?

The air seemed to thicken as they stood hunched over
in the middle of the helicopter, staring at each other. The
howl of the wind and the steady beeping of the heart-
rate monitor twirled around them like a symphony.

Brian chose that moment to stir, crinkling the space
blanket and setting off the monitor alarm. Luca's hand
dropped as he started guiltily and immediately switched
his attention to the stretcher.

Luca placed his hand on the pilot's shoulder.
'Hurting, Brian?'

Brian's eyes drifted open and he gave them a goofy
smile. 'Nope. Everything ish wonderfullll,' he slurred.
'That morphine is gooood stuff.' And his eyes drifted
shut again.

Mia, who was once again checking Brian's foot
pulses, smiled. Obviously the pain relief was working.

'How are they?' Luca asked.

'The same, I think. The foot seems a little cooler,
though.'

They resumed their seats, Luca wrapping himself in
a space blanket as well. He checked his watch. 'Nearly

four-thirty,' he said as he peered out the rain-spattered window.

They sat in silence for some minutes, both looking out at the watery blackness. 'This wasn't quite how I imagined my first visit to the Blue Mountains would pan out,' Luca murmured.

Mia's gaze slid from the window to his profile. 'I recommend driving next time.'

There was a pause as their eyes met and then they both laughed. Mia's stomach rumbled. 'Are you hungry?' She grabbed her backpack from its hidey-hole. The foil of the space blanket crinkled with her every movement. 'There's usually some exceedingly fattening, sugar-loaded snacks in here.'

She gave a triumphant whoop when she located two chocolate bars and handed him one. She tore off her wrapper and sighed as she savoured that first sinful bite. 'To think, this could be the last chocolate I ever eat.'

Luca glanced at her sharply. 'Don't talk like that.'

Mia shrugged as the other lasts competed for equal placing. Last time smelling eucalyptus. Last time seeing rain.

Last time being with Luca.

She wondered if she confessed to these crazy new feelings whether Luca would pretend that he reciprocated. He could renege when they were safely back in Sydney, she wouldn't hold him to it, but if she was about to meet her fate then…why not utter the words?

Because she didn't want her last moments filled with an awkward silence and an even more awkward Luca trying to figure out how to let her down gently before they crashed to a fiery death.

Or worse—watch him lie to her.

Yes, he wanted her. But that was different from love. And, faced with her own mortality, nothing less would do.

She sighed again. 'Just being realistic.'

Luca shook his head. 'We're in a stable position. Air Control has our ELT signal. We just need to wait out the weather and then they'll get us out of here as soon as they can.'

Mia nodded. Listening to the sure, steady note in his voice, she believed him. 'I know.'

They finished their chocolate serenaded by the moaning wind and the rhythmic beeping of the monitor. Luca shut his eyes briefly and let his head flop back against the headrest. The fine crinkle of the space blanket sounded like crickets chirping as he shifted to get comfortable, stretching his long legs out into the confined space.

His legs brushed hers and he lifted his head. 'Sorry.' He grimaced as he shifted them slightly to one side.

'It's fine,' she murmured.

Their gazes locked and for the longest moment they just sat and watched each other. Luca was the first to break the connection.

'So…you've never seen *Swan Lake*?'

Mia didn't say anything for a minute. Then she just shook her head. 'Have you?'

He nodded. 'My grandmother adored things like that. Opera was her first love but she enjoyed ballet too. And she insisted we all be well versed.' He smiled at the memory. 'She took me and my sisters to Rome when I was twelve because it was playing at the Teatro dell'Opera.'

Mia remembered he'd mentioned having sisters before. She heard the affection in his voice and felt a corresponding ache of longing deep inside. Her life had been far from family outings to the opera and ballet.

'You have three sisters, right?'

'Yes.' He toyed with leaving it at that but was surprised by the urge to confess all. 'And a brother.'

His accent thickened and Mia heard the regret in every syllable. He'd mentioned he'd been ostracised and she could hear the pain in every husky nuance. How terrible to have lost an entire extended family. Two people had been hard enough.

'What happened, Luca?'

She'd told him she hadn't wanted to know. And she hadn't. But that was before feeling the power of a love so deep that, even now, despite its newness, it was nestling in to her bones, bedding in for the long haul.

Now she wanted to know everything about him.

She wanted to know it all.

Luca hesitated at her soft enquiry, knowing the answer involved a trip down memory lane. And he'd just flown halfway round the world to come back from there. But somehow, with his recent trip back to the scene of the crime and the potentially dire situation they were in, it didn't seem so confronting.

In fact, it seemed kind of cathartic.

And in this strange metal cocoon, perched in the treetops of an ancient forest, it seemed as if they were the only two people in the entire world. Despite the beeping of Brian's monitor, the occasional staccato chatter from the radio and the ever-present potential for disaster, the atmosphere was intimate.

Maybe it was the rain—the whole dark, stormy night

thing—but somehow the mood was conducive to con-fidences and deep dark secrets.

And it was Mia. The one woman he instinctively knew would understand. But where did he start?

CHAPTER TEN

MIA watched and waited. She could see Luca was grappling with some demons and she held her breath, hoping like crazy he'd open up to her.

'I fell in love for the first time…' Luca paused. 'The only time…when I was sixteen.'

Mia steeled herself against the jab to her chest. He seemed so definite. So absolute.

He snorted. 'At least, I thought I had. I think lust or infatuation is probably more appropriate when I think about it now.'

Mia tried to ignore how the spike of jealousy hurt. *It was an ancient love affair, for crying out loud!*

'She must have been a hell of a girl,' she said, forcing lightness to her tone, and turned to look out the window because she couldn't bear to see what love looked like in his eyes. Not when it was for another woman.

He nodded. 'Oh, yes. Her family was an old, important family in Sicily and our two families had had a deep and abiding friendship for generations. She was promised to my brother.'

Mia's gaze snapped back to his. 'Promised? Like an arranged marriage?'

Luca smiled at her shock. 'Yes, Mia. An arranged marriage. This is Sicily where the old ways still rule.'

Mia blinked at the strange concept. 'But…you fell in love with her instead?'

Luca shook his head. 'As well.'

Oh. Mia felt goose-bumps on her arms as if the wind had found its way in again and blown right up beneath the blanket. There was nothing as heart-wrenching as brother against brother. She hunched into the space blanket a little more with a corresponding ruffle. 'Ah.'

Luca gave a grim nod. 'Yes. Ah.'

She quirked an eyebrow. 'Were there pistols at dawn?' she joked.

Luca gave a half-smile. 'No. That might have been quicker.'

Mia sobered. 'It was bad.' She wasn't sure if it was a question or a statement.

Luca nodded. 'Marissa and Carlos had a tempestuous relationship. He was twenty-three and she was eighteen when the engagement became official. He worked in Rome and was away frequently so Marissa and I hung out a lot. And when they were together they argued frequently then made up again. I think they both loved the drama of it all. And I…'

Luca paused as he remembered how love-struck he'd been. 'I watched like a desperate puppy from the sidelines. And when she came to me and said that they were done and that it was me she'd wanted all along… I didn't question her motives. It didn't occur to me that she would be disingenuous. That I was some pawn to make Carlos jealous.'

Luca shook his head. What a fool he'd been for

Marissa. What a stupid, naive fool. He glanced at Mia and marvelled at how little it suddenly seemed to matter.

'And then Marissa got pregnant and she told Carlos, who she apparently was still seeing, that the baby was mine. She told me it was his and the families came to loggerheads...' Luca shrugged. 'It was like the Capulets and the Montagues times one thousand.'

Mia couldn't really laugh at the joke. She could sense Luca was just skimming the surface and could only begin to imagine the repercussions.

'So who was the father?'

Luca shrugged. 'She miscarried and it became a moot point.'

'I'm sorry,' Mia murmured. 'That must have been hard for you. Losing a baby at any stage is difficult.' She'd been ten when her brand-new baby sister had been stillborn and that had been truly awful. 'And you were so young.'

Luca was momentarily taken aback. His family had been too angry at the time to acknowledge the emotional impact on him, let alone support him through it. Until today his grandmother had been the only person who had understood how much grief the incident had caused him.

He nodded then paused for a moment to pick up the thread of his story. 'A massive rift developed between the two families and it was only Marissa and Carlos's engagement that kept them together. I became the scapegoat.'

Mia felt his pain right down to her toes. And finally she understood his compassion with Stan that first night, a man who'd loved a woman that hadn't been faithful.

'But…surely your parents, your sisters…? They're your family…they're supposed to love you. No matter what.'

Even as she said it she felt a fraud—her parents had certainly forgotten all about what they were supposed to do, bogged down in the quagmire of their grief and anger.

Luca shook his head. 'Sicilians don't forgive very easily and I learned right then and there that love is no guarantee of anything. That any relationship, no matter how strong, can go toxic. I was sent to live with my grandmother in Palermo and as soon as I was out of school I left and didn't go back.'

'Until this week.'

Luca nodded. 'Until this week.'

'Was it hard…seeing them again? Your brother. And Marissa?' Luca shook his head. It had been a relief. Seeing Carlos and Marissa together no longer hurt. 'No.' Mia wished he'd elaborate. *Was he still in love with her?* But she shied from asking it, too frightened of the answer.

'Was there any mellowing?'

He shook his head. 'I was pretty much persona non grata.'

An almighty gust of wind seemed to shake the helicopter and her anger swirled inside the cabin with as much potency. 'That's not fair.'

Luca shrugged, looking out the window. 'Life's not fair. But I'm very pleased, very grateful to you, that I went. That I got to say my goodbye. Nonna anchored me during a very turbulent period in my life. To my shame, I don't think I appreciated that till many years later. I was angry for such a long time.'

Mia watched his brooding profile as he seemed transfixed by rain spatter patterns. 'I'm sure she knew.'

Luca nodded. 'I hope so.' He sat staring out at the inclement abyss for a moment before turning to her and saying, 'I've never told anybody this. I'm not really sure why I'm telling it to you.'

All he knew was how right it felt.

Mia gave a small smile. No matter what, she did not want to read too much into such an admission. People were never the same on holiday or just before plunging to their deaths in a helicopter.

It was practically an unwritten law. 'It's okay. Near-death experiences tend to encourage confidences.'

Luca chuckled. 'Maybe you're right.' He sobered before pinning her with a speculative stare. 'Your turn. What makes Dr Mia McKenzie tick?'

He knew there were things, deep-seated things, that made her the wonderful, non-cuddly woman he'd come to think of as naturally as he inhaled and exhaled.

It was Mia's turn to look out the window as his question made her squirm. She wasn't so sure she wanted a man who thought every relationship had potential for toxicity to know her deepest, darkest stuff.

'Same things as everyone else, I guess,' she hedged.

Luca watched her avoid his gaze. Right...so this wasn't going to come easy. But he was suddenly desperate to know what made her the woman she was. Why she didn't stay the night. Why she didn't cuddle.

Why she was looking anywhere but at him.

'Okay. Let's start with an easier question. Why did you become a doctor?'

Mia barely suppressed a snort. How could he know the answer to that question was about as entwined with her baggage as was possible? She glared at him. 'Why did you become a doctor?'

'A child nearly drowned in a lake near where my grandmother lived when I was a teenager. I helped revive her. I knew then and there I wanted to be a doctor.'

Of course. Trust Luca to have an answer. She only wished hers was as cut and dried.

Luca leaned forward in his chair, placing his elbows on his knees, and the foil crinkled. 'Come on, Mia. I told you mine.'

The beeps of the monitor seemed to mock her every thought. Oh, what the hell…

She glanced out the window again. 'My mother had a baby. A stillborn baby, when I was ten.'

Mia didn't want to be sucked back to that time but here, in the darkness, surrounded by the fury of mother nature, it seemed impossible not to be. 'One minute I was going to have a baby sister to dote on. The next minute she was gone. The doctors were so good. Kind and compassionate. Not just to Mum but to me too. I guess I made up my mind then.'

Luca watched her as she stared intently out the window as if the meaning of life was lurking in the treetops. 'That must have been a hard time in your life. Your parents must have been devastated.'

Mia snorted. 'You could say things were never quite the same again.'

Luca frowned. 'They didn't make it?'

Mia shook her head. 'My father walked out a few weeks later and found himself another family. My mother took to our couch and zoned out for the rest of my life. Last time I checked, she was still there.'

Things suddenly became much clearer for Luca. The

most important man in her life had deserted her at an age and during a time when she'd needed him most. And her mother had been too grief-stricken to fill the gap.

'I'm sorry,' he murmured. 'You were just a child. You didn't deserve to be abandoned like that.'

Mia could almost feel the intensity of her ten-year-old pain as she stared out the window. She rolled her head to look at him. 'I hated him for so long.'

Luca shrugged. 'But of course. You needed him and he wasn't there for you. Or your mother.'

Mia gave a harsh little laugh. 'My mother.' She shook her head. 'My mother let me believe that he was the bad guy. That he'd found a better family. But she lied to me for years.'

'Oh?' Luca frowned.

'I found my mother's file when I was a med student working at The Harbour. The baby wasn't my father's.'

Mia rolled her head back to face the window. The find had been cataclysmic and still sucked her breath away.

'I confronted her about it. She admitted that Dad walked out because he'd found out about the baby's paternity. She didn't defend herself or apologise for letting me think the worst of him. She just said that I didn't understand what it was like to be married to a man who worked twenty-four seven.'

Luca watched as a range of emotions flitted across her face. Her emotional fragility after the Stan incident suddenly tightened into crystalline focus. It must have stirred up all those old childhood hurts.

'Did you…did you contact your father…try and reconcile?'

Mia bit down on her lip—she would not cry. No matter how hard that particular part in the saga had been. No matter how polite and distant her father had been. He'd been hurt too deeply both by her mother and by her own refusal to have anything to do with him over the years.

'I did. But it was too late…the damage had been done. And he had three little children who adored him. Frankly, I was a painful memory that he'd put away in a box somewhere.'

The rawness in her voice caught him somewhere right in the middle. His solar plexus. *His heart?* His family's abandonment of him seemed to pale in comparison. At least he'd been older, more emotionally equipped to deal with it. 'I'm sorry. That can't have been a good time in your life. Especially when you were in the middle of your studies.'

Mia gave a little laugh. 'You could say I went off the rails for a while there. A lot of booze and partying. A lot of hooking up with men who I always thought wanted more but were only out for casual sex. Which led to more drinking.'

Ah, so that's what she'd been referring to when she'd told him she'd once liked alcohol a little too much. And maybe it also explained her reluctance to get involved in anything more than a one-nighter. Mia had taken firm control of her life.

'You did well to stop the spiral,' he commented. Mia nodded. Luca had chosen a good word. She *had* been spiralling. Into self-doubt and self-loathing. Each new man, each drink, had made her feel more and more sullied.

'I failed a major exam. Had to resit it. It scared me

silly. I suddenly realised that there was no point throwing away my future over a past I couldn't change.'

Luca nodded. 'Yes.' It was a lesson he'd had to learn too. 'It seems you and I have a lot in common.'

'Oh?' Mia quirked an eyebrow as she looked at him again. 'You got all boozy and floozy too?'

Luca chuckled. 'No. Well, no more than any other angry young man, I suppose. It took a while to realise that I couldn't change what had happened. To accept that my family were never going to take me back. But once I did, it sort of freed me a little.'

Mia studied his face. 'So that's it, you're totally Zen with the whole thing?'

Luca smiled. 'No, not totally. Let's just say I'm a work in progress.'

Mia's heart filled her chest as she smiled back. 'Guess that makes two of us.'

They smiled at each other for a moment then Brian groaned. Mia checked his pulses as Luca administered another small dose of morphine. And when they sat back down again they settled into a companionable silence, each caught in their own thoughts.

Mia yawned. 'We should get some sleep,' Luca suggested.

She nodded. She wasn't sure if it was the confession or the hour but she was suddenly bone-deep tired. And it seemed like the most natural thing in the world to shut her eyes as the man she loved shut his.

Mia wasn't sure what time it was when she woke. Or even what had woken her. But watery daylight lit the inside of the chopper and there was a strange buzzing, crackling noise that she didn't think was coming from the rustling of the space blanket.

She came fully awake as Luca leapt up, muttering, 'The radio.'

And then it was all stations go. No time to feel embarrassed about spilling all their private, closely held secrets in the dark or to analyse what opening up to each other meant. To work out where they stood. Or even to retract them.

No time at all.

The weather had settled and the rescue chopper was fifteen minutes out.

Forty-five minutes later, Mia was harnessed to a rescue officer, dangling over the drizzly treetops, looking down at a wrecked helicopter and a calm, solid Luca. Her eyes filled with tears as her heart swelled so large and full it felt like it was going to burst from her chest.

He was everything she'd ever realised she needed. But he'd only ever loved one woman. And maybe he still did. He certainly thought that all relationships had the potential to go toxic.

Just her luck that when she finally fell in love it would be with someone as damaged as herself.

Luca awoke with a start, vaulting upright. It was dark and he was momentarily disorientated. He'd been dreaming about Mia dangling over a dark, swirling, freezing mist. About her screaming his name as her hand slid from his and she fell.

His heart pounded like a freight train as he realised he was in his room. He glanced at the clock—six-thirty.

But was it morning or evening?

And what bloody day was it?

He flopped back against the mattress, taking deep breaths, forcing himself to calm down. It was just a dream.

A really bad dream.

Mia was safe. Brian was safe. They were all safe.

Mia…he'd lost track of her in the whirlwind that had descended on them the minute they'd set foot on the helipad at The Harbour. Whisked away for tests and debriefing and questions from all kinds of different official people and dozens of people dropping by to wish them well. When he'd finally been told he could go, there'd been no sign of Mia and Evie had told him that she'd taken Mia home and tucked her into bed.

His first instinct had been to go to her. But he'd checked it. She needed to sleep. Just because she'd opened up to him, didn't negate that they'd both been through a trauma and been up most of the night.

So he'd headed for his bed too. And despite his conviction that his speeding mind wouldn't allow him respite, the combination of the jet-lag and adrenaline had him out for the count within minutes of his head hitting the pillow.

But now he was awake. Wide awake. And he knew why. He knew why with every thud of fear still echoing in each heartbeat. He knew why he was dreaming about Mia. Why the overwhelming panic and despair at losing her—in the crash, in his dream—had woken him from deep and utter exhaustion.

He was in love with her.

He'd foolishly thought that they were just a casual thing. That they were having a bit of fun. Some great sex, a distracting flirtation.

But obviously his brain hadn't been listening.

Because while his body had been enjoying itself he hadn't realised his emotions had become involved. That their entire relationship had been based on a series of emotional connections—interlocking, weaving them together.

Stan and the emotional tumult of his case—for both of them—had been the first connection. Being held at knifepoint had been the catalyst for their initial sexual liaison. Sure, he'd dismissed it as a very nice, very surprising turn of events. But it hadn't been the uncomplicated one-off he'd been fooling himself it was.

It had occurred after a highly charged emotional incident.

And then later, when they'd worked together to save Stan's life, they'd forged an even deeper bond.

His grandmother's death had ramped it up a little more. Forced them to an even deeper level of emotional intimacy without him even knowing it. She'd been there to comfort him. To hold him. To tell him to get his butt on a plane and go to her funeral.

That had been more than just sex, no matter what she'd said.

For heaven's sake, she'd stayed the night. She never stayed the night. *She didn't even cuddle.*

And then there was last night. Sharing that near-death experience and then opening up to her, like he'd never done before. Unburdening all the ugly things about his past he never spoke about. Listening to her as she'd unburdened hers.

He'd been pretending it was casual. Having a great time with hard and fast sex, indulging in the physical to override anything deeper. But somewhere along the way it had become more than that.

For him anyway.

He loved her. And it didn't frighten him. He didn't want to run from it like he had in the past. Maybe returning to Sicily had laid some ghosts to rest. Maybe it was almost dying in that helicopter crash. Maybe it was *Mia* almost dying in that helicopter crash.

But he wanted to live. He wanted that grand love poets had written about. And he wanted it with Mia. His scarred, scared Mia.

He didn't want to live another day without it.

Mia woke to a terrible racket. She'd been so tired when Evie had finally dragged her home and pushed her into the shower, not even thoughts of Luca had been enough to keep her awake as she'd collapsed naked into bed.

It took her a moment to realise the racket was coming from the front door. 'Go away,' she groaned as she dragged the pillow over her head and shut her eyes again.

'Mia? Mia! Open up!'

Mia sat up as the voice registered. *Luca?*

'Mia!'

Luca's urgent tone penetrated the fog of fatigue. She was throwing back the covers and pulling on a robe before her sluggish brain even registered her purpose.

'Mia!'

'Coming!' she called as she hurried out of her bedroom, tying the robe firmly at her waist, half tripping over a discarded shoe on the way.

Why on earth was he pounding her door down? Her heart rat-a-tat-tatted in time to the knocks as it romanticised his presence. But she doubted he was knocking like a madman to tell her he loved her. More likely the building was on fire.

Which made her unaccountably grouchy.

She reached the door and snatched it open. Her breath caught in her throat. He stood before her in track pants and a hoodie, his feet stuffed into thongs, his hair rumpled, that stubble still peppering his jaw, a blanket mark reddening one cheekbone.

The man had never looked sexier.

'Where's the fire?' she snapped, because it was that or do something really silly like invite him into her bed.

She'd meant it when she'd told him they couldn't keep sleeping with each other. She couldn't love him and only have some of him. Know that he was waiting for the whole thing to go toxic.

Luca took in her tousled blonde hair and the outline of her breasts beneath her gown and smiled. 'You look good,' he murmured appreciatively.

Mia gripped the door at the lust she saw glittering in the deep brown depths of his eyes. 'I sure hope you didn't wake me for that.'

Luca smiled. 'Can I come in?'

'Luca,' she sighed. She was not going to be sucked in by that sexy smile.

'Please.' He spread his hands. 'Just for a moment.'

Mia almost shut the door on him. She was tired and at a really low ebb. Didn't he know she wanted nothing more than to curl up in bed with him and sleep for a hundred years?

Why didn't he just leave her alone?

Hoping she wouldn't regret it, she stood back and inhaled as he passed. She hadn't meant to but he smelled so good she let his aroma wrap around her like a warm cloak. She stood by the closed door, arms folded, as he strolled to the centre of her lounge room.

Luca turned to face her. She seemed remote. Both physically and emotionally.

That didn't bode well.

He took a step towards her. 'I figured out why I told you all that stuff last night.'

Mia regarded him warily. She hoped he hadn't figured out why she'd told him her stuff. The only way she could keep her dignity here was to hide her feelings. 'Really?'

He took another step. 'I've known somewhere deep inside for a while that you understood me, truly understood me, and I thought that it was just our family issues, our unhappy pasts uniting us in a way that few people could relate to.'

Mia nodded. She'd recognised him as a kindred spirit almost from the beginning.

'But it's more than that, Mia. You got under my skin, sneaked up on me when I wasn't looking. I was fooling myself that we were just keeping it casual but I was wrong.' He raked a hand through his already rumpled hair. 'I've been walking blindly down this track towards you all along and it's only now that I see what's really happening.'

Mia's heart started to thump erratically in her chest. What was he saying? That his toxicity sensors were twitching madly? That he was getting too close and it was time to get as far away as possible? 'Oh? And what's that?'

'I'm in love with you.'

Mia didn't say anything for a moment. She didn't

move. She didn't breathe. In fact, she was pretty certain her heart even stopped for a few beats.

'Mia?'

'What about Marissa?' she blurted out, because that was way simpler than the crash of other thoughts and emotions that were churning inside her.

'Marissa?'

'You said she was the only woman you ever loved.'

Luca frowned. 'I was sixteen. And infatuated. That wasn't love. I knew that the moment I saw her in the church in Palermo last week. I was a boy with a crush. What I feel for you…in here…' Luca patted his chest. 'It's a thousand times deeper, wider, stronger. You're the one I want to talk to, make love to, wake up to.'

Luca watched her face as she grappled with the news. She looked like she was fighting it. Trying to come up with ways to block it out. Block him out. He covered the distance between them until he was standing within touching distance.

'I know that you think you can't do this—have a relationship with someone. That it's not you. That you're not the *sleeping-over* type…'

'Me?' Mia scoffed, arms still firmly crossed. 'What about you? Aren't you afraid this will go toxic too? Because I'm not going to get involved with someone who's waiting for me to slip up or who's out the door at the first sign of trouble wearing a gas mask.'

Luca, buoyed by the concession that she might actually be thinking of getting involved with him, placed his hands on her shoulders and rubbed his thumbs against the polar fleece of the thick robe.

'I'm not saying that this doesn't scare me, that it's not new territory, but as you said last night I can't let an unhappy past, one that I can't change, ruin a chance at a happy future. Neither of us can, Mia.'

Mia felt tears well in her eyes. This couldn't possibly be true, could it? *Could he actually love her back?*

'Oh, Mia,' he murmured, drawing her against him. 'Don't cry, Mia. I love you.'

Mia shut her eyes tight as his accent washed over her like syrup and she allowed herself a moment to inhale the essence of him. Less than two months ago she hadn't even known this man. Just last night she'd realised the utter depth of her feelings for him. And realised he couldn't love her back.

Could she have been wrong?

'This is just the near-death experience talking.'

She tried to break out of his grasp but Luca held her tighter. Her voice was muffled against his shirt but he heard every word.

'No, Mia, no.' He eased her gently back. 'It may have been the jolt that removed the blinkers from my eyes, but this isn't sudden. I've known deep inside, deep in my heart since that night in the on-call room, that you were special. That you were more than just another woman.'

The sincerity in his eyes and in his husky accented voice called to her on a primal level. She laid her head back on his chest as she allowed the possibilities to bloom. 'I thought we were going to die last night and that I'd never get the chance to love you.'

Luca hugged her close as her words sang like an opera in his heart. 'You love me,' he said.

He'd hoped, he'd wondered, he'd wished. But to hear her say the words meant more than his next breath.

'I didn't want to,' Mia murmured.

Luca chuckled as he stroked her hair. 'Well, it's just as well we don't always get what we want.'

'Oh, Luca.' She pulled back and looked into his eyes, oozing love and joy. 'I love you so much, I couldn't bear anything to happen to us.'

Luca placed a finger across her mouth, shushing her, knowing what she was thinking. 'I'm not your father, Mia. And you are not Marissa. We're us and we won't make the same mistakes.'

And then he lowered his head and drifted the sweetest, softest kiss across her mouth she'd ever experienced. Her eyes fluttered closed and she sighed.

'Promise?' she murmured against his lips.

Luca chuckled. 'Promise.'

EPILOGUE

Two weeks later a limousine carrying Luca in a tuxedo and a glamorously dressed but blindfolded Mia glided to a halt outside the Sydney Opera House.

'We're here,' Luca announced.

Mia laughed. 'Luca, for the last time, where are we going?'

'Patience,' he teased, kissing her nose. 'Patience. Although we could just drive around in the back all night...' he dropped a kiss behind her ear '...and christen the seats...' His lips nuzzled her neck.

Mia laughed and pushed him away playfully. 'Oh, no. No way.'

The door opened and Luca grinned at the chauffeur. 'Okay, then, let's go.' He helped Mia out and once she was standing steadily he removed her blindfold.

Mia blinked as the illuminated sails of the Opera House filled her vision. She smiled at him. 'We're going to see a show?'

Luca smiled down at the woman he loved. 'The ballet, actually.'

Mia looked at the tickets he thrust into her hands. She read the fancy printing several times before it registered. She looked up at him, the man she loved, so tall and handsome and so, so hers.

'*Swan Lake*,' she whispered, hugging the tickets close. 'Oh, Luca…thank you.'

Mia beamed up at her Italian angel. She wasn't sure when she'd stopped seeing the devil but tonight all she could see was a pair of luminescent wings and a bright golden halo.

And he was all hers.

* * * * *

MILLS & BOON®

Why shop at millsandboon.co.uk?

Each year, thousands of romance readers find their perfect read at millsandboon.co.uk. That's because we're passionate about bringing you the very best romantic fiction. Here are some of the advantages of shopping at www.millsandboon.co.uk:

* **Get new books first**—you'll be able to buy your favourite books one month before they hit the shops

* **Get exclusive discounts**—you'll also be able to buy our specially created monthly collections, with up to 50% off the RRP

* **Find your favourite authors**—latest news, interviews and new releases for all your favourite authors and series on our website, plus ideas for what to try next

* **Join in**—once you've bought your favourite books, don't forget to register with us to rate, review and join in the discussions

Visit **www.millsandboon.co.uk**
for all this and more today!

MILLS & BOON®
By Request

RELIVE THE ROMANCE WITH THE BEST OF THE BEST

A sneak peek at next month's titles...

In stores from 16th October 2015:

- **Ruthless Milllionaire, Indecent Proposal**
  – Emma Darcy, Christina Hollis & Lindsay Armstrong

- **All He Wants for Christmas...** – Kelly Hunter,
  Natalie Anderson & Tori Carrington

In stores from 6th November 2015:

- **In the Tycoon's Bed** – Maureen Child,
  Katherine Garbera & Barbara Dunlop

- **The McKennas: Finn, Riley & Brody** – Shirley Jump

Available at WHSmith, Tesco, Asda, Eason, Amazon and Apple

Just can't wait?
Buy our books online a month before they hit the shops!
visit www.millsandboon.co.uk

These books are also available in eBook format!

15/05